Everlost

Also by Brenda Pandos

The Emerald Talisman
The Sapphire Talisman
The Onyx Talisman

Everblue
Evergreen

Everlost

Mer Tales ~ Book Three

By
Brenda Pandos

OBSIDIAN MOUNTAIN PUBLISHING

This novel is a work of fiction. Names, characters, places and incidents either are a product of the authors imagination, or used fictitiously. Any resemblance to actual events, locals, organizations, or persons, living or dead, is entirely coincidental and beyond intent of the author. No part of the book may be used, reproduced or stored in retrieval systems, or transmitted in any form or by any means, electronic, mechanical, photocopying, recording, or otherwise, without written permission of the author. The author holds all rights to this work.

Text Copyright © 2013 by Brenda Pandos.
All rights reserved.
Everlost: A novel/by Brenda Pandos

Cover design and layout by the author herself.
www.brendapandos.com
Cover Images Fotolia.com
© Elena Schweitzer - Fotolia.com,
© Subbotina Anna - Fotolia.com

Published by Obsidian Mountain Publishing
www.obsidianmtpublishing.com
P.O. Box 601901
Sacramento, CA 95860

ISBN: 978-0-984983537

10 9 8 7 6 5 4 3 2 1
Printed in the United States of America

To Janille Dutton, for being you.

And to all the mermaids who think their tails are less than perfect, you're valuable and worthy of a promise. Choose someone who will treasure that gift.

*"If he loved you with
all the power of his soul for a whole lifetime,
he couldn't love you as much as I do in a single day."*

-Emily Brontë, Wuthering Heights

1

Bait

Tatiana swam toward the palace, spitting out the bits of flesh that had found new homes between her teeth. She moaned as her head ached, buzzing with a dull grogginess.

Great seaweed! She thought. *What possessed me to bite that poor merman's arm? Gahhh. One kiss and I'm a—a flesh-eating monster? Seriously?*

With an extra hard flip of her tail, she propelled herself faster to wash her mind of the horrible act she'd just performed; the webbing of gems interlocked and fastened to the fabric of her promising dress weighed her down in the current. The drugs lingered, still affecting her muscles, and Fin's pleas to leave Natatoria tugged at her mind. The closer she came to the palace, the more the longing to see Azor consumed everything, taking away all the regret. She loved Azor and her life was here, in Natatoria, now.

She hoped Azor wasn't injured—of course, he wasn't dead, she'd feel that—but he could be hurt. Mermaids had doused the interior of the hall with octopus ink just as the rebel who'd grabbed her had dragged her out. She knew what the ink would do—she'd used it when she'd inked Azor's compound to bust Fin from the dungeon. Like magic, the mermen's bodies lost awareness and they all fell unconscious, floating like bobbers in the water. Once they all woke up, they'd be mad as a school of hornet fish and ready to continue the fight.

Two of the King's guards sped in her direction at lightning

speed.

"Princess!" one called out.

Tatiana tipped her head to the side. Who was he calling out to? Turning around, she expected to see Princess Girraween or Garnet behind her but saw neither.

The taller of the two stopped first and bowed his head. "Azor is worried and—"

A small laugh bubbled from her lips. He was addressing *her*—she was a princess now. She almost stopped him from being so silly when Azor's voice sliced through the water.

"Tatiana! There you are!" Azor hovered outside of the western palace entrance, his hand on his forehead. "What are you doing out here?"

At his glorious voice, she pumped her tail and left the guards in her wake. His sinewy muscles, dark eyes, goatee and raven hair took her breath away—her promised mate. She stretched her arms out, never happier to see anyone in her life. "Azor, you're safe."

He remained stiff, not returning the hug. She backed away, confused. "What's wrong? Were you injured?"

"What's wrong?" He wrinkled up his face in disgust and turned his shoulder away from her. "Do you even have to ask that?"

She blinked, nursing the sting to her ego as the guards passed and swam inside.

"Are you mad at me?" she asked.

"I don't have time to explain the obvious and once the ink fully fades, you'll help restore the palace to its previous splendor with the other servants."

"What? But—I didn't do this."

He swiveled and closed the distance between them. "Are you trying to tell me that that wasn't *your* father arguing during our ceremony? That *his army* didn't attack the King?"

"Army?" She swallowed down her anxiety. "I didn't even know he'd returned from his mission. My father is not a traitor."

"He stormed the palace!"

"I was in the palace with your mom and sisters, preparing for the ceremony all day. I had no clue what my father had planned, let alone that he'd returned. But I didn't go with them. I chose you. Didn't you see that merman pull me out of the palace?"

His eyes narrowed as he appraised her for a dark moment. "You expect me to believe a rebel merman, loyal to your father, took you *against your will*?" he snarled, revealing his razor sharp teeth. "That's highly unlikely."

"Yes," she said meekly with a gulp.

Disbelief lit his face. "Well all I can say is you're lucky you've picked the right side, Princess, and have come back to me— unless you're a spy."

"Never," she said breathlessly.

He continued to scowl, making her stomach ache with dread. "Doesn't matter anyway. The others won't last long in hiding, especially with a reward for their capture."

Her heart squeezed. It would be darn near impossible to track her parents now that they were in Tahoe, especially since most mers were too afraid of humans to go on land. But a reward? This was already going too far.

"What reward?"

"I'll offer my sister Garnet's hand, of course." His conniving smile turned her stomach. "My sisters can finally promise now that I'm no longer unmated."

She stared at him, confused. Natatorians didn't value money like humans did. The ocean provided shelter, food and the occasional sunken treasure, and there was very little one needed to barter—beyond a few luxuries like fruit, an air bubble, a lava stove, or a finely crafted garment. Title and importance, however, was an entirely different story.

"They've had to wait? For you?"

Azor puffed out his chest. "I'm the only male heir to the throne and without a queen, I couldn't secure my rightful place. My father made them wait just to be sure. Royal blood needs to take the throne, not some guppy spawn from a bottom-feeder my sisters would pick." He sighed, a contented smile full on his face. "And now that I've got you, the title is within reach—that is, once I have a male merling to ensure the blood line continues."

He pulled her in close and kneaded her stomach, mussing the fabric tangled on the gems of her promising gown. The warm water from his mouth washed over her stunned expression. She'd just become a princess an hour ago and now he'd have her leading the mer world as queen. She wasn't ready for that kind of responsibility. Surely they'd spend years as prince and princess, taking trips and purchasing things for their home in exotic places, before having to take the throne. But with his swagger, he acted as if he'd rule tomorrow, which was preposterous. As far as she knew, King Phaleon was in terrific health and the title would only be passed upon his death.

Azor's bravado faded and he let go of her upon spying Badger.

"Sir, sorry to be a botherin' ya, but I have some news ya might fancy," said Badger as he approached from the direction of the Tahoe gate.

Tatiana's mind swam, anticipating what he'd say. Hadn't he been in the ceremony room moments ago? His niece, Lily, was there to promise Fin, after all. Or was he a rebel, too? The drugs made her memory fuzzy until the kiss. Azor's glorious kiss.

Badger's eyes focused tightly on Tatiana and his concern snapped her from the blissful thought.

"And ..." Azor finally said, twitching his tail impatiently. "We don't have all day."

"Yeah. So, I got me Lily girl outta harm's way, when I been seein' yer lass, I mean, the Princess, bein' dragged off by one of those vermin, so I tried to swim after to stop 'em. But she do right nice fightin' 'em off herself, and all—"

Tatiana held her jaw stiff in an effort to keep her mouth from flying open. Did Badger see she'd bitten the rebel? And what about her parents? Fin? They were there, watching before they escaped to Tahoe.

"Get to the point, Badge," Azor interjected.

"So, I thought you'd be wantin' to know she'd be quite loyal to ya, and all dat."

"Well, isn't that nice of you." Azor perched his eyebrows upward, eyeing Tatiana with surprise. "Is that it?"

"Yes." Badger held up his chin, remaining straight-faced.

Tatiana looked away. Watching Badger's conflict confirmed her own slippery predicament. Loyalty to Azor and the kingdom meant she'd need to disown her parents, that they were the enemy now. Her shoulders sunk. How could she do that? They were her family.

"Come, Tatiana," Azor barked.

With her tail trailing low, Tatiana followed slowly, unprepared for what she'd see. The ballroom was in shambles—holes in the walls, statues missing appendages, others toppled on the floor in rock heaps. Healers attended to shaken-up guards scattered around the room. On the other end, Queen Desiree, in her regal purple gown with glorious white hair floating about her, barked orders to the servants to clean the mess. Girraween and the other princesses hovered behind their mother, startled and aghast at Tatiana's arrival.

She tried to ignore them and searched for Azor, who had disappeared in the mix of mers. But the princesses weren't the only ones gawking. All eyes had found her, staring with condemnation and anger. This had been her father's fault—her fault. Tatiana fidgeted in the current, moving to a space in a darkened corner.

Nearby, Uncle Alaster swam in with her cousin Colin, in a mad rush, calling for Azor. Her heart lurched, knowing they'd report back about her parents, about Fin.

"My good-for-nothing brother stormed the basement with spears. Threw a punch at Colin and then tried to impale me." Alaster gestured to Colin's perfectly good eye. "Nearly killed us. Then the son of a bass pushed us through the gate and disabled the release lever. We couldn't get back in. We're lucky to be alive."

Azor's quiet fury at their news terrified Tatiana while Alaster mumbled apologies. Would Azor try to go after them now that the gate was sealed? This would give her parents time to leave on foot in the morning. She secretly wished she knew about this lock. It would have come in useful when she'd broken Fin free from the dungeon. As it was, they'd spent the entire night, unsuccessfully, avoiding capture from Azor and his goons.

Azor yelled at the group of nearby soldiers to assemble. "We must go now, before they get anywhere on foot!"

Panic coursed through her as his men swam past with spears and tridents. If they got through, would they injure her family? Kill them? She moved her tail, intent to follow—all the way to Tahoe if she had to.

"Tatiana!" yelled Queen Desiree.

Tatiana ignored her and chased after the weapon-wielding mob. She pounded her tail harder, unable to keep up due to the heaviness of her gemmed dress. The cave opening leading to Tahoe eventually grew closer, and her heart sped up. Why did her old home feel like enemy territory?

Azor's head flicked back and upon seeing Tatiana, he slowed, turning around with a scowl.

"Go back to the palace, Tatiana!"

"No, please. Don't do this."

Azor glared. "Go home, now!"

As she grabbed his arm, determined to latch onto him like a starfish, a wall of churning white water ricocheted from the gate's opening and blasted into them, pushing Azor's body into hers. They clung to each other as another earsplitting boom rocked the water and shot fire all around them. She watched in horror as the cave mouth crumbled and collapsed shut.

"Holy crawfish!" she yelled, gripping to him tighter. "What was that?"

The sand ballooned around them and slowly settled down like fine snow. The other mers were floating haphazardly, clutching body parts and their heads.

Azor mouthed something as childlike fear crossed his face, but she couldn't hear him or anything beyond a loud buzzing.

"What?" she asked, realizing she couldn't even hear herself. Warm liquid poured out into the water—blood. Her blood. She shrieked, or at least she tried to, as knives carved pain through her scull starting at her ear.

Azor pulled her tighter into his body and rocked her gently. She sank into his chest, filled with pain, yet enthralled to be encased in his glorious touch. She could feel his body reverberating, one from his escalated heartbeat and the other from something he was saying. She assumed they were words of love and thankfulness they'd survived. She imagined he'd apologized, and vowed to call off the hunt now that the gate wasn't traversable. Most important, she imagined he told her he loved her with all his heart—and would forever.

Bits of silvery material floated down from the cerulean ceiling like falling stars, as the crystal ball freed itself and glided gently down behind a group of mer houses. Half of the sunlight tunnels dimmed, leaving them in the dark. Her eyes adjusted as bubbles bounded upward from the collapsed gate and escaped through new large fissures.

They held onto one another for a second longer, then Azor pushed her away. She watched his features darken when green-cloaked Dradux guards swam up with scythes in their hands.

They were all speaking with large hand gestures, but she heard nothing. Only incessant ringing. Blood vessels popped out of Azor's neck as he motioned to Tatiana and the damaged gate.

Then reality hit. If she hadn't have stopped Azor, she would have lost him. The thought pulsed a shiver up her spine. From nowhere, tears poured uncontrollably from her eyes and she couldn't stop the sobs. The men gawked.

"What?" she said, embarrassed. "Azor almost died."

Azor shook his head, said something to the men, then tugged at her arm. The men gathered the injured and swam off in the other direction.

"Can you hear okay?" She pointed to his ears.

He nodded, but pursed his lips and latched his arm around her torso, pulling her through the current. Why didn't the blast affect him? Were his eardrums thicker? Mermen and mermaids were so different.

She let him lead her away into the darkest corner of Natatoria—his compound. The silvery spires came into view first. Something was different, though. The huge stone pillars, that contained the great whites between the mouth of the Pacific gate and Azor's compound, had crumbled into piles of rock in his yard.

The sharks were free.

2

Sea Sponges

Azor shoved Tatiana into the entry of the compound and slid the heavy stone door shut. She whirled around, stunned he'd left her side, and tugged at the iron handle in a panic, unable to lug the monstrous thing open.

"Azor!" she screamed, fearing he'd become shredded into chum if he stayed outside too long. "Get back in here!"

She scrambled over to the window and wrapped her fingers around the bars, scanning the outer corridor for him. The tail of a great white whipped in the current, disappearing in the direction of the palace. She held her breath, waiting for Azor to reappear. Sharks, mindless zombies of the water, craved mer flesh, especially their blood.

A hand gripped her shoulder from behind. Tatiana squealed and jerked away. A girl with black eyes and onyx hair held up gloved hands as if Tatiana had pulled a gun—a servant. Her lips moved and her smile faded into distress. In sadness, she studied Tatiana's torn promising dress.

Tatiana held her ears, the pain maddening. "I can't hear you. There was an explosion."

A concerned frown covered the girl's face before she slowly swam closer. Filled with uncertainty, Tatiana lowered her hand and allowed the sweet girl to shift her tresses aside and assess for damage. At the edge of her long flowing nightgown, Tatiana saw one of the flukes on the girl's tail was missing, indicating the reason for her servitude.

Typically, only the severely maimed—or worse, the orphaned—were royal servants. Though sacrificing your life to the royal family was deemed honorable, everyone knew the real reason why they'd been *volunteered* to serve—no one wanted to promise their "perfect" child to the maimed for fear their genes would carry on to their offspring. And orphans, the lowliest of the mer, whose mothers weren't discussed and fathers were unknown, had no one to petition their hand. Gloves hid the fingers of servants as a symbol of their commitment not to promise.

Tatiana tried not to gawk and rubbed her ring finger instead. The coveted white tattoo hadn't had time to appear yet and Tatiana couldn't wait to see the proof of her eternal bond to Azor.

The girl finished her exam and gestured for Tatiana to stay. Then she swam past the mermaid statue in the foyer and disappeared through an arched doorway. The statue looked familiar. One she'd remembered being in the outer courtyard before. Had he moved it? Twin beams of light illuminated the statue's bare breasts from hidden sun tunnels in the ceiling. Tatiana couldn't stop staring at her, feeling inadequate about her own anatomy.

In the servant's absence, a chilling emptiness consumed Tatiana. She moved inside farther and her gaze panned the interior of the Prince's home, realizing this was hers now, too. Though wide and spacious, the inside lacked décor—a direct opposite of the palace's lavishness. A stone table surrounded by rock stumps for chairs stood before a hearth, glowing from trapped lava behind the gel cover. Above, bluish light from sconces illuminated bones of fish heads on one wall and weapons resting in harnesses on the other. Straight ahead, down a long hall flanked with arched doorways, were the iron doors to the dungeon—the ones she'd broken Fin out of not too long ago.

Incessant ringing assaulted Tatiana's brain. Then vertigo set in, spinning the room. Quickly, she rested her backside on the nearest stump and clutched her queasy stomach. Where was Azor? Why hadn't he returned?

Unable to stay upright, Tatiana doubled over, wishing her body would heal itself already. Gloved fingers prodded at her shoulder. Tatiana looked up as the dark-haired girl produced two fluffs of cotton and put them into her ears. A warm sensation flooded into Tatiana's skull and traveled down her neck. She hummed in relief as the horrible ringing lessened.

The girl then showed Tatiana a green seed and motioned she eat it. Nauseous and riddled with fresh memories of the effects of the healer's drugs on her earlier, Tatiana declined.

"I need to stay alert and wait for Azor. We need to help him. Where are the guards? He can't defend himself alone. Not against sharks." Tatiana eyed the wall of tridents and spears, tempted to grab one and lead a rescue attempt herself. Her body, on the other hand, veered sharply to the right and Tatiana practically toppled off the stump.

The girl grimaced and held out the seed more urgently. Her lips moved and she pointed to Tatiana's ear. "No—help you."

At the vision of Azor being torn limb from limb, Tatiana's heart pumped harder, amplifying the pain with each excruciating beat. She doubled over, cupping her ear, and moaned. The girl forced the seed into Tatiana's mouth and, desperate for a reprieve, she swallowed. Within seconds, relief and sleepiness overtook her.

The girl tugged on Tatiana's hand and led her past the naked mermaid statue, through the arched doorway. On the left, Tatiana discovered a kitchen, and on the right, more doorways covered in seaweed strands that led somewhere else. At the end of the hall, a hole was cut out in the ceiling. They glided through easily to the second floor. The same eerie blue glow illuminated another hall lined with iron doors, ending in a set of two at the end.

Tatiana yanked her hand free. "But what about Azor?"

The girl's mouth curled into a frown. She shook her head and spoke slowly so Tatiana could read her lips, "Gone—to the palace."

"But how? All the sharks!" Tatiana ran her hand through her hair, forgetting the multitude of pins and golden chains that had held her tresses for the happiest day of her life. A few launched errantly into the current like falling stars, but Tatiana didn't care. Azor needed her.

Numbness deadened her limbs as flashes of her last visit to the compound surfaced. The thrill of breaking in, her heart racing like mad, the ink, the dumbfounded guards passing out, the fumbling of keys, the effortless escape from the dungeon, freedom with her brother in Tahoe, short-lived freedom that seemed a lifetime ago. Azor's compound stood empty today. Where were the guards? Had they all attended the ceremony?

Again, the servant girl persuaded Tatiana to go with her and took her by the arm. Tatiana almost pulled away, but the warmth through her gloved fingers was comforting. Together, they floated into the closest room, the fight melting inside.

On the floor was a grouping of sea sponges in a perfect square. Tatiana wanted to laugh, and probably would have if her lips weren't so anesthetized. She'd rather sleep in the current than rest on slimy sponges. In truth, she'd rather not sleep at all. There was a rescue plan they needed to execute.

The servant ignored her hesitation and motioned she lay on the sponge bed. Without warning, blackness drenched the room, enveloping everything around them. An odd sensation rolled over her and her body tilted parallel to the floor. Something heavy draped over her fin and settled her slowly to the floor.

Muffled voices outside the door woke Tatiana. Groggy, she sat up and winced, gaining her bearings. The sunlight filtering through the window was dim—morning perhaps? Sponge slime covered her skin and face. She wiped off the goo, then pulled the fluffs from her ears and almost squealed in joy. She could hear without the incessant ringing.

"Nothing's changed," Azor said in the hall, "I promise you."

"But..." The longing in the female's voice froze Tatiana in place.

"You know the delicacy of the situation. If I could have done things any other way, I would have. Just be patient. I have a plan," he finished.

Tatiana strained to hear, her joy he'd survived the hungry sharks short-lived. Her heart constricted like a fist. Only men occupied the compound and female servants. Who was this woman and what *situation* was he referring to? After another moment of silence, she flipped the woven kelp blanket off with her tail and swam to the door, pressing her ear against the crack.

"Azor?" she called out before opening the door.

An empty hall greeted her. From the first floor, angered voices from mermen filled the water. Anxious to see Azor and the source of the commotion, Tatiana swam down through the porthole. She had so many questions. What had happened? Who had he spoken with in the hall? Why hadn't he checked on her? But most important, when were they leaving for their honeymoon? She closed her eyes and corrected herself: promisetide.

In the main room, a dozen mermen milled about, stinking up the place with their fishy musk. Problems surrounding the destroyed gate and the sharks dotted the mermen's conversation. Jealousy arose in Tatiana as she scanned the area for the woman, finding no one.

"I say we go through the Pacific gate if we can't reopen Tahoe's in time," a man yelled from the other room. "We've already shown those sharks who's boss!"

Tatiana's chest jolted at the mention of Tahoe. She snuck past the mermaid statue to the corner and peered around. Mermen cheered and clanged their metal weapons against one another as if toasting glasses, happy to go after her parents and her brother. She recognized none of them, save Badger. Their eyes met at once and his bearded lips remained still, his eyes apologetic.

Upon seeing Azor, everything faded as her blood sang through her veins. Like a sunrise, she wanted to bask in his love, feel his arms around her, enjoy his tenderness he'd briefly shown after the explosion, and get to know every inch of him.

A few others saw her and fell silent, glaring at her and her white promising gown. Azor turned to find the distraction and frowned. Her shoulders sank at his disapproval.

"Tatiana! Go back to your room!" he yelled with a jab of his finger.

The rest in the room quieted and stared. Her mouth turned dry like a desert. Shocked and hurt, she choked down a swallow of seawater to loosen her vocal cords.

"I-I can hear you just fine," she said.

"Oh." He dipped his head to the side. "Well, Love... this meeting is for men only. So why don't you go find something else to do."

She frowned at his lack of concern. Never mind the fact she wanted alone time with her new husband. Their last interaction involved his suicide mission through shark-infested waters. As the stares continued to linger, she waited for him to suggest, at the very least, a short conversation in private.

"Azor? I'd like to talk—"

"Later," he said, his voice clipped.

She winced at his harshness then turned with a loud huff, but not before she locked eyes with *him*—blue-grey eyes she could pick out anywhere. The merman's gaze returned to Azor, his jaw clenched tight as if he didn't notice they'd recognized one another. She could have sworn he'd been the one—the rebel who'd dragged her from the palace, the one she'd bitten.

She immediately searched his forearm for signs of a bite wound, but he moved his arm out of sight. Her body iced over. What was he doing here?

3

Friends and Rebels

Jacob moved his arm out of sight, his heart racing. Yes, his wound from Tatiana's bite had not fully healed, but with everyone else's cuts and wounds, it didn't stand out—except to her. A tremor hit his fin, remembering her attack—fierce and fiery, and oddly a turn on. And yet she still stared, questioning.

She saw me. She knows.

He locked onto Azor, well… more like burned holes into him, and concentrated to keep his breathing easy. Visions of what Azor had done to Tatiana the day prior continued to gnaw at his gut and boil his blood. He couldn't believe, even after Jack interrupted the ceremony, the asshole still kissed her.

He fingered his trident, keeping track of Tatiana in his peripheral vision. If she'd suspected something now, just wait until she found out Jacob was to be her bodyguard. He smiled slightly, imagining her response.

At the sound of the stone front door leading outside scraping against the floor and opening, Jacob turned and straightened his shoulders.

No!

Darrellon, the leader of the King's guards—the Dradux—appeared with a smile on his face. Behind him he towed a string of rebels, all chained and recently flogged. Jacob's muscles tensed, ready to spring into action. Badger clasped his shoulder.

"Wait, son," he mumbled.

Wait? Was Badger mad? He, Badger and the rest of the

undercover rebels here could take Azor and the enemies out, even though they were outnumbered two to one. They could free the rebels—free Tatiana—and be the heroes. Badger just needed to give the word.

Jacob stared into the helpless faces of the men, his friends, when he saw Maugin, a Council member's daughter among the group. She bowed her head in an attempt to hide her face, while furtively scanning the room through her veil of hair.

Outrage swelled in Jacob's chest and his fins bristled. He turned, the point of his trident aimed at Azor's chest when Tatiana swam from her hiding place, glaring.

"What have these people done to deserve this?" she demanded of him.

Azor's head whipped around and he clamped onto her arm, pulling her into the hall past the statue. Jacob watched them carefully as the commotion of the room picked up in volume.

With a lift of his chin, Azor frankly replied, "This is not your concern, Love. Let me handle the rebels while you adjourn to the privacy of the sitting room upstairs."

"The rebels?" Conflict stretched over her face and she yanked back her arm from his grip. She gestured, appalled, at the line of injured mer. "This is inhumane and these people did nothing wrong."

Azor moved closer to her, his poisonous barbs extending. Jacob, noting the hostile stance, left his seat and floated closer. He'd stab Azor outright before he'd allow Tatiana to be abused in any way.

Azor only lifted his chin and smirked. "They've admitted to their crimes of treason and must fulfill their punishment. It's only a few days in the dungeon, that's all."

"Treason? For helping my father?" she asked.

With quick movements, Azor pulled her close and brushed his lips against her hair, making Jacob want to vomit. And like magic, she softened, her eyes glazing over. Azor traced the neckline of her dress with his finger. "You should probably go change out of this dress, don't you think?"

She nodded, leaning into him with a look of longing in her eyes. "Okay."

What the—? Jacob couldn't believe his eyes. Where was all the fire he knew she had? This was an atrocity. She needed to tell Azor where to stick his so-called punishment and free her people.

With a smile of victory, Azor kissed her temple and then left to deal with the prisoners. Jacob worked to keep his face indifferent, smirking only slightly when Azor nodded his direction. Helplessly, Jacob watched Tatiana's bliss evaporate and she floundered in the current, a mix of sadness then disgust on her face.

That's right, Tatiana. He's a snake and doesn't deserve you, Jacob thought. *Fight the promise and give him hell.*

Her blue eyes bore into Jacob once again, hitting him with a raised eyebrow. A hot bolt of lightening zinged down his tail and he turned away, caught. He fought to catch his breath, dialing down the internal heat that had blazed temporarily out of control in his body. What was it with this woman that she had such an affect on his self-control?

He focused his attention on a messenger boy who'd swum up beside Azor and whispered in his ear. Azor's grin vanished, his color graying slightly. "I'll be there shortly," he told the boy before he addressed Blanchard. "Have the rest of the sharks been contained?"

"As far as I know, yes. We'll put up more permanent bars tomorrow," he said. "Is there a problem?"

"There's one that we didn't…" Azor looked over his shoulder at Tatiana and paused, as she peered from behind the mermaid statue, gripping the plinth with white knuckles.

Blanchard nodded, anticipating what Azor was to say anyway.

"As for the prisoners, set up a guard detail. I'll interview the ones who haven't confessed later." Azor's face hardened, and he turned to his charges. "Men, scour the city. Anyone who's wounded, or was unaccounted for during the ceremony, find them. Bring them here for questioning. Grommet, Eron, Cyanen, Peridge, and Badger, come with me."

Jacob closed his eyes for a second. Of course Azor would, unknowingly, summon most all of the secret rebels for assistance.

As his friends passed by, they exchanged knowing glances. The plan was that if anyone's life was in jeopardy, they'd overthrow the palace and take over. Otherwise, they were to wait for Jack to return with backup. Jacob had expected only days would pass, but now with the Tahoe gate demolished and Azor's growing Dradux squad, he had no clue when that would happen. They didn't have time to wait, especially where Tatiana was concerned.

Jacob noted Tatiana still hung in the shadows, watching everything, when Xirene swam up behind her and led her away to the kitchen.

"Come away from the warriors, Princess," the ebony haired healer said. "I'm sure you're hungry after your long day."

Tatiana quit protesting when the girl struggled with her deformed fin to pull her forward. The thought of food sickened her, but she did need space to think.

Ugh! She cursed herself again for her weakness. Under Azor's touch, Tatiana's brain turned to mush, unable to process, let alone carry out a functioning thought. There were mers in the dungeon, locked up for trying to stop her promising ceremony, taking the blame needlessly. She had to do something.

In the kitchen, two other mermaid servants were arranging plates on a granite table in the middle of the room—both brunettes. Behind them a huge slab of shark meat bled into the current. Tatiana imagined the head would join other rotting trophies on Azor's wall. *Oh the joy.*

"Princess," they said, bowing their heads.

Tatiana recognized them immediately and smoothed her hands down the front of her white gown, now torn and missing most of its gems. They'd helped her get ready for the ceremony—but only after she'd been drugged and cooperative.

"I—thank you," Tatiana said to the healer. "My ears feel so much better."

"Good." She grinned and pulled a plate from the grouping, and handed it to Tatiana.

Tatiana tried to lift her lips in an appreciative smile, but leered instead. *The last time you gave me something, you drugged me to sleep, you slippery little grunion.*

"What did you use to heal me?" Tatiana watched the healer closely, hoping for a snippet of fear to flood the water.

Squaring her shoulders and lifting her chin a notch, she casually stated, "Just something I whipped together." Her smile didn't touch her eyes, just as cold as Azor's compound.

"And the sleep aid?"

The healer cocked a brow. "That's never happened before. Your constitution is most *delicate*."

Tatiana smirked. *Delicate, my fin.* She took a seat and removed the woven lid weighed down by colorful rocks attached at the edges. On her plate was a live lobster nestled within a collection of green plants and an orange. Her mouth watered at the site of the golden ball that took flight into the current. Fruit, a true delicacy in Natatoria.

"Careful," the yellow-tailed brunette warned, "don't let that sucker get away."

Tatiana wasn't sure if the girl meant the orange or the lobster. Thankful the claws were tied, Tatiana put the lobster under the lid and snatched the escaping orange and tore off its rind.

"Didn't you help me get ready earlier?" Tatiana asked her, embarrassed she couldn't remember her name.

"Earlier?" The healer interrupted, cocking her head.

"Weren't you at the palace yesterday, Xirene?" the blue-tailed brunette asked. "For the ceremony?"

Xirene flipped her dark hair and looked away in disgust. "No. I was here."

The blue-tailed brunette cleared her throat. "I'm Shanleigh and this is Coralade, Princess. Yes, we did help you get ready to promise Prince *Azor*." His name floated off her tongue like a butterfly.

Coralade swished her blue tail and giggled a quick, "hello," before she continued with tearing greens. Behind them, Xirene cleaved the shark's flesh.

Tatiana worked to keep her composure. Mentally she once again tried piecing together who the woman in the hall earlier could be. Another princess? The Queen? The jealousy surged inside her once again. Why hadn't Azor informed her of this situation? And why were there unsupervised female servants allowed in the compound anyway, and so close to the adjoining barracks? No proper mermaid would be caught here alone, knowing about the temptations of wayward guards, the main reason for the dating parlor and chaperones in the first place.

"Do you all live here?" Tatiana asked.

"No, well, not yet. Maybe…" Coralade tucked a lock of hair behind her ear as her eyes darted coyly to Xirene. "Depends if the infirmary overflows to the conservatory. And with all the extra *unpromised* guards in the barracks now…"

Shanleigh nudged Coralade. Together they giggled.

"That's enough." Xirene hovered in the current, looking down her nose at both of them. Shanleigh and Coralade exchanged anxious glances and went back to work. "I don't know why the Queen sent these two. They have a bad habit of being loose-lipped and disrespectful."

"Are there really that many injured?" Tatiana asked.

"No. Coralade would like an excuse to be in close proximity to the guards. For that reason alone, I'll never allow her to stay here. I can't understand why I've been issued bottom feeders for help."

Tatiana caught Coralade waggling her tongue out of Xirene's view and withheld a smile. Instead, she focused on the orange rind floating in the current, angered and frustrated. Though she'd never dreamed she'd be promised to Prince Azor—the man she'd despised and every mermaid loved—now that it had happened, she wanted nothing more than to be together with him, away from the drama and onlookers. But between the rebels being arrested and the gate explosion, the divide between the people kept increasing—as well as the divide between her and Azor. More servants moving into her home meant her secret wish was far from coming to fruition, not to mention Azor having more to deal with.

Tatiana sighed. "Were many hurt by the blast?"

"A few of Azor's guards were, but they've all been attended to. Men have stronger eardrums." Xirene said with a syrupy smile. "Though, it seems poisons were used on blades during the skirmish. Poison that our blood doesn't want to heal as quickly."

"Oh?" Tatiana said softly, running her hand through her tangled hair. "I didn't know such a poison existed."

"Yes, well…" Xirene paused and cleared her throat. "It's supposed to be outlawed. Makes the healer's job more difficult if you don't know what you're doing."

Tatiana lowered her orange, wanting to ask more questions, but getting her intel from servants didn't seem proper or entirely accurate—considering the gossip mill at the palace. Maybe later, once she stopped by her home to pick up her clothes, she could visit the palace and ask Princess Girraween.

The servant girls continued to work in silence, as the tension grew thicker.

"I'm finished. Should we serve the men now?" Coralade asked as she pulled the hair-stick from her bun and fanned her brown hair around her shoulders.

She took off her apron and Tatiana gasped, noticing she wore nothing but her white servant skirt, trimmed in blue over her blue tail. Coralade lifted her tray stacked high with plates and began to swim to the doorway.

"Wait! Where are you going?" Tatiana blinked in shock at her blatant nakedness.

Her face blanched. "To serve the meal."

"Without a top on?"

"I—" She raised the tray to cover herself and looked to Xirene in a panic. "Azor likes us to be natural in his presence."

Tatiana clenched her jaw and glared at the three of them, appalled. To her shock, both Shanleigh and Coralade were naked under their aprons, confirming the gossip floating around at mermaid school.

"For the love of seaweed, do you have no propriety—with the rumors, and—?" Tatiana bit her lip. She didn't want to mention the threat of tempting pregnancy. Many an orphan were birthed from unknown women and delivered by servant mermaids to the orphanage. "I don't care what you did before, you will not be topless in my mate's or any guard's presence here in my home. Do you understand? You're to be chaste at this compound, no excuses."

Coralade and Shanleigh looked sheepishly at one another as they replaced their aprons and mumbled a quick, "Yes, my lady," in unison.

As Xirene shooed both girls out the door, Tatiana pushed her plate aside, her appetite further ruined. No wonder the guards enjoyed living here. A visual brothel, with a half-naked statue in the foyer that freely advertised it.

"I expect you to enforce my wishes." Tatiana sized up Xirene, noticing she wore a white frock practically covering her whole body.

"I wouldn't think of having it any other way." Xirene bowed before retreating to the hidden back rooms of the kitchen.

Tatiana's eyes slipped shut. She had no idea what had happened within these walls before, but things were most definitely going to change, starting first with the dress code and then with the prisoners. Azor would be getting an earful once he came home.

4

Leviathans and Oranges

Tatiana swam into the front room, curious to see where the blue-grey-eyed rebel had gone. After scanning the room, she spied Coralade rubbing her tail against him. Oddly, jealousy hit her, until she noticed he seemed annoyed with her flirting, even pushing her away. His dignity intrigued Tatiana momentarily, but as she approached, his eyes caught hers and his gill flaps stopped moving.

Caught you red finned, Tatiana thought with a smirk.

She swam full force, determined to discover if he did in fact try to steal her from the palace, when she noticed newly placed golden bracers emblazoned with the Natatorian insignia on his arms. His jaw tightened as his eyes met hers, piercing into her. And instead of fear, his gaze lay thick with the secret and a hint of smolder.

He rose from his seat and tipped his head. "Princess."

Her heart skipped a beat, her cheeks flushing. After her assault on him, she couldn't believe he'd look at her like that, not to mention she was promised. Even still, she couldn't collect herself. She looked away and smoothed down the tulle wisps of her gemmed promising dress, embarrassed she still had it on. Confusion clouded her mind, one for her reaction to him, but also in lack of proof. Without a bite mark, she couldn't be sure if he was the one.

"Princess. I'm glad to see you've met Jacob."

Her insides jumped at Blanchard's voice. She swallowed hard.

Jacob remained stoic, eyes now cast downward.

"Not formally, but then again I have no idea who any of these men are that are occupying *my* living room. Don't the barracks have a hall for them to commune in? They're stinking up the place."

"Of course, milady." Blanchard straightened himself. "In light of the recent attack, we're fitting those chosen with armor so they're prepared to serve the kingdom at a moment's notice. That frees the Dradux so they can directly serve the King. Though I know they're annoying to you, the guards are here to keep watch over the prisoners."

She wanted to roll her eyes and laugh at the absurdity of his statement. Like she needed protection from the rebels. The Dradux, on the other hand, she most definitely didn't want to be alone with. The ones who allowed parasites to latch onto their tongues and occupy their mouths—she shivered at the thought.

She returned her attention to Jacob, the sneaky little anemone fish. He'd slid right into the compound undetected. *What are you up to, Jacob?* Little did Azor know before fitting him with armor, he'd ditched the black rebel robes and bandaged his arm just in time. If only she could take one peek under that sliver of gold to make sure.

Blanchard cleared his throat, gaining Tatiana's attention. "And in light of your abduction, you're being assigned a personal bodyguard as well. Jacob will personally make sure you're safe until the threat is over."

She turned to Blanchard, aghast and practically laughed. Was he kidding? "Threat? What threat?"

"I heard a rebel abducted you, correct?"

She squinted in disbelief and chuckled, eyeing Jacob for a response. Technically, rebels were on her side. The irony was, they assigned the very rebel who *had* abducted her—she couldn't believe her ears.

"I really don't think that will be necessary."

"Yes, it is, Princess. With everything that's happened, it's hard to know who to trust."

Her lips pressed into a line unappreciative of Blanchard's subtle implication that she was a rebel as well. Her father had defended her honor; that was the truth. She wanted to shout their innocence across the hall so everyone would hear, especially the guards who continued to glare at her.

"Fish sticks!" she said. "No one is going to bother me. I don't need a bodyguard. I have Azor."

Blanchard's face hardened. "Prince Azor will not be able to provide round the clock protection."

"And poor Jacob must have a family or something." She glanced at his finger for a promise tattoo, finding nothing. "This is silly. With all the guards here at the house…"

"I'm only following the Prince's instructions. You'll need to take it up with him if you disagree."

She clenched her jaw, refraining from arguing further. *Oh, you bet I will*, she thought.

Blanchard bowed before leaving to speak with someone else. Jacob remained quiet as the eyes of the other mermen watched her with glaring mistrust. In Azor's absence, she felt vulnerable—like she was the enemy. Would they lock her up eventually and say it was for her protection?

Without another word, she swished her tail and escaped past

Ms. Sea Urchin and her tatas to the second floor. Unsure where to go, she hid in her room. If she could have locked the door, she would have.

Alone, she drifted to the window, reality sinking in, and the tears came. Since she was a little merling, she'd dreamt of the day she'd promise to the love of her life. Never did she imagine a war would stem from that union. A terrible war that pit brother against brother and her lover, not even on her side, wouldn't find time to comfort her.

She sobbed into her arms until she drifted off to sleep, exhausted.

Hours later, Tatiana's eyes popped open and she shook her head to gain her bearings. Never had she slept this much in her life.

Sunlight dimly filtered into the water outside her windows, but she couldn't be sure of the time, or even the day. Alone in her room, her heart sank like a stone. The lonely quiet of the house hit even harder. Where was Azor?

She swam out of her room and peered down the empty second-story hall. Identical rooms like hers lined the corridor, ending at a set of double doors. The master bedroom, perhaps? She wondered why Xirene hadn't put her to sleep in there yesterday. She swam forward and bit her lip, carefully pressing open one side of the massive doors.

"Azor?"

The huge room loomed before her. In the center was a large

dais covered with bright green moss—she assumed the Prince's bed, but no Azor. Scary carved faces of snakes and demons lined the walls and looked down on her in disgust, like an intruder. She slithered slowly inside and ran her hand over the back of the door to close it. Something sharp cut into her hand and she pulled away, biting back a scream. On the back of the door, carved into the iron, was a leviathan's mouth, jutting out at her. Cradled in its teeth was a human baby. The monster's snakelike body, thick like a redwood trunk, trailed along the walls of the room ending in a tight coil wrapped around a human woman as she reached for her child in desperation.

Tatiana's chest clenched tight in hysteria. Her eyes darted back and forth, processing the meaning of the dreadful carving. In a flurry of terror, she fled from the room, unable to handle, let alone witness, the frightful sight. Tatiana froze in the hall, gulping to catch her breath. She'd known Azor hated humans, but this? His true disdain shone in all its horrific teeth and snarls—in his bedroom of all places. She closed her eyes, clutching the neckline of her gown, and willed her thumping heart to slow.

Logically, this would be enough evidence to bolt—swim through the Scotland gate, or even through the sharks to the Pacific—and never come back. Before the promise, she'd never stay with such a monster, one who'd had such disregard for humans and for his own kind, and yet the promise wouldn't let her fathom leaving him now, blackmailing her and rendering her useless when bathed in the beauty of his glorious presence. How could her mind and body be at such odds with one another?

She pressed her thumbs against her temples, trying to force

her brain to think straight. At entertaining the thought of running away, her skin broke out in gooseflesh, her heart rate accelerating. Never. She couldn't. She was bonded to him, hook, line and stinky sinker.

"Oh, dear Poseidon. Why?" she whispered before she slipped down the porthole.

Downstairs guards snored, slumped onto the floor with spears dangling loosely in their hands. She traversed farther down the forbidden hall, cautious not to disrupt the current. On her left was a big meeting room and farther down, the archway leading to the barracks. To her dismay, the room was empty. Across the hall, though, was an arsenal filled with weapons and armor—enough for every merman in Natatoria. She stopped and stared at the vast collection.

Sad groans pulled her attention to her left. She eyed the dungeon doors, wondering how many arrested merman lay shackled behind them. She swam closer and placed her trembling fingers on the iron latch, finding it unlocked.

How easy it would be to help the prisoners escape, she thought.

"Do you need something, Princess?" a male voice asked.

Her entire body jolted—caught with her hand in the proverbial cookie jar, but she didn't dare turn around. *Jacob.*

"You mustn't go into the dungeon. It's not a proper place for a lady."

She snorted softly at the manipulation behind his words, but kept her hand firmly planted in an act of defiance, hoping he'd go away. "I appreciate your concern, Jacob, but this is my house now, and I'll go where ever I want."

"I object."

"You object?" She chuckled. "Sea stars! Who made you my keeper?"

He swam to her and placed his hand gently on hers. Surprising to her, his warmth sent a tingle across her skin. She gasped and pulled away.

He responded and drew his shoulders taut. "I'm responsible for you, and I don't feel it's safe for you to be around the prisoners."

"They can't hurt me."

Jacob grimaced. "It sends the wrong message."

"To whom?"

"To your people."

She looked away from his blue-grey eyes and swallowed hard.

"All the mers are my people, or are you accusing me of being a traitor, too?"

"Of course not, Princess. But, please." He motioned she move away from the door, careful not to touch her a second time.

She held her spot. "Are they being cared for? Fed?"

"Yes."

"And the girl?"

"She was released earlier into her father's custody. She was at the wrong place at the wrong time." He stretched out his arm towards the front of the house. "Princess. Let's go into the other room. Can I get you something? Are you hungry, perhaps?"

Seriously? The thought of a guard serving her food humored her. She bit back a smile, tempted to laugh at his lame attempts of distraction, but composed herself instead. "Actually, I'm looking for Azor."

Jacob exhaled, his eyes losing focus for a beat. "The Prince has yet to return from the palace."

"What's taking him so long?"

"I'm not sure." His jaw clenched and she found it odd he didn't look directly at her.

"What aren't you telling me, Jacob?" she demanded, swimming closer to him.

Jacob cast her a quick glance. "Nothing."

She squinted, her lips curling down in disbelief. "Will you go check on him and find out what's taking so long?"

He lifted his chin and Tatiana couldn't help but notice his washboard abs flex.

"No," he said, determined. "I won't leave you."

She shook off her attraction to his physique and balled her hands. "Seriously? Fish fry! There are a bazillion guards here to keep me *safe,* if you haven't noticed."

She almost laughed at how incredulous that sounded considering—even while she fought with Jacob—they snored through their argument.

"Shhh," he said sharply, tugging her by her elbow to the front room. "I'd love to assist, but I have my orders. If something were to happen—"

She pulled away. "I know. You'd be hung by your scales. Blah blah blah. Tube worms! I need to know where my husb—mate is. I am the princess, remember," she whispered, hard.

"How could I forget?" he said glibly.

She fisted her hands when Jacob wouldn't budge. "Then take me to the palace if you must *chaperone* me," she whispered, the edge to her voice hard.

"No."

"I decree it."

A small smiled tipped his lips. "You don't have the authority."

"Try and stop me." She swam past Jacob to the front door in determination. "You're my bodyguard, be one."

"Princess, don't be foolish." He wrapped his hand around the bottom of her fin and held her there.

"Unhand me. Now!" She whipped her tail away from his grasp and swirled around, glaring. "You can't touch me and you can't keep me prisoner either."

Jacob took up a trident in his hands and moved in a flash to block the front door. "I have my orders and I'll do what's necessary to keep you from leaving."

She zipped up to him and tugged on the arm bracer covering his left forearm. "Like putting on these silly things? So I can't bite you again?"

Surprise crossed his face for the slightest second before he covered his angst with an empty expression. "Princess, contain yourself. This is unbecoming."

"Unbecoming? Poseidon! You sound like my mother. And I recognize you." She pointed at his nose, their faces inches from one another. "I know who you are."

His gaze unfocused as he looked over the top of her head at the stirring guards scattered around them, jaw clenched. "So what if you know who I am," he said quietly. "Are you going to turn me in? So I can be flogged and arrested just like the rest of the men who stood up for your honor, for your rights?"

Tatiana gasped and her eyes grew momentarily before she centered herself. How dare he manipulate her when all she wanted was her mate?

"You weren't able to contain me then and you won't now," she hissed and took up another trident leaning against the wall, aiming it at his chest. "Move aside."

Jacob's hard expression softened as he eyed the trident. He shook his head with a peculiar grin.

"Are you serious?"

"Yes—" but before she could attempt to use her weapon, Jacob pulled the trident from her hands and swiveled her around, pinning her hands to her sides. He placed his other hand over her mouth. His body, hot and strong, pressed up against hers. A flicker of want sparked inside her. She'd never had a merman hold her like that. Only fabric from her dress and his man skirt was preventing them from accidentally…

"Don't," he whispered in her ear. "You'll wake the household."

Her breath caught in her throat until guilt overcame her fantasies. She pushed out her claws from her fingertips. With a flick of her wrist, she tried to swipe at his body when the door behind them scraped against the floor, opening. Jacob let go and distanced himself, falling into a bow.

"Captain."

"What's going on in here?" Azor commanded, his gaze darting between the two of them.

5

Sting

In relief, Tatiana swam up to Azor's side, taking his hand. "I'm so glad you're here. Tell this guard that he isn't allowed to touch me again. Ever!"

Azor scowled. "Jacob—explain yourself."

Jacob raised his head. "The Princess wanted to leave the compound against your orders and she wouldn't take 'no' for an answer, sir. I restrained her."

Azor turned to Tatiana with a fierce look and dropped her hand. "Is this true?"

The smug smile melted off her face. "What orders? I had no knowledge of this."

"You're not allowed to leave, especially not when our kingdom is at war, hence the reason I've assigned Jacob to watch over you."

She sucked in a startled breath at the words "watch over you." "This is ridiculous. War?" *Not to mention the occupants in the compound are far more hostile than anyone in Natatoria could be,* she thought.

"Yes, Tatiana. War. And my father, thanks to Jack, is fighting for his life at this moment. And if he dies, Poseidon help us all. No one will forgive you after that, even if it does make you Queen."

The water whooshed out her gills and she moved backward in the current, stunned.

Azor caught her surprise. "You didn't know yet?"

"How would I know? You haven't told me anything since the explosion, and then you just disappeared earlier today. How did my father injure the King?"

He laughed acrimoniously. "Jack's explosion freed the sharks and one took off half the King's fin."

She shook her head, sinking to the floor. This couldn't be true.

Off to the right, Jacob shifted his body in the current, his eyes downcast. Did he know and chose not to fill her in? Tatiana wanted to scream at both of them, at the injustice, at how things kept putting a bigger wedge between her and Azor's happily-ever-after. A sad moan escaped from her lips instead.

Azor yawned and arched his torso. A cracking sound prickled across the water. "I'm tired and hungry, and don't want to argue about this anymore. Jacob is here to stay, so you had better listen to him. And bring food to my room. Now." He swam past her toward the second story porthole and disappeared.

She gulped down the bile crawling up her throat and caught Jacob's apologetic eye. She turned away with a loud humph, maddened by his pity.

"Good night, Princess," he said as she swam toward the kitchen.

She almost told him he could stick his sympathy up his vent, but bit back her retort. She swallowed her tears and searched through the rock shelves for something to serve her mate, finding nothing. Her eye caught the barely touched meal she'd left on the table earlier.

She grabbed a tray with utensils and swam up the porthole, not before eyeing the naked maiden in the foyer. A tempting thought to remove her dress and serve her new mate topless, like the servants often did, crossed her mind. Too embarrassed, she decided against it.

As she approached the door, her stomach lining ground together like sandpaper. Was it too much to hope he'd pull her into his arms, say he loved her, and promise everything would work out after this horrible unending day? If not, she'd have to live with the constant ache she felt from his disapproval. And now with the King's injuries, how could he forgive her? *Dumb sharks.* Why did Azor have them at all? Did he never think they might break out of their cage at some point? She groaned and vowed to make things right again, beg for forgiveness, something.

"Azor?" she asked as she entered the doorway. The idea of spending the night in his creepy room wasn't on her list of places to have their first romantic encounter together. Determined, she lifted her chest and ignored the gargoyles, vowing she'd be a dutiful mate and enjoy herself anyway.

Azor's head was tilted against the granite headboard, eyes closed. His dark fin spread over the end of the bed. He'd removed his skirt and armor, lying there practically naked. Tatiana's heart thudded harder and she looked upward, not ready to gaze upon the part that made him a man.

"I'm here," he said, annoyed.

She swam up with an eager smile. "I found you a lobster and an orange."

He grunted and took the tray, placing it on his lap. She blew out a sip of water, glad the tray covered him at least. Without a thank you, he pushed aside the knife and fork, and cast off the lid. With wolfish bites, he ripped into the flesh of the live lobster, ignoring its wriggling fits of pain. Then he sent the empty carcass flying into the current, before grasping for the orange halves.

"Someone's eaten off this." He crushed the delicacy in his fist. Tangy juice filled the water, making Tatiana's stomach sick. "Get me a fresh one."

She opened and closed her mouth, wanting to tell him that it had been her orange and she'd only had one slice, but she didn't want to anger him any further.

"Okay," she muttered.

She returned to the kitchen and checked more thoroughly, finding nothing. Apparently, the army had devoured everything in sight, including the entire shark carcass. She fisted her hair. *Where is Xirene when I need her?* What was she going to do?

After a few minutes of fretting, she returned to the second floor empty handed. Quickly, she unbuttoned the back of her dress and wriggled out of it. She placed her palm on the door, ready to push it open, when an idea hit. She unfastened a long section of tulle from the dress's train and wrapped it around her back and over her breasts, making a bow in front.

With her homemade lingerie on, her heart thumped wildly.

"Azor?" she whispered with a coy smile, pushing open the door.

He'd shifted to his side and his tail zigzagged over the width of the moss. Gills ruffled on his neck between each loud snort.

With a small flick of her tail, she glided over and let her gaze rake over his sculpted body. Tiny iridescent scales covered his torso and thickened at his waist, spreading into a shiny ebony tail—powerful and muscular. But now that she could finally see his *thing*, she wasn't all that impressed. Though she'd never witnessed a merman's privates before and had only seen drawings of male parts in Ash's health book, she'd expected something larger than a tubeworm. How did something so squishy work anyway? Sure, Ash had explained the birds and the bees to her, but fishy style? That appeared to be something completely different.

She bit her knuckle and waited for him to stir. When imagining her first time, she'd hoped Azor would be lucid, at least. And besides gyrating her hips in a mating dance to sweeten the water with pheromones, she was clueless in what else to do to seduce a sleeping merman. With the gargoyles looking on, dancing was the last thing she wanted to do. Then a horror story from mermaid class came to mind. Rumor was Ms. Gumboot's ear mishap hadn't been an accident after all. Someone said her mate let his sharkish side take over and he bit her during a moment of passion. Would Azor do the same if she tried to tickle his *thing*?

She gasped, semi revolted and chose to sit next to him. She gently raked her fingers through his lustrous hair, fanning out the dark strands in the current. All they needed was time together and all doubts she had about their differences and compatibility would vanish.

Azor rolled over with a grunt and pinned her down with his heavy tail. The spikes of his pectoral fin dug into her lap, cutting her scales. She muffled a gasp and unpinned herself from his appendage, rubbing at the bleeding cuts on her tail.

Maybe sleeping in separate beds was a good idea.

No, she told herself. *This is part of being a dutiful mate.* She swam to the other side of the bed and gathered her courage. Spooning next to him, she nuzzled her nose to his ear this time.

Finally, he chucked and reached for her, mumbling something under his breath. Hoping he'd take her into his arms and give her the grand experience everyone was always so hush-hush about, she positioned herself.

His hands made contact with her tulle covered boobs first. She willed away her trembling limbs and held her breath, waiting for him to pull her in tight, ushering her into bliss. But Azor squeezed, too hard.

She yelped and jerked away.

He continued to grope with his hands as if looking for something, eyes still closed.

"Riri," he mumbled, "get back over here, you vixen."

Riri? Tatiana floundered, confused at the name, but assumed he was dreaming. Protecting her chest with one arm and her closest ear with the other, she slid her fin over within his reach.

His eyes fell open and he groggily stared at her, half-lidded. She smiled and revealed her chest to him, hoping he'd undo the bow.

"I'm here for you," she said, her mouth dry and her heart doing jumping jacks on her empty stomach. "Wrapped as a present."

He stared at her chest for a beat, and then his lips pulled down. "What are you wearing?"

Wide-eyed, Tatiana felt her insides jolt. He didn't like it—how could he not? She suddenly wished she'd at least looked in a mirror first. Was she hideous? She glanced down at her breasts, confused. They appeared perky and presentable, as far as she could tell.

However, in the time exchange, Azor's eyes flipped shut and he flopped backward, rolling away from her. Tatiana stared down at him, trying to process what had happened, her self-esteem crushed. Bubbles made their way up to the ceiling from his backside vent, bathing her with a fowl stench she could taste on her tongue.

He started snoring again and the creatures on the walls mocked her disgracefully again. Then, from out of nowhere, his tail whipped around and wacked her in the backside, nicking her with his poisonous barb. Like a car without breaks, her body careened sideways through the water toward the leviathan on the door. She squealed and held her hands out, bracing for the impact.

As she stopped herself from narrowly missing the monster's teeth, fire spread down her tail and ignited her fin on the inside. She whimpered, withholding her sobs, and rubbed out the burn. She glared at Azor. He'd slept through everything. Cursing under her breath, she took the hint and pulled at the water with her hands, dragging her dysfunctional tail out the door, never feeling more humiliated in her life.

6

Priorities

Tatiana rolled over and opened her eyes at the murmurs coming from the first floor. Her ratty dress floated above her like a ghost, minus the gem-covered overlay that was resting on the floor. Pain from her dorsal fin flared once again.

"Holy crawfish." She reached for her aching appendage and had prompt flashbacks from the night prior. Did Azor even remember what happened?

On her mental checklist of things never to do while trying to seduce Azor, WEAR TULLE was listed on top. *What a sack of sea slugs. But he did like Grandma's shell encrusted bra I wore at the top-secret meeting.* Imagining the jangling top activated the synapses of her brain. Maybe a secret dinner for two, in a secluded place where Azor could get his mind off of work—without eyes and ears invading their privacy, was the key. And chocolate covered strawberries. She tapped her lips with her finger. Where would she find those in Natatoria? Maybe Sandy could help or she could pull some strings with her old buddy Dorian.

Then, after Azor's appetite was sated for both food and other things, she could promise to cook food like that for him all the time and serve him topless—with an air bubble installed, of course. She could read and write, not to mention paint. *Sea stars*, at the thought of cooking, her untransformed human toes curled. He'd love her forever just for her pancakes.

The creak of the iron door made her heart hiccup. She looked up, hoping Azor had come to apologize, and bit her lip so she wouldn't spill the crabs about the magnificent dinner she'd planned.

"Princess?" Xirene asked before she entered the room.

At her voice, Tatiana's hope deflated.

"Yes, come in," she said with a huge sigh, then remembered she still wore the tulle bow across her chest. She swam up, snagged the dress, and held it over her homemade lingerie.

"Breakfast." Xirene carried in a plate of food and set it on the bed, the same tray Tatiana had used the night prior. Her stomach soured at the embarrassing memory.

"You didn't have to. I could have come down." She turned her back to Xirene and shimmied into the dress, reminding herself to pick up more clothing today.

"The morning has been busy with the planning meetings. I assumed you didn't want to eat with all the guards wandering about, since you slept late." Xirene swam over and helped fasten the buttons on her dress.

Slept late? She glared at the dim lighting outside, angered she had no way to tell the day or time.

Xirene continued. "Can I bring you something to do today? Sewing, perhaps?"

Tatiana pouted before she popped a fresh blueberry into her mouth. Cooking, yes, hand sewing, no way. She remembered the disastrous vest she'd made for Azor for the festival—partly because she'd tried to make it ugly—and suppressed a smile.

"What are the big plans?"

"Oh… the guards are reattaching the crystal ball and rebuilding the shark fence," Xirene said, flitting around the room as if to look for something to do. "Along with other things—all boring stuff."

"Hmmm." Tatiana popped another berry into her mouth. "Actually, I need your help with something."

She stopped, eyeing her warily. "You do?"

"I'm going to my parent's house today, to get clothes, but to also set up a romantic dinner for Azor. I need you to cover for me, then send him to my house at, say, six o'clock."

Xirene open and closed her mouth in quick succession. "I don't think that's such a good idea, Princess."

Tatiana chuckled "And why not?"

"Well, with everything." She shook her head and tsked.

"What do you mean, *with everything*?"

Xirene fiddled with her white gloves, pulling them taut around her elbow. "Azor wishes you to stay here, where you'll be safe. And I don't feel right—"

"Safe?" Tatiana tilted her head. "Come on, Xirene. If Jacob escorts me, how would that be dangerous? I could dress like a Dradux—cover my head. Maybe Coralade can help?"

"About your parents' house." She looked down and gulped. "I've been meaning to tell you. There was… an accident."

Tatiana's limbs fell limp. "What do you mean, an accident?"

"When the ball fell, it crushed a few houses. Your parents'… I'm sorry to say… was a casualty."

"What?" Tatiana sucked in a deep breath; her fin sunk to the floor. "Why didn't anyone tell me?"

"We… we weren't sure how to tell you." She flashed an apologetic smile and patted Tatiana's shoulder. "And… everyone knew they wouldn't be back, and you live here now—I'm sorry."

Tatiana turned and closed her eyes, unwilling to lose it in front of Xirene. "Oh."

"I'll leave you alone." Xirene slipped out of the door.

Tatiana wanted to die. Though her home didn't have much as far as memories, her mom had brought priceless keepsakes from Tahoe. And if Tatiana never saw her parents again, only her memories would remain. She at least wanted to see the damage—see if she could rescue anything, though most everything would be ruined by the water.

"Gah!" She couldn't stay cooped up in this room anymore. She was beginning to go stir crazy and her hibernating legs itched for room to breathe.

Jacob greeted Tatiana with a smile when she entered the hall. "Princess."

She startled in surprise. "Jacob?"

"At your service."

She pressed her hands to her sides, grazing the place Azor had stung her the night before, and refrained from flinching. "What are you doing here?"

"I'm your bodyguard. I go where you go."

She pursed her lips. "More like an electronic leash."

Jacob's mouth twisted. "Electronic leash?"

"Never mind. Human thing. So, what gives?"

He still kept a puzzled expression.

"Forget it." She swam to the porthole, done with small talk.

Jacob blocked her path, spreading his flukes over the passage. "You can't pass."

"And why is that?" She perched her hands on her hips.

"It's just better you stay in your room. You don't need to be bothered with—"

"With what?" She huffed. "The big plans? I'm already in *the know*, so… move aside."

"How about a game of Carfunkle?"

"Carfunkle? You can't be serious." She laughed. This wasn't the time to offer the merling version of marbles. "What do you think I am, ten?"

Jacob flustered. "It's just a suggestion—to help you pass the time."

"I don't need to be protected from overhearing the details about the palace repairs, Jacob. I'm not a delicate flower."

"It's not my request." He moved closer to the porthole and flared the spikes on the sides of his fin. "Please, Princess."

She eyed the spikes warily, the last jolt with Azor a little too fresh in her memory.

"Or you'll what? Hurt me?" She laughed temporarily until remembering the heat between them when he'd restrained her—her cheeks flushed.

"I'll do whatever is necessary."

She glared, wishing she had laser eyes like the mermaid movies often depicted.

"Azor!" She yelled through cupped hands. "AZOR!"

The voices stopped on the first floor. Azor appeared in a flash. Tatiana smiled when she saw him, hoping he'd straighten out this misunderstanding, but he didn't return her happiness.

"What is going on here?" Azor said through his teeth.

"Jacob won't let me go downstairs."

"I know," Azor said, "I told him to keep you up here."

She pursed her lips. "You did? But why?"

He grasped her by the elbow and pulled her into the room.

"It's for your safety."

Though she'd wanted his touch more than anything, she pulled her arm away and laughed. "My safety? Seriously?"

"Yes," he said earnestly.

"We're in your dumb compound. Who's going to attack me here? A moray eel?"

"It's not a matter of protection..." Azor looked away momentarily. "But of trust."

"Trust?" She dropped her hands. "Xirene said you're talking about repairs, right?"

Azor closed his eyes for a beat. "No, Tatiana. The daughter of the rebel leader cannot be seen overhearing the plans involving the rebels. It sends the wrong message."

"The wrong message?" Her mouth gaped. "Well, wouldn't our relationship send the wrong message? No?"

"Well..." Azor flipped his tail nervously.

Tatiana leaned in. "I thought you were going to hold the rebels for a few days and then let them go. I mean, we were just promised. We haven't even celebrated our promisetide, or... done anything, yet." She looked upward at him, eyes twinkling, hoping he'd get her underlying meaning.

"Yes, but there have been rumors there will be another attack." Azor's eye twitched. "And with my father out of commission, it's my duty to deal with this. There will be plenty of opportunity for celebration when all of this is over. So for now you must be patient. I'm needed most here."

Her shoulders dropped and she pressed him with an angry scowl. "Your wife needs you most."

"Wife?" He laughed and rolled his eyes. "The human ways have clouded you and your parents' judgment. If you would have been raised in the colony, we wouldn't be having this problem in the first place. You need to learn your place among the mers, starting with me."

"Or what? You'll take me to Bone Island?" She guffawed. "I don't even feel like you're promised to me. You haven't kissed me once or told me you love me."

Azor raised his brow. "I've been a little busy, if you haven't noticed."

"Too busy to acknowledge your new *mate*?" She tightened her eyes when annunciating the official mer term.

"I've acknowledged you as much as I'm afforded and I don't allow my feelings to overrule me."

"Oh, right. Sure you don't." She balled her hands into fists. "And yet you've managed to direct all your anger and blame on me for what my father has done. How's that for keeping your feelings in check?" She turned her back on him, unwilling to allow him the satisfaction of seeing her lip quiver.

He swam over and touched her shoulder.

"Don't say that," he said softly.

He began to pet her hair and rested his chest against her back. She rolled her eyes shut, the fire dousing under his touch. Their bodies pressed up against one another and she ached for him to take her into his arms and away from the madness.

She reached around and clenched onto his backside, wiggling her hips against his, launching a few of her pheromones in the water. "Then show me."

Azor's body tensed and he kicked his tail, dragging Tatiana

backward in the current with him. When she didn't let go, he extricated his body from her hands. "Tatiana, please. I need to go. We can do this later."

"Later?" she asked with a laugh. "I think something's seriously wrong with you."

Azor's nostrils flared and he flew at her, and flattened her body against the wall, trapping her hands above her head. "Don't insult my restraint."

Tatiana's pulse leapt in her throat. She could see in his eyes he wanted her, that he just needed an excuse to call off his duties for the day. Her hips swirled again in the mating dance.

"But I want you," she whispered.

His chest heaved, his face conflicted, before he succumbed to her. Hungrily, he pressed his lips to hers, pressing his taut body against her. She wriggled her hands free and wrapped them around his neck and up into his hair. He gave in to his wants, deepening the kiss further.

"I do… want you, Tatiana," he said in her ear, the water whooshing from his lips, forced and warm. "I just need my men to trust me, that's all. Cooperate with Jacob until this is all over and then I'll make it up to you. Can you do that for me?"

She closed her eyes, her head spinning, and pushed down her selfish desires. "Barbados?"

He laughed, playfully. "We'll see."

"Fine, I guess so. But you're mine tonight. Promise me that."

"Yes, of course." He finished with a quick kiss on her forehead and turned to leave.

But given a tiny morsel when she'd been starved of his affection, she couldn't let him go just yet. She caught his hand

and pulled him back to her like a rubber band. Her mouth pressed eagerly to his as her hands moved to run down his chest and to find the top of his manskirt. Fumbling to unbutton the top, she wove her tail around his. His eyes opened wide in shock.

He yanked his head back and pushed her off with his hands. "Ta—Tatiana, what are you doing?"

She pressed an impish smile on her lips. "Just an appetizer of what's to come later."

Azor's head whipped around to the door. A silver fin with a missing fluke flashed past the cracked doorway. He turned to Tatiana and scowled, like they'd done something naughty.

"Don't do that in public. It's not proper," Azor scolded as he left the room.

Confused and still turned on, Tatiana blinked, trying to process what had happened.

Public? What—?

"We're in our own house," she called back. *And serves Xirene right to get an eyeful, the little snoop.*

But Azor didn't return.

"Azor?" Tatiana called, "I'm not done talking to you."

As she entered the hall, Jacob slid over, blocking her path to the porthole.

Her cheeks flared, knowing he'd been in the hall this entire time. "Where'd he go?"

"Princess." Jacob bowed in a heavy nod.

"I don't want your sympathy, Jacob," she said with a scowl. "And why are you here anyway? Pretending to care about Azor's cause? So much so you're protecting his mate?"

"I'm here just as you are. Pretending." He cocked his head,

challenging her.

"Pretending? I'm promised to—"

"And that means you let your feelings, however wrong they may be, overrule what is right? That's not the girl Jack bragged about," Jacob interrupted.

Tatiana flexed her fin. "What is that supposed to mean?"

"If your father were here right now, would he be proud of your choices? Would he say well done for begging the attention of the one who stole your kiss and mistreats your people?"

Her hand flew to her mouth. "You have some nerve, traitor."

"Traitor." He chuckled and shook his head. "I guess the promise does brainwash a mermaid. I'd hoped, for Jack's sake, you'd feel differently."

Unwilling to take any more of his insults, Tatiana swam up into Jacob's face, grabbing ahold of his chest plate. "You have no right to judge me, Jacob. You have no idea what I'm going through right now. This wasn't my choice and if my father didn't—"

Jacob thrust his jaw upward. "You're father came to your rescue. Don't blame him for standing up for your rights."

Her lip quivered, her insides exploding in heat and anger. She withheld swiping her nail across his cheek and instead pointed at his face. "You may have been able to con Azor and become my bodyguard, but I don't have to like it and I will most definitely be keeping an eye on you."

He quirked a smile. "I wouldn't have it any other way."

"Oooh!" she grunted before flipping her tail to disappear into her room.

With a hard shove, Tatiana pushed the iron door shut and

flung herself onto the woven kelp bedspread, mad as a hornet fish. What did Jacob expect her to do? Fight with Azor and make him see reason? Or what? Take up a trident and rescue the mers herself? And his audacity to bring her dad into the argument. Ugh! She pounded her fist against the bed, anger and frustration swimming in her brain. Jacob had some nerve lecturing her, considering they couldn't just let the rebels go. And as it was, Azor had put his work above her needs anyway, more worried about Xirene seeing them than letting his inhibitions free.

She moved to the window and grasped the cemented bars, pressing her forehead to the smooth rock. Off in the distance, mermen worked to reinforce the spires, and over the ridge was her family's home—destroyed. Somewhere in the rock face, the tunnel to the Pacific Ocean loomed. If only the sharks weren't there, maybe she'd give Azor a well-deserved scare and exit through the Pacific gate to the Sacramento River and on to Tahoe—home. Her mom would know what to do. She missed Fin and Ash so much. Most of all, she missed her life on land, the sun, the wind, and her freedom.

She tugged the bars and grunted, finding them well cemented down, when a shark swam her way. She backed up, heart pounding, as the beast's lifeless eyes deadpanned her, good and hard. Tatiana momentarily forgot her greatest defense, her siren scream, and cowered in the corner.

"Get out of here, fish brains," she said.

It startled, then rammed its gigantic grey torso against the wall before swimming out of sight. She caught her breath and reassessed her feeble plan. The only way to maneuver past the sharks was to siren, and that would give away her plan before she could even embark on it. She slid to the floor, her head in her hands, lost.

After a stint of self-pity, she nixed the idea altogether. A visit to Tahoe without Azor's knowledge was stupid, and her parents were long gone by now. She had to hope once the drama died down that Azor would spend more time with her. That was the magic behind the promise, or so she was told. And Jacob… she didn't know what she'd do about him.

A pile of beaded fabric waved in the current from the floor, probably Xirene's ditched delivery. Bored out of her mind and sick of wearing her promising gown, Tatiana rummaged through the stuff and picked up a needle.

7

Abandon

Jacob flinched at the sound of Azor's fist slamming on the table as another argument broke out. The smell of fear filtering in the water could mean only one thing. Azor had insisted they were to go through the Pacific Gate to capture Jack in Tahoe, no excuses.

Jacob eyed Tatiana's door warily, then slid down the porthole for a closer look. Through a water vent, Jacob watched the Council shift nervously at the table in Azor's war room. Darrellon—the most disgusting of all the Dradux guards—and Alaster were the newest members of the shrinking group. Darrellon, too good to join them at the table, wore the hood of his green cloak over his head, and leaned against the wall in a dark corner, fingering his scythe. Under the hood, all Jacob could see was a hint of his eyes and the occasional flicking of his parasite over his lips. At the sight of the disgusting thing, Jacob's vent puckered.

"But what about the sharks?" Alaster asked as he scrutinized the others, as if to check if they could feel his fear.

"Cassava poison on the barbs will stop them if they're feeling brave," Azor said with a challenging glare toward Alaster. "Are you with me, or are you going to slither out on this one?"

"Of course, Captain," Alaster said, puffing out his chest. "I just want to be sure, after the King was injured—"

"Must I remind you that if you were doing your part in minding the gate, the explosion would have never happened?"

Alaster frowned. "How was I to know my slimy brother

rigged the gate with explosives?"

"That was quite a thing to overlook." Azor pitched his brow. "I'm shocked you're not eager to lead the convoy from the Pacific Ocean to the Sacramento River. It's your territory after all."

"Of course, Captain. I wouldn't have it any other way," Alaster said with a hesitant smile. "If you deem that to be the best way to go about this. Of course, there's always the option to reopen the Tahoe gate."

"Reopen the gate?" Fendole, the eldest Council mer interjected. "We don't have the merpower, or the explosives—"

"Nor the time," Azor interrupted. "Yes, later we'll shackle up the rebels and make them clear the Tahoe gate, but for now, we need to apprehend Jack and assert our authority. The citizens are watching and if we don't squash this, who's to say the rebels won't grow in numbers and lead a revolt and overthrow the kingdom? Our only option is the Pacific Gate. It's the closest body of water to Tahoe."

The group murmured in agreement, but Alaster wasn't the only merman who was concerned. Most of the Council members were bathed in worry, which was to be expected. After their King had lost his fin to a shark, they'd be idiots to swim through the enclosure with only spears. Why didn't they just have a mermaid siren for them? Or did Azor want this convoy to go through undetected? But more important, could no one sense the fear like Jacob could—covering it up with useless nonsense?

Jacob surveyed the nine members of the Council. With his and Badger's seat recently vacated, and two others arrested as rebels, only Grommet and Fendole remained undetected, secretly loyal to Jack. If the others didn't speak up and stop cowering under their scales, they'd be looking for new positions in Natatoria. Maybe it was already too late. Azor had already begun to make decisions without them, adding more Dradux as his henchmen to carry out his wishes.

Upon a slim majority vote to swim through the shark enclosure, Azor left the war room. Jacob returned to the porthole entrance, expecting Azor to beat him there to grovel for Tatiana's forgiveness. Instead, Azor swam into the kitchen.

Jacob waited, watching for Azor to return as the others could be heard milling about into the opposing hall with the occasional banging of armor and weapons. He glided over to the main room, curious. Outfitted mermen applied thick bright-green poison to the tips of their spears. Jacob's stomach churned—cassava poison was supposed to be illegal. At least it was when Jack and the King were on the Council.

The time ticked on, yet Azor still hadn't returned from the kitchen. What was he doing? Did he have any intention of telling Tatiana what he was up to? That he was leaving?

Jacob sighed and leaned up against the wall, questioning his choice in this assignment, questioning his sanity. Yes, he'd promised Tatiana's father he'd keep watch over his daughter, but Jack couldn't have prepared him for this. Sure, he knew things would get ugly considering he'd developed feelings for Tatiana, but he'd never expected Azor to act so callously toward her. What in Hades was wrong with him? Could Azor not see the beautiful woman before him? Her smile, her spunk, her beautiful deep-blue eyes, her amazing body. If Tatiana were his, she wouldn't get a moment's peace—well, maybe to eat and occasionally sleep. But it was as if Azor wasn't even a man, let alone promised to her. His focus was solely centered on revenge. For what? Jack had only wanted Fin and Tatiana to choose their mates—nothing worth starting a civil war over.

And then Azor's constant lies, like he only pacified her so she'd behave—to abandon her again for… Jacob couldn't be sure what else could be more important. But still, he was secretly pleased for his own selfish reasons. If there was anything more than the little contact Azor gave her now, Jacob would have to flay his chest right there and cut out his soul.

And yet again, Azor would leave without saying where to or for how long. And she'd crumble, questioning herself when she should be irate at the lying loser—all because of a stupid kiss. Jacob palmed his hand through his hair. *Madness, utter madness.*

He fought the urge to swim to her room, subdue her somehow, and abduct her again. He'd happily endure more siren screams and bites to help her see reason, to free her from Azor's power. And he preferred that feisty side of her.

More importantly, he'd heard rumors of people who'd fought their promise if they weren't happy or were mated to someone who'd somehow survived Bone Island and were never reunited. They'd overcome the pull; they'd moved on to another. Tatiana could do that as well, if she truly wanted. She didn't need to be chained for life to such a sociopath.

Grommet swam up to Jacob, breaking him from his spiraling thoughts.

"We're going, man," he said under his breath. "Azor thinks Jack purposefully pushed Colin and Alaster through the gate before rigging it to blow. And I bet Jack thinks he's got time, too."

Jacob breathed harder. "We need to get him word. Where's Badge?"

Grommet rolled his eyes. "Who knows? After he was kicked off the Council for being beta, I lost track of him yesterday. With everything going on, Azor's gone a little wacko since the ceremony. He's not only increased the guard, but the Dradux as well. He saved the grunt jobs for the betas whose alibis cleared. I bet Badger's probably training in the yard with the younger ones like always, or worse—elder duty."

Jacob withheld a laugh. Badger loved heckling the little kids and with Azor out of his hair, he could easily slip away to his mate's cousin Dorian's gate and warn Jack via phone without anyone noticing.

"I'll take care of it," Jacob whispered. "Just… you know."

They gave each other a knowing smile. Since they were merlings, Grommet was king of making trouble and passing the blame onto someone else.

Azor emerged from the kitchen, distressed. He caught Jacobs's eye. *Is his skirt on backward?*

"I'm leaving for a few days. Tell Tatiana I'm… Hades. That she needs to sit tight and I'll be back in a few days. I'll make it up to her. Keep her from doing anything stupid, if you know what I mean." He rubbed his goatee, thinking. "I'll have my mother fetch her tomorrow and bring her to the palace. That might help her adjust better."

Jacob nodded, fighting a grin. If anyone was about to do anything stupid, it was Jacob. *So much could happen in a few days when you leave your promised mate alone, Azor.* While watching Azor tie back his hair with a cord, Jacob thought of how easy snapping his neck would be.

He closed his eyes. *Patience, Jacob. Patience.*

Without another word and none the wiser to Jacob's deception, Azor left the compound with his minions in tow, and Jacob returned to Tatiana's door. He waited for the shriek. Maybe he'd be lucky. Maybe she wouldn't see.

Twenty minutes later, Jacob's prediction came true.

"Azor!" Tatiana screamed from within her room. "What are you doing?"

Jacob's pulse pounded as he waited a beat longer. He couldn't burst into her room unannounced, unless…

At her siren scream, he quickly pushed open the door and Tatiana swam full force into his chest plate, knocking him back into the current. She let out a groan, rubbing her head.

"Princess. Are you okay?" Jacob steadied her, wary of her claws, as she fought to swim around him.

"They left—with Azor—through the sharks. He's not safe. He can't leave!" Her words tumbled from her trembling lips. "He promised."

Jacob sighed, the ache of watching her fret was overwhelming. "They'll be back. Don't worry."

"Back?" Her voice spiked an octave. "He said he needed a day. Where is he going? Why?"

She swam past him, through the porthole, not waiting for an answer. The entire place had emptied except for a few mermen guarding the front and dungeon doors. She yanked on the metal handle, unable to open it.

"Open these doors right now!" she demanded.

The guard on her left only watched with a smirk on his face.

"Didn't you hear me? By order of the Princess. Open them!"

"No," Jacob said somberly, resting his hand on her shoulder. "You're to stay here. Azor will be back soon."

"Where is he going? To—?" The fear in the water matched her face, chilling his bones as her frantic eyes darted from him to the door—like a caged animal knowing the slaughter was coming. She grabbed onto his arms, begging. "We have to warn—"

"I know," he said quietly.

At the opposite end of the hall, groans flowed freely from the dungeon. Tatiana dropped his arm and turned as Sandy, Badger's mate, exited through the doors. She wiped her hand across her brow when she caught sight of Jacob and the Princess.

She quickly bowed and retrieved an empty basket off the floor. "Jacob, how's your—?"

"I'm fine, Sandy. Thank you," Jacob said quickly, his hand grazing the arm bracer covering Tatiana's bite. He'd failed to mention to Sandy that day that Tatiana had been his attacker when she'd bandaged him. He proffered his arm to her, anxious to pass word of Azor's plan. "Can I escort you out?"

"Oh, thank you, Jacob. That would be nice."

Sandy smiled and swam forward, then stopped. Tatiana, frozen in a trance, remained planted directly in her way. Jacob knocked into Tatiana's tail when she didn't move aside, breaking her from her spell.

"Sandy," she finally said breathlessly, "nice to see you again."

"Yes, it is. It feels like it's been ages with everything that's happened."

The Princess gulped and eyed the dungeon door. "What are

you doing here?"

"I came to deliver messages to the prisoners from their families. Part of their punishment is no visitors, so the Queen has allowed me to come once a day to bring food, at least until they've served their sentence."

"Of course," the Princess said, straightening up. "That's very kind. I wish they didn't have to suffer at all, it's really not…" Her eyes hit the stone floor as her words trailed off.

"Don't blame yourself, sweetie. This wasn't your fault." Sandy gave her a sympathetic look. With a quick tilt of her head, she clued Tatiana in on a guard listening. "We haven't seen you around the palace. Is newly promised life treating you well?"

Jacob restlessly flicked his tail, annoyed at the small talk.

Come on, girls. Jack doesn't have all day.

"As well as can be expected, considering …"

Jacob grimaced at Tatiana's lie; her promising was far from the happily-ever-after any mermaid would have wanted. He could remedy that for her—now—if he were confident he could contain her teeth and talons first.

"Yes," Sandy said and smiled sweetly. "Well, I best be on my way. Hopefully I'll see you at the palace later."

Jacob straightened with a slight smile and readied himself to solicit her help out of the guard's earshot.

"Oh, why don't you stay for…" —Tatiana fidgeted and looked to the kitchen, sweeping out her hand—"dessert, perhaps?"

Sandy blinked in surprise as Tatiana clearly gnawed on her lip. Jacob's nostrils flared. *What are you up to?*

"Sure," Sandy said, her eyes darting in question to Jacob.

"Perfect." Tatiana turned to Jacob, raising her brows. "Sandy is a long-time friend and I'm in need of some company since I've been alone this *entire* time. And Azor's—well, you know, MIA—so, if you don't mind."

Jacob remained straight faced. "You don't have to ask my permission. Sandy is always welcome." Tatiana gnawed at her lip and he entertained a brief fantasy of taking her cheeks between his hands and kissing her, because in all honesty, that's what she needed most.

"Great." Tatiana arched her eyebrows. When Jacob didn't move, she shooed him with her hand. "You're dismissed, Jacob."

Jacob inwardly chuckled at her spunk and moved to the front door. But as soon as the girls disappeared into the kitchen, he relocated to the foyer, and remained out of their sight, but close enough to listen in.

"Where's Xirene?" Tatiana asked.

"Out," Shanleigh grumbled.

Jacob recalled Xirene's rushed escape earlier after interrupting the two in Tatiana's room and he blocked out what the reason could be, assuming Xirene had the same problem he had—misplaced affection.

The conversation oddly paused and the smell of freshly cut fish tainted the water.

"Are there any blueberries left over?" Tatiana asked.

"I don't know." The annoyance in Shanleigh's voice angered Jacob and the urge to remind her she spoke to the future Queen rocked him, but he stayed outside the doorway, determined to chew her out later.

"Could you go look?" Tatiana asked, a little more pointed.

"Yes," Shanleigh quipped.

At the silence, he wondered what the ladies were doing, when he heard Tatiana whisper.

"Azor and his army just left to go to the Pacific Ocean. I'm worried he's going to find a way to get to Tahoe. I need to warn my family."

Jacob blinked in shock and then smiled at her resourcefulness.

"Will you help me?" Tatiana asked.

Sandy answered, "Of course. We'll get them word. Don't worry."

Tatiana's voice returned to a normal level. "Thank you, Sandy, for everything, especially for your kindness to the jailed rebels."

One of the guards snapped up his head and Jacob realized her mistake—twice she'd shown mercy within earshot of those who gossiped and questioned her loyalty.

"Yes, Princess," Sandy said before her voice quieted. "A word of advice," she whispered, "don't let anyone see your concern for the rebels. You needn't worry about them. I'll handle their well-being. Remember, in these hard times, appearances are everything. No one wants you accused of treason."

Tatiana's voice faltered. "But I'm royalty."

"And not above the law and the lies." Sandy's voice hardened in warning. "Trust no one," she said softly.

Their conversation paused for a beat, and then just like that, their chatter changed to the promising ceremony, redecorating the compound, and the like.

After several minutes, Shanleigh finally returned, interrupting them. "I'm so sorry, Princess. I couldn't find any leftover blueberries. Will these raspberries do?"

Jacob could imagine the state of raspberries underwater, even fresh ones. He fought everything not to barge in and smack

Shanleigh across the face for her disrespect.

"Thank you," Tatiana said sweetly. "Don't let me keep you from preparing the fish."

At Tatiana's sweetness, Jacob's anger defused. He marveled, even in times of great distress, she remained kind, even to the servants. Sudden rustling at the table alerted Jacob the kitchen chat was over. He glided nonchalantly to the door, pretending he was there the entire time.

"Done already?" Jacob asked with a fake cheeriness.

Tatiana stuck out her tongue playfully.

The two ladies hugged, and Sandy swam to the door. Tatiana hovered a little too closely while Jacob lifted the metal bar, releasing the door. He assumed Tatiana wouldn't lose control in front of Sandy, but he still positioned himself so Tatiana couldn't slip away. If only the guards weren't watching. He could so easily allow her to run, with his help, of course.

Sandy bid a quick goodbye and swam off. Once Jacob locked the iron back in its place, the panic Tatiana had managed to cage spread menacingly across her face. He could imagine her thoughts, especially since her separation from Azor would be for an unknown length of time. Fear swirled an ugly finger around them and Jacob grimaced. He wanted to help her, comfort her. But mostly distract her.

"I'm going to my room," she said quickly, lifting her chin. "Goodnight."

He cringed, knowing night was hours away, but she swam away before he could respond. He redirected his anger to the mermaid in the kitchen. Before he paid a visit to the barracks, Shanleigh was going to wish she'd checked her attitude at the door.

8

Examination

A sweet, gentle voice woke Tatiana from her slumber. She expected to see her mom, but instead looked up into Queen Desiree's light-blue eyes framed in white-blonde hair. Her body shuddered awake.

"My Queen." Tatiana sat up with a gasp, wondering if she should bow or what was the proper way to address her.

"Oh, don't be alarmed, my sweet," the Queen said with crimson lips. "It's just me."

Tatiana's heart sped to full throttle, alerting her tail to move. Like a bird, she perched on a nearby chair and quizzically looked around the room. Next to the queen, the lithe blond healer who'd drugged Tatiana the morning of the ceremony hovered in the current. Her not-so-innocent gaze studied her and Tatiana wondered what her mother-in-mer was up to.

"Azor mentioned you haven't been feeling well," the Queen said.

Tatiana furrowed her brow. "I feel fine, my Queen."

She smiled weakly, embarrassed they'd found her here instead of in Azor's bed. She actually wished the healer could mend what was ailing Azor—his inability to bond with her officially.

"Well, that's good to know, because your sisters have missed seeing you at the palace and are asking why you haven't come around to visit."

"They're not mad?"

"Mad? Oh…" Her words trailed off as she swam to the window, glaring at the sharks in the distance. "This entire situation has become most unfortunate because of the accident. The King is healing slowly and hopefully he'll feel strong enough to resume taking audience soon and put all the accusations to rest. In the meantime, I've asked Azor to remove the sharks so they don't escape again. I see they're still here." Ice laced her voice.

"Is that what he's doing? Getting rid of the sharks?" Tatiana asked, her voice growing shrill. She absentmindedly rubbed her aching left ear. With her strained relationship with Xirene, she hadn't had time to ask for another dose.

"No," she said coldly.

Tatiana kept her eyes downcast, warring with herself about whether to apologize on her father's behalf or not. Would that only put him in the crosshairs again? No one had outright accused him of blowing up the gate, but the timing was suspicious.

"I have something else to discuss with you," the Queen continued quickly.

Tatiana kept her head low, her heart pounding, prepared for the worst. The Queen's surprise visit hadn't been to check up on her after all. Her worst fears were coming true. Imprisonment for her parents' sins, perfect timing since Azor wasn't there.

"My son and I have vastly differing approaches to this problem, and I want to test a theory."

Tatiana gulped again. *Test a theory? What did that mean?*

"I believe your presence at the palace will show a united front after everything. Because I trust you, so should everyone else. A show of support that I've forgiven and forgotten, you see. That your union has been blessed and so has your future." She nodded to her young servant, who swam over with a smile.

"I'm going to check you over," the girl said in a lilting voice.

"Check me for what?"

"I heard you were hurt from the blast—your ear," the Queen interrupted.

"Oh," Tatiana reached up and touched her ear, "yes, it's still sore."

The healer's large bugged-out eyes sent a shiver down Tatiana's fin. She turned Tatiana's head to the side with her gloved fingers and peered into her ear. From her apron, she pulled out a weed and shoved the mangled pulp into the sore ear. Twigs poked the delicate skin lining the canal, making her wince. Relief wasn't as quick or as wonderful as when Xirene had treated her, but the pain lessened nonetheless.

The girl continued, checking Tatiana's tongue and eyes, then kneading her hands over her ribs, making her giggle. And then, without permission, the girl removed Tatiana's top and studied her breasts.

"Hey," Tatiana said with a squeak and covered herself with her arms. "Is this really necessary?"

Tatiana held her hand out for her top she'd handcrafted the night prior. The Queen blew out a breath of water and grimaced, acting as if her servant had merely inspected cantaloupes at a farmers market.

With the Queen's nod, the healer gave Tatiana her top back.

"We must make sure you haven't been infected with the Ichthyopthirius multifilis," the Queen simply stated.

"What? On my breasts?" Tatiana startled at the accusation, knowing the "ick" parasites showed up as white spots on one's gills first. "I highly doubt it."

Tatiana quickly fastened the button in the back and eyed the healer suspiciously.

"May I feel your abdomen?" the healer asked with a smile.

Tatiana looked to the Queen in a plea to which she merely gestured with her hand. "Please, let the healer finish."

Tatiana clenched her fists and lay on the bed. "I promise you, I don't have the ick."

Both women remained quiet, intent on studying Tatiana's body like she was on display at the zoo. The healer's hands kneaded her scale-covered stomach, pressing all around the area under her bellybutton.

"Hey, that tickles," Tatiana said, squirming.

The healer gave the Queen an insightful look before motioning that she roll over. "I'm almost finished."

Tatiana groaned.

"Please cooperate." The Queen smacked her tail, impatient.

Tatiana rolled over, wishing the exam would end soon, and felt the healer examine her spine, checking each vertebra. The healer pressed into her skin where her tail started and tugged on Tatiana's scales with a hum. Then with a quick lift of the cloth encircling Tatiana's hips, the healer squished her fingers into the spot where only her mate should ever touch, releasing her mating scent into the water. Tatiana flipped her tail and slid out from the healer's probing touch.

"Hey! What are you doing?" She pulled the cloth down to cover her cloaca, angered.

The healer pulled her head back, stunned, and looked to the Queen. "It's all part of the exam."

"Please, Tatiana. It's to know the condition of your female system." Queen Desiree pulled aside her long white tresses and leaned in. "Aren't you curious to know if all your parts are functioning properly?"

Parts? The Queen made her sound more like a starfish than a person. "I'm sure they're working just fine, thank you."

"Are they?" Queen Desiree pushed up her brow, giving Tatiana a knowing look. "Now let's not kid ourselves. If that were true, you wouldn't be here... alone, would you?"

Tatiana froze in her spot, her mouth agape. Salt in her wounded heart. The reason for the examination settled into focus. Azor must have said she had the ick to get out of why they weren't celebrating their promisetide. And now, after the examination, the Queen knew full well that wasn't the case. She blamed Tatiana's inability to seduce him as the culprit. She felt weak, her fin slowly flattening against the ground.

"Don't despair. Having a beta-mer as a mother, of course you don't know these things. You should have come to me sooner. Many have issue when it comes to the act. I'll set up a private class with the mer matrons. They'll show you the dance. Then when Azor returns, you'll feel more confident." The Queen smiled innocently and patted her arm. "Now, collect your things and come with me to the palace. There is a lot to do."

Tatiana clamped her mouth shut and tried to wash away the humiliation. The Queen might as well have stamped "frigid" on her forehead, and her cheeks caught flame under her skin. If it wasn't so embarrassing, she would have confessed to the Queen her failure to please Prince Azor wasn't because of her lack of trying.

A male cleared his throat in the hall. "Princess?"

Jacob. At his voice, she really wanted to die. She already knew his displeasure in her appeasing Azor, but did he know, too, that she hadn't done it yet? Did the entire palace know? Was everyone talking about her supposed *ick*?

She buried her face in her hands.

"Princess?" he asked again. "I'm ready to escort you."

Tatiana pressed her eyes shut, determined not to let Queen Desiree ruffle her, and reopened them with new resolve. Azor's obsession with work clearly had prevented him from consummating their union, and the *ick* was a kinder excuse for why they weren't pregnant yet—so much better than saying he was too busy. Could that be the real reason? The only reason? She groaned at the thought.

But she knew, after their brief tryst yesterday, it wasn't a matter of desire. Guilt from indulging in pleasure over his duties had prevented him from giving into it. And then snoopy Xirene didn't help. If she didn't get his mind off of work, her barren womb would raise suspicions. Most newly promised couples were pregnant within the first week, unless something was physically wrong, or one partner was a beta, which usually made pregnancy difficult to achieve. A week hadn't passed, well, not yet. Was the entire kingdom counting? *Oh, Poseidon.* If she didn't look pregnant soon, she'd be labeled defective.

Her eyes rolled back into her head, her stomach churning. No. She'd help Azor get his focus off of work and onto her. Somehow. He'd chosen her after all and she'd make him proud—

and soon—before she was doomed to be… replaced.

At the thought of watching another mermaid cling to his arm and bear his shoal, she wanted to vomit.

Sea stars, she moaned on the inside.

"Princess?" Jacob asked again. "We shouldn't keep the Queen waiting."

"Yes," Tatiana said warily as she swam out of her room with a fake smile and her head held high.

If Sandy was able to get the message to Dorian, Azor wouldn't find her family and he'd come straight home to Natatoria. Then she'd make him want her—as soon as he returned. Once she became pregnant, she'd flaunt her full belly for the entire kingdom to see, the first being the Queen. Then everyone would be happy, too happy to punish the rebels, too happy for war.

9

Birds and the Bees

The entourage of merfolk exited out the front doors of the compound in a massive school; the Queen and ten or so of the guards surrounding her in front, while Jacob and Tatiana hung in the back. Jacob's straight face and alert eyes weren't typical of his normal self at the compound. Being a secret rebel, she could see how he'd be uncomfortable, but his fearful reaction unnerved her.

"Are you okay, Jacob?" Tatiana asked in a low tone.

Jacob continued to survey the landscape, never once looking at her directly. "Yes, Princess. Just stay close to me. Never wander alone in the palace."

Her lips curled into a smirk. This is what bothered him? She wanted to snort at his over-protectiveness and constant attempts to poke his tail into her business. Instead, she saluted him to be funny. "Sure thing, Captain."

He squinted at her for a brief second as if to say, "Stop joking around and wise up." The deep grooves in his scowl hit her like a smack to the cheek.

Tatiana broke eye contact and glanced across the horizon at the palace. Desolate and quiet, not a single mer was in sight. An eerie feeling crept over her as an earlier conversation she'd overheard between Shanleigh and Coralade sunk in. They'd said the mer matrons had refused to sing, in mourning for the jailed rebels. And since Azor had accused all beta-mers without alibis of treason, no one knew how long the punishment would last—making everyone crazy with worry. But to experience the void of song left a deep yearning inside Tatiana. She choked down her own melody that bubbled behind her quivering lips.

The group swam in unison to the northern side, where only royalty entered. Being newly mated, this was her first time using this entrance and a strange excitement tickled inside her. That was until she saw the guards. Light from the room sparkled down into the water from the extra large opening in the palace floor; illuminating two figures cloaked in green, holding their ghastly scythes—Dradux. As she surfaced into the room, passing through their oyster stench, she inhaled the air and shook off their vampiric appearance. Did they always guard the royal entrances?

Before her, a white marble floor stretched the length of the room. Queen Desiree slipped behind the sea grass privacy curtain, phased into legs, and walked across the floor without missing a beat. With a quick unclipping of her skirt's train, the soft shush of sparkling fabric fell like a waterfall down behind her long legs.

Jacob and the rest of the guards reached for sunbeams from the sun-tunnels in various places and leapt up onto the floor as well. Tatiana followed Queen Desiree's lead. Behind the curtain, she basked in the sunlight and marveled as the scales faded from her skin. But at the sight of her bare thighs, she recalled she'd never fashioned herself a complete skirt and tugged down at the small swatch of cloth tied around her hips.

Panic seeped into her as she peeked out from behind the sea grass and scanned the emptying room for help. She couldn't join the Queen's audience practically naked.

Jacob softly grunted when he motioned she exit.

"I can't," she whispered.

He furrowed his brow. "Why not? The Queen is waiting."

"I don't have a skirt on," she whispered, hard.

Jacob's cheeks flushed, then he pinched his eyes shut. "Dang it, Princess."

He looked around in desperation and motioned a servant girl over. They whispered to one another, but the girl merely gawked. Each passing second squeezed Tatiana's chest tighter. She needed to follow the Queen without disruption.

The servant girl jumped into the porthole pool. With a wiggle of her hips, she produced her own skirt.

"H-here," she said with an outstretched hand.

Tatiana blinked, disbelieving this girl gave up her skirt, in front of the Dradux below, no doubt.

"No, I couldn't," Tatiana argued.

"I'll get another. Just go!"

Tatiana reluctantly took the skirt and let the curtain fall. She inspected the dripping white skirt hemmed in blue. She couldn't enter audience with a servant's skirt on, nor could she arrive naked. With a quick jerk against the blue fabric, the offending trim pulled free like perforated paper.

Perfect!

She pulled on the skirt and tied the purple swatch at her waist as an accessory, and with a quick jump to her feet, she was ready to run to the audience room if need be. Her locked-up legs had a different idea. Slipping on the marble in her bare feet like she were on roller-skates for the first time, she toppled forward, hands splayed to catch her fall. Jacob darted forward and swooped his arms around her waist, catching her just in time.

"I've got you, Princess," he said softly, setting her upright.

Tatiana's cheeks flared, not from embarrassment, but the rush flooding across her skin from Jacob's touch. She smiled and smoothed her hands down her skirt before attempting another go at walking. Jacob proffered his arm instead, which she took, and caught herself hoping for the same thrill.

"Right this way, milady."

Tatiana turned to the girl in the pool and mouthed a, "thank you," to which she smiled.

The Queen had already settled onto her throne, ready to engage the first mer citizen when Tatiana entered the chamber. All heads were bowed and Tatiana quickly lowered hers as well.

"Oh, yes. There you are." Desiree motioned Tatiana to sit in an empty chair at the end of the row of princesses. Tatiana grinned, happy to meet her approval. Then the Queen's eyes fell down to Tatiana's skirt and her smile melted off her face.

"Um… Girraween, sweetheart, please help Princess Tatiana find something more presentable to wear."

"Oh, yes." The Princess perked up and bounced over to Tatiana, grabbing her hand, but not soon enough.

A small gasp escaped the lips of the occupants in the room as they turned and stared. Tatiana's cheeks practically ignited in response. The only thing she needed to finish her servant attire was a pair of white gloves.

Oblivious, Girraween pulled Tatiana through the halls of the palace past rooms Tatiana had never seen before. The vast expanse shocked her, especially since she'd been under the impression that most of the palace was underwater. They passed a library with ceiling to floor bookshelves, flanked with busts of prior Kings. At the sight of the rows upon rows of books, Tatiana practically salivated, envisioning herself snuggled in an oversized chair, drifting off into another world—a human world she loved and missed—and wished she and Azor kept residence there instead of the waterlogged compound.

Girraween didn't notice Tatiana's longing and pulled her through the endless maze, stopping before two white wooden doors on shiny brass hinges shaped like fleur-de-lis.

"Here," she said, opening one side. "This is my room."

Lush white carpet covered the expanse of a room bigger than the first floor of the Tahoe house. Couches lined the walls filled with a variety of stuffed animals and the center featured a four-poster bed with a lacy canopy.

The Princess ran over to her humongous closet with mirror-covered doors and threw them open. Skirts and tops of every color and length were squished into three levels of hanging space like tiers of a wedding cake. On the floor were shoes—expensive designer shoes—of every type imaginable.

"Where did you get all of this?" Tatiana asked breathlessly, eyeing Girraween's bare feet.

"Land." She chuckled, as if her wardrobe swam up and beached itself at the northern porthole. "Where else, silly?"

Of, course. "Wow. I didn't think the King allowed his princesses on land."

"No, the meanie, but royalty does have its privileges." She winked.

Before Tatiana could enquire further, Girraween was at her

side, unbuttoning her skirt. "I can't believe you'd even wear this. Like, eww." As she attempted to remove the skirt entirely, Tatiana stayed her hand.

"Oh. I'll do it." She buttoned the top button and eyed the door, expecting to see Jacob lurking in the hall. "I... I didn't have a choice," she continued. "My clothes are at my house—"

"You're swimming around the guards *uncovered*?"

"No, of course not," Tatiana stammered, "I was wearing this." She untied the belt and held the swatch up, letting it unfold.

Girraween huffed. "That little thing? Sea slugs, we need to get you some clothes!"

When she ran to her closet, Tatiana darted over to shut the door so Jacob wouldn't see or hear them. Oblivious to Tatiana's concerns, she began tossing out garments one after the other. Tatiana dropped the swatch to the floor and kicked it under the bed, before she attempted to catch the onslaught of fabric and beads.

"Cease fire!" Tatiana called out as she hoisted the heavy pile onto the bed.

Girraween laughed and began to help her put on the first garment. As she unsnapped the back of her top, memories of the snooping healer came to Tatiana's mind and she pulled away.

"Thank you," Tatiana said as she disappeared around the dressing curtain. "I've got it covered."

Within moments, Tatiana returned and spun around in a green number.

"Oh, that's cute." Girraween squealed in glee, as the fabric fluttered around Tatiana's ankles. She tossed her another garment. "Try this one."

Tatiana smiled and returned to the curtain. After ten wardrobe changes, a patch of raw skin formed under her arms from the sequins and it became clear Girraween wasn't finding a proper dress for the audience; she was a bored and tenacious princess wanting to play dress-up.

"This is perfect, really." Tatiana smoothed her hand over the yellow chiffon fabric.

Girraween frowned. "Are you sure? Because I think this pink one brings out your eyes."

"No, really. I'm fine."

"If you insist." Girraween threw the garment on the mountain of clothes and plopped herself on the bed. Then she slapped her hands down, suggesting Tatiana sit. The floral cotton print reminded her of her comforter at home, sending a pang of longing for her family and Ash through her gut.

The Princess pulled a hairbrush from her side table drawer and began working out the knots in Tatiana's hair, pulling out a wayward beaded pin from her promising ceremony. "When was the last time you combed your hair?"

"Um..." Tatiana thought. "I guess my promising ceremony."

"I know you're underwater all the time, but you really shouldn't let it get like this," she said, yanking down on the brush. "So, what's it like?" she asked.

"What is what like?"

"Being promised, silly."

Tatiana forced a fake grin. "Um... it's been okay so far, though, I haven't had much time with your brother... since the ceremony."

"Oh, right, that." She gave a coy smile. "I told you everything would be better once you got promised."

Tatiana's breath hitched, remembering back to mermaid school where she'd often complained about Azor. "Yeah, it's been dreamy," she said nervously, wanting to change the subject. "Too bad he has so much work to do."

"Oh, I know." She pawed through a box of hair ties. "If mermaids ran Natatoria, there'd never be any problems. Women know how to get along so much better. And if the men get outta hand, we ink them—just like that."

Tatiana chuckled to be polite. If the King was fair, she wouldn't have an issue with men leading. But equality and the freedom to pursue one's dreams as a female was highly discouraged in Natatoria. As future queen, she hoped she could change those practices.

Girraween pinned up one side of her hair before attacking an unruly tangle, ripping at Tatiana's scalp.

"Ouch." Tatiana winced.

"Oops, sorry." She giggled. "So, what's… you know…" her voice lowered to almost a whisper, "mating like?"

Tatiana launched into a coughing fit, choking on her spit. The Princess waited, eyes wide, as if she'd asked about the water temperature outside. "I… I don't think I want to be talking about this."

"Why not?"

"It's… private."

"Well…" She looked away and brought her hand to her mouth. "This is horrible of me to say, but Pearleza told Linise that you hadn't—you know—done it yet."

"Pearleza?"

"My mother's healer." She smiled proudly as if the gossip she spread wasn't about her sister-in-mer who sat directly in front of her. "I overheard them just as you arrived. Linise is my maid."

Tatiana inhaled deeply; the air felt extremely drying in her lungs. "Of course we've done it."

"I knew it! That's what I thought. Pearleza doesn't know a dang thing. She just likes to stir up drama. Do you think you're pregnant yet? Ooh, that'll stop everything." She bit her lip.

Visions of running from the palace and swimming far away racked Tatiana's mind. Her worst fear *had* come true. How could she show her face in the palace knowing everyone knew she and Azor hadn't done the deed?

"Yeah." Tatiana felt her eyes glazing over. She needed this to stop—she needed to help Girraween start a new rumor. One that involved someone else.

"So … how'd you do it? Fishy style?" Girraween's eyes grew. "Or the *naughty*?"

"Girraween!" Tatiana cleared her throat as her mouth turned into a sand dune.

Ignoring Tatiana, she laughed and pulled out peacock feathers from a big box and rambled about the mating habits of the mers before chaperoning laws. But there was no way Tatiana would share about any type of mating—most definitely not the human way.

"I know mers say they don't do the *naughty*, but where else do they do it if not in their bubbled homes, you know? Have you ever wondered that? Of course with the compound, there isn't an air bubble, but still, I was hoping you'd tell me because it's all so foreign to me. I mean, where do your legs go? Do you have the same parts?"

"Uh... don't you think your mother should talk to you about this? I don't feel comfortable—"

"My mother? Heck no. You're the only one, Tatiana. Please. All my sisters are chaste, and I'm surrounded by stuffy mer matrons. No one will tell me."

She held her hands prayerfully and shot doe eyes. Tatiana gulped, staring fearfully back at her. Even if she'd wanted to share, she hadn't much of a clue herself.

"It's pretty special," Tatiana finally said.

She frowned. "Special? Not fun? Fin tingling? Mind blowing?" She lay back in her pillows, clutching one to her chest, and stared dreamily at the ceiling. "Utterly romantic?"

"Eh-uh yeah, those things, too." She pitched up her lips in a huge smile, hoping she'd satisfied her curiosity.

"Hmmm." Girraween sounded slightly disappointed. "Well, I'm hoping you *are* pregnant and have a boy merling so I can finally go to the dating parlor. I'm so tired of being locked away from life." She sat up quickly and tossed the gold colored throw pillow. "To finally, you know, do it."

Tatiana blinked at her, still confused why the King made them wait to be promised. Girraween looked at least eighteen. "Why can't you go to the dating parlor?"

"Daddy wouldn't let me." She straightened and furrowed her brow, speaking in a masculine voice. "Girls are to be pretty pictures: nice to look at, but shouldn't speak. The royal blood line always continues through the males, because men make the best leaders, blah, blah, blah." She snorted and rolled her eyes. "Oh... that reminds me. I want to see your fleur-de-lis."

Girraween pawed at Tatiana's waistline. Tatiana turned happily; anything to get off the topic of mating.

The Princess huffed. "It's not there yet. Weird."

At her words, Tatiana turned to look at her hip, too. She was right. The royal mark that magically appeared after one kissed a royal hadn't shown up.

Tatiana chuckled nervously and felt her ring finger—the white tattoo was taking its time to come as well. "Maybe it's like the promising tattoo?"

Girraween took a peek at Tatiana's finger, then her own hip, inspecting the royal mark she'd acquired at birth, before returning to Tatiana's hair.

"Yeah, maybe." She shrugged, then with a quick flick of her comb, she twirled and pinned each tendril of Tatiana's hair into a massive up-do surrounded in peacock feathers. "I'll have to ask my mom."

At the mention of Queen Desiree again, Tatiana's heart plummeted. "Don't you think we should return to the audience?"

Girraween faked a yawn and threw down the brush. "Do we have to? This audience stuff is such a bore. I miss our make-up and hair sessions at mermaid school so much. Wasn't that fun, back before you were promised?"

Tatiana had to agree, though the other mermaids were jealous backstabbers at the time. She didn't think she could return now that she was a mer matron. Beauty school was for the unpromised to learn how to snag a boy.

"We should get back."

"Fine," Girraween huffed. "I'll have these garments taken to your room. But you need to ask Mistress Wynie to craft you some of your own. The staff notices these things and oh how they love to talk."

Tatiana smiled, secretly confused why Azor didn't have Wynie come to the compound earlier when he knew she hadn't anything to wear. Girraween held out a mirror and Tatiana studied her reflection. If only she weren't underwater for her promising day, her hair could have looked this fabulous in feathers. Sadness interrupted her thoughts, reminding her of her issues with Azor.

Tatiana left the room just as Linise entered. Through the closed door she heard Girraween bark orders to clean up and deliver the dresses. At that moment, Tatiana vowed to never talk to her servant in the same manner; that was if she were ever assigned one.

10

Lavish

Jacob straightened when Tatiana left Girraween's room, his eyes briefly sweeping over her. She noted he hid a smile. Or was it a smirk? Was he mocking her? Dressed in yellow and surrounded by feathers, she suddenly felt a little ridiculous.

Behind him, the servant girl who'd shared her skirt earlier, stood at attention.

"Oh," Tatiana said once spotting her, "your skirt. I'll go fetch it—"

"N-no," the girl rattled off. "No bother. I-I'm fine. I-I've got a-another one."

Her stuttering interrupted Tatiana's concentration and she worked to keep a straight face.

"This is Nicole, your handmaiden here at the palace," Jacob said, as if to rescue the both of them. "She can show you to your room."

"I have a room?" Tatiana's mouth gaped open, then snapped into a frown. This confirmed Azor wasn't coming home, at least not today. "Oh, okay, I guess."

Jacob studied her, confusion on his face.

Tatiana ignored him and added, "Nicole, sorry about earlier… and thank you for sharing your skirt."

Nicole did a double-take. "You're quite welcome, Princess."

With a spring in her step, she took the lead as Jacob followed. Tatiana, lost in sadness once again, walked behind the two of them, worried what Azor planned to do in Tahoe. Had he wanted to find her parents? Arrest them? Though hanging out in the palace was better than his dungeonesque compound, she loathed the continual waiting.

Her eyes, though, had other plans as they zeroed in on Jacob's gait, having never seen him in legs before. Biting her lip, she marveled at his shoulders. Much different than Azor's, more toned with a wicked tribal tattoo hugging his shoulder. His waist was smaller, too, setting off the V of his torso. The lines of his sculpted back muscles moved and contorted in such beautiful ways. At his waist, two dimples pressed in and out, winking at her from his black skirt that hung low on his hips. And his calf muscles as they popped out with each step. Had she even seen Azor's calf muscles?

I bet he's got a sexy butt, she thought. *So much fuller than Azor's flat butt.*

She bit her knuckle, wondering if Jacob had ever been naughty with any of the servants.

"Tatiana?"

She snapped out of her trance and dropped her hand. Jacob and Nicole had stopped before two white doors, and watched her peculiarly.

"We're here," Nicole stated with a slight nod. "Would you like me to open your door?"

"No, I've got it." Tatiana pushed her thoughts aside, and turned the knob.

The room took her breath away—beautiful furnishings and floor to ceiling windows framed the gorgeous underwater landscape of Natatoria—decadence beyond her wildest imagination. She walked to the bed and trailed her hand over the silken blue threads and puffy pillows, wondering why Azor lived like a freaking sea hermit. The ceilings were gilded in gold and embedded with stones of every color, sparkling brilliantly upon her. Spinning in a full circle, she took in the rest of the room as its warmth enfolded her.

"I-I hope it is t-to you're liking, ma'am."

"Yes, Nicole, far better than I'd ever imagined." Tatiana sat in front of the vanity on a plush cushioned chair and studied her feathered hair.

"It's stunning. Don't you think, Jacob?" She turned to find him in the doorway. His eyes darted from the table where Tatiana sat, to the bed.

He grimaced. "It'll do."

"Will it ever." Tatiana laughed at his continual stoniness. "I wonder what the guard quarters look like." She quirked a smile, teasing him.

"I won't need a room. I plan to remain outside your door when you need rest."

What? Are you a vampire or something? She searched his face, confused he'd forgo good sleep. With all the guards in the palace and the Dradux at the main entrances, she was in the safest place possible.

He continued to study the room, but not in an admiring sort of way—with more of a scrupulous glare. Like at any moment a flesh-eating zombie would jump from the closet and eat her brains.

"And there's no other way to enter this room but through this door, correct?" He hit the frame hard with his palm, startling

Tatiana.

Nicole folded her gloved hands over her skirt and nodded. "Ah, as far as I know, y-yes. I mean, someone could break a window, I guess."

The thought of staying alone in such a vast room suddenly unnerved Tatiana. "And you certainly won't be staying in the... servant's quarters. Right, Nicole?"

"Normally, I sleep in the c-conservatory, but since I'm to serve you, I'll sl-sleep h-here."

She pointed to a closet-sized room next to the main door. Inside was only a cot and dresser.

"That's your room?"

"Yes, miss. M-most comfortable." She curtsied to the Princess. "And quiet. The conservatory can get loud at times."

Though happy she'd have someone nearby, Tatiana didn't understand Nicole's gratitude. And with all the vacant rooms they'd passed, why were servants to sleep in a stuffy room filled with bunk beds anyway? What were they all for? A statement of wealth? The lavishness seemed more like a waste—another pretty bobble on Natatoria's bracelet, tucked away in a jewelry box no one would ever see.

It was as if the servants' deformities or lack of living parents were their own faults. And the worst part being, the royals hadn't really earned the money. Born into wealth and status, they'd used their laws and freedoms to sell sunken treasure to purchase their human trinkets.

The cogs in Tatiana's mind synchronized as another mission became clear. Once she was queen, she'd compensate servants so they could earn the finer things if they wanted, even live outside of the palace, and be promised. They didn't need to be punished further by working for free.

Tatiana turned to Jacob, eager to tell him her future plans. At his scowl, she refrained.

She padded barefoot across the carpet toward him. "I'll see about getting you a cot, or maybe an adjoining room."

"No." He met her eyes with determination. "I'm fine standing guard outside your door."

"But you need to sleep."

"I'll sleep when I'm dead."

Sunlight refracted from his eyes, and zinged into her like lightning, weakening her knees. She abruptly looked away, embarrassed. Though his continual presence should have annoyed her, his constant attention to her needs, even at his expense, flattered her. And though she'd never admit it publically, she was beginning to enjoy him being there.

She shook it off, reminding herself of his job and her promise. Jacob's dedication stemmed from his reverence to her father, for which she couldn't fault him. But why? Did he know something about her father's future plans that she didn't? Was her father planning to return and overthrow the kingdom?

The thought startled her. If Jacob didn't support Azor, then why was he still here? Why didn't he follow her father and leave? One thing was for certain, no matter how much she wanted to trust Jacob, she'd never let her guard down. If given the chance, she knew he'd abduct her and she'd never see Azor again.

"You better get back to the audience," he said quietly. "Your absence will be suspicious, especially if Princess Girraween returns before you."

"You're right." Tatiana straightened her shoulders and gave herself a once over in the mirror before she darted past him into the hall, shaking away her conflict.

◦

The audience resumed and Jacob returned to pace the hall. With an empty stomach and a full mind, he couldn't concentrate. The line of mers stretched down and around a corner, seamless and unending. Though he knew it was their custom, he cringed each time the next mer begged to speak with the King, or Prince Azor. If they only knew that if they praised the Queen for her attention, she'd be more generous in giving what they'd ask for.

The needs were all the same: extra food, access to the fountain of essence, or the request to visit a prisoner. Baskets of food were issued until they ran out, and small vials of essence were administered to the injured—not nearly enough to heal someone. The most annoying was listening to the mer matrons wail when denied access to visit their mates in prison. Jacob knew it was a front to show weakness of the rebel's wives, but after the thirtieth scream, Jacob's head was pounding.

But Tatiana didn't know the plan and with each new citizen, she struggled to keep a straight face. He wished he could have told her, but with her loyalty to the promise and Azor, he wasn't sure if she could be trusted. The rebel alliance had been formed as a backup so the King's overstretching tyranny couldn't take over their lives. Jack wanted to round up the banished survivors from Bone Island, the Lost Ones, before they confronted the throne. And unless anyone was in mortal danger, they were to appear beaten so Azor would let his guard down.

Once lunch was announced, relief covered Tatiana's face until she spied the seating chart. Queen Desiree had placed Tatiana at the end of the table next to Princess Garnet. The snobbiest of the princesses. Jacob knew Garnet wouldn't welcome her, nor say a word.

Hungry and irritable, Jacob wished he would have eaten with the other guards in the kitchen, but didn't want to leave Tatiana's side. Confused momentarily, he wasn't sure where to stand and settled against the wall behind Tatiana's chair. He stared straight ahead, breathing from his mouth. If the rebel wives had to endure separation from their mates, he could endure thirty minutes until the next audience.

The other guests chattered freely, as curious eyes of servants continued to gawk at Tatiana. The chair at the opposite end of the table, facing the Queen, remained empty—Azor's perhaps? Queen Desiree bowed her head and closed her eyes. The table grew silent and followed her lead.

"All mighty, Poseidon. Heal the King and our city. Give mercy to those who suffer," she said, her voice monotone. "Help us through this difficult time and grant me wisdom to know who is friend and who is foe. Amen." She exhaled sharply and motioned to the head chef.

Servants appeared and presented plates overflowing with greens and baskets of bread. Jacob clenched his fist, his stomach rumbling at the smells. The two pieces of fish he'd had at breakfast burned through him hours ago. And his distrust of the guards in the palace and the unfamiliar routine hadn't allowed him time away from Tatiana. If Nicole hadn't snuck him a snack earlier, he would have passed out from hunger by now.

Tatiana munched hungrily on her greens, unable to wait for those around her to be served; Jacob knew this to be her first meal of the day.

"What's this?" Queen Desiree asked, throwing the bread basket into the hand of a nearby servant. "It's stale and where are my croissants and jam?"

The servant girl bowed her head. "I'm sorry, my lady. Prince Azor has forbidden leave of Natatoria and with the rations we've administered, we're short on flour—"

"Forbidden leave of civilians, yes, but mer matron Phelomenda has my permission to exit the gate with armed guards as usual, for food and supplies. If this was in question, why hasn't anyone spoken to me of it until now?"

"Yes, but—"

"But what?" she yelled and the entire table hushed.

Jacob recalled Azor's last decree at the compound before he left—to booby trap the gates and spread rumors that Jack had planted more explosives. The rebels knew that wasn't the case, but if they didn't heed the warnings, their fatal injuries from barbed wires coated in cassava poison would stop them first. Azor's faulty logic didn't leave room for the food needs of Natatoria. No one wanted to cross through a gate, especially the orphaned servants who'd lost parents to dynamite accidents in the past.

The servant lowered her head even further. "What if there's another explosion, my Queen?"

"What? Nonsense." She raised a brow and shot a look of disdain to Blanchard before addressing the servant. "I'll have the gates inspected. There's nothing to worry about." She blew out a hard breath. "Blanchard, assign mer matron Phelomenda a team to pick up supplies. And inspect the gates—at once. This is ridiculous."

Blanchard bowed his head and quirked a smug smile. "Of course, my Queen."

Yeah, sure you will. As Azor's lapdog, Blanchard had no intention of dismantling the poisonous nets covering each exit, even for food. He'd only stuck around to keep an eye on things and report the decrees Azor might need to undo.

Jacob shifted his weight from foot to foot while Tatiana ate with her eyes low, keeping to herself. So far, in spite of all the gossip about her failed union, she'd managed to stay in the Queen's good graces.

A few spaces down, Princess Girraween's voice filtered over the hum. She laughed with those around her, and pretended as if all were well with Natatoria. Queen Desiree, on the other hand, remained stoic and deep in thought as she pushed her meal around with her fork. Only the occasional hard look or gruff retort broke her concentration. The Queen, jovial and normally smiling, was the softer side to Phaleon's hard rule. Without him, she'd had to assume a tougher role and was cracking under the strain. Jacob didn't know how much longer she'd be able to handle the pressure.

The same went for Tatiana. Under the glares of the mer and whispers behind her back, her confidence was wavering. Jacob closed his eyes and cursed the promise. He'd known Queen Desiree to be strong in the presence of adversity, but apart from approval of the King, the promise molded her into a spineless jellyfish.

Pick up your head. Show them you're stronger than this, Jacob silently pleaded to Tatiana. *You're to be queen.*

"Could you please pass the salt?" Princess Garnet said, startling Tatiana.

"Oh, of course." She handed over the salt, and waited a beat before replying, "Nice meal."

Garnet dusted her soup, then smiled before dipping her spoon. Jacob held his breath for Tatiana's sake, but Garnet said nothing further. Jacob wanted to kick Garnet's chair for her rudeness.

The main course followed, broiled lobster tail and scallops, and Jacob's stomach rumbled louder as he salivated over Azor's plate. Tatiana turned with a concerned frown and motioned to the empty chair at the end of the table.

"No. I'm fine, Princess," he whispered.

She stared at him and pressed her lips. "Then go to the kitchen, at least."

He eyed her coldly. "Turn around."

She huffed and complied, but kept eyeing the plate at the empty seat. He vowed to never allow himself to become so starved again. *Just a few more minutes.* He breathed a sigh of relief when the servants started to clear away the dishes.

"Who's this for?" Tatiana asked the servant before he could take the plate of untouched food away.

"Prince Azor, ma'am."

"But he's not here."

The servant gulped and flashed a nervous look at the head of the table. Once again he tried to take the plate and Tatiana delayed his hand.

Stop, Tatiana, Jacob yelled internally. He refrained from resting his hand on her shoulder and squeezing.

Tatiana leaned in closer to the servant, "Please save it for me, then."

"But, I—" the servant began.

"No," Jacob murmured under his breath.

Tatiana turned to him with a persistent frown. "Then go eat in the kitchen."

Jacob clenched his jaw, unmoving from his spot.

"Tatiana? What seems to be the trouble?" Queen Desiree asked. The table hushed.

Tatiana whipped her head around and straightened her shoulders, standing. "I was wondering what would happen with this uneaten meal."

She smiled. "They discard it, of course."

"Even with the scarcity of food? I'd rather someone eat it." Tatiana said. "Like… my guard, Jacob."

Jacob bristled. Had she no tact?

The Queen's smile vanished into a smirk. "Your guard is to eat with the servant staff."

"But Blanchard—"

"Blanchard is first in command when Prince Azor is away. And since you're new, I'll excuse your insult to me and this table."

Jacob stared straight ahead as all eyes fell on him and then to Tatiana. He couldn't have imagined anything worse for her to say at her first meal as princess.

The Queen's heated stare lingered on Tatiana for a beat

longer, sinking in. Then she stood and threw her cloth napkin onto her half-eaten plate of food, and stormed out of the room in a huff.

The room collectively gasped and Tatiana sank into her chair. Once the conversation picked up, she pushed her uneaten greens around her plate with her fork and all Jacob could hear was Garnet's low cluck. It took all his concentration not to backhand the tiara off the snob's head.

11

Disappointment

Audience resumed and Tatiana sat on her brocade throne with her hands in her lap, hoping to fade into the itchy fabric tickling her back. The Queen conducted business far more curtly than before lunch, and Tatiana couldn't help but blame herself.

So stupid.

She hadn't meant to upset her, but with the obvious waste of food, she couldn't handle listening to Jacob's stomach a moment longer. Was she trying to impress her guests? Show that even though they'd run out of peasant rations, royalty didn't need to worry? How could they not see the obvious in front of their faces with the low numbers of fish outside and the servants scared stiff to pick up supplies?

Then after the meal ended, Jacob dashed out of the dining room first, without even so much as a look. Tatiana knew she'd get an earful later, but she didn't care. She wasn't going to sit by and let perfectly good food go to waste. Tatiana glanced out to the hall once again, hoping to give him an apologetic glance, but didn't spot him.

However, as more mers confirmed the terror the explosion had caused, Tatiana wanted to disappear into the cushions of her throne. And without knowledge of who was in support of whom—her father or the King—the Queen had the public fountain in the square sealed off completely. Only the royal healers were allowed to dole the vials from her private bath.

Though many mer matrons, like Sandy, acted as healers, without essence they were useless against the poisons. Xirene and Pearleza were the only official healers that Tatiana knew of, and because of that, a huge task loomed before them.

After dinner, Tatiana retired early and crawled into bed mentally and physically exhausted, but not before Jacob let her have it.

"My well-being is for me to worry about, Princess," he'd said. His bitter tone stung her ears and crushed her spirit when all she'd wanted was to make sure he'd eaten something. Unable to reason with him, she'd abandoned him in the hall and slammed the door.

The tears fell into her silken pillow. Her insides were numb, first with embarrassing Jacob and now with her longing to appease Azor. Was it so horrible to want to cocoon herself in his arms? She couldn't deny any longer her real fears, that he'd find and arrest her parents. Why was that more important than their relationship? And what if he succeeded? Could she be with a man who'd so diligently brought her parents to his warped sense of justice?

She pinched her eyes shut, her breath taken away. The fact Azor remained away for so long had to be good news. Or was it?

She thought of her family, of Ash and 'Fin. She missed them so.

"Please. Let them be safe," she mumbled into her pillow.

And though she couldn't stop her worry, her heavy eyelids fell shut and sleep overcame her quickly. But not the peaceful rest she craved.

Running from swarms of stinging bees rattled her dreams.

Continually they stung, over and over, creating a deep throbbing pain in her lower back. She tried to open her eyes to escape them without any luck.

And what seemed like minutes later, the sun-tunnels brought in the morning light. Tatiana rolled over to stretch and a stabbing pain radiated from her hip.

Sea stars. What the—?

A brown mark stained her skin. She leapt from her bed to the full-length mirror and quietly whooped. The coveted fleur-de-lis had finally made its appearance.

She traced the strange mark while biting her lip. No one had said it would hurt coming in, but then again, the only royal who'd acquired a mark from a promising kiss and not from blood was Queen Desiree. Maybe she'd ask.

Then Tatiana glared at her hand. Why hadn't her ring tattoo appeared then?

"Oh," Nicole entered the room and eyed Tatiana's hip, then smiled appreciatively. "Good morning, Princess. Sorry I didn't wake you sooner. You were sleeping so soundly. Shall I fetch your breakfast?"

Soundly? Holy Crawfish! Tatiana wanted to express the opposite, but the fleur-de-lis had lightened her mood.

"Yes, Nicole. Thank you. And get a little extra, please." Tatiana nudged her head toward the hall.

Nicole winked in understanding and darted from the room. Satisfaction flooded Tatiana as she shrugged off her sleeping gown. A famished bodyguard wouldn't do her any good and with Nicole's regular deliveries, she'd get him to eat one way or another. She couldn't help but crack a smile. Had that jellyfish

Garnet even missed her at the breakfast table this morning?

She laughed, then put on an outfit from her closet—the pink beaded one Girraween fancied—and tugged the waist of her skirt down to show off her fleur-de-lis. In the reflection of the mirror, something shimmered from her dressing table. Tatiana turned and froze. In a bed of silk sat a small jewel-encrusted crown.

Did Nicole bring it with her earlier? Tatiana knew she wouldn't have missed it yesterday. Gingerly, she approached the treasure as if it would sprout wings and fly away, and pulled the delicately entwined silver from its resting place. The gems, arranged in flowers next to metal leaves, shimmered in the light. Should she wear it today?

Her hair, resembling a peacock that had flown through a tornado, needed serious help. She tugged out the feathers from yesterday and pulled the brush through her blonde hair. The loose tresses fell softly around her shoulders. With lithe fingers, she nestled the crown on her head.

Its beauty took her breath away, along with the responsibility.

"Queen Tatiana," she said softly as her heart thumped harder.

Anxious to show someone, she popped her head out of the doorway.

"Jacob?"

He startled to attention. "Princess. Good morning."

She waited a beat for him to notice, but his eyes quickly glazed over and slid shut.

"I'm having Nicole fetch breakfast. Have you eaten yet?"

"Oh, I..." His eyes flittered open and he combed the hall with a frown. "She did?"

"She's picking up extra, but if you insist on refusing to share, you can leave to eat in the kitchen," she said while fluffing her hair, trying to draw attention to her crown. "I think I'm fine here. I don't see any bad guys lurking in the hall—well, maybe a small one behind that vase over there. You can get him on the way out."

Jacob didn't even smirk. He shook his head. "I'll wait."

"Wait for what? Are you even awake?"

He lifted his head and grunted, stretching his arms above his head and twisting his torso. His biceps flexed around his ears, making Tatiana's head swim. She stared a moment too long, imagining herself snuggled in next to his rippling chest.

"I am awake, and don't worry about me." Jacob slid into a runners stretch.

Worry? She snapped from her trance and pushed aside her hair, trying to recall what they were talking about. *Oh, right. Breakfast.* "Fine, then I'll force feed you half of mine in a few minutes."

She turned, but he took her arm, recapturing her gaze. He stood and his eyes suddenly burned into hers, sharp and quick. "Do not assume for one minute you're safe here. I said not to worry about me."

She swallowed down her gasp, startled at his abruptness, and shirked off his hand. "Yes, but you need to eat at least. I can't have my bodyguard famished when I need him, can I?"

He exhaled heavily, closing his eyes. He paused, gaining his composure. "I am far from famished, Princess. I'm taking in sustenance just fine."

Yeah, with my help, she thought smugly, her eyes darting down his impressive chest.

"Suit yourself." She smirked. "Don't you think you're overreacting a little? Who's brave enough to come up against the Dradux to kidnap me?"

"Don't assume the Dradux are on your side, Princess." His eyes wrinkled at the corners.

Tatiana frowned. Yeah, she hated the creepy Dradux, but they served the King. They'd die to protect him. She shook off the worry.

"What did the Queen want with you last night?" he asked abruptly.

"Oh, I don't know. But when I woke up, I found this." Tatiana stretched her neck and held her head high.

He quickly glanced at her head and remained irritated. "Hmmm."

"What?" She touched her tiara. "Is something wrong?"

"No." He frowned and rubbed his chin. "We should go back to the compound today."

"You act as if I've been given free reign because the Queen has let me out of the dog house. And that so totally hasn't happened," she said adamantly. *As if that were my decision whether or not I could leave to begin with.*

Jacob's eyes squinted. "Dog house?"

Tatiana quirked a smile and nudged Jacob in the side. "You've never heard of dogs?"

"Well, of course I have, but what do their houses have to do with the Queen?"

She laughed. If it weren't for the fact dogs couldn't survive the trip to Natatoria, puppies would be roaming the halls, looking for patches of grass to pee on right now.

"Serpents, it's just a human expression. It means… I hope to stay in her good graces, especially after she's given me this." She touched her crown.

"Hmm." He shook his head, annoyed again. "I'd like you to decline audience and make arrangements to return to the compound. This morning."

"Why?"

"I have a bad feeling—"

A squeal down the hall interrupted them. Girraween ran and embraced Tatiana, practically toppling her over. "Oh, Tatiana! You're up. You missed breakfast. And ooooh! Look at your crown!"

She jumped up and clapped, then took Tatiana's hands and twirled her in a whole glee-filled circle, like children.

"I overslept."

"Overslept?" Girraween laughed like what she'd said was absurd, then sobered up. "You're feeling okay, right?"

"I'm fine."

"Well… you've done it. You've caused another stir. Everyone thinks you might be pregnant already. Isn't that wonderful?"

Jacob crossed his arms, flexing his biceps, and returned to his spot against the wall. Tatiana couldn't stop her cheeks from flushing and she kept from looking directly at him. Of all people, Jacob knew she and Azor had never slept in the same room, let alone done *it*. Why was everyone so keen on her womb anyway? *Maybe leaving* was *a good idea,* she thought until she remembered Azor. He'd come to the palace, looking for Tatiana first, then report his findings to his mother. She didn't want to miss him, or the news.

Azor's prolonged absence still punctuated her mind with worry. She couldn't live in the middle of a family feud her entire life.

"Possibly," Tatiana mumbled in a lie, trying to return to the present. She hoped her admission of pregnancy would quell the gossip temporarily until she could get Azor alone to seduce him.

Tatiana caught Jacob's raised brow at her lie.

"That'll prove Pearleza wrong." Girraween pulled on Tatiana's hand. "Come on. We need to hurry."

Tatiana stole her hand back. "Nicole is bringing me breakfast first. I'm starving."

"Oh, right." Girraween patted Tatiana's tummy. "You're eating for two now, or maybe three! Just hurry. Mother won't be happy if you're late."

Tatiana cringed, considering she'd just returned to her good graces, proof being in the crown.

"Late to mermaid school?" Tatiana hoped.

Girraween laughed again. "No, silly. School is cancelled for now. We must be present at the audience. It's practice for your future." She winked, eyeing the crown again and oohing.

Tatiana sighed in disappointment, but feared angering her mother-in-mer further. She bit her lip and stared at Jacob. How could she ask to leave now? However, another day of ceaseless glares while the mers begged assistance of a male leader who was incapacitated made her head hurt. Maybe Azor would come home and save her from this nightmare today. Then they'd go home to the compound like Jacob wanted.

Nicole arrived and brought the breakfast tray. Tatiana shoved a bit of jelly-slathered biscuit in her mouth and hummed before

Girraween managed to drag her away. Jacob reluctantly followed, but not before Tatiana made him eat the other half of her biscuit.

Through the vast window in the audience room, Tatiana counted the blue grenadiers as they swam by. Only the smallest of the schools were left—a terrible sign. If the fear to venture through the gates remained, the mer population would starve. Hunting in open sea was needed for bigger game fish that didn't like swimming at Natatorian depths—like salmon, tuna, grouper and dolphin fish.

"Tatiana."

Azor's voice made Tatiana practically jump out of her skin and she scanned the hall for him. Beads of water rolled down his muscular chest and stomach, pooling at his feet in the doorway. At the sight of him, she forgot everything she'd been upset over—basking in his glorious presence.

She rose to her feet, her breath held. He crossed the room to her. Collectively, everyone held their breath along with Tatiana until his lips met hers in a passionate kiss. Her legs quivered and she wrapped her arms around his shoulders, finding the soft wet hair at the nape of his neck. He was here, touching her, and she was finally whole again.

"I've missed you," he whispered in her ear.

"Azor," the Queen said sweetly. "Good to see you're home."

She dismissed the anxious group of awaiting mers with a wave of her hand. "Blanchard, take these citizens out. We'll resume after lunch."

At the groans, Azor yelled for "silence." In the hall, Tatiana could hear soft pleas to speak with Prince Azor, but the guards ushered them away. Tatiana's heart broke with each tortured face disappearing around the corner and out of sight.

Queen Desiree stood from her throne and walked over to hug her son. After their embrace, Azor intertwined his hand with Tatiana's. She beamed, hoping they wouldn't have to stay long under the Queen's watchful eye.

From the hall, Jacob glared. Her stomach tightened. Of course Jacob would be angered at her happiness to see Azor. What did he expect her to do? Yell at him in front of everyone? Azor was her mate, after all, and she the understanding wife. She'd pick her battles and this wasn't one of them. With a flick of her hair, she focused on Azor.

"Son," Queen Desiree said, her eyes darting quickly to Tatiana. "I'm sure you have lots to share. Let's go talk in my private chambers, shall we?"

Tatiana squeezed his hand tight and followed, glued to his side. They walked into the hall and her heart pounded, wondering about the news. Was her family safe? Had he returned empty handed?

Azor stopped and nuzzled her ear. "I'll be right back."

"What?"

He kissed her cheek and touched her nose. "Wait for me in your chambers. I'll be there shortly."

He dropped her hand and her arms fell limp. How could he just leave like that again? Bar her from the conversation? She wanted to know where he'd been, what had happened. Did he find her parents? Would he pardon them? But her mouth, just like her legs, wouldn't work, the humiliation was overwhelming. And just like that, he walked around the corner, out of sight.

Stunned and shaking, she gathered her courage and smoothed

her sweaty palms down her skirt. She wouldn't allow the rumor mill anything new to chew on. A queen would never crumble; Tatiana would prove the same. She was strong, even in disappointment. Azor had a job to do and she'd allow him freedom to do it.

With firm steps, she moved down the adjacent hall, away from prying eyes. She lifted her chin and turned to Jacob, barely holding onto a shred of sanity. "Would you escort me to my room?"

With a heavy nod, Jacob replied, "Of course, Princess."

12

Fleur-de-lis

Tatiana walked down the stark corridor with Jacob next to her, lost in her own world. With each step, the weight of everything bore down on her shoulders—the secrets she kept along with the lies. She longed for more than just a promise with Azor, longed to be his confidant, to be his best friend.

She fought everything inside her not to run to the Queen's private chambers and demand they include her. Why couldn't she know what happened? If he'd captured her parents, she'd find out. Better to tell her himself, than let the rumor mill do it.

She fisted her hands, furious at him, and turned down the last hall on the right. The door to her room cried out as a beacon, a safe haven where she could crumble into a fit of tears out of view of Jacob. As she twisted the knob, Jacob called out.

"That's not your—" But he stopped speaking.

Tatiana blinked out of her thoughts and stepped barefoot into a room three times the size of her own. In the center was a huge oak four poster bed. The King lay in the middle of it, eyes closed.

She gasped and backed up into Jacob's body, ready to retreat when the King turned, his eyes locking on her.

"Hello?" he asked, his voice tired and weak.

Her hands shook, one for disturbing him and two for the sight of him. His skin, pale and weathered, hung loosely on his deteriorated muscles. He wasn't reminiscent of the powerful king who'd just conducted her promising ceremony a few days ago.

"I'm sorry—my mistake, I didn't mean to—I'll leave." She dipped into a quick curtsy.

"Tatiana? Is that you?" A smile spread on his face. Grunting, he pressed his hands downward and wiggled his hips to adjust himself upright. Tatiana could see there was nothing under the sheets below his hips—a creepy emptiness.

She hid her gasp, averting her eyes back to his, then to the floor. "Your Majesty, I know what you're about to say and I sincerely apologize…"

"For what?" The King laughed. "Visiting the King? Please. Come talk with me. Do you have good news?"

She stood, stunned. He wanted to talk with her? The King? This couldn't be the same man who'd just force-promised her and threatened her father; the one in charge of all of Natatoria.

"I—I," she stuttered and gulped down her words of more apologies, her tongue stuck as if in peanut butter.

"Come." He motioned to the chair next to him. "Sit with me and tell me all that's happening in Natatoria. Are you and my son finally happy?"

Her chest heaved, her legs numb. Didn't he hate her? Shouldn't he? Or maybe this was a trap. A way to get her to spill what she knew.

"Yes, I'm happily promised to Azor," Tatiana lied, trying hard to cheer up her face as she warily scanned the room for hidden Dradux guards. When no one sprung out to seize her, she moved to retrieve a chair. The King gasped behind her. Tatiana swiveled around, ready to spring for help. "What's wrong? Are you ill? Should I get the healer?"

"No," King Phaleon said, eyes wide as he composed himself.

"I—it's nothing." He looked off to the large windows beyond her, his eyes losing focus. "I've been wondering how she—managed to—never mind. I'm rambling." He cleared his throat, regaining his smile. "Why has Azor left his pretty mate wandering the halls of the palace anyway?"

"Uh-mmm." Tatiana inhaled deeply, her heart pounding. She sat down and gripped the cushion under her thighs to stop them from quaking. Was this a test? How could he not know where Azor had been?

She closed her eyes and murmured, "He's with the Queen."

With a tilt of his head the King sighed and clasped his hands in front of him. "Yes, of course. Last I'd heard, he'd left for Tahoe. How'd that go?"

Her breath quickened at the confirmation. "I'm not sure."

"Did he find your family?"

"Hopefully, no."

"Yes, I'm sure the kingdom will breathe a collective sigh of relief if that were true—they do love Jack." He shook his head, murmuring, "Foolish boy."

Confusion continued to swirl about her. Foolish? Did he mean Jack, or Azor? The ultimate decision of her parents' fate lay in the king's hands after all, according to Azor.

"What will you do with them?" she asked with a hoarse throat, eyes low.

"Your parents?" The King chuckled. "If Azor actually manages to catch them, nothing, if I have any say."

Nothing? She bit the inside of her cheek, unsure what he meant exactly. With the fight, then the explosion, and now his injuries, why was he so willing to let it all go?

King Phaleon sighed. "I'm *dying*, Tatiana, if you didn't know. My voice no longer matters."

Tatiana blinked in shock. "You—you don't seem like you're dying to me."

"You and Queen Desiree are so optimistic." The King laughed jovially, as if disbelieving her honesty. With a reddening face, he clenched his fists and cursed under his breath. "Little do you both know how quickly things can change on the eve of power."

Tatiana pulled her head back sharply at his abrupt anger. She pressed her lips to stop herself from asking questions.

"I'm not faulting you for my injuries, so stop looking at me like I'm going to scalp you. I'm…" He dropped his head. "I owe you an apology, my child."

Her eyes, as big as saucers, fell to her quivering hands now clenched in her lap. The fear to speak any further overcame her. This couldn't be real. Was he sincerely apologizing?

"No, sire. Please, I beg of you—" She moved to the floor on her knees, clasping her hands. "I—we—what happened with your fin—so tragic."

His hand reached out and touched her shoulder, cold but soft. "Please, stop groveling, and sit. I blame no one but myself."

She blinked up at his genuine smile pressed into the wrinkled leather of his cheeks. Slowly, she returned to her chair.

"Tatiana, you're such a sweet girl. I should have never allowed Azor to manipulate—" He stroked his beard and slowly closed his eyes. "Jack has always been the wise one, and I, the fool. And I betrayed our friendship over the lust of a woman, and then again to a thankless son. I thought your union would help mend things and bring our families together once again. But only now that I'm laid up here, do I see my ignorance. I wish I could tell Jack in person and convince Azor to... ah, Hades."

Tatiana couldn't believe her ears, that he'd actually accepted fault for the forced-promising and banishing her father over it. Was he saying he'd tell Azor to stop going after him. Had the accident given him brain damage?

"I—" Her mouth hung opened.

"And now I'll pay—with my life, I imagine."

Tatiana blinked, astounded. "What do you mean? You'll return to the throne soon after you mend. A little sun, or fresh water perhaps."

"Red Tide!" The King cursed and Tatiana slammed backward into her chair in fright. "My time is over! You will be queen soon, and you must listen!" He pounded his fist against a book engraved with his name in gold letters on his nightstand. "I would have never guessed, without knowing the look myself, that my son would betray me, even after I've given everything he's asked for. So I've written down the truths in this book to show you the way you must raise your son. To teach him respect and the history of our people, mistakes and all. His heart must desire to serve the people. It's my unborn grandson who's the future of Natatoria's salvation. I beg of you, please! Do you understand?"

Tatiana's breath caught in her throat. What was he saying? That he disapproved of how Azor turned out? That he'd somehow betray the King? And what did he mean she'd be queen soon?

"But you're fine," Tatiana squeaked out.

The King harrumphed and flipped back the blankets revealing two stumps mid-thigh, scarred and bulbous. "As if I could rule like this—with these things. You're too young to know the prejudices of our people."

Tatiana's hand flew to her mouth. "Oh, dear Poseidon."

"Poseidon be damned; he had nothing to do with this." He returned the silken covers to his non-existent legs. "This is my doing—or undoing. To think in all my eighteen years—" The King's eyes met the ceiling before he pressed his lids shut. "That I've ruled that long and learned so little. That I'd betray my own father, not thinking my son would do the same—like all those before me. Knowing my son, you will need to be *creative* in your persuasion, and not as naive as the Queen and I have been."

Tatiana fidgeted nervously in her seat. Had he no faith in Azor, or himself? He believed he wouldn't return to rule. "Your Grace, pardon me, but I don't know what to do with all of this."

"I know. Just... accept my apologies and learn from my mistakes." He held out the book to her.

Tatiana's lips pursed, accepting it. "Of course, my King."

"And please bring me your beautiful son, so that I might see him and wish him great wisdom before I go."

"Of course, my King." Thinking of the future, she rubbed her stomach. Then tears pricked her eyes at the thought of her merling never knowing his grandfather.

His eyes lingered at her hand before his body went limp. He fell into the pillows behind him. "I wish I had more time."

His voice was merely a whisper.

"Rest, sire. I can come back later."

"Please, one more thing..." he whispered. "Come closer, child."

Tatiana rose from her seat and approached. The King blinked

slowly and his eyes looked off into the horizon, his mind not with her. Tatiana grew worried watching him, as if he'd expire right then.

"Lean closer." He clasped her hand.

And she did.

13

Crazy

Tatiana's screams sent Jacob charging into the King's room; the knife normally hidden in his boot was unsheathed and pointed outward, leading his attack.

"Princess!" he yelled.

But Jacob wasn't prepared for what he'd see. Within the King's grasp was Tatiana's neck, his lips dangerously close to touching hers.

"Stop! Phaleon!" she grunted, shrieking again, pressing with all her might against his chest. "STOP!"

"Don't fight me," he begged. "It'll be quick—you must let me. You must!"

"No!" She clawed at his chest, but as a human she had no talons. "Jacob!"

Jacob sprinted to her and pried Tatiana out of the King's hands. With a shove, he pushed the King aside. Pointing his knife at the King, he watched his body flip over, almost toppling off the other side to the floor. The King cursed, lying on his back, pawing to cover his torso with the sheet.

"Get back, soldier!" he bellowed. "Guards!"

Jacob's hand froze. He couldn't believe his eyes. The King's legs were missing. Pity stopped his need to strike and end his life. He backed away, pushing Tatiana behind him, prepared to fight the Dradux who'd come to the King's aid.

Jacob scanned the walls for another exit. But neither a

Dradux, nor anyone for that matter, appeared. Why was he left unguarded?

King Phaleon recovered, panting. "This isn't what it seems," he said, his eyes wild.

"I know what I saw." Jacob's steely eyes scoured the King. He took Tatiana's hand, leading her from the room.

"No!" the King yelled, "I need Tatiana—it's for my grandchildren. You don't understand. Please, Tatiana. Allow me one kiss."

Without a single look back, Jacob shut the door, silencing the King. He scanned the hall before taking the Princess's face in his hands. With great care, he studied her. Then he touched her arms and patted down her sides. "Are you okay? Did he hurt you?"

Large tears formed in her blue eyes.

She stared, unblinking. "H—he…"

"I know." Jacob wiped away a tear with his thumb, sick at what the King almost accomplished. Her lips trembled and all Jacob wanted to do was quiet them with his own—smother them with loving kisses and promise her he'd never let that happen to her again—if they were together.

"I don't understand," she whimpered.

He dropped his hands as his conscience took over and closed his eyes to think. The worst was yet to come, and they didn't have time to waste. He needed to take her far away from Natatoria—now.

"We only have one choice. We must leave," Jacob took her hand and led her down the hall toward the northwest entrance.

Tatiana dragged her feet, stopping him. "No. I mu—must tell

Azor first."

Jacob swiveled around, facing her. At the mention of Azor's name, anger flushed through his body. How could she still give this asinine family her allegiance?

"Azor?" He palmed his hair, exasperated. "Don't you see? The King assaulted you. And once he tells someone I attempted to kill him, we're dead—I'm dead. He's sick—and he's crazy. My fate is in his hands. They'll lock me up and then I won't be with you to stop that from happening again. I won't allow it! Do you even know what I wanted to do to him when I saw his filthy hands on you?"

Tatiana's face crinkled in worry. She pressed her lips and Jacob realized he'd said too much—she wasn't his to be so possessive of. "I—I know, but Azor. He asked me to wait. We'll be going home and…"

Jacob gritted his teeth, his heart pounding. "Tatiana. Stop letting your promise lead you and listen to yourself."

"I know." She pinched her eyes shut. "Maybe I am crazy. But from what the King said, I don't think anyone is even listening to him anymore."

Jacob's features froze. "What did he say to you?"

She looked away, confusion crossing her face. "So many things about… about…the past kings and his disappointment in Azor." She scanned the floor, searching for her words. "I can't even make sense of it—it was all so jumbled, but he did apologize. To me and for what happened to my father. He doesn't want to punish him for the shark attack, or the incident at the palace, or the explosion. He blames himself."

"He what?" Jacob spouted a sardonic laugh.

"He does, for allowing Azor to convince him to force our promising, and then for betraying the friendship he had with my dad."

Jacob stood, dumbfounded. "Well, now I've heard everything." He tisked and shook his head. "A little convenient when all he wanted to do was *kiss* you, don't you think? I know the King and he's never repentant. Was there no one in his room attending to him?"

"No," she said, sadly. "It was as if they'd stuck him there to die."

Jacob pressed his palms into his temples. *Damn promise!* Why couldn't she see reason? This wouldn't be the only incident—many more would come and he couldn't handle it if anyone succeeded in harming her.

"I still think we should leave," he said evenly in one last-ditch effort.

She looked up at him, imploring. "I'm sorry, Jacob. I won't leave without Azor."

Jacob clenched his jaw. "Won't or can't?"

She pinched her eyes shut and sighed. "Just go, Jacob," she said, with sadness in her voice. "I'll be fine."

"Like just now? I told you this place wasn't safe and if I wasn't with you—" Jacob bowed his head, regaining composure. She'd be the death of him.

She stared at her hands, silent.

He couldn't believe he was about to let her stubbornness win. He had no choice. She'd only leave kicking and screaming, and that wasn't really an option.

"No, Princess. Where you go, I go."

"Thank you," she said softly.

14

Vacation

Jacob said nothing further the entire walk to her room. Alone, she lay on her bed and stared at the ceiling, too numb to cry. The bruises on her neck had vanished under the quick healing of her mer blood, but the aftermath of what happened hadn't yet. Hours had passed since Azor left with his mother and the assault kept replaying in her mind. With what the King said, she had so many questions, none of which she felt comfortable asking Azor.

"Tatiana?"

She snapped into the present and turned toward Azor's silhouette in the doorway, curbing her desire to run to him. She clenched her jaw instead. After everything, he'd need to earn her affection first.

"You're finished?" she asked, her voice drenched in sarcasm. "Nice of you to stop by."

"You're not happy to see me?"

As he entered her room, she tried her hardest to still her shaking limbs and stay mad. His soft, dark hair fell gently to his shoulders and all she wanted was for him to shut-up, kiss her, and tell her he was taking her far away from Natatoria.

"Did you find my parents in Tahoe?" she asked instead.

His face fell. "No."

Relief filled her, but she hid that from her expression. "Did they leave?"

"As far as I know, yes."

He walked closer and her heart pounded. He took her hands

into his and abruptly yanked her to her feet. "Let's not talk about the trip, okay?"

With a rush of rough movements, he encircled her in his arms and pressed his body against hers. She remained ridged, determined not to give in. Though her soul celebrated with his touch, she managed to subdue its all-encompassing power. She wouldn't reward his niceness after he'd lied multiple times and abandoned her. Not to mention the other atrocities inflicted on her from his mother and father.

"You left me out," she said, her tone biting.

"I know." He traced a circle on her cheek with his finger, through the wet trail that ran to her chin. "I'm sorry."

She gulped, her strength wavering, and turned her face to the side. "And you told your mother I had the *ick*."

"What? No, I didn't." He laughed into her hair. His other hand slid down over her waist, cupping her backside. "Where were we the other day?"

Her breath caught unexpectedly and she closed her eyes. "You cannot leave without telling me where you're going or when you'll be back."

"I said I was sorry." His whiskers brushed her skin as his lips traced her jaw to her neck. Goose flesh broke out along her skin, her breath quickening.

"I don't forgive you," she whispered.

"Hmmm..." he said, nipping at her neck. "That's too bad, considering you smell so enchanting."

Her head swirled with his own musk mixed with the evergreens and water of Tahoe. Home.

"You can't leave me, then expect one simple apology to make

everything okay."

"You're right." He tugged on her earlobe with his teeth. "I was only checking on your parents for you, to calm your nerves, but they'd left and I'm not entirely sure where. Maybe you'd know."

"Probably the safe—" She winced as his bite pinched her skin. She closed her eyes, swallowing in the rest of her statement, working to clear her head of his seduction. Though she wanted to tell him the truth, she wouldn't. Any information about the safe house in Florida would lead Azor right to those who'd successfully helped mers escape Natatoria's tyranny.

"Safe?" He nuzzled her hair and pulled her in tighter, molding his body against hers.

"Just somewhere safe," she spluttered.

She finally relaxed into him and grew anxious for him to actually kiss her lips instead of tease her neck with his tongue. But at the roughness of his hands and the hard metal of his armor pressing into her, she recoiled, reminded of the King. Soon enough, the after-effects of the promise took hold and swam in her head instead. For the briefest of moments, she forgot everything: the rumor mill, Pearleza's earlier exam, the suggested mating dance class, King Phaleon's confessions and wanting lips. They all faded into a distant memory. Azor was what she'd wanted: his love, his acceptance, his body against hers.

And as if he'd read her mind, Azor removed his armor and pressed all of his weight onto her tiny frame, forcing her to lie on the bed. Her heart raced at the thought of being together, and as humans do—so naughty. Her wiles as a woman weren't broken after all. They'd only needed time alone, away from all distraction, to start their lives without a care of the world around them. No caste system, no servants, no titles or expectations of babies, no power, no death. Just their kiss and their touch.

Azor worked his lips down her chest and fumbled at unhooking the back of her top.

"Let's run away," she whispered, her wish slipping out off her tongue involuntarily.

His fingers froze and he jerked his body up. "What?"

She hiccupped, realizing her mistake, and smiled coyly. "Or not."

Azor dropped her to the bed and stood, a parental glare replacing his desire. "Run away? Are you insane?"

She moved up onto her elbows, trying to coax him with her knee to lay on her again. "It just seems like a good idea considering," she stalled, her voice quivering. "We could come back after everything smoothes over—take an extended promisetide in the Canary Islands."

"Our place is here, with *our* people. We don't have the luxury of a promisetide, especially not now." Azor huffed and pushed his dark hair from his eyes. "We're going to be king and queen sooner than you think"

He eyed her belly and then gritted his teeth.

She froze, remembering King Phaleon's prediction. "What do you mean?"

Azor laughed. "Like my father has any desire to live now that he's," Azor gestured wildly, "finless and barely able to swim. How can he lead when he looks no better than a servant?"

Her throat constricted, knowing the direct opposite to be true—he wasn't dead, he was very much alive. "Why does that have to matter?"

"It matters tremendously."

"Then change that archaic prejudice and show that accidents happen but it doesn't change the person inside."

Azor's eyes pressed into slits. "It's not that easy."

She grimaced, not really wanting the King, wild and insane, to remain on the throne, but angered at Azor's narrow-mindedness. "Don't you mean it's easier for you to take the throne and let your father wither away?"

He closed in on the space between them, angry grooves marring his beautiful face. "Mind your tongue, Tatiana."

She blinked back her tears and smoothed down her bunched up skirt with her hands. How could he be so wonderful one minute and such a monster the next? Maybe he *was* just like his father in more ways than one.

Tatiana popped up from the bed and tried to act natural when Nicole scurried into the room. She began to pull Girraween's second-hand clothing from the closet and stuffed it into a garment bag.

Azor spun around. "What do you think you're doing?"

Nicole startled, eyes wide, then bowed low. "Your h-highness. I ap-pologize. I didn't realize—"

"You walk in without knocking?" he asked, his voice growing gruffer. "I should have you flogged."

"I-I didn't know you were here. I'll leave."

Tatiana moved in front of Azor and laid her hand on his arm, wanting to absorb his anger.

"Don't be upset. I allow Nicole to come and go as needed."

"A shut door should always mean you knock first. What if…"

He didn't finish, only glared harder at her servant.

Tatiana lifted her head. "I recall another servant of ours committing the same crime. Did you flog her?"

Azor grimaced, and whipped his hand from hers. He stared at the open bag full of borrowed clothing. "What's this?"

"I-I was p-packing for the Princess," Nicole said in almost a whisper.

"Packing?" His gaze swung to Tatiana. "Are you going somewhere?"

Tatiana laughed nervously. "Home, silly. To the compound."

Azor cocked a brow momentarily. "I thought you'd want to stay here, considering the situation at the compound."

"Stay here?" Tatiana's voice raised an octave. "No. I... you're moving back to the palace?"

"I'm not king yet," he said with a smirk. "I don't know why I didn't think of it sooner. You seem far more at home here at the palace. Then you can socialize with your lady friends and mentor with my mother. It's important you learn what it's like to be queen. She said you're taking nicely to your new title; even wearing your crown, I see. You'll be far less bored than at my stodgy compound."

Her breath, stolen from her lungs, wouldn't make words come to her mouth. He couldn't be serious. Stay here? With the gossip and the lies?

"Oh, Tatiana. Don't look at me like that," he said, pulling her into his arms. "It's not like I won't see you everyday. Actually, you'll see me more than you do at the compound. And unless things become too demanding, I'll stay nights here with you." His hands gestured to the room. "It's so much more *human—*

just like you like."

Tatiana couldn't stop the disappointment swelling in her chest, her mouth unwilling to speak. He was distancing himself from her—all to build an army against those who were loyal to her father.

He smiled coyly. "Then Jacob can come back to the barracks with me and train the next round of guards coming in."

"No," she said quickly, clutching her neckline.

After the assault, she didn't want to ever be alone in the palace again, and Jacob, though frustrating at times, was the one true person who cared about her well-being. He'd been there, sacrificing his very life, even when he could be arrested for what had happened. He still never left her side, for any reason, even when he really didn't need to.

"No?" Azor laughed. "I thought you couldn't stand Jacob."

"I—" Tatiana swallowed hard. "I mean, no, I want to be with you. I go where you go." The haunting words Jacob had just said to her slipped from her lips and felt oddly wrong.

"Hmmm." His eyes fell into slits. "You understand what that means, don't you?"

She looked up at him, meekly, her heart pounding.

He remained stern. "You must stay out of my way and not question me when I leave."

She lowered her head. "I understand."

"Fine, get packed quickly. I plan to leave within the hour." Azor exited the room, leaving Tatiana's mind spinning and her heart aching once again. Could she really stay promised to this man? A man who put everything before her? A man whose priorities meant punishing those who'd helped her father? A man who didn't act promised to her? She swallowed down her pride and held back her tears.

The rumpled comforter under her bag mocked her. If she hadn't suggested they run away, they'd be snuggling together in the afterglow of love instead of arguing. She might have conceived. A baby would heal the colony—blessed news, a new distraction. But the thought of Nicole interrupting would have been ultra embarrassing. He would have most definitely flogged her if that had happened.

Tatiana sighed and tried her best to shrug off the disappointment. They could start back up later tonight. After a whole day of briefing with his mom, he had to be tired. Butterflies reignited in her stomach at the thought. Tatiana quickly helped Nicole pack a few of her things, too, and together they stepped into the hall.

Azor gave one intolerable glance to her servant. "Where do you think you're going?"

"I-I assumed." Nicole lowered her head, casting a sideways glance to Tatiana.

"You assumed what?"

Tatiana walked over and kissed him on the cheek. "Nicole is my handmaiden, Azor," *and my only servant ally.* "I want her to come with me."

"You have a servant."

Tatiana snorted. "Xirene? I'd think after what happened, you would have gotten rid of her by now."

Azor's face tightened. "No, Tatiana. Xirene is responsible not only for the barracks, but for governing my household as well."

She jerked her head backward in surprise. Shouldn't that have become Tatiana's job? "Well, then Nicole can help her with the household chores. I mean, the guards have been eating us out of house and home."

He looked Nicole up and down like she was cattle.

"Please?" Tatiana's voice lilted.

Azor exhaled hard. "Fine, but one mistake and she's gone, got it?"

Nicole nodded and retrieved their bag. Tatiana ran to Azor's side and looped her arm into his.

"Thank you," she said.

Over her shoulder, she gave a sly wink to Nicole. Behind her, leaning against the wall with his arms folded, Jacob scowled. Tatiana sucked in a breath. She'd been right. No one ever came for his arrest. But still, his judgment lay thick behind his eyes. Eyes that said she shouldn't put up with Azor's treatment of her, that she was more valuable than being merely arm candy.

She looked away, focusing on Azor. Her life was with him, and whatever he could give had to make her happy. Jacob needed to accept that she could be loyal to both—be the peacekeeper. And they were finally leaving the palace like he'd wanted.

Blanchard and a group of Dradux joined Azor, Tatiana, Nicole, and Jacob at the northern entrance. The need for such protection surprised Tatiana. Like Azor was king already. Did he expect an attack outside of the walls of the palace? A waft of oysters hit her nose, gagging her. Out of the water, the Dradux stunk. Once under the water, the stink faded as Azor took the lead, hand in hand with Tatiana.

Giddy with excitement, she imagined how their special night together would start. Maybe a private dinner, or they'd forgo everything and immediately go upstairs. But the closer to the compound they swam, the more curt Azor's responses were to Tatiana's small talk. Upon entering the doorway, he dropped her hand altogether.

15

Overstepping the Bounds

Tatiana's heart plummeted at the crowd of golden armored guards in the front room.

With a wave of his hand, Azor said, "Direct your servant to take your things to your room. I'll be there shortly."

"Excuse me?" Tatiana fought the terrifying déjà vu and focused on the obvious. Why wasn't he directing his guards back to the barracks?

The soldiers all turned and watched, their faces a mix of curiosity and scorn. The heat of their stares prickled her nerves.

Azor leaned in closer, eyes tight, and pulled her into the foyer past the statue Tatiana had affectionately coined Ms. Sea Urchin. "I thought we had an understanding."

"But you're not going to dismiss them? Haven't you done enough already today?"

Azor scowled. "I need to know what's happened in my absence. I will come upstairs as soon as I'm finished."

Courage surged inside her when staring into his dark eyes. "I'll tell you what's happened. While you were on your mission to find my father, the citizens were lost without a leader, fearful of more explosions, and heartbroken without their mates. They won't hunt for food, and weird injuries keep popping up that can't be healed by our blood. Okay?" She scowled. "It's a mess, but I'm done waiting. You're next item of business is me!"

Azor pulled his head backward in shock. "I see," he said,

thoughtful. "Well, then…"

He trailed his finger down her arm and wove his hand around her waist, pulling her in tight. A shiver of excitement flared across her fin, interrupting her brief tirade. Tatiana let out a small humph, but felt her body tremble and resolve weaken.

She stiffened her lip. "And I haven't quite forgiven you, yet."

"You will later," he whispered in her ear. "Do you have something to wear that's sexy… for tonight?"

She closed her eyes and tried to remember why she was so angry a minute ago, her heart performing flip flops. "Um… maybe."

"Then go put it on," he said with a coy smile, "and I'll be there in a minute." He pushed her on her backside into the hall.

She glided away from him, her mind aflutter, and headed for the second story porthole. In the kitchen doorway Xirene hovered while watching Azor, unease drawn on her face. Tatiana hadn't seen her since the incident a few days ago and assumed she'd be off attending to the wounded. Oddly, she wore a green polka-dotted, loose-fitting dress that flared in the current, as opposed to her typical skirt and matching top. Tatiana's eyes lost focus staring beyond her polka-dots flittering in the current.

Why was she allowed to wear something other than the approved servant attire and why was she at the compound? She couldn't have possibly finished her healing duties. Tatiana took one glance over her shoulder to gauge Azor's reaction to this infraction, and caught him longingly watching Xirene in return. Then his eyes instantly darted to Tatiana.

He cleared his throat and straightened his shoulders. "Thank you, Love. I'll be there soon."

"Don't keep me waiting," Tatiana said, with a quick swivel of her hips.

She landed Xirene a glare before swimming up the porthole. *That girl has got to go.*

Once in her room, Tatiana tried to rush Nicole, helping her unpack her things in her "dressing room," in order to get prepared for her big night with Azor. The current, though, took the lighter items afloat and required rock weights to hold them down.

"Don't feel bad about having separate rooms. It's nothing to be ashamed of," Nicole said, eyeing Tatiana warily as she placed a rock on the last *floater*. "Do you know the Queen has a separate room from the King as well?"

"What? We don't have separate rooms. I—there isn't any closet space in Azor's room."

"Oh, my apologies," she said, lowering her voice. "Pardon my asking, but I heard Prince Azor has some rather shocking carvings in the master bedroom."

"Not any more revolting than that Ms. Sea Urchin in the foyer." Tatiana fake laughed while sitting on the side of her sponge bed, trying to stay light-hearted and patient, wondering how long she could keep up the ruse to Nicole. "Yes, his design flare is very *different*. I'm hoping once things settle down, I can get to redecorating, starting with a bubble, at least on the second floor. Rock weights won't do for my wardrobe," she said with a nervous giggle.

"Oh?" Nicole's eyes darted to her hands. She began to clean an unseen spot on her gloves.

"Why? Do you think that's a bad idea?"

"No," Nicole cleared her throat, like she knew something but was worried to share. "You might ask him first."

Tatiana cocked her head and lowered her voice. "You've been serving in the palace for a while now, correct?"

Nicole nodded.

"Then maybe you know why his compound is so drab. Was it originally only meant to be an addition to the barracks? I can understand his need to stay here to keep an eye on things until they smooth over, but as king and queen, I'd expected we'd live in the palace."

Nicole continued to scrub at her glove as she swayed on her seat. "Prince Azor's fond of the old way."

Tatiana scoffed. "I know that. I was just hoping he'd change a little for me, or at least give me my own section to do with what I want."

"Maybe." Nicole bit her lip. "He's always been like this, even when he was little. This compound was his idea, actually, and the sharks…" She stopped abruptly.

Tatiana furrowed her brow. "You knew Azor when he was little?"

"Since he was born." She sighed and leaned her chin in her hand. "I'm ancient, Princess."

Tatiana laughed. "Ancient? I highly doubt that."

"I'm twenty-eight."

"You don't look a day over eighteen." Tatiana cocked a brow and laughed. "Who would know?"

"Well …" She held up her left hand and wiggled her gloved ring finger. "Being unpromised, I pretty much am a spinster."

Tatiana sucked in a breath and Nicole turned away,

embarrassed. "I'm sorry, Princess. I-I shouldn't have said anything. I overstepped my bounds, again. You can send me back to the palace if you want. My m-mouth always g-gets me in t-trouble."

And just like that, Nicole's stuttering returned. She flitted up off her seat and flicked her tail, hand outstretched to the door.

"No." Tatiana moved in front of her and motioned she stay. "It's fine. I understand and I don't agree with keeping servants unpromised if they'd rather not. How is any of what happened to you, your fault?"

Nicole clasped her gloved hands together and Tatiana wondered if her stuttering granted her servitude. And then she thought of her age in relation to Azor's. At ten years apart, that would mean Nicole would have been a servant at ten. *What?*

Then the answer popped into Tatiana's mind. Nicole wasn't maimed, she was an orphan—the product of a hidden secret deep within the dark corners of Natatoria. Her ears turned red in response.

Nicole sighed. "At one time, promising was my dream until my parents died in a mining accident when I was eight." She swallowed hard, hesitating as Tatiana watched with rounded eyes. "I didn't have any other family to care for me, so I was taken to Dori, the royal nursemaid at the time. Pearleza's and a few of the others' parents also died. Gracious King Merric didn't want us to suffer and there were no other orphans at the time, so we were cared for with the Princesses. But once Prince Phaleon took over and the *problem* started, an orphanage had to be built." Nicole looked away.

Orphans. Tatiana had heard rumors that servant girls

frequently arrived at the doors of the orphanage with *lost* merlings. Unclaimed, they were raised then turned over at fourteen, when they could serve. Tatiana had suspected servant girls, often un-chaperoned, might be persuaded to mate in secret places with slick talking guards who'd promise to take them away—never kissing them. But that fairytale never happened and as a result, the Queen was never without an influx of help.

Nicole continued on, disrupting Tatiana's thoughts. "When Azor was born, Dori mysteriously disappeared and Mistress Zerelda took over the new orphanage. Then, when we were deemed of age, we were assimilated into servitude."

"I'm so sorry," Tatiana said breathlessly. "That's horrible."

Nicole sniffed, the water washing away her tears. "Thank you, Princess, for your kindness," she whispered. "We were told by Mistress Zerelda that our parents must have done something hideous for Poseidon to judge us so cruelly."

"What?" Tatiana gasped. "No, Nicole. Poseidon had nothing to do with that." Tatiana huffed and shook her head. "It was an accident, like you said."

Nicole gulped and looked down. "King Merric was injured and almost died as well. But he was weak after that, and once Prince Phaleon had his son, he too all but disappeared. I remember my mother, a beta, would praise at what a gracious leader King Merric was and how he cared about all mer, never treating anyone differently."

Tatiana blinked, reminded of King Phaleon's warnings and his insistence she teach her son history. Her parents rarely spoke of Natatoria as it was, and being on land, she'd been separated from current events. Hopefully she'd still be able to get his book and read about the secrets of the past, but the thought of running into the King made her shiver. "I'm so sorry, Nicole. Truly sorry."

"Thank you. And it's an honor to serve you, the future queen."

Tatiana's stomach contracted. What if an accident had killed her father when he widened the Tahoe gate years ago? Would she be fitted in gloves and serving another future queen? She had to do something. She had to stop this archaic lifecycle hurting her people.

At the door creaking open, Tatiana startled, expecting Azor. Xirene popped her head inside.

"Sorry to bother you, Princess. I'll show Nicole to her quarters now, if she's finished unpacking your things."

Xirene's eyes panned the room, then smugly eyed Tatiana's yellow skirt. Did she overhear Azor ask her to change?

With a glare, Tatiana rose in the water. How dare Xirene flaunt her disrespect. Twice she'd entered her room without announcing herself, and this would be the last time.

"I don't care what you've done in the past, Xirene. You're not to open my door without my approval of your entry, do you understand?"

Xirene's eyes flew open wide. "Y-yes, Princess."

"Such a crime could lead to a flogging, Azor has informed me."

Xirene's chest heaved, her eyes hitting the floor. "Yes, Princess. I apologize."

Tatiana looked over to Nicole, flashing a smug smile. If only she knew the torture she'd endured from Xirene this entire time.

The reprimand served Xirene right for ogling Prince Azor, then overstepping her bounds as keeper of the compound.

"And what are you wearing? This isn't acceptable attire."

"I-I'm sorry, milady. With everything, I haven't had time to do wash."

"Wash?" Tatiana laughed, before pity took over. Faces of the citizens asking for help flashed across her memory. "Oh. Yes. That's understandable, considering... Apology accepted."

Xirene bristled. "Can I show Nicole around the compound and explain her new assignments?"

Tatiana caught Nicole fidgeting in the corner, her eyes low as well. It was then that Tatiana's mistake became clear. Nicole didn't know the nit-picking and interference Xirene had caused Tatiana. She'd only witnessed Tatiana burst into unprovoked rage over what: intrusion without knocking and improper attire, offenses Nicole and Tatiana had committed themselves.

Tatiana's chest fell forward as an apology burned on her lips. In one interaction, she'd done the direct opposite of what she'd claimed she'd wanted to do, confirming she'd always regard Nicole and the others as lowly servants.

"Yes. That would be fine."

Nicole smiled weakly. She swam out of the room behind Xirene, her arms hanging limply down below her.

Tatiana blew out a sad breath, and moved to watch the sharks out the window. She wanted to take back her comments to Xirene. Normally she'd never be this rude to anyone, let alone a servant, but Xirene had a way of getting under her scales.

Off in the distance, the sharks mocked her. Even after the Queen had demanded Azor seal them outside the gate, they swam in defiance, waiting for another time to attack.

Everyone was overstepping their bounds in the kingdom: Azor, the King, Xirene. When would it end?

Tatiana sifted through her clothing, looking for something enticing to wear. After the tulle incident, she was intimidated to do anything unconventional. If only she'd had Grandma Sadie's shell encrusted promising top.

After an hour passed, Tatiana grew impatient. She jetted out of her room and down the porthole, swimming headfirst into Jacob's chest.

"Oomph." She sculled her hands to right herself. "We have to stop meeting like this." She smiled coyly, hoping he wouldn't insist she return to her room.

"Hmmm…" he said, running his hands through his hair.

She craned her neck to look over his shoulder, finding an empty room beyond Ms. Sea Urchin. Voices filtered in the water just beyond, but she couldn't decipher anything.

Jacob stiffened and kept a straight face. "Azor isn't finished debriefing yet."

"You think?" Tatiana propped her hands on her hips and let out a long breath.

"He said he'd be up soon." He tilted his head, his lips in a tight line.

"Sure he did." She pushed her tail, swimming around Jacob, and looked for something to busy herself with so she could listen in.

On the ceiling, two orange starfish caught her attention. With a quick flit to retrieve them, she attached the invertebrates to Ms. Sea Urchin's tatas and laughed on the inside.

A giggle from the kitchen caused Tatiana to swivel around.

"That's a good one," Coralade said with a thumbs-up.

Nicole smiled too, but the happiness didn't touch her eyes, stealing away Tatiana's joy.

The girls returned to their work in the kitchen, but Tatiana didn't feel comfortable joining them. After her altercation with Xirene, and the fact the girls knew she was waiting for Azor's private attention, she had to show the wait didn't bother her. Under no circumstance would she let the maids have more kindling for their gossip.

She turned to Jacob, head held high. "Just let Azor know I'm waiting in his room."

A quick forced smile lit her lips before she swam through the porthole, down the hall, and shut herself inside his room.

The creatures once again made her shudder. Their glaring eyes made her think twice about removing her top. Instead, she propped herself on her hip, pressing her arms together to show cleavage and fanned out her tail to show all the colors. The faces leered, sending out hateful vibes with their eyes. Tatiana shut her lids tight to block the condemning stares, listening to the muffled voices downstairs. Her heart thundered away as she waited.

Then she had a better idea and zipped to her room to retrieve some clothing. The gargoyles needed a makeover.

16

Pancakes

At a low rumble, Tatiana opened her eyes with a start. Light from sun-tunnels filtered into the windowless room, illuminating the heads she'd draped with her clothing the night before. She blinked, gathering her wits, when the bed came to life on its own and shook beneath her.

She swam into the empty hall, panicked. Like always, Jacob had been standing guard, but today—when an emergency happened—she couldn't find him.

"Jacob?" She traversed down the hall, calling his name again.

"Princess?" Jacob's face appeared at the porthole, eyes alert. "Is something wrong?"

"Didn't you feel that?" She placed her hand on the wall to confirm if another had hit. "I think I cursed Natatoria after all."

Jacob hid a slight smile.

"This isn't funny. I just felt an earthquake."

Jacob shook his head. "No… it's dynamite."

"What?" After Nicole's story the evening prior, her heart hammered faster. "Dynamite? Who's using dynamite?"

Jacob sighed. "Azor. Who else?"

"What? Why?"

Jacob pulled his lips into a tight line. "He's reopening the Tahoe gate, that's why." With a quick shrug, he swam off.

She pressed her palm on her forehead then flitted down the porthole to the first floor, mad as a hornet fish. Ms. Sea Urchin's uncovered tatas distracted her momentarily before Shanleigh's voice filtered in from the kitchen, halting Tatiana in her spot.

"All this blasting is giving me a headache," she said.

"If the royals want it opened so badly, then they should do it their dang selves," Coralade interjected. "The hard way, with pickaxes."

A chorus of giggles followed.

"Y-yeah," Nicole said, her voice shaking. "It's just so d-dangerous. The rebels have f-families."

Tatiana moved in closer; the fear behind Nicole's voice constricted her chest.

"But the rebels should open it considering it was their leader who blew it up to begin with," Shanleigh said.

"True," Coralade agreed. "Give them the pickaxes."

Coralade snorted.

"How long is their sentence anyway?" Nicole's shy tone hinted she didn't agree.

"I heard a month," Shanleigh said, hushed.

"I heard no one goes home until all the rebels turn themselves in," Coralade said.

As Jacob swam by with a stack of tridents in his hands, Tatiana straightened and tried to act casual, preening her hair in a mirror. He gave her a puzzled look before he disappeared down the hall. She blew out a breath and returned to the doorway.

Shanleigh continued, "I think they deserve what they get—defying the King like that, over what? A promising to Prince Azor? Limping limpets, no wise parent would deny the Prince their daughter's hand. But, *no-o-o*, T gets to *ch-oooo-se*—"

"She doesn't know how good she has it," Coralade said. "I

mean, if she doesn't want him, there's a line of mermaids who would, including me."

"And I'd be in the front," Shanleigh trilled. "But I heard they don't even stay in the same room."

Tatiana withheld a gasp. Azor hadn't returned to the master bedroom like he'd promised the night before, and his common practice of avoiding her, along with her barren womb, was front page news of the palace's tattle tribune. Her internal heat turned up, bubbling the water next to her skin.

"They don't?" Coralade responded. "Well, Pearleza said that they haven't even done it yet."

At the snickers, Tatiana's blood pressure skyrocketed. She fisted her hands and readied her fin to swim in, when Shanleigh added.

"He should make her wait considering she thinks she's *too good* for him. Honestly, the nerve."

The heated water whooshed over Tatiana's gills. *Too good for Azor? Is that what the palace thinks of me?*

"And have you seen how *you-know-who* reacts when he gets too close to T?" Coralade lilted.

Tatiana's breath caught. Did they mean Xirene?

"I think someone's a little jealous," Shanleigh crooned then a squeak followed, as if someone had pinched her. "Stop it, Coralade."

"What?" she laughed innocently. "I'm just saying that I'd take Chauncey in a fin-flip."

"Uh-huh," Shanleigh said. "Even Grommet... or Jacob. *Hubba hubba.*"

Visions of strangling Shanleigh and Coralade overcame

Tatiana.

Coralade tsked. "Jacob's a bore. He never leaves T's side to have any fun."

Tatiana clutched her neckline, her pulse zooming in anger. How dare they speak about the royals, the rebels, and Jacob that way? She put her hands on her hips, ready to confront them when Xirene swam from the front door, her arms loaded down with baskets.

"Princess," she said with a frown. "Can I help you?"

Fear radiated from the kitchen, along with a few gasps. Tatiana smoothed her hands down the front of her blue skirt, trying to appear calm. She'd had enough of their forked tongues. They'd learn first hand how high-and-mighty she could get when she tossed them out on their fins. But the walls of the house shook again.

"Holy!" Coralade shrieked. "When will they quit already?"

Another frantic gasp came from the kitchen—this time filled with terror.

"You okay?" Shanleigh asked.

"Y-yes, fine," Nicole whimpered. "The blasting. It's just like before—"

At Nicole's distress, Tatiana knew stopping Azor took priority. She'd deal with Coralade and Shanleigh's vitriol later. With a quick flit to the front room, she caught Jacob's eye.

"I'm going to the Tahoe gate. You coming with me?"

He nodded, though his frown said he'd rather polish the weapons than escort her. "Yes, Princess."

Thankful that he didn't put up a fuss, she refocused her energy and rehearsed what she'd say to Azor. He'd get an earful, not only about the blasting, but about where he slept that night.

Jacob stopped before he unlocked the front door. "You can't go out. Not without this." He produced a thin, blue iridescent hooded cape.

She took a long look at him, shocked he'd insisted she wear such a beautiful garment, and smiled. Maybe they had made progress in their friendship.

"Thank you, Jacob," she said appreciatively, until a horrid stench of rotten fish filled the water. "This reeks."

"I know."

"You know?" Tatiana wrinkled her nose, attempting to remove the offending garment. "I'm not wearing this."

Jacob stilled her hands and tied a bow at her neck. "You will if you want to see Azor," he said, blue-grey eyes sliding into her, "You'll wear this. No exceptions."

Tatiana stared back. Argue or obey were her only options. And if she stayed to argue, Azor could hurt someone.

"Fine," she grumbled and swam past him outside.

Through the current, Tatiana whipped her tail hard, anxious to get to Azor before another blast blew. Jacob followed behind, eyeing the horizon. Upon crossing the clearing, she could see a row of shackled prisoners handing rocks to one another. Within seconds, another blast sent bubbles zipping out of the hole up to the ceiling of Natatoria. Instinctively, she cupped her hand over her sore ear.

Then, she saw Azor, dark hair waving in the current. The water once again rippled from the heat blazing off her skin.

"Azor!" she called out.

He turned in surprise as the water shimmered, vibrating

again. She held her ears, expecting the blast to burst her eardrum. Azor's eyes burned first into Tatiana's lithe frame, then Jacob.

"What are you two doing here?"

"Seriously? Rockfish!" She frowned, propping her hand to her hip. "I should be asking you."

Azor pressed his brows together, his glare ping-ponging between them. "Jacob, take her home. Now."

"No!" Tatiana latched onto Azor's arm and pulled him away from the onlookers. Temptation to choke him besieged her. She put her face inches from his. "You said you'd come to bed last night. *Promised me* you would, and you didn't. Now you're here, without even so much as a good morning. To what? Open the gate?" She pressed out her claws and dug into his skin.

"Hey," he barked, whipping his arm away. "Keep your talons to yourself, woman."

"I'm done! With this and with you!"

"Tatiana, Love," he said his voice softening. He approached her with his hands raised. "I came to bed last night, but you'd fallen asleep. And this morning, I wanted so badly to kiss you, but you looked so peaceful, like an angel."

She blinked in confusion. "Angel?"

"Yes, Love," he said, cupping her cheek.

The same ache returned; the thrill and delight from his touch. She fought him, closing her eyes, willing away the curse of the promise. She'd get her point across one way or another. "My parents have left. Leave Tahoe be."

He lingered for a moment, then recoiled, wrinkling his nose. "You stink."

Her cheeks heated. She cast a glare at Jacob, who pivoted

away—studying the crew at the mouth of the Tahoe gate. But at the absence of Azor's touch, she could finally concentrate on what she'd wanted to say.

She clutched her fists, gaining courage. "This is dangerous and silly. Someone could get hurt."

"Like I care if a rebel beta or two gets singed." He blew out a chuckle. "It's their leader's fault that…" He stopped himself and rubbed his goatee, jaw clenching.

"You don't know that for sure. It could have been…" She clamped her mouth shut when Badger's name came to mind. She wouldn't sell him out after he'd proved his loyalty to her family. "Uncle Alaster."

"Alaster?" Azor laughed. "No. This has nothing to do with your *parents*. We have assets in Tahoe we must attend to."

"What, a house? My father built that, and the charter business and everything else in and around that house. Those assets belong to my family."

"We bought the land, which means the assets belong to us." With a dark expression, he continued. "Don't make this a bigger issue than it needs to be. There's no other way into Tahoe and I will reopen the gate; it's as simple as that."

Tatiana laughed coarsely. The King's words about a foolish son came to mind and she couldn't agree more.

"Did you know Nicole and other servants lost their parents to a mining accident when they were only children?" she hissed. "I'm sure these explosions are giving them and all the servants a huge vote of confidence. They're already afraid to get supplies as it is—"

Azor puffed his chest forward; his pectoral spikes flared. "All of that is none of your concern, Tatiana." He smirked. "But if you insist on sticking around, please do so out of view of the rebels. Your presence is confusing."

"Confusing?" She perched a brow. "As future queen, I care about all mer: beta, rebel, maimed and the orphaned. And dynamite is dynamite. If the servants are terrorized, who's going to get your mom her coveted croissants and fresh berry jam?"

His smile remained. "Maybe she'll have to eat fish like the rest of her kingdom."

"That's if we have any left in a few days." Tatiana huffed.

His eyes hardened into a scowl. "I refuse to argue with you. Your father forfeited everything once he defied the King and I will reopen the gate."

"My father did nothing wrong and your actions aren't fixing the problem. It's only making it worse! If you'd only listen to your father and stop this before it's too late!"

He cocked his head back and snarled. "It's not up to you. Ever!"

"Ughhh!" She turned her fin in disgust and kicked her tail toward the compound. She'd expected him to chase after her, or at least call out her name, but he yelled for Jacob instead. Heartbroken, she sped off blindly, leaving them in her sand-filled wake.

⁓

Her heart stuttered and mind whirred. She couldn't return to the compound, not after the sharp-tongued servants sliced her up like sushi. This would only add to the gossip mill, though they'd know soon enough when the explosions didn't stop. Her words to him were nothing. With another pump of her tail, she turned east and headed for her old house. Maybe in the ruins she could salvage what was left of her stolen life. Maybe there an answer to her problems would arise.

Upon rounding the last row of mer houses on Percophidae Lane, Tatiana gasped. Unscathed and pristine stood her home, just like she and her mother had left it right before the promising ceremony.

"That little piranha," Tatiana mumbled under her breath as she swam in for a closer look.

The furnishings and familiar smells greeted her with open arms, and she threw off the stinky jacket and spread herself across the floor. She inhaled, bent her knees and wriggled her toes, thankful spiders couldn't take over like they would in her Tahoe home. At her song of joy leaping off her tongue, a crab skittered across the floor and Tatiana laughed, thinking of Fin—his hated underwater version of spiders.

Immediately, Tatiana dashed to her room and put on her favorite pink tulle sequin skirt, then hustled to the kitchen and whipped up a batch of vegan pancakes (due to a lack of eggs and milk) and brewed a pot of hot coffee. The delicious smells danced with one another and tickled her nose. She ate with a peaceful smile, the first one in a long time, until a twinge of guilt hit her.

Though she'd meant every word she'd said to Azor, dread over her delivery took hold. How would they unite a kingdom when they couldn't even get along? Or sleep in the same bed, for that matter?

She groaned into her hands. Lies… all he told were lies. He'd promise one thing and do the total opposite, then expect his apology would smooth things over. If she returned to the compound now, he'd win and she'd virtually be in agreement of his poor treatment of her. Why, in spite of his cruelty, did the promise have such an unfair hold on her heart and her actions and not on his? Only briefly would she have moments of clarity, like in the heat of an argument, where she could see what an ass he really was. But then his touch turned her to a spineless jellyfish, addicted to him like a drug. She'd hated him once. She wanted to remember her feelings, use them to help her think clearer. Azor clearly showed there was a way to control oneself, master the art of the promise. What was the secret?

Maybe distance was the key. What if she hid at her parent's for a while? Would he finally care? Miss her? Worry to the point, he'd realize his mistreatment of her? There was no reason for him to pursue her parents anymore. Sure, the King suffered because of a chain of events he admitted he started. But hadn't Azor talked to his dad yet? Asked for advice on how to lead Phaleon's kingdom, at least? Surely King Phaleon would mention he'd seen Tatiana, that he'd asked her forgiveness, that he no longer wanted to press the issue. Besides, the sharks were Azor's doing. If they'd been held on the other side, in the Pacific Ocean where they belonged, and not in Natatoria, the King would be ruling today. Azor and Tatiana would be on their promisetide.

At the thought of a vacation, she closed her eyes and moaned. Fruity drinks and playing tag with the dolphins floated in her mind, along with intimate things only the promised do. *If only.*

Ash and Fin drifted in her mind. They'd be at the Florida safe house by now, starting over. Had any of the runaway mers given them an update on what's happening in Natatoria? Did they care? Ash and Fin would be head over fins in love, and her parents... well, apart for practically a month, they'd be just as bad. And in their minds, they'd probably thought the same of her and Azor—but nothing could be further from the truth. Did they even miss her?

After how she'd treated them when they'd only wanted to save her, they'd know it wasn't a good idea to return. And with news Azor might be hot on their tails, they'd never risk coming back anyway. To know they'd accepted her choice and moved on without her hurt. Was this her punishment for wanting to become human? For wanting such a selfish dream?

She pushed away her half-eaten plate, her appetite ruined. If only she and Fin had successfully escaped when she'd broken him out of Azor's dungeon. They'd all be together in Florida, preparing to attend Florida Atlantic University with Ash, and peace would have inhabited Natatoria. Everyone would have been so much better off.

She stared at the time zone clock in the kitchen and bit her lip. Would this be her life? Constant waiting, pining, begging, and fighting? What would happen after she bore a child? Would Azor steal away her son? Warp their sweet merling's mind to be mean and cruel like he was? She couldn't bare the thought. And then with the servants watching and gossiping, bets on how she'd handle the responsibility, handle the stress, handle the throne.

No.

Then the solution crossed her mind, an escape from all the madness. She could simply leave. She already knew where her family was. Once in Florida, her parents could convert her and she'd forget everything, all the blame, madness, treachery—that is if they forgave her. The thought thrilled and sickened her.

At the plan, her eyes drifted to her mother's waterproof bag tucked neatly in the rock cabinet over the lava stove. She didn't need anything for the trip—only the heirlooms that were special to her family. Her gut tightened and twisted, the thought of leaving Azor exhausting. Though life under the sea had proven to be nothing but heartbreaking, could she honestly go through with it and leave him?

Before she could chicken out, she grabbed her cup of coffee and moved to her room to pack her things, one of which was *Little Women*. At the thought of Meg, Jo, Beth, and Amy, she missed Ash, her best friend and sister-in-mer; her heart pounded faster. She packed her journals, her paints, and cookbooks. The growing, intense fear screamed from her soul, squeezing her chest and inflicting her with dread. She continued on, blaming Azor. His pigheadedness was the reason she was leaving. Maybe now he'd finally understand how serious her threats were. A lifetime of loneliness seemed a fitting punishment.

Like a small hurricane, she whizzed through her room, scooping up bikini tops and skirts from her closet, when her beloved pink sparkly bag flopped to the floor. Inside was a collection of memories she'd made with Ash. As she clutched the purse to her chest, she vowed she was making the right choice. This and the rest of her belongings could only be enjoyed on land—with the wind in her hair, the sun on her face, and the sand between her toes. Freedom. A life of her own.

She stuffed the pink purse into the waterproof bag and lugged it to the porthole. With a soft thud, the bag hit the floor. Tatiana took a deep breath and stared at the shimmering water.

What are you doing?

She teetered, the task daunting. Could she leave? Would she leave? Maybe all Azor needed was a few hours. Yes, that would wise him up. She just needed to wait him out. He'd eventually come looking for her and be sorry. Wait it out. Win.

She sat on the couch, her bag in her fingers, and pulled her feet up. She'd prove a point. This time, she'd be stronger than the promise. Had to be.

17

Too Late

Frantic, adrenaline pulsed down Jacob's fin as he swung his tail, cursing at himself for insisting she wore the scent-covering cape. If Tatiana wasn't at her parents' house, he didn't know what he'd do. Escape, too. Or die trying.

He'd watched her vanish over the dunes toward the compound, but she'd never arrived. She'd been missing a day. An entire day and no one, not even the rebels, had seen her. Did she get mad enough to run? Did she somehow get past the Dradux and the cassava drenched nets and escape out of a gate? The thought of Tatiana in the hands of the Dradux, especially Darrellon, made him want to punch something. Poseidon help anyone that dared touch her.

Secretly, he hoped she'd escaped to Florida. He knew about the safe house and figured Tatiana did too, but with the iridescent hooded cape covering her scent, he couldn't track her. And before he left Natatoria, he'd need to be certain she'd left. There was no coming back.

He hadn't thought until now to check her parents' house. Rumor was the crystal ball had damaged the home and others beyond repair. At this point, he'd check anywhere. And like a singing beacon, Jack and Maggie's house stood at the end of the lane—untouched. He darted up the porthole, took in the sight of Tatiana on the couch, and practically passed out on the floor in front of her.

"Princess? Thank Poseidon you're safe." Lying on his back, his chest rose and lowered from his breaths. "I've looked everywhere. You don't know how terrified..."

Jacob's eyes glazed over before he closed them slowly, thanking the heavens above, then he cursed them. She'd stayed in Natatoria—wild and frantic like a dying fish—for Azor. He scolded himself for his over-protectiveness in insisting she wear the cape. His eyes scanned the floor and saw her bag near the porthole.

Bag? Had she intended to leave?

Jacob quirked his head, imploring. "Why didn't you return to the compound?"

"I—uh." Her mouth moved, but she said nothing further.

Rocking on her seat with unfocused eyes, she tightly wrapped her arms around her legs. Everything inside him wanted to pull her into his chest, nuzzle his nose in her hair, and whisper everything would be okay. She'd packed, but didn't leave? Why? Was this only a stunt to get Azor's attention? Jacob closed his eyes in remorse. The fool had barely cared she'd left. He didn't even form a search party.

Jacob knelt before her. "Princess, please. Don't ever disappear like that again. I must know where you are at all times. There are those who'd want nothing more than to harm you, do you understand?"

At the mention of hostile mers, Tatiana snapped out of her stupor and laughed. "Like the King?"

Jacob inhaled and blinked slowly, remembering the horrible incident.

"Yes..." Though the peaceful nature of the mer had been

tested, Jacob didn't think anyone was desperate enough to ransom Tatiana for freedom of their jailed mate. But the guards—especially the Dradux—would cop a feel or attempt a lick just for bragging rights.

"I know everyone hates me. They think I'm a spoiled brat and undeserving of the Prince's affection... but to harm me? Who'd be so cruel and hateful?" She glared at his arm, the place where she'd bitten him. A chill ran across his spine, remembering that day. She sucked in a tortured breath. "Your rebels? As revenge for my father abandoning them?"

"No... they care for you, Princess, just like they care for your father."

"Of course you'd say that." Tatiana recoiled further onto the couch. Her eyes sparked, accusing. "Where is my mate anyway? Is he even looking for me?"

Jacob's chest flexed. After Azor found out she was missing, he called off Jacob's search party. He'd told everyone he didn't want to give attention to her tantrum, calling her a spoiled merling in front of the guards and servants, that she'd come home and beg for forgiveness eventually.

"No. Azor isn't looking for you. He thinks you're throwing a tantrum."

Tatiana blinked, disbelieving. "What?" Tears suddenly trailed her cheeks.

Jacob cringed, wishing he'd been less direct. Her eyes, puffy and swollen, told him she'd been crying and most likely lay awake all night. He inched closer, offering his palm. She glared into him with frustrated helplessness.

He looked deeply into her eyes. "You don't have to put up

with this, with him."

"And then what? Leave?" Her lip quivered.

Jacob gestured to the bag. "Looks like you'd already planned to do so."

"How could I leave, Jacob?" She laughed coarsely. "I can't even last a night without freaking out."

"You can do it, Tatiana. I believe in you. You're strong."

She pressed her eyelids shut and shook her head. "How do you know that? You don't even know me."

Jacob smiled. "Did I tell you I was with your father on the mission? He told me about a girl who was incredibly smart, who wouldn't let anything stand in the way of her dreams. Of her bravery and desire for truth. One who loved people and was a friend to all." He leaned in "The only thing he forgot to mention was how beautiful you are."

Tatiana's eyes popped open, her cheeks growing pink. "Don't say that."

"Why not?"

Tatiana stuttered. "Because it's not true, and…" She gulped down a sob. "My father would be horribly disappointed in me. He probably hates me."

Jacob sighed. "No, Princess. He's planning to come back for you."

"What?" Her chest heaved.

"He doesn't want you here, dealing with a tyrant who isn't even capable of love."

"Wh—?"

"Don't deny it." Jacob gritted his teeth. "I've watched how he treats you. Like a possession. He's using you, Tatiana. You're a pawn in his game. His mission is to find Jack and punish him by beheading him in the square. He's increased his guard, arresting beta-mers, and using illegal poisons. And he's planning his coronation, even though you haven't given him a…" He looked away, disgusted.

Her breath came out quick. "No."

"But you can get away. Leave him. Leave this. I can take you to Florida. I know where the safe house is. Then we can tell your dad about everything."

She gasped and their eyes met. A fire crackled between them—one of loyalty, of understanding, of unity, of purpose. He'd gotten through to her, finally. He rose, and held out his hand, ready to go. Ready to leave.

As she reached for him, his mind raced with his plan. Dorian still had control of the Scotland gate, and since the distance took hours to traverse, even at merlightning speed, and Azor hadn't paid much attention in securing it, they should be able to escape undetected. The cape would cover both their scents, leaving no trail, and once in Loch Ness, they could backtrack to Florida. They'd be free.

His hand wrapped around her slender fingers, sending a bolt of desire through his body. At her trembling, he knew she'd been fighting her growing feelings for him, too. He'd seen how she'd looked at him, reacted to his touch in the past. The heat between them was undeniable and with Azor's absence, Jacob could break the promise spell and heal her broken soul until she wanted to kiss him.

She pushed to her feet, hope in her eyes. Jacob stared at her lips, wishing she'd ask him now. He'd kiss her. He'd treasure her forever.

Her tongue darted out, licking her lips, when her mouth curled into a frown. She dropped his hand. "You're lying to me, Jacob. This can't be true."

"What?" Jacob's face grew pained. "No, Princess. It's all true. The last thing I want to do is manipulate you. Your safety is my only priority."

"Right," she sneered. "Your only priority? You've made your position pretty clear. And if my father is coming to attack, he'll take Azor out. He'll murder him. How is that any better?"

Jacob gritted his teeth. "Princess, listen to yourself. Must I remind you how Azor treats you? He doesn't even care enough to come find you."

"He's busy," she said, throwing her shoulders back. "And all you've ever wanted was to take me from Azor anyway. My place is here, with him."

At her refusal, he wanted to tell her the truth, that it wasn't just his loyalty to her father that fueled him. He'd become attached to her, grown to care for her deeply, and Azor's mistreatment was driving him mad.

She thrust out her jaw, speaking between her teeth. "He may not be the man I dreamt of being with my entire life, but I won't let my father hurt him."

Jacob rubbed the back of his neck, working to keep his cool. How could she still, after everything, defend this *asshole*? "Please, Tatiana—"

A loud exhale at the porthole interrupted Jacob.

"Tatiana," Azor said, breathless. "There you are."

And in one small turn of her head, Jacob watched her

expression change. Tears trickled down her cheeks as her body wobbled forward, arms limply outstretched.

"I knew you'd come for me," she whispered.

"There, there," Azor said, jumping from the porthole, and phasing midair. He scooped up her legs and she fell against his shoulder. "The scare is over. Let's go home."

With a splash, they were gone. Jacob fell to his knees, reaching out to the empty air that had just held her. She'd been there, within his grasp, and willing to go. They could have disappeared far away from the danger… and he messed it all up.

"Argh!" he yelled, pounding his fists into the floor. "Damn you, Azor!"

The mind-jacking power of the promise had tricked her once again. He pinched his eyes shut, shaking his head. Why had he expected anything different? Hope she'd fight back? Choose him instead? None of this should have been a surprise. She'd never leave him, even with everything. If only he was guarding someone else—anyone but her. He palmed his hair and breathed out a harsh breath, before he stood and dusted off his hands.

He had to return, like always, and resume the role as protector. And it was going to kill him.

18

Angelfish

Inside the compound, Coralade and Shanleigh were a flutter of conversation like their sister had returned from the dead while Nicole hugged onto Tatiana's neck. Jacob shook his head in dismay. Would Tatiana see through those two at least? Did she already forget their vicious gossip?

His eyes met Nicole's—Tatiana's only true ally in the compound—and she breathed a sigh of relief, mouthing a, "Thanks".

Jacob tried to grin in return, but felt sick inside. Yeah, he'd found Tatiana, but he hadn't saved her from anything. Nicole would soon learn the hell this place was.

"There," Azor said as a snap rung through the water.

Jacob's head whipped to their location.

Tatiana smiled, fingering a delicate gold bracelet stamped with the Natatorian royal symbol. "It's lovely. Thank you."

"I'm glad you like it." Azor grinned.

Jacob's heart hammered, hiding his glare under a straight face. This wasn't a present, but a restraining bracelet—one filled with poison—and if she left the depths in Natatoria, she'd be dead within hours without the antidote.

As the mermaids admired the bracelet, Azor moved closer to Jacob with a knowing grin. "I can't have my little precious angelfish wandering off now, can I?"

Jacob clenched his jaw. "Don't you think she should at least know?"

"And ruin this moment?" Azor shrugged, surprised. "She needed a pretty bobble for her wrist, after everything. I have to ensure the safety of my possessions, as I'm sure you can understand. With the Tahoe gate about to be reopened, one can't be too careful."

"But she'll die if someone abducts her." Jacob's tone, controlled, hid his desire to rip out Azor's beating heart.

"Then I suggest you make sure that never happens." Azor knocked Jacob in the chest, flashing him a condescending look before returning to Tatiana's side.

As Azor led Tatiana to the porthole, all Jacob could see was red. *Murder would end this.* He calmed his gills while the servants returned to the kitchen and the guards to the barracks. Azor would be in his room with her, kissing her, touching her.

Jacob gripped his trident harder. It took all his self-control not to race upstairs and slaughter him now. How did Azor even know Tatiana was at her parents'? And why did he decide to look for her then? He'd made Jacob look like a liar.

"Smooth," Grommet said, swimming over to where Jacob hovered in the water.

"Leave me alone," Jacob grunted.

"I thought you'd finally done it," he said, cocking an eyebrow.

"Yeah, well…"

"You're one sucker fish for punishment." Grommet punched Jacob in the arm. "Well, you look the part at least. No one would know where your true loyalties lie."

Jacob laughed. "I need to put in for a transfer."

Just then, the front doors of the compound opened.

"Get yer girlie hands off me, yah thieven bloke."

Jacob and Grommet swiveled around. With shackled hands, Badger yanked on the chain from an unseen assailant. Jacob felt the blood drain from his face as he tried to appear calm.

Then, from nowhere, the end of a javelin pummeled Badger's face, whipping his head backward. Blood and a lone tooth took flight into the water from his split lip.

"Quiet, traitor," Blanchard seethed as he lugged Badger into the foyer.

Azor swam in from upstairs and a wicked smile spread over his face upon seeing the newest arrival.

"We caught him returning from Scotland. He was seen on land using a telephone," Blanchard informed him.

"I knew it," Azor said while tapping his lips with his finger. "Only a matter of time 'til your true disgusting self showed, beta."

Badger spit out more blood. "Why don't cha let me outta these here shackles and then be accussin' me proper. I'd fancy you a pop in the kisser before you knew what was comin', ya panty-wearing coward."

"Don't talk like that to the Captain," Blanchard bellowed and reared back to hit Badger again. Jacob flinched, ready to stop him.

Azor quickly intervened. "Leave him, Blanchard." He swam up and got in Badger's face. "Maybe one day you'll get your wish, old man. But until then, you'll rot in jail."

"I did nothin' wrong. You have no proof," Badger spat.

"I could have you jailed for your disrespect alone. Who were you calling in Scotland, Badger?"

"Yer girlfriend and she be wantin' her panties back," he said, giving them a bloody sneer.

Azor pulled his eyes into slits; all of his prior happiness disappeared from his face. "Lock him up."

Jacob worked to calm down his heart rate as outrage swirled in his gut. Inside, his heater revved out of control, boiling the water around his arms. His muscles ached in restraint, the temptation to stab Azor and free everyone from his miserable existence coiled in his fingers. He could do it and Grommet would have his back. He gave Grommet a nod, ready to pounce, when another group of mers flooded into the hall, pulled in by the Dradux.

Badger caught Jacob's eye and shook his head, calling Jacob off.

"Yer makin' a mistake, Azor. Mers don't take kindly to martyrs and class warfare," Badger seethed.

Azor ignored him and swam past, giving Jacob an appraising look before heading out the front doors. "Lock the rest of them up. I'm going to the palace."

Jacob nodded shakily, watching another moment of opportunity fade. Badger gave him a quick smile before disappearing behind the double doors. The Dradux followed Azor and the rest went into the dungeon. Once the front room emptied, Jacob pounded the butt of his trident against the stone floor, cursing himself for not taking the opportunity.

"It wasn't time yet." Grommet gave a sympathetic look.

Jacob cast him a sideways glance. "I had him, right there. An open shot."

"Yes, but then the others would have kindly slit your throat in return."

"I don't care anymore, Grommet. I need to stop playing it safe."

"But what about Tatiana?"

Jacob closed his eyes and sucked in the briny water, wondering what she was doing upstairs alone. "We're running out of time."

"We're biding our time," Grommet corrected.

He thought about his foiled plan to leave with Tatiana. With spies watching the gates, they would have been caught, he would have been dead. Then Tatiana would be alone with these snakes. "Damn Blanchard."

Grommet clapped Jacob on the back. "Stay positive. We still have the upper fin."

But the panic swelled inside Jacob, the loss of power suffocating.

"How? Our numbers have dwindled and the people—they're practically starving. Once they hear Badger's been arrested, all the Queen has to say is she'll grant pardons to anyone else who turns in a rebel, and we're sunk."

Grommet's face hardened. "And commit communal suicide? They'd be branded traitors on both sides. Not worth it. No one has been escorted to Bone Island yet. Azor is all hiss, no bite. We have to stick to the plan and wait for Jack."

Jacob's pectoral fins flared. "I can't just wait."

"Jack's coming and he has friends on the outside. They're bringing weapons and poisons, and then we'll bust everyone free from here, ambush the palace, and set Tatiana as Queen since she's royal now. And when that happens, you'll be fighting a horde of mermen to get your hooks into Azor. She'll be as good as yours after that."

Jacob laughed at the thought of being king. "So optimistic."

"You have to be strong, and on guard for the future queen of the new Natatoria."

Jacob looked down at his hands. "She thinks I'm lying to her."

"It's the promise. Don't worry about it."

Jacob stretched his bicep, flexing the scared bite mark. "She thinks I just want to abduct her to punish her for staying with Azor."

"You always hurt the ones you love."

Jacob shrugged, thinking of how sexy her feisty side was, before he slugged Grommet in the chest. "Knock it off."

He backed away, hands up. "I'm just putting it out there. And rumor is Azor hasn't even spent one night with her yet. Bet they're not even bumping uglies, if you ask me."

Jacob's fanned his fins, spikes pointed outward. "I'd like you to kindly stay out of her bedroom, if you don't mind."

"I'm just saying, it's a little odd. She doesn't sleep in his room either, from what the girls say." He pointed over his shoulder to the kitchen with his thumb. "They've got a peephole."

Jacob wrinkled up his face. "What—?"

"I'm just saying… it's odd."

"News flash, Grommet. There've been no rogue promisings, if you're trying to suggest something."

"Az hole is a son of a bass, but if Tatiana were mine, you wouldn't be able to keep me away from her. And thank Poseidon he's not tickling her regular, or you'd be one mad hornet fish. And you know they're definitely not—" he pounded his fists together twice, "doing the *nasty*."

Jacob shoved into Grommet, hard. "Shut your mouth right now, or I promise I'll—"

Grommet held up his hands as Jacob flipped his trident, pointing it at his chest. "Okay. Sorry. I'm just suggesting he ain't really promised to her and when the time comes, you might have only one choice."

"To run?"

Grommet eyed the trident warily. "No, stupid. To kiss her."

Jacob blinked at him, then shook his head and laughed, lowering the weapon. "How in the heck will that solve anything?"

"Well…" He smirked. "Maybe it'll clear her head for a bit so she can see she doesn't feel anything for that slimy bag of sh—"

"Clear her head?" Jacob pulled his shoulders taut. "No. More like mess with mine. Didn't your mother teach you anything about the bond?"

Grommet rolled his eyes. "Well it's either that, or waiting for Jack to come back and—" he drew a line over his throat.

Jacob leaned forward, threatening. "If I kiss her, it won't be because she needs a distraction. Got it?"

"Suit yourself." Grommet laughed, then swam off.

Jacob's breath sucked in short, his heart racing. He turned and looked to the porthole. Sure, Azor was being a dick, but he'd never perform promise polygamy, not with his responsibilities and ambitions of the throne. Jacob would rather think him a cold hearted snake incapable of love. And right now, in Tatiana's condition, kissing her wasn't the answer. Not only because he would want her all the more, but because she'd know his true feelings. Then she really could hurt him. No. Jacob had to remember his kiss was powerless in the shadow of her bond to Azor.

There were only three ways he'd kiss her. Most important, because she wanted him to, second, because Azor was dead, or third, she'd somehow broken her bond to him. Nothing else could sever that. And at this rate, with how she defended Azor under the promising spell, that would never happen.

He'd have to shut it all off and wait. Hope he wasn't fooling himself. Or he'd go insane.

19

Feathers

Upon surfacing through the porthole, Azor lifted Tatiana into his arms and carried her past her room and down the hall. She squealed on the inside, trying to keep her composure, reminded of the human custom of carrying one's bride over the threshold. Was this the moment? The one she'd been waiting for? She smiled, finally happy. Jacob had been so terribly wrong about Azor.

At the double doors, he paused. "Close your eyes."

Tatiana's heart thumped wildly and her lids slipped shut. What did he have planned? Her hair danced with the fluidity of his movements. A soft clang of iron signaled he'd shut the door. "You can open them now."

She peered momentarily into his dark eyes and startled. Somehow she'd expected blue-grey ones to peer back at her instead.

"You okay?" he asked quickly.

"Yes, I…" She turned and her voice hitched in her throat. Billowing blue fabric hung over the gargoyles head and a white silken sheet lay on the bed.

He cleared his throat. "I took the hint my décor made you uncomfortable."

"Oh." She put her hand to her mouth, remembering she'd hidden their disfigured faces with her clothes the other night.

Sconces filled with blue light lit the way to the bed like a runway. Small colorful fish darted about almost in a fireworks display around them. The only thing missing was a little music to capture the mood.

"It's so lovely." Her lips pulled into a smile.

"Good." He took her hand and led her to the bed. "With everything that's happened, I figured it was the least I could do… to make it up to you for being so *distracted*."

Tatiana's soul sang at the words. Jacob's lies hit harder. Azor had been concerned and her plan had worked. He'd finally seen she was worth spending time with, so much so that he'd made things romantic. She trailed her fingers lightly down his chest; her man in shining scales was finally ready to be her mate. "I—thank you. It's so beautiful."

"Just like you." He sat and sculled his hand on the sheet, inviting her to sit.

She floated down, her hands trembling. She felt so inept—inexperienced. His confident smile warmed her and she soaked in the sight of him—his hair, his smile, his teeth. She wanted to exude that same confidence, do something bold. Movies where women brazenly took off their tops came to mind. Should she do the same? Or just start by performing the mating dance? Or both?

She floated up, reaching behind to undo the button, when Azor stayed her hand. "Let's take things slow."

He produced a red strip of cloth and waved it in the current, before he wrapped it over her eyes. She bit her lip, trying not to giggle, plunged into semi darkness. "What are you doing?"

"You'll see," he said with a throaty voice.

His tongue was at her neck, tracing her collarbone, his hands caressing her stomach and hips. A loud gurgle radiated from her throat, making an obnoxious burp.

"Sorry," she apologized as her cheeks heated.

"Hmmm," he said, halting his hands. "I have an idea."

She held her breath, waiting for him, a bundle of nerves.

"Open your mouth." His voice was at her ear again.

"Okay."

A tingle of what he'd do rolled deep in her belly. Something smooth and oval was placed on her tongue. She broke the skin with her teeth, tasting sweet—a grape.

"That was a grape. Too easy."

"How about this one."

She quickly chewed and swallowed the grape, the last piece too bitter for her liking. Was the grape spoiled? She opened her mouth for the next delicacy. Bumpy and small, she knew right away.

"A raspberry." Again, something sour lingered after she swallowed.

"Try this one," he said, his lips tugging on her earlobe.

Citrus and tang filled her mouth. "An orange. Too easy."

Tiring of the game, she reached for him unable to find him in the current, preferring his taste in her mouth instead.

"When do I get to feed you?" she asked, her tongue suddenly lazy.

"In a minute."

From nowhere, a blueberry popped into her mouth and she chewed, but ripped off the blindfold shortly after. "My turn."

Azor hovered directly above her. He waggled his finger at her. "Uh uh… I have another game."

Before she could protest, he snatched up her wrists behind her back and wove the tie around them, binding her.

"Oh, my." She giggled, a silly flighty sound to her ears.

He slid behind her, his lips traveling from her ear down her neck. She wiggled as his whiskers tickled at her collarbone.

"Stopppp," she squirmed.

He took down the straps of her top, trailing his finger where fabric met skin. "What's down here?" He purred with his chin on her shoulder.

Tatiana snuggled into him, her inhibitions lowered. "Why don't you find out?" she said, her words slurring.

"Hmmm…" He trailed his hands down her chest, then around to her back and stopped at the top of her skirt, unbuttoning the button.

With swift movements, he swiveled her around by her hips and laid her flat on the bed. Her head swirled in glee, the room spinning. "Wheeee," she said, exaggerating the E's on purpose.

He caught hold of the band encircling her waist and tugged. She giggled, shimmying her hips, and a plume of pheromones launched into the current around them. Azor's face contorted, a grimace almost. Tatiana laughed, surprised by his odd reaction.

Once the skirt was free of her, she knew what would happen next. She tried to watch him over her shoulder, but the pair of Azors hovering over her—zigzagged and blurred in and out of focus.

"Hold still," she said, trying to grab him, then remembering her hands had been tied. "This isn't fun. I want to touch you."

From nowhere, he produced a feather duster worm in his hands and a devilish smile on his face.

"No!" she squealed. "Don't touch me with that."

He tickled her fin then moved up slowly to her backside. She shrieked, boarding on a siren scream.

"Okay, okay," he said, tossing the feathered thing into the current. "Don't siren or Jacob will come."

She laughed, her eyes rolling back into her head, and thought of Jacob—jealous Jacob with his blue-grey eyes and tussled brown hair. Wouldn't that interruption be embarrassing?

But she didn't care. Her body, vibrant and alive, zinged with electricity. Her eyelids, though, felt more like dead weights. She willed them open, wanting to see Azor as he touched her. Or was he touching her? A million little soft flutters ticked her scales, all over. She loved this soft, delectable space where the hurts faded—where she was finally happy—free.

She reached out for Azor, her arms magically unpinned, but couldn't find him. She couldn't even find the strength to open her eyes to look. Encased in warmth, she didn't care. His scent was heavy in the water and she'd never felt this magnificent.

20

Secret Places

Jacob lingered at Azor's door, warring with himself about opening it, just to look in on her. After he'd escorted her upstairs, she'd slept the entire afternoon, missing dinner. Her soft sleep-induced murmurings had to be enough to comfort him.

He let the notion go and slithered down the porthole. Why did he insist on torturing himself? He should just go to bed and leave the worrying up to the Prince, but he couldn't. Things didn't add up.

When Badger had arrived, Azor seemed more concerned about his arrest and returning to the palace, than rejoining his lover. And he'd left her side so quickly—minutes really—and didn't seem all that much *happier*. And even at the late hour now, Azor hadn't returned from the palace. What kept him so preoccupied?

Could Grommet have been right? Jacob shook his head, pushing that idea away once again. Azor couldn't have committed promising-polygamy and kept it hidden this entire time. Otherwise there'd be a jealous—if not pregnant—mermaid ready to claw Tatiana's eyes out and difficult to keep quiet. No, Jacob would rather think Azor's heart was too hard for true love.

"Jacob," Grommet whispered. "What are you doing up so late? Catch some sleep. I've got the doors."

"Yeah," Jacob yawned. After searching for Tatiana the entire night prior, some shuteye would be favorable. "Thanks."

Jacob swam past Grommet with a nod, thankful to have such a good friend.

"Hey, ahhh…" Grommet said slowly. "Have you been to the dungeon since you've been back?"

"No. Why?"

"Maybe you should check out the newest arrests."

Jacob scowled. Most all of his fellow rebels had already been arrested, sans Grommet. And watching Badger dragged in wearing shackles was hard enough. He swam inside anyway, but Grommet couldn't have prepared him for their latest arrestee.

Jacob's mouth slipped open as he stared at the merman caged before him. "Jax?"

Jax popped an eye open, gaining focus. He smiled. "Brother. Nice to see you again."

"You're supposed to be …"

"Yeah, I know. Dead." Jax shrugged. "The King can't keep a good merman down, or should I say up?" He chuckled, pointing to the ceiling.

Jacob gave his brother a quick once over, trying to get past the shock. The last time they'd seen one another was at dinner with their parents before everything happened—the accusation of treason and his brother's sentence to Bone Island. Yet he hovered there in the current—alive and smiling, no less.

Jax palmed his hand through his hair and the black gleam on his finger caught Jacob's eye. He blinked slowly, registering the meaning.

"You're promised?" Jacob asked.

"Nothing gets past you, does it? Babysitting has made you observant."

Jacob ignored the insult, a hint he'd been getting an earful from Grommet, and continued, "When did this happen?"

"After I kissed a girl, how else?"

Jacob grabbed the bars. "Don't mess with me, Jaxon. Tell me who."

"I will. I'll tell you everything, but I need you to get me out of here first," he whispered.

His grip slacked on the bars and he glanced down the row of his caged rebel friends. Most were sleeping, except those closest to them—all wanting to be freed, all wanting to go home. He gritted his teeth. The price the rebels needed to pay to ensure everyone's freedom hit an all time high now that Jax was in custody. How could he secretly get his brother out without raising suspicions?

Sure, the undercover rebel guards had planned to free everyone if they ended up tied to trees on Bone Island, but his brother? If he'd escaped there already, Azor wouldn't send him back. The next step would be a public execution. They'd need to organize an escape sooner—possibly before Jack returned.

The golden cuff encircling Jax's wrist caught his eye and his shoulders sank—identical to Tatiana's, only larger.

"I can get you out, but I need a key to the cuff first," Jacob finally said, pointing to the golden bracelet.

"So? Get me one."

"Azor's got it."

Jax gritted his teeth. "Then break 'em with pliers or something. They're made of gold." He tried gnawing on the metal with his teeth.

"Don't do that! They're filled with poison."

Jax threw up his hands. "And let me guess, Azor has the antidote, too?"

Studying Jax's wrist made Jacob suddenly remember seeing one on Fin. How'd he get out of Natatoria alive? Did Jack have the antidote? "Yeah, but I have an idea."

Jax's face brightened. "Good. What?"

"Uh..." He looked around for Badger, but didn't see him. "I need to talk to Badger."

"Can't. He's in solitary. Guarded by the Dradux."

Jacob sighed. "Of course." He tried to recall if he'd ever mentioned the cuff to Badger or not.

"If you can get me out, then why's everyone locked up anyway?"

"It's not time yet."

"Time? Are you kidding me? You've got a fine army right here that can take over Natatoria or high-tail it out and you're waiting?"

"It's tricky, Jax." Jacob landed his impatient brother a glare. "The timing needs to be right."

"You mean you need to wait for Jack so you don't lose your precious babysitting job," Jax said, with an eyebrow waggle.

"Don't think just because you're inconvenienced, you can start barking orders. There are more lives at stake than just yours."

"Inconvenienced?" Jax met his glower. "I could die in here, Brother. So, figure this out and soon. I don't have a ton of time."

Jacob exhaled hard, his gills flapping in the water. He controlled his tongue, reminded of Tatiana's mood swings from her promise. "Why did you come back anyway? You were free."

"Ah," he shrugged. "I have my reasons."

Jacob pinched his eyes shut. "It's the girl, isn't it? You came back for her."

Jax looked away. "Maybe."

"Who? There haven't been any rogue promisings—"

At Jax's coy smile, everything clicked into place. Before he'd been wrongly accused of treason, all Jax talked about was Princess Galadriel. After his banishment to Bone Island, Jack was assigned on the secret mission—one to find the lost Princess. Together, Jack's men had made a quick detour to Bone Island to free his brother, yet he wasn't there. And when they'd ended up finding Galadriel in Florida of all places, she seemed edgy and cranky. And he'd remembered her fisherman's tale of how she'd lost her left ring finger from a tangled net.

"Don't tell me you kissed... Galadriel?"

Jax shrugged with a guilty smile. "Face it, brother. We love rich royal blood, don't we?"

"Poseidon." Jacob scrubbed his hand over his face. "Was that your crime of treason?"

"But you found her, right? I heard Jack came back. He wouldn't have returned empty-handed."

"How could you hear about Jack's mission but not about anything else?"

Jax flew at the bars. "Is she here? Or not! Answer me, Jacob."

Jacob's nostrils flared. "No. She's not here. She wanted to stay in Florida. Jack returned to stop Tatiana's promising—and failed—if you didn't know."

He groaned. "Florida. Ughhhh." Jax fell backward in the water and splayed both hands over his heart. "I knew it. Dang it!"

"But she wants to be converted."

Jax bolted upright. "What?"

"I don't know. She's fickle… and crabby."

Jax grabbed the bars. "No, dude. Don't mess with me. I want out."

Jacob looked hard into his brother's eyes. "I will. I need time though."

"I'm going crazy in here. It's been too long. She needs me, or she's going to do something stupid. If she converts…. I don't know what I'll do."

Jacob didn't think he needed to worry. Galadriel had been far from cooperative when they found her and knowing the real reason behind her erratic behavior, everything clicked. She couldn't return to Natatoria promised to a convict, and to be converted would mean losing him forever. She'd been waiting for Jax to find her.

"She's managing. I had no clue."

"No clue? Hello?" He wriggled his ring finger. "Nothing gets past you, big brother."

"She's missing her finger, from the accident."

Jax's smile vanished. "What accident?"

"She said it was a rope or a net…"

Jax growled, fisting the bars again. "I'm gonna kill him!"

"Who?"

"The King, that son of a bass."

Jacob sucked in a rush of water. Would the King really remove her fingers just so no one would know the truth? He shook his head. "The King's not doing so great."

"What?"

"Jack blew the Tahoe gate and the blast knocked down the shark fence. One got to him before we could contain them all."

Jax's anger exploded into caustic laughter. "Karma is a freaking bitch!"

Jacob looked away. "I guess you could say that."

He wondered what bad karma followed him, protecting a woman he loved and watching her pine for the attention of a heartless workaholic.

In a moment of silence, he heard her voice—Tatiana's—coming from within the compound. At first he thought his sleep deprivation made him imagine it, until she called for Azor. His shoulders slumped.

"I gotta go. We'll talk more later." Jacob swam from the dungeon into the house before his brother could reply.

He tried to think of an excuse for why Azor wasn't home while he scanned the main room. A frantic gasp from the kitchen grabbed his attention. Fear had flooded the room, but she was no longer there. Then through the doors of the servants' hall, he saw her, banging on Xirene's door.

"Princess," Jacob whispered.

She swirled around, eyes wide. "What?" She hissed, eyeing him up and down.

"You shouldn't be back here."

"And why not?"

"This is the servants' quarters. It's unfit for you—."

"Mind your own damn business, Jacob." She jutted out her jaw.

Jacob pulled back, hurt by her tone.

Just then the door before them opened. Xirene appeared

wearing a white nightgown that floated around her fin in the current. She yawned and rubbed her eyes with a gloveless hand. "What's wrong, Princess? Do you need something?"

Tatiana's eyes scoured Xirene, as if looking for evidence. With a shove, she pushed Xirene aside and swam through the doorway, disappearing through a hole in the ceiling.

Her terror-filled voice echoed in the room. "Azor? Come out this instant."

Azor? Jacob looked to Xirene, whose face flashed horror. She zipped past him, through the porthole behind Tatiana. Jacob's heart beat hard, one for the accusation and then for the secret air-filled room. Xirene's and Tatiana's wet feet slapped against the floor of the room.

"Princess! Leave my room at once!"

At Tatiana's grunts, he clenched his jaw, unsure what they were doing. As an unpromised merman, though, he wouldn't dare enter a maid's room, but he couldn't allow this to continue.

"Princess," he called through cupped hands. "Please, leave Xirene's room. Don't do this."

Something wooden hit the floor, smashing into pieces.

"He was here, wasn't he?" Tatiana demanded. "Tell me the truth!"

"I don't know what you're talking about." Another loud thud followed.

"Don't lie! I heard him!"

"He isn't here!" Xirene snarled. "Get out!"

A shriek propelled Jacob's tail, lifting him up and through the porthole.

"Princess," Jacob called out as he emerged into the air-filled room. Then he saw Tatiana—long lean legs connected to bare bottom.

She turned, and in a flash he saw her—beautiful and forbidden—before she yanked the bed sheet to cover herself.

He gasped then disappeared under the water with a splash, darting through the hall into the kitchen, past the statue, and toward the front door. With a quick heave of the iron latch, he was outside the compound and over the ridge. He tried to think of something else, anything else. But he couldn't. The memory of her beautiful curves replayed in his mind and when he closed his eyes, he entertained the snapshot over and over, only he was with her.

Why wasn't she wearing a skirt?

Of course he'd allowed himself to imagine what that secret place would look like—but to know, and to have a visual to go with it. She'd been the most beautiful woman he'd ever laid eyes on before, but now? This? To be so close to her, teased like that, when she was forbidden; Azor's.

The sad reality hit him and his hands fisted a clump of kelp fronds. He yanked hard with a groan, wanting to shove them down Azor's throat, when a sick feeling settled over his scales. If Azor found out he'd seen the Princess naked, he'd kill him.

Flaring his fin, he slowed in the current, and stopped. He bowed his head. Running would show his guilt, not to mention leave Tatiana unguarded, and staying… could he stay? Chance getting arrested? He closed his eyes, exhaustion taking ahold of his body. There were more lives than just his to consider. He turned to look to the compound. No one was coming to arrest him. And other than Xirene and Tatiana, no one else knew.

With a lump in his throat, he kicked his fin to return to the compound. He had no choice. He had to take the gamble.

21

Favorites

Tatiana's chest heaved as she stood on the wet rug, covering herself with the sheet. Had Jacob really just seen her naked? She knew she should feel embarrassed, or even violated for his mistaken glance, especially after they'd fought. But she didn't. There was something in his face, his eyes—his carnal want. And ashamedly, she liked it. She could enjoy him watching her like that forever.

Xirene's fist remained perched on her hip. "Azor is not here," she said through clenched teeth. "And I suggest you put some clothes on."

Tatiana eyed her room and then turned to the porthole—anger melting away. "My mistake," she conceded in defeat. She ditched the sheet and dove into the porthole.

Back in the kitchen, all that remained was a healthy dose of Jacob's fear from his retreat. She could understand why, considering Azor wouldn't take his infraction—that was her fault—lightly. She closed her eyes, trying to gain composure, her heart sprinting. If only this was a simple accident, things could continue on as if nothing had happened, but Xirene was there—her wide eyes took in Jacob's reaction to her nakedness. And now, fueled with anger over Tatiana's accusations, Xirene had a reason to tattle. *And just when things were improving.*

Tatiana swam past the mermaid statue into the hall and grazed her hand along the ceiling. Xirene's secret air-filled room had been there, hidden on the other side of the second-story hallway wall this entire time. She bit her lip, retracing her steps. What was she trying to prove? What had she expected to find?

Laughter had sliced through her dreams, happy and playful. She had awoken, expecting to be lying next to Azor, and startled to find herself alone. The sounds then pulled her from Azor's bed into the second-story hallway and she'd pressed her ear to the adjacent wall. Azor's voice mixed with a woman's flooded her ears.

Recalling the rumpled sheet in Xirene's room, Tatiana's chest rose and lowered with dizzying breaths of water. How dare Xirene deny what she heard! There was no way Tatiana was mistaken!

Tatiana swiveled around, ready to find Xirene and scratch her eyes out, when Azor swam through the front doors. Alert and agitated, he startled at the sight of Tatiana.

"What are you doing swimming around without a skirt on at this hour?" he asked with a frown.

Her cheeks heated at the accusation. He'd been the one who'd taken off her skirt earlier, before she'd fallen asleep. It was only because she'd heard laughter on the other side of the wall that she'd darted out of the room unthinking, her backside uncovered before him now. But she wouldn't let this distract her from confronting the truth. He and Xirene were together, doing the *naughty*, even when he'd hated all things human. She couldn't withhold her rage any longer.

"Where have you been?" she seethed.

He glared at her, insulted. "I was at the palace, of course."

Tatiana studied him, looking for an indication of a lie. "Doing what?"

He sighed and rolled his eyes. "This again?"

"Yes, *this again*, until…" She gritted her teeth, then sucked in a breath once Jacob swam through the doors, freezing her lips in place.

"You have no right to question me," Azor said.

Tatiana swished her tail nervously in the current, wishing she had a skirt on. Jacob's concerned eyes flickered to her for a beat, making her heart race again. A different tug plagued her now—she worried about Jacob's punishment for seeing her this way. "Nothing. I woke up and you weren't there. I heard your voice, but I must have been wrong. I'm glad you're home."

Azor squinted then finally looked over his shoulder. His gaze landed on Jacob. "Why were you outside?"

Jacob clenched his jaw. "Checking the perimeter."

Azor's eyes formed into slits. "Unless my mate leaves, which should only be authorized by me, you will *not* leave the premises, ever. Understood?"

"Don't talk to him like a child, Azor," Tatiana interrupted.

He hit her with a glare. "I'll talk to him however I choose."

"He's not your slave," she said, through her teeth.

Azor barked out a mirthless laugh before he grabbed Tatiana by the arm, ushering her farther down the hall. "You will keep your mouth shut and go get dressed."

"Azor," Jacob warned, his voice low and threatening.

"Unhand me, you lumpsucker," Tatiana growled.

He gripped tighter, his voice hard. "I can make things very difficult for you, Tatiana, if you don't obey me."

She laughed evilly. *News flash. It's already unbearable.* "Like giving your female servant an air bubble over your own mate? Try again."

Though her insult should have surprised him, Azor's face remained taut and unchanged. "How is Xirene's bubble any of your concern?"

"Maybe my hunch was right." She pitched up her brow, ready to confront him. "Maybe I did hear *your* voice."

Jacob's fear floated over Tatiana's nose, making her keenly aware he was nearby and listening.

"You better not be insinuating anything. Xirene has been a good and faithful servant for many years. She needs a dry place to mix her herbs. The bubble was the least I could do."

"And me? What about my needs?"

He laughed. "I've met your needs, or don't you remember earlier?"

She pulled her arm away and hissed. Beyond him tickling her tail with the dreaded feather worm, she remembered nothing.

"Actually, I don't. You…" her mind whirred. The sour taste clicked. It was like the green seed Xirene had given her the first night. "You drugged me to sleep, so you could… leave? Go to her?"

"I did no such thing. And we did *do it*." He recoiled as if making love to her was the worst thing imaginable. "How can you pin your inability to stay awake on me? It's insulting that you can't even remember."

Disgust flushed through her at the thought of him mating with her when she wasn't lucid.

She flung his arm away. Something in her snapped. At his words, his cruelty, at his lies. "You'll never touch me again. I don't care if you need a son to rule."

With a whip of her tail, she pivoted and readied herself for a retreat through the porthole when he grabbed her wrist.

"I don't need your permission to impregnate you." He roughly grabbed her and pressed her against the wall, rubbing his groin hard against hers. "I could take you right here if I wanted."

"You wouldn't," she whispered, horrified, knowing Jacob was right there, watching.

Azor scoffed, casting one glance over his shoulder. He let her go. "Of course I wouldn't. I'm not an animal. Just know your place and get some clothes on."

He pushed her aside and swam through the porthole to the second floor. Her chest heaved with adrenaline and she fought to relax her gills.

Jacob remained in the foyer, his grip tight on his trident, blatant concern etched on his face. She turned her face away, embarrassed, but firmly kept her backside pressed against the wall, her privates hidden from his gaze. She knew how immature she looked, first with accusing her servant of cheating and then getting caught in the nude as a human. She willed him to go away—leave her to sort out her feelings.

Jacob didn't move. He watched her for a long time, finally extending his hand to her, palm up. Another invitation to leave, the second offer within twenty-four hours. She stared at it, then at the yearning in his grey-blue eyes. Should she go with him? Freedom could be just beyond the suffocating walls of the compound, just beyond Natatoria. He'd take her to her father, if she wanted, convert to human to escape Azor. Temptation rocked her. Then she gulped down a sip of water and leaned against the wall to think.

There were consequences and implications in taking his hand. After his reaction in Xirene's room, she knew why he took the bodyguard job in the first place. It wasn't just his loyalty to her father that fueled him. He'd developed feelings for her. It was the reason he never complained, never left her side, and hovered in the current now, offering her another chance to escape. And if she did go, she would condone his behavior—this treachery against the royal family, against her promise, against the rules. Alone, there'd be nothing stopping him from taking her as his. He'd be no better than Azor or the King who tried to steal her kiss days ago.

Besides, everyone would think her crazy to leave the Prince; give up the chance to be queen, and with her bodyguard, of all people—a scandalous crime. Labeled a cheater, she'd tarnish the honor of being chosen as a princess and abandon the kingdom when the mer needed her most.

Closing her eyes, she twisted Azor's golden gift around her wrist. Though attracted to Jacob, she knew the longing from the promise would never rest if she left Azor. She hadn't been able to even last a day—wild with worry the last time. But the laughter kept playing in her mind, chipping away at the hold over her soul. Though she didn't catch them, she knew they were together. The thought of Azor choosing Xirene over her crushed her like a flower in a hail storm.

Too weak to decide on her own, she opened her eyes to Jacob, hoping he'd make things easy on her and just abduct her from this nightmare. She wouldn't fight him. She'd go willingly this time.

However, when she opened her eyes, he was gone.

22

Gossip

Jacob lay awake on his bed in the barracks, his body exhausted but his mind a live wire. When Tatiana twisted her bracelet, he almost heard the lock of her heart slamming shut, and he didn't stay for what was to happen next: to watch her swim through the porthole, to know she'd go toward Azor's room, to hear her beg his forgiveness and offer herself to him. He'd rather die first. Proof he was wrong. Proof, even with Azor's hateful treatment of her, she couldn't break the hold of the promise.

But Azor had lied. His scent hadn't come from the palace, as he claimed. Just swimming from that direction himself, they should have crossed paths. His deception made Jacob wonder. Had Tatiana's worst fear been the truth? Did Xirene's room have another exit?

But what baffled him was why Azor would jeopardize the crown and sleep with Xirene? Sure, he looked the other way when his guards toyed with the mermaid servants, but he'd never allow himself to do the same—not when he could spawn a child with the royal mark. He'd rather think Azor wasn't capable of love. Tatiana's kindness and compassion should be more than enough for any merman. Not to mention her human body—which Jacob just had the privilege of seeing. Instead, Azor chose to starve her of his presence, of his acceptance, for what? Revenge?

If only he'd followed Azor's abhorrent stench to its location before the seas diluted it. Then he would have evidence, showing Tatiana the true animal that he was. However, he would have been too late. Jacob knew his presence prevented Azor from taking Tatiana against her will right there in the hall as a means to punish her. Carnal and brutal, he'd assert himself to show his power over her and most likely plant his seed. And if Jacob happened to witness that, he wouldn't be able to control himself.

Tatiana's reaction, though, saddened him. Unbelievably, even after Azor's disrespectful threats and flimsy alibis, Tatiana remained submissive. Jacob's faith had hit an all-time low. Where was the real Tatiana? The girl Jack couldn't stop talking about? The one who he knew could be stronger than the promise?

In the silvery light of the morning, Jacob returned to the main room of the compound, ready to relieve Chauncey. He stretched his tail, working out the aches and pains. From the little sleep he did get, his body hadn't restored itself. His skirt, even after cinching it up another notch, hung low on his waist.

The front doors were unguarded and a giggle from the kitchen told Jacob why. A quick flit of two entwined tails—the bright blue of Coralade's and the dull grey of Chauncey's—gave them away. As Jacob approached the kitchen, he saw Chauncey's hands pawing her, practically mating with her against the worktable. Jacob shook his head in disgust, especially after knowing Chauncey had fathered three orphans in the past two months.

Where was Xirene? She'd never allow this abhorrent practice to happen right in her kitchen.

Jacob retreated out of sight, then cleared his throat before swimming into the kitchen. The two broke apart like opposite sides of magnets. The cloying stench of pheromones swirled thick around them.

"Yes," Coralade said, while tying her apron. "Breakfast will be ready within the hour."

"Good to know," Chauncey grunted, then swam past Jacob with a cocky sneer. "Pretty uneventful night…"

Yeah, right. "Thanks for taking my shift."

"No problem," he said with a surly smile and disappeared around the corner.

Jacob waited a beat before turning to Coralade, withholding his snide comments. She looked up at him, shooting bedroom eyes through her long green lashes. "Good morning, Jacob."

"Where's Xirene?" Jacob asked sharply.

"She and Shanleigh are at the palace picking up today's rations. Is there something I can do for you?"

She wiggled her tail in rhythmic time. Her pheromones ignited in the water once again with the slightest hint of the mating dance. Jacob sculled backwards.

"Control yourself, temptress." He eyed her warily. "I should have Xirene send you back to the palace for your indiscretions."

She straightened up and stopped churning the water with her hips. "You're one to talk."

Jacob squinted in surprise. "Excuse me?"

Coralade's wicked smile curved the corner of her lips. "Peeping in on the Princess." She petted one index finger down the other and purred. "Naughty, naughty."

Jacob's jaw clenched. "Says who?"

"A little sunfish told me there was quite a scene last night."

"You heard wrong," Jacob said quickly, fanning the water to dilute her scent.

Coralade smiled in victory, then stiffened, her full attention at the doorway to the kitchen. Azor's stench hit Jacob before he turned around.

"Have you seen Xirene?" Azor asked with concern.

Jacob flexed his fingers, still angered at the prior night's events, and worked to remain straight-faced. Azor stared hard at Coralade, wrinkling his noise in disgust. He hit Jacob with a curious look before his pectoral fins flared.

"Well, have you?"

Coralade piped up first, pressing Jacob with a knowing smile. "She was up quite early this morning, from what I'm told."

Azor's eyes narrowed. "I don't have time for your games. Just tell me where she is."

"Yes, Prince," she said with a curtsy. "She's at the palace, of course. Picking up food rations for today."

Without another word, Azor blasted through the front doors. Jacob watched him, curious. Why was he in such need to find Xirene that he couldn't wait for breakfast? He glanced back to the porthole, wondering about Tatiana, and saw no one.

With a quick flick of his tail, he moved to the front door and closed it in place. He turned to spy Coralade watching him with a bashful smile. She winked, then disappeared into the kitchen.

He stretched his neck and back in an attempt to be nonchalant while his insides churned. What bothered him wasn't the impending awkwardness that would come once he saw Tatiana. It was Coralade. If she knew what had happened, everyone knew. And once Azor found out he saw her nude as a human, Jacob was as good as dead. Were the Dradux on their way to arrest him right now? Did he dare run?

He continued to watch the porthole, anxiety snaking through him. This wasn't the first time he'd had a close call: first, when abducting the Princess from Azor after he stole her kiss and then rescuing her from the King's assault. Had he run out of free chances?

At the sight of a purple tail at the porthole, Jacob's heart lurched momentarily until Nicole emerged with an empty tray.

"Good morning." She flashed him a cheery smile.

Jacob returned the sentiment, his pulse lowering to a normal beat. That hadn't been the first time he'd mistaken her for Tatiana, their tails being so similar.

"Anything happen last night?" he asked curiously, probing to see if she'd heard the gossip yet.

"Last night?" Nicole's eyes grew.

Jacob leaned forward. "Yes, with the Princess."

"Oh." She giggled, smoothing her free hand down her white skirt. "Nothing that I know of. After her night away in her family home, she must have been right exhausted. She's been asleep ever since." Nicole cracked a smile and winked. "In her room, no less."

Aghast, Jacob sculled backward in the current. "What are you suggesting, Nicole?"

"Nothing." She pressed her lips together, looking away. "Just in c-case you'd w-wanted to know her whereabouts, that's all."

Flustered, she flitted to the kitchen. Plates clattered against the counter. Jacob paused, eyeing Tatiana's door from the porthole. Had she not gone to Azor's room? What had happened after he left?

When the main door ground against the floor, Jacob's body jolted. He palmed his trident, ready. He wouldn't be arrested without a fight. But only Shanleigh swam inside with boxes of food in her hands. Jacob blinked, annoyed at his jumpiness, and lowered his weapon.

She quickly rubbed her tail up against the guard's fin at the doorway, soliciting help with her delivery, and Jacob's shoulders reclined against the wall. After that, the girls' giggles and titters wouldn't be contained in the kitchen during their preparation of breakfast. Curiously, though, none of them mentioned why Xirene hadn't joined them or the events of last evening.

He looked up at the starfish on the ceiling, wavering in indecision. If only he could go back in time and wait before seeing his brother in prison. He could have prevented Tatiana from entering Xirene's room and taken back his mistaken glance.

His mind entertained the vision of her body once again and his fins shivered in pleasure. He didn't feel ashamed for wanting her. He'd fight heaven and hell for her, knowing a day of his love was greater than Azor could give in his lifetime. Forced to wait, he wondered if his fate would mirror that of his brother Jax. Bone Island, then ultimately, death.

As time ticked on, guards milled in from the practice field to eat and Nicole checked in on the Princess once again. By midmorning, Blanchard and Chauncey wrangled a row of cuffed prisoners from the dungeon for the final removal of rocks at the Tahoe gate. Neither Azor nor Xirene returned.

The same scene repeated at lunch and the prisoners returned to the dungeon to be served their one meal of the day. Jacob's gut twisted at the sight of his comrades, their bodies smaller than before, the crazed look in their eyes from worrying about their fate. He'd join them soon enough, locked away, awaiting his punishment for who knows how long.

Lost in a daze, Jacob didn't notice Grommet approach.

"Snap to it," he said with a surly smile.

Jacob groaned and blinked slowly. "This has been the worst day."

"Duuude," Grommet said, while clapping his friend's back, "could have been a whole lot worse, considering."

Jacob frowned. "Considering what?"

Grommet's eyebrow twitched. "It's all anyone can talk about. Tatiana accusing Xirene of bumping uglies with Azor, and you seeing her naughty bits in the process." He clucked his tongue while making a gun with his finger. "Man, wish I'd stuck around to see *that*."

Jacob shot him a glare. "Yeah, where'd you go last night, anyway?"

Grommet rubbed his ear. "Oh, that… after you went to the dungeon, I… had to go to the dungeon for a sec."

"Seriously?" Jacob huffed. "I trusted you to keep an eye on things. And you could have stopped her from leaving the second-story. Now I'm going to be arrested."

"Psscht. I doubt it. Azor's in another world and no one wants your job… well, maybe now they'd consider it." He hummed with a knowing smile. "For now, you're safe. Lucky dogfish."

Jacob scanned the faces of the guards. Their looks, ranging from "way to go" to "dead merman swimming," suddenly made sense. "Where's Azor anyway?"

"They finally opened the gate, so I'm assuming he's in Tahoe. Seems his sister Galadriel might be there as well."

Jacob's jaw dropped. "What?"

"Yeah—converted and everything. Kind of crazy, if you think about it. Jack had her right under his fin this entire time and didn't know it."

Huh? This can't be right. Galadriel was in Florida and a mermaid when he last saw her. And as of last night, she and Jax were still promised. He, of all people, would be the first to know if someone had converted her, loosing his connection to her. Then who could this girl be?

Grommet stretched and yawned. "So anyway... nothing's as good as your peep show, so enjoy the stardom."

"What about Xirene?"

"Word on the current is she moved out. Don't need the jealous mate and accused adulteress living under the same roof, that's for sure."

Jacob sighed. In spite of everything, he would miss the herbs she added to their meals. Better than the stuff they served the guards at the palace. He had to look on the bright side. Maybe with Xirene gone, Tatiana would be happier.

Upon spying Nicole with Tatiana's lunch tray in hand, Jacob raked his fingers through his hair and waited for a report on the Princess's well-being.

But within seconds, Nicole returned with a worried look on her face. In her hands were two uneaten plates of food.

"Why isn't Tatiana eating?" he asked.

"She says she's not hungry."

Jacob's fists clenched. If Azor hurt her, Tahoe be damned,

he'd go ballistic and rip Azor's fins off right now. "Is she ill?"

Nicole shrugged. "From what I can tell, she's okay. Depressed, maybe. Should we notify Prince Azor?"

"No," Jacob said quickly. "He's busy. I'll handle it."

"Okay." She swam past him, but within seconds, she returned from the kitchen in a frenzy. "The knife is missing from her tray."

Jacob pumped his tail hard to propel him through the porthole and lugged open her door, unannounced.

Tatiana gasped and straightened, hands tucked behind her back. "Hades, don't you know how to knock?"

"Princess," he said, eyes wild, searching the room. "Please, let me see your hands!"

"What—? No!"

"Just show me what you have behind your back."

"Get out of here, Jacob!" She pointed with one hand, keeping the other against her fin. "After last night, I don't ever want to see you again."

Jacob clenched his jaw, wounded by her words. "Princess, last night. I didn't mean to—that was very—I shouldn't have—I—" But a suitable excuse or apology wouldn't form logically on his tongue. "Damn it."

Her shoulders dipped forward, her spirit relenting. "That's not what I'm talking about, and how were you to know Xirene had a bubble, and then my skirt…"

Jacob bowed. "It will never happen again."

She laughed scornfully and shook her head. "You're right, it won't."

He frowned, confused, but approached her, determined to

take the knife. "That doesn't warrant you doing something rash. Show me your wrists, Princess."

"What?" Tatiana backed into the corner, still holding something against her leg.

He put out his hand. "I want the knife."

She gave him an incredulous look before revealing the knife. "You think I'm trying to kill myself?" She laughed. "Already changed your mind after the *girl of strength* lecture. Who do you take me for, Jacob?"

Jacob backpedaled in the current. "No—of course not."

She shook her head and grasped the hilt. With a turn to the horizon, she looked off in the distance. The sharks passed with feigned aloofness. She let out a small sigh. "Go ahead. Give me today's lecture about how stupid I am to be with Azor."

Jacob opened and closed his mouth. "I just want to know why you kept the knife."

"To stab Xirene, why else?" She laughed sadistically.

Jacob tilted his head. "That's not funny. She's not even here anymore."

Tatiana arched her brow. "What—? Oh, great. It'll be my fault for that, too, and then once Azor finds out you saw me…" She waved the knife across her neck. Her cheeks reddened and she quickly flipped her tail nervously. Beige colored sand ballooned in the water. Then Jacob spotted a tiny hole in the wall between two bricks. He stiffened.

"I know things have been tense," he held out his hand, "but you don't have use for a knife."

"I'm not giving it to you," she said more firmly.

"You'll never get through the mortar in time before Azor

returns, and what about the sharks?"

She pursed her lips. "Won't I though? As if he'll notice. Maybe you were right Jacob. I am his pawn."

"I won't allow you to escape."

Strained laughter pressed from her lungs. "You mean, I can't escape unless I go with you," she said more forcefully. "Fish sticks! I know what you're really trying to offer me, so don't try to deceive me, Jacob. I've figured out what you want, and it's what you've wanted since the moment we met."

Jacob reached backward with his tail and pushed the door closed. "Princess, your safety and happiness is all I want. And that means you can't go through the shark tank."

"Or what? I'll die? I doubt he'll even miss me. At least the sharks will want me."

Jacob's pulse hammered in his veins. He wanted to tell her he wanted her. That he'd love nothing more than to help her escape, if she'd just allow him time to retrieve his trident. But the bracelet Azor slapped onto her wrist glared back at him along with her disdain. He'd treat her like gold, but she didn't want him to come. The fact she'd rather die than have Jacob escort her showed she didn't care for him at all.

He bowed his head. "Please give me the knife."

She turned in a huff. "Leave, now."

Jacob swam to her in a flash and wrapped his arms around her torso, trapping her arms. She hissed, flipping her tail and snapping her teeth. Her fight was weak, unlike the first time, but the heat wasn't. Like before, a spark ignited between them— hotter. His want seized his body as he felt her hot glow against his scales. She had to feel their attraction. He controlled his urge to bury his nose in her hair, to kiss her neck. He merely held her until she stopped thrashing.

"Drop the knife, Tatiana," he whispered calmly in her ear.

"Call me, Princess!"

"Drop the knife."

"No!"

"We'll find another way out of here, just drop the knife."

"I said, no!"

Jacob clamped her wrist, forcing open her hand. She grunted, fighting him harder than before, then eventually the knife dropped to the floor. Jacob immediately let her body go and snatched the knife. She flared her tail, smacking him across the face, and swam to the opposite corner, massaging her wrist.

"Get out," she barked, then pointed to the door. "Get out!"

Her siren scream blasted him into the closed door. He fumbled at the knob and flew down the porthole within seconds, knife safely in his fist.

23

Sharks

"Princess!"

Tatiana sucked in a startled breath as she opened her eyes, expecting to finally see Azor. Jacob's terrified face peered down at her instead.

"What's wrong?" she squeaked, gaining her bearings, sweeping her eyes around Azor's room.

After their fight earlier, she'd moved in to Azor's room rebelliously to wait for his return.

"It's an ambush!"

"An ambush?" Tatiana sat up; all her anger from their earlier fight melted away, replaced now with fear. "Here? Now?"

"Yes. I need to get you out of here." He studied the walls for a moment and grimaced at the carvings. But quickly dismissed them and held her gaze, hand outstretched.

She took it and swam with him to the hall, too scared to question him. Grunts and feral cries of war, along with weapons clashing, resounded from the floor below—similar to what she'd heard at the promising ceremony with Azor. However, the frustration and hate-filled sounds revealed no one wanted to spare any lives today. Death was the agenda.

Tatiana clung to Jacob's arm in fear. "What do they want?"

"Shhh," Jacob said.

At the end of the hall, Grommet hovered over the porthole, two crescent-moon knives in his hands. He gave Jacob a nod and

Tatiana's heart lurched.

"I'm not going down there," she whispered.

Jacob escorted her to a neighboring guest room, sliding the iron door shut behind them. He then pulled a nearby rock cabinet to hold the door in place, sealing them inside. A safe room.

Though sturdy, she didn't think the cabinet would keep the murderous horde out forever.

Tatiana grabbed onto Jacob's bicep tighter. "What are we going to do?"

His jaw clenched and he gently moved her aside. "This," he said in determination. In an instant, he'd swiveled around and wacked his tail into the wall with a grunt.

Tatiana squealed, bordering on a siren scream. Jacob put his finger to his lips before he wacked the rock wall again. Then he took the flat end of his trident and tested the bricks until one moved. He smashed his tail once again and three fell free to the other side.

Tatiana listened by the door to the sounds growing louder. "Are they rebels?"

"Not rebels."

"Then who are they? Why are they here?"

Jacob stopped for one moment to eye her. "I'm not sure, but they're here for you."

Tatiana gulped, unable to catch her breath. "Where's Azor?"

"Conveniently in Tahoe."

As Jacob continued to bust out rocks, creating a small rectangular hole, his plan became clear. They were going to escape through the shark tank.

The sight of the great whites circling in the distance through the tiny hole dissolved any courage she had mustered. Yes, earlier she'd planned a delusional romantic and dangerous attempt to escape through the shark tank to the Pacific with maybe a close call—all as a stunt to gain Azor's attention. Now, with the blood and fear she smelled in the water from downstairs, and the beasts with their dead eyes circling closer and closer, she was paralyzed with fear. They'd eat her the moment she left fin of the compound.

"I can't go out there." She clutched at her throat. "I don't care if you're with me, or not."

Jacob frowned, knocking the last rock free. "You were all charged and ready to escape earlier. What changed?"

"Reality," she said softly, fins shaking.

Jacob took a deep breath. "Well, I'm sorry to say, sweetheart, you're better off with the sharks than facing what's in here."

She studied Jacob quizzically. "You say that like you're not coming with me."

"I can't. My brother is trapped in the dungeon. I have to free him first."

In shock, Tatiana froze. He wasn't coming with her? What happened to, "where you go, I go?" She blinked, waiting for him to tell her he was joking. But Jacob merely held out his trident to her.

"It's simple. Just strike one and the others will feed on it, leaving you freedom to escape."

Simple? Wide-eyed, she stared at the weapon, refusing to take it. He placed the trident in her palm and positioned his body next to hers. Heat, like earlier, pressed into her as he wrapped his hands over hers and jabbed the trident forward and twisted. "Like this."

She gulped and allowed him to control her movements, short and jerky.

"Twist after you stab, then yank backward. That'll create the most blood."

Blood. Her head swirled. Her father had showed her how to shoot a gun once, but this? Stabbing an animal—one with razor sharp teeth that fed off of her fear, that would kill her in an instant if she missed.

"Just..."—he closed his eyes for a beat—"do not siren, unless there's no other choice. Do you hear me?"

She whimpered, slowly shaking her head. Was he really not going with her?

Jacob ignored her hesitation and pulled the shimmering cape from his utility pack, the one she'd worn before. Fastening the cords around her slender neck, his warm fingers rested at the hollow at her throat to tie the bow.

Finally, he slipped the hood over her head and placed his hands on her shoulders. With deep, penetrating blue-grey eyes, he held her in his gaze. "I want nothing more than to go with you, but I can't. You have to do this without me, Tatiana. I believe in you. You're strong and you're a fighter. Please, live, for me... and for your kingdom."

Of all of his proclamation, the "for me," resonated most in her mind. Though earlier, she'd called his bluff about what she'd suspected, and he'd ignored it. This sealed it. An admission from his lips. His soft, full lips. Guarding her wasn't just a job to him anymore. He cared and wanted her to escape, to live.

She gulped down her hesitation, at the feelings stirring in her belly. Sure, she couldn't deny his sexy abs and amazing physique were hard not to lust over, along with his enchanting eyes that pierced her to her very core. But was that all just a physical reaction? Did she care deeper, too?

But now, she knew Jacob's heart—his kindness, his mercy, his faithfulness and dedication. A far cry from Azor's lust, lies, and hunger for power. Only a kiss held her captive, and now she knew there wasn't anything worth being loyal to. She *could* choose. She *could* leave him.

Then something inside her popped—like a busted light bulb. Warmth and hope flooded into that dark place, into her starving soul, dissolving Azor's hold. He hadn't given her a piece of his soul after all, just a hopeless dream, a placeholder to occupy her heart. She clutched her chest and blinked, opening her eyes as if for the first time. Instead of guilt, she saw the truth—a forced chemical attraction, and then all her previous thoughts of Azor before he stole her kiss surfaced. At how much she loathed him: his despicable character, his arrogance, his crude and rough gestures, his disregard for everyone, too many offenses to think about. But Jacob, his inner light brought her out of her fog set in by the deception. Surprisingly, she cared for Jacob, more than friendship. Overwhelmingly, so much more.

Free from the weight of the promise, she studied Jacob's lips, desiring to feel them against hers. To wrap her tail around his. To feel his heat close to her always.

Kiss me, Jacob.

Jacob waited a beat as fear twirled around them in an awkward dance. His fear. Why would he be afraid?

Just kiss me already.

His chest rose and fell, the desire ardent on his face, his eyes matching his desire—hot as embers. She wanted to ask him, to tell him it was okay. But her lips, as if the last place the promise had hold, were paralyzed and refused to speak her deepest desire.

Something heavy rammed into the door behind them, startling them. She yelped as a gruff voice followed, demanding they open up. Jacob released her.

Tatiana's body began to quake. "Please come with me, Jacob."

"I'll come as soon as I can," he said, grabbing her shoulders one last time. "Go to your parents' house and stay there no matter what happens. Secure the porthole. Don't allow anyone in but me. I *will* come for you. Do you understand?"

"Yes."

"And that bracelet Azor gave you is filled with poison. If you leave Natatoria, it will kill you," he said quickly.

She gasped at the revelation, wanting the dreaded thing off her wrist. The agony, fear, and determination filling his stunning face, stopped her. And instead of kissing her lips, he brushed his mouth against her forehead. His skin, warm and soft, sent a delicate tingle up her spine. Then he grasped her hips firmly and helped maneuver her body through the tiny hole in the wall.

Tatiana's heart leapt when he let go. She swiveled around, ready to swim back through when Jacob stacked up bricks behind her.

"Go," he said firmly, his eyes pained. "There isn't time."

To her right, a curious shark caught notice and approached. Whipping its tail nonchalantly, it propelled itself in her direction. Shifting upright, she pressed herself against the wall, trident tilted outright.

I know how to use this and turn you into a chum bucket if you come closer.

With a thrust of the sharp metal out toward the shark, too scared to speak, she willed her fear and the beast away. At the last moment, the shark twitched and slid its sleek and scarred body over the roofline to the left side of the compound.

Tatiana caught her breath. *That's right. Best stay far away from me, ya big sea sack.*

She remained against the wall and listened. Jacob refilled the hole in the wall, effectively eliminating her last-ditch escape route. Her stomach twisted sickly. Why hadn't Jacob picked a room with a window? And why, after everything, had he abandoned her to a shark-infested tank? Being with the sharks couldn't be safer than being inside.

"Red tide," she mumbled, rising slowly upward to peek over the roofline. Three black hooded figures with scythes swam in from the distance. She slipped back down and hugged the wall, studying the first story roof below her. For the moment, only the sharks could see her.

While she waited, fear and blood filtered into the water through the downstairs windows. And as if someone had just sprinkled fish food, a horde of sharks darted her way. Beyond them, at a hundred yards off, the door out of the shark enclosure loomed in the distance. She had to get there—and fast.

"Where is she?" a gruff voice said. Her head snapped around, and she pressed her ear to the wall.

"Who?" Jacob asked, a smile in his voice.

"Don't mess with me. I'll take you down first and then find

her hiding place."

Tatiana shrieked at the reverberating sounds of metal hitting metal, her pulse quickening. Panic overcame her. She'd finally discovered who was worth living and dying for, and if Jacob died, it would be her fault. She had to get him help.

Inching to the right, Tatiana kept her back to the granite spires, clearing the second story. Below, she spotted the windows and encircled her cape around her body, hoping to blend into the environment. But more sharks circled, attracted to the blood from the battle. Tatiana was running out of time. A quick dart directly through the circling sharks would be the fastest way to escape.

Somewhere from inside she heard a merman yell, "Stand firm." She curled into a ball and waited, expecting someone to catch her, but nothing followed. Her heart zoomed faster.

Mustering all her courage, she replaced the hood that had fallen off her head and pushed off the spire for the doorway. On her left, a shark caught notice and changed its course. Fright plagued her lips, a scream waiting restlessly on her tongue. She could siren and scare them away, but then the enemy would locate her and Jacob's acts of courage would be for nothing. She clamped her mouth shut, swimming hard with the trident ahead of her.

At the last second, she swiveled around, backing into a granite spire and held out her trident towards the shark. Two more sharks entered the pursuit.

Three? How could she fight three?

"Back," Tatiana gruffly whispered, thrusting the trident, almost a parry between them. "This is my dance space and that is yours, got it?" she said jokingly in an attempt to lessen her fear.

They menacingly circled, mocking her, closing in with each pass. One knocked against the metal door with its tail to her right, rattling the lock, while the other approached, grazing her tail on the left. She met the oncoming intruder with a fierce jab to its leathery underbelly, barely puncturing its skin. It flicked its tail and headed upward, circling around for another pass.

With the trident firmly in her hands, she attempted more humor. "I'm vegan. I don't taste good."

She inched slowly to the door and twitched her tail sideways. Once she had the lock within her grasp, she blew out a relieved breath and shook it. The button, rusted solid, wouldn't depress.

"For the love of the Kraken!" Her heart rate spiked.

Suddenly, a whole mouth of jagged razors flashed out of nowhere. She squealed and ducked; her hands blindly jabbed the trident forward. She pressed her eyes shut and flared her fin into a fighting position. A thick cloud of bloody water clung to her gills and Tatiana coughed. She held onto the trident, jerked back and forth in the current like a bucking bronco, when the pole yanked free from her hands. A tail roughly shoved her into the spires one way, then something smacked her hard on her waist from the other. She shielded her head with her hands, waiting for the pain that didn't come.

Tatiana finally opened her eyes. Through the red fog, the shark reared back, flipping and twisting with the trident stuck out of its snapping jaws. And just like Jacob had said, the others zeroed in and began to savagely rip apart their fallen comrade in a rolling red ball of froth and fins.

Tatiana grabbed onto the door, her hands shaking. The lock

magically clicked open, freeing the doors, then fell into the dark depths below with one final shimmer.

She blinked, stunned, then opened the doors and swam through. Behind her, a shark's tail smashed into the door, swinging it wide. She quickly grabbed the rough metal and slammed it back into place, holding it shut. Without the lock, she had no way to secure the doors. Again, grey bloodied bodies hit the metal, rubbing her palms raw. She needed something to secure the door shut, but what?

The tie on her cape caught her eye. She yanked one side free and wrapped the twine where the lock had been, making a Trucker's Hitch knot, like her father had taught her on the boat, but one thrash of the sharks tail broke the twine free.

Tatiana yelped, sculling back in the water. A shark, angry and hungry, came at her, teeth bared.

Her siren scream was about to leap off her tongue when a shriek like never before tore through the water. She held her ears, the noise drilling in her skull. And like cockroaches, the sharks scurried through the Pacific gate and disappeared.

Tatiana looked off to the compound for the source, unable to see through all the blood. As far as she could tell, no one appeared to be coming.

24

Parasites

Jacob took one final look at Tatiana before sealing the hole. He ached inside, his chest heaving with an adrenaline rush. *Please don't let this be the last time I see her alive.* Stuck between a rock and a hard place, he had no choice. He'd never forgive himself if something happened to her—but in here, especially with the Dradux lurking, she'd surely die or at least she'd wish she were dead with what they might do to her first.

He pushed aside the cabinet to free the door and pulled a knife from his utility belt. Readying his stance, he waited for the Dradux to break into the room at any moment. Within seconds, the door flew open.

"Where is she?" Darrellon growled.

"Who?" Jacob gave him a half-shrug.

"Don't mess with me." Cassava poison clung to Darrellon's scythe. He flashed his yellow teeth and waggled his parasitic tongue. "I'll take you down first and then find her hiding place."

Jacob grimaced at the parasite and readied himself for the attack. He'd known the Dradux regularly practiced stinging one another to build immunity to the poison. Darrellon might be immune to his poisonous barbs, but he'd carve up as much of his flesh as he could on his way down.

"Be my guest," Jacob said, raking his fingers, palm up. "Come and get me."

Jacob kept a clear distance, wary of Darrellon's paralyzing

barbs.

"My pleasure." Darrellon laughed and cocked back the scythe to strike, when a curved knife hooked around the blade.

Grommet.

In Darrellon's startled surprise, he yanked hard to free his staff when a second crescent-blade sliced through the water, catching Darrellon's throat. In one swipe, his hooded head lopped off into the current, falling end over end, exposing his true appearance. Dreadlocks floated around the lines of his scarred face, fringed with rows of rings pierced on pasty white skin.

Disgusted, Jacob watched the parasite squirm free from Darrellon's bloodied mouth, as if it already knew its host wasn't going to provide anymore.

"Sick," Jacob said under his breath. "Thanks, man."

"Don't mention it," Grommet said quickly, handing Jacob his other crescent-moon knife. "Where's the girl?"

"Out of the shark tank, I hope."

Grommet's eyes grew. "Really?"

Jacob sniffed the water and smelled blood—lots of it. He wasn't sure if it was Darrellon's, or coming from elsewhere, but he wouldn't think the worst. He couldn't.

"She'll be fine with my trident." Chilling grunts and groans filled the water; a mermaid's siren from below set his nerves on edge.

Horror covered Grommet's face. "Dude, we need to get down there."

"How many of them are there?"

"I don't know. Ten, fifteen, maybe." Grommet's fear accosted

Jacob's senses, practically shaking sense into him. "It's a blood bath. Once Darrellon swam through and headed to Azor's room, I dropped a cabinet over the hole, knowing we could take him. The algae scum are freaking using cassava against us, man, their own comrades."

Together, they swam to the sealed porthole, but not before Jacob looked out the window. In the distance a shark writhed, a trident sticking out of its mouth. He struggled to see Tatiana through the cloud of blood or the metal door leading out. Had she'd gotten away? Was the blood only the shark's?

Something beat against the floor, smashing the bricks away. Then a loud shrill, louder than any mermaid's siren, vibrated the current—but it wasn't female. Both Grommet and Jacob held their ears.

"What the heck—?" Jacob pinched his eyes shut, afraid his eardrums would burst. Then the entire building shook as something hit the side of the compound.

"I told ya they're animals."

Jacob looked at him, fearful. "What was that noise?"

"I don't know, but we better do something before I pee my skirt like a girl."

"Wait," Jacob said quickly, feeling the wall directly across from to him. "I have an idea."

Jacob swam to Darrellon and pried the scythe from his dead fingers. He aimed at the wall opposite Tatiana's room and cocked back the blade. On the third whack, tiny air bubbles rushed through the hole. Then an explosion of air blew bricks outward, revealing the backside of a hidden room, Xirene's.

"What the—?" Grommet said, dumbfounded.

"I knew it." Jacob entered the now entirely flooded room.

A wooden trapdoor on the floor flipped open, dislodging a rug and revealing another porthole exit.

"Go," Jacob said, with a firm point. "Find Sandy. Tell her what's happened and that we need ink and lots of it, then go to Tatiana's house. It's the last one on Percophidae Lane. Tell her to pack her things. I'm coming."

Grommet's spine stiffened. "No."

"What do you mean no?"

"I'm not going without Nicole."

Jacob blinked at him, speechless.

"I know what you're going to say, but..."—Grommet clenched his fists on the hilt of his blade. "We hit it off and—" At another siren, Grommet palmed his hair. "I have to go find her!"

Before Jacob could argue, Grommet swam down through Xirene's private porthole and disappeared into the kitchen.

Jacob stared at the empty porthole, confused. Nicole? The noises in the hall cleared his focus. He needed to get to the dungeon and the fastest way was through the shark-tank. He kicked his tail and returned to the guest room. With his scythe, he busted out the rocks once again. Tatiana's flowery scent hit his nose. Panicked, he shot a look off across the tank to look for her. Not a shark or Tatiana was in sight.

Quickly, he replaced the bricks and swam below to the backside of the dungeon. In the wall, a huge hole had been knocked clean. Inside, fear surrounded him and through the red haze he looked at the cells.

"Jax?" Jacob whispered, swimming to the first cage. Another siren gripped him, and he hoped Nicole and Grommet were escaping. "Jax, are you in here?"

Grunts and weapons clashing against one another echoed from inside the compound. Feeling along the bars, he moved parallel to the floor. Fleshy bits of something grazed his hand and Jacob pulled away as a severed arm bobbed by in the current.

He knocked it away and pressed his body to the floor, wishing he would have stolen Darrellon's black robe to better conceal himself, when it hit him. He wore a rebel robe, not that of a Dradux. Were they there to look like rebels?

With his fingers, he inched his body to the doorway for a better look. Through the veil of the blood, he could barely make out a figure. When they turned, he pressed himself to the floor, accidentally knocking his tail against the opened door.

"What's that?" a male voice asked. "Go check it out."

The water swished around his head and Jacob held his breath. A barb nicked him in the back and he stifled a groan. Pain seized him like a cramp.

"What the—?" someone above him said.

Jacob lay still and played dead. A laugh mocked him as another painful zap hit him in the side. This time Jacob couldn't subdue his reaction. He whipped his tail, propelling his body upward. He poised his scythe, challenging his attacker to try stinging him again.

Through the red vapor, Blanchard's smile came into view. He, too, was dressed in the black robes of a rebel, but Jacob knew he wasn't one. Blanchard pointed his scythe at Jacob while eyeing his weapon.

"Jacob," he said evilly. "Alive, I see."

"I should say the same of you, rebel."

"Yes, I guess I am." He quirked his head. "Where's your girl?"

My girl? At the irony, Jacob had to laugh. "Far from here, I hope."

"Or maybe not," Blanchard cocked his brow as another siren hit the waters, he then nodded, his eyes darting to a place behind Jacob.

Jacob charged, ready to slice open Blanchard's throat if he didn't tell him where Tatiana was when heat speared Jacob's back. He coughed, clutching his chest, and looked down at the red gushing in billowing bursts around shiny metal tinted in green, protruding out of his chest. Laughter filled the water as Chauncey came into view. Then two Chauncey's danced in a circle following a third, like a figure eight, before everything went to black.

25

Tricked

Anxious to get Jacob help, Tatiana darted off toward the palace, then she slowed. If the attackers weren't rebels as Jacob claimed, then who were they? Was the palace under attack, too?

Azor's scent hit her nose and she halted. He'd been there, moments ago. She scanned the horizon and neighboring houses for him, tempted to at least call out a warning. Why didn't he come home first after visiting Tahoe?

A group of mermen in black hoods appeared to her left. She ducked down, still sniffing the current. Her cape's stink, though, quickly covered everyone's trail. Others had swum by too; their scent thick like oysters. Her heart pounded as she pressed herself against the wall. Though dressed in black, they held scythes, which struck her as odd. A violent weapon, they had only one purpose: to chop off the assailant's head, and she hadn't remembered the rebels using them during her father's ambush.

With the oyster scent, the scythes and dark hoods, everything clicked and her heart galloped at the realization. Were the Dradux appearing as rebels so Azor would have another infraction to add to their growing list of crimes? "No," she whispered as fear coursed through her. If they caught her, they surely would want to kill her to make it all the worse.

With a kick of her fin, she high tailed it home. Through the porthole, she surfaced like she'd crossed home plate and phased into legs. Still in a fit of panic, she eyed the couch, tempted to move it over the entrance. But upon scanning the interior, she noted garlic lingering in the air. A tiny blue blanket lay on the couch next to a white oval pillow with decorative bows on the edges. The loveseat had been moved to the other side of the room as well. All things she hadn't done.

"Hello?" she called feebly. She dropped her cape to look for a weapon to protect herself.

Tiptoeing into the kitchen, she pulled a knife from the chopping block, noting a bowl of fresh fruit, assorted greens, and pastries she'd only seen served on the fancy tables at the palace lay strewn on the countertop.

"Azor?"

She hadn't smelled his scent at the entrance, or anyone's scent when entering her home. Who would come here to find shelter? Move in? Yes, her parents weren't coming back, but trespassing was unheard of in Natatoria. This was still her family's house.

"Jacob?"

At the silence, she tiptoed down the hall, looking inside each doorway, blade pointed outward. The blood pulsed heavily down her shaking arms, making the knife wobbly. She wished for the sense of smell in the air, so she could know if she truly were alone.

"I'm armed! Show yourself!"

Again nothing. Not a noise, not a scratch. She spied her room, then her brother's, finishing at her parents'. Clothing lay on the floor, but no intruder. A relieved breath slipped from her lips, and she lowered the blade.

Her mother's soft white robe, or at least what was left of it, lay on the floor next to a skirt missing half its ribbons. Had the intruder stolen the fabric to make the pillow? *What nerve!*

Tatiana grabbed the items, evidence of the intrusion, and marched to the kitchen for a second investigation of the food. Her heart stopped when she spied her mother's waterproof bag.

Scattered onto the tabletop were her clothes, books, paints, and her diary opened to the last entry she'd written, in English of course.

Dear Diary,

I hate Azor so much. The way he keeps watching me, like all he wants to do is mate with me. I'm not even a person to him. Just an object. And the fanfare when he arrives. Holy Crawfish. It's disgusting and the mermaids have no tact. They beg for his attention with their fancy tattoos, revealing tops, and beaded hair, just to be ignored. I bet they'd bare their boobs to him in an instant, if he asked. Rumor has it the servants do that already for him. Makes me want to vomit.

And then it's "you're so lucky, Tatchi," "I wish he'd promise to me," and "has he asked you?" It's like I'm already his. Sea serpents. Who would want him? To think of his icky, sticky, vile, licky, fish lips on mine or worse—his hands! UGH! Tahoe! Take me away. I miss Ash so much. The sun. The air. The beach. What I wouldn't do for a soy latte at Starbucks right now.

Can't the Festival be over with already? Then in front of Poseidon and everybody, I can finally tell him "NO!" Or wouldn't it be perfect if he had a garment malfunction on his vest and two perfect circles fell off of his clothes on accident? See how he'd like it if his nipples were exposed for all of Natatoria to see. Wouldn't that be a sight?

Thank you, Diary. You're the best!

Tatiana traced her fingers over the words, then closed the book. Here it was in black and white, all her feelings, all her disdain, and yet, after one empty kiss she'd forgotten everything. How could the promise do that to someone? She picked up the book and threw it across the room, angered Azor had had so much control over her. Light reflected a golden gleam off the bracelet mid-throw. With a featherlike touch, her finger grazed the Natatorian symbol. Did it really have poison in it? She tried to slide it from her wrist, but couldn't; the clasp locked tight. Inside, a soft shushing hit the metal—liquid. Poison.

She gritted her teeth and slumped at the kitchen table, holding her face in her hands. The bracelet proved Azor had masterminded everything. Did he guess she'd figure out he *was* cheating and wanted to ensure she wouldn't leave? Was the ambush his final stab at controlling Natatoria? Grinding the rebellion out of existence by framing them? He was going to kill her.

With a loud gasp, someone emerged into the porthole, startling Tatiana. Her insides jumped and she palmed the knife, holding her breath, afraid who it could be. At the silence. She tiptoed into the hall, her heart rate thundering in her ears.

"Jacob?" Tatiana asked softly.

Tatiana heard another gasp before a splash—the intruder's retreat.

She ran to the empty porthole and plunged her face underwater. The corner of her cape dangled next to her, masking the intruder's scent.

"Red tide," Tatiana cussed, tossing the cape in the corner.

She peered outside through the one-way glass, seeing no one.

225

Should she dare go out? With the Dradux ready to mer-nap her again, she couldn't chance it. Instead, she pushed the coffee table over the hole, and heaved a heavy rock cabinet on top.

"There," she said shakily, knowing only a mer with Hulkish strength could lift both off at once. "Try and get me now, lampreys."

Sitting on the couch with her legs folded up in a ball, she sat with knife in hand and waited.

And then the lost feelings surfaced, the suffocation that haunted her in the compound. The voice that said she'd never measure up. That she didn't deserve happiness. That even Azor, who'd hounded her affection relentlessly, had cheated on her with Xirene and now sought to kill her. If she survived somehow and Jacob never returned, what was she going to do? She couldn't believe he wouldn't come for her. He had to, otherwise she'd be hunted and everlost in Natatoria—forever. And then the tears came.

26

Edge of Death

"Is this her?" a garbled voice said from the dark.

Jacob turned, or tried to turn, but found his neck refused to obey his wishes, and his eyelids were glued shut.

"No, you idiot—"

Azor. Jacob knew he was in Hades now, and he couldn't move to kill the bastard. With each small breath, fire raced deep in his chest, pulling at his lungs. A groan escaped his lips.

"Well, her fin's the same color," the goon whined, sounding like Chauncey.

"That was her maid, for Poseidon's sake. Don't you know what the Princess looks like?"

Nicole. Was she alive? Did they have Grommet, too? Was he dead?

"Hey, Captain. This one is still alive," another voice said.

Jacob focused all his might to open his eyes, unable to.

"Who is it?" Azor asked, his voice closer.

Jacob's body flopped over as if of its own volition and cool water rushed over his gills.

"Oh, it's just Jacob," Chauncey said, his breath reeking of oysters.

Anger pulsed through Jacob and he wanted to reach up and strangle the jackass. What did he think he was? A Dradux now?

"Heh," Azor said mockingly. "Look at him. He's one lucky bastard."

"I thought I killed him," Chauncey said. "I'll finish him off for you."

Chauncey, you traitor. Wait till I get my hands on you.

"No," Azor said quickly. "I—I need him. If he hangs on, send him to a healer."

Jacob willed himself to open his eyes, to fight. Say something at least, but he couldn't. Death's grip had its hooks wrapped around his limp fin, waiting for his soul to release. Whatever pinioned his chest wasn't doing so through his heart. His blood, he imagined, with deep determination to live, healed what tissue it could around the weapon.

Chauncey whined, "Come on, Captain. Are you sure? He did… you know, see T's naughty bits."

Azor laughed evilly. "And you could have, too. Played with them if you wanted, but that would have required you to find her first, which you didn't!" Azor's voice morphed into an angry bark. "I can't believe she's not here!"

Jacob felt something nudge his fin. "Someone must have told him our plan."

"How? No one knew but us."

"He had the second floor all sealed up initially, and then Darrellon. Did you see his head?" Chauncey tsked.

"Yeah, well," Azor grunted, sad almost. "There's no exit upstairs, so that *one* must have been the decoy so she could get away."

"But what about Xirene's room?" someone else asked.

"There's no outer exit, I said!" Azor sounded more adamant. However, there *was* another exit—Jacob had covered it up with Xirene's bed once they'd found it.

More fire spread down Jacob's torso as he worked to flex his fin—something popped in his spine. He groaned.

"Just let me finish him off. He'll never join us. He's sympathetic to the Princess. We don't need him."

"We do need him," Azor said, voice hard. "He'll be a witness against the rebels. Then they'll pay—all of them. But not until I find Tatiana."

"But he saw me. He knows."

Azor paused a beat. "Well… after he wakes and tells me where Tatiana is, you can dispose of him."

Jacob's skin crawled. Azor's vitriol proved he wasn't promised to Tatiana, couldn't be. Was Xirene his secret lover after all? Had he had everyone fooled? With Tatiana hearing them laugh and the secret trap door leading outside, it all made sense. Azor could come and go, and no one would know. But how'd he get away without her conceiving? Was she sterile? He knew Azor to be a son of a bass, but set up an ambush to mer-nap his mate and frame it on the rebels? He'd kill him, if he lived.

Silence followed, and Jacob's feeble mind drifted.

Too easy to sleep. To just let it all slip away.

27

Twin

Reminded of all the previous waiting, Tatiana's gut ached and she began to pace. She'd grown tired of time's double-edged sword, passing too quickly in good times, and painfully slow otherwise. After being free from her promise to Azor, she never wanted to feel so trapped by someone again. But why wasn't Jacob here? Something had to be wrong—terribly wrong. Listening to the eerie silence beyond the walls, she wished for a song, even a sad one. Something to break the monotonous quiet.

Instead, a song of regret, soft and low, birthed off her tongue. Quiet, so as not to travel outside. The echo reminded her of when her mom used to sing—when she cleaned or made dinner. Even in the shower in Tahoe.

She snuggled in the soft blanket and sang the Natatorian anthem, then a few human songs she knew. *Twinkle, Twinkle Little Star* and *I See the Moon*, when a frightening thought hit her.

What if Jacob wasn't coming back for her? What if he'd staged the ambush and only planned to break out the rebels, leaving her behind?

She sat up and clutched her chest, rising to her feet. He'd promised he'd always be there for her, saying, "where you go, I go." But this time he hadn't. He merely pushed her into a shark-infested tank with only a trident, leaving her alone.

Had he grown tired of her? Maybe the fear of arrest over the naked incident made him run. Or that she'd continually refused his pleas to leave: in the palace, the compound, here. She gulped back her tears, dragging her bare foot over the spot he'd knelt, remembering everything. She could have left with him then, before Azor fitted the bracelet on her. Had Jacob finally given up on trying to convince her?

"No," she whispered. He couldn't. Not now. Not when she'd finally freed herself from the bond. But his warning not to siren, when that's exactly what someone else did, hit her hard. He'd made her escape alone because he couldn't tell her the truth. That he'd finally decided to leave Natatoria without her.

She scanned the house again for a sign, a clue he'd been there, and ran to the kitchen. Had he left her the food?

She clutched the counter, overwhelmed with dread, when a cramp crippled her leg mid-thigh. Her thoughts immediately went to Fin. A flash hit her eyes, blinding her. Water. Blood. Kids voices heckling her. Then the pain shot like fire, seizing her muscle.

"Oooh owww!" she screamed, grabbing at her leg. The pain burst stars in her eyes and the world spun topsy-turvy. Everything faded to black.

28

Awake

Falling through the air-filled blackness, Jacob tumbled head over fin, clutching his chest as the blood spurted from the open gash, oozing and red. He screamed in pain, but nothing would come from his mouth. And the ground, rushing at him at such speeds through watery eyes—he could see it now—closer and closer. He'd die and this nightmare would all be over, all for nothing.

Jacob's body jolted. He yelped, the pain careening through his ribs.

"Whoa, don't move, Jacob," Sandy's hand pressed gently on his shoulder. His rushing pulse rocketed through his veins. "You've been injured and you're healing. I know it hurts, just take deep breaths. It'll be over soon."

Jacob took small sips of air; his eyes remained firmly shut. The air smelled dank and dusty, like leather and pipe smoke. He pried his eyes open and stared at an old chandelier attached to a brick ceiling. A dull thud repeatedly hit at his temple.

"Where am I?" he asked, his voice horse. He panned to Badger and Sandy examining him in concern.

His hand grazed the white bandage drenched in sparkling blue liquid across his chest.

"You're at our house," Sandy said, while squeezing his hand.

"Good to see the squirrely-get has his father's spunk, eh?"

"Badger," Jacob said in relief, throat crackling. "You're out?"

"Aye, I am." Badger knocked his burley hand on Jacob's foot.

"Good to have ya back."

Jacob inhaled deeper and looked around for others, finding no one. "Where is everyone? What happened?"

Badger bobbed his head. "That quiet orphan boy took one look at the Dradux comin' to skewer us and he let loose. Screams like a maid, I tell ya." He rubbed wildly at his ear with his index finger. "But packs a wallop'n like a tank."

"Screams?" Jacob asked, his mind askew.

"Ferdinand. Ya know. That kid that used to hang out at the practice field, organizin' the weapons. He don't talk much."

Jacob's eyes glazed over with a slow blink. "Oh, right. Ferdinand. He broke you out?"

"Right outta solitary." Badger's beard lifted with his smile. "Ya'd never know it, but his yockers are bigger than all of us gits put together. I'm sure Azor's vent cheeks are pinched right about now once he sees what Ferd did to the dungeon."

Jacob remembered the big hole in the wall, at least.

"And Jax?"

"Jax?" Badger clasped Jacob's shoulder. "I don't remember see'n 'im. Right bloody mess in dat there shite hole. I could barely see me hand in front of me face. After Ferd broke me outta me cell with his tail, me and the rest of 'em plundered the armory and fought our way out. From there we scattered. I didn't even see you."

Jacob closed his eyes and rubbed his forehead. When at the compound, there wasn't anyone inside the cells that he could see. He must have just missed them. "Poseidon."

"I'm sure he broke out with the rest." Badger straightened his shoulders.

Jacob slowly raked his hand through his hair. Jax, was a catfish with his nine lives, but he'd need to get the bracelet off before leaving for Tahoe or for Florida to find Galadriel. And avoid the cassava barbed nets. "How'd I get out?"

"Grommet brought you to me," Sandy said with a soft smile. "He told us everything. He said he created a diversion so he could sneak you out of that secret door you two found."

"And Nicole?"

Her lips turned down. "No. She'd lost too much blood and…"

Jacob pinched his eyes tight, the past returning in snippets. The blood. The sirens. "Where is Grommet?"

"He went back. With the jail break, he thought it best to stay undercover. Said he'd check on Tatiana for you, first."

"We have to go," Jacob moaned, trying to sit up.

"Whoa." Sandy and Badger moved forward with their hands outstretched for him to remain flat. "Your insides are arranging themselves. You must not move."

"But Tatiana," Jacob said with a groan, grabbing his ribs.

"Yer not goin' anywhere, lad," Badger said quickly. "As long as she stay put, she'll be fairin' until we can get the supplies and weapons to escape. Besides, you need a bit more time."

"No, we can't leave her there," Jacob growled. "The Dradux weren't at the compound to kill off the rebels. They were after the Princess. A staged ambush to look like us so Azor could pin it on the rebels. Grommet had to cut off Darrellon's head to stop him from killing me to get to the Princess. But I'd managed to help Tatiana escape through the shark tank and…" He lay back, eyes rolling into his head in exhaustion. "She's waiting for me and Azor will know to look for her at her parents' first."

"Aye," Badger said, palming his hand through his hair. "That nutter. I understand him hatin' us, but why would he want to hurt his Princess? He needs her so he can be king."

Jacob moaned softly, too tired to explain about his theories with Xirene. "We owe it to Jack to take care of his daughter—Azor can't get to her before we do."

"Hmmm—" Badger said, scratching his beard. "Fine, then. I'll go."

"No. I'll go," Sandy said quickly.

"It's too dangerous. You're both wanted mers." Jacob let out a huff. "I'm her bodyguard. She's my responsibility."

"Aye, but with yer ribs busted and yer lung a mendin', ye ain't goin' nowhere fer awhile. I'm goin' so quit yer bellyachin'."

"You can't Badger. If they catch you…" he groaned, struggling to sit up. "I'll do it."

Sandy pressed down hard on his shoulder. "You'll do no such thing. Lay flat, you hear me? I didn't waste my precious essence to have you end up a cripple."

Jacob stopped struggling and relaxed into his pillow.

"Don't you be worryin'," Badger said with a tap to Jacob's shoulder. "Sandy's got a little ink left. She'll be back in a pinch. And I'll keep me eye on ya. I need to brush up on me nursin' skills anywho."

Jacob raked his hand through his hair, frustrated with Badger's lack of concern. "But she has the bracelet on, too."

Badger held up his wrist with a surly grin. "Aye, we all do, mate."

Sandy sighed, shaking her head. "Don't worry, Jacob. We have enough herbs stored to make an antidote for everyone, even the Princess. Now rest. I'll go."

Jacob closed his eyes and pounded the table he lay upon, stuck in a worthless body, healing. He didn't have time for this. He had to get to her. Didn't they see the disaster at the compound? If his injury took Tatiana from him... he couldn't bare the thought.

Jack's plans be damned. There'd be hell to pay, and Azor would owe it... with interest.

29

Lovely

Frustrated cursing and muffled commotion woke Tatiana with a start. She stared up at the ceiling of her parents' home, a vision of Fin in her mind.

Fin?

She listened harder, wondering if she dreamt she'd heard a voice, and felt down her leg, expecting a mass of hot blood pooling around her. Though she found nothing, her sixth twin sense wouldn't stop alerting her something was wrong with Fin.

"Riri, this isn't funny. Come here and move this thing, please."

Azor. Tatiana gasped at his cordial yet impatient tone filling the hall.

With a shake of her head, she sat up. She winced as if her leg would hurt, but felt no pain. Only the dank taste of dirt filled her mouth. She tried to swallow the grime away.

"I wanted you to be careful, but this is a little extreme. You shouldn't even be lifting things in your condition. Please, lovely, help me. I'm trapped and I miss you."

Lovely? Miss you? Tatiana rubbed at the knot on the side of her skull, still thinking she was hearing things, before slowly maneuvering to her feet. Their last interaction ended when he'd threatened to impregnate her. Then he'd disappeared in the morning without a word before the ambush. How did he even know she was here?

"I have more food, and you won't believe what happened at the compound… complete bloodbath like you thought," he continued. "I'm going to have to make sure there's Hades to pay, considering what they've done to the place."

Food? Bloodbath? Her heart leapt at the words. How did Azor know ahead of time what Jacob and the rebels were planning unless… the ambush really happened. *Jacob.* She shuffled to the living area, stars flickering in her vision as she walked to discover the truth.

"Come on," he whined. "Are you sleeping? I don't have long. I need to return and schedule a search party. I can't believe…" At her entrance, Azor's mouth froze half-way open, his eyes wide. "Tatiana?"

Tatiana glared at him, one hand holding her head and the other firmly resting on the wall. "I assume you were expecting someone else. Riri perhaps?"

"H-how'd you get here?"

Tatiana faked a laugh. "Swam, just like you did."

He blinked a few times, his mouth flapping on its hinge. "You need to come home."

"To a bloodbath?" Tatiana perched a brow. "I think I'll pass."

Azor gained composure. "It's all clear now. The rebels involved were apprehended. But I'm so glad you're safe. We've been looking for you."

She squinted at him and everything clicked into place, sickening her. He'd set up the ambush so he could be with Riri.

"And…" He lifted his box of food, setting it on the porthole ledge. "I thought you'd be hungry… Love." He smiled weakly.

She laughed again at his lies. "What happened to *lovely*?"

"Lovely, Love. Same thing." He held out his hand. "Are you okay?"

Instead of taking his hand, Tatiana staggered over to the couch, falling into the cushions. "Who's Riri?"

"Riri? I don't know."

She leveled him with a glare. "Do you think I'm an idiot? Who is she?"

"I don't know what you're talking about. I don't know any Riri."

Tatiana snorted. The food, the moved furniture, the pillow, everything. It wasn't Jacob, but Riri who had moved in and made herself at home.

"Is Riri the one you're cheating on me with?" Tatiana asked plainly, holding up the pillow.

"We've already been through this," Azor said adamantly.

"Have we?"

"Yes, and frankly, I'm sick of hearing about it. First it's Xirene, now it's Riri."

"You're such a horrible liar, Azor." Tatiana cocked her head to the side. "We both know they're one and the same. And maybe I wouldn't have to accuse you of cheating if you slept in your own bed and stopped treating me like a freaking pariah!" The pillow sailed across the room and glanced off his head.

"Well, maybe if you didn't start fights with me every time I came home—"

"You're not going to turn this around on me." Tatiana gritted her teeth.

"Please, Tatiana. Lift this monstrosity off the porthole and I'll explain everything and make it up to you, right now."

"You'll never touch me again," she sneered.

Azor grunted in his attempts to push the table off the hole. "You're in shock over what's happened at the compound and hearing things. And why are you holding your head?"

"Shock? I'll say. I just found out my mate has been making a fool of me. We're done, Azor."

"Please," he said, grunting again, this time gaining leverage. "I care about you more than anything. And with this revolt, I've decided both of us need to move into the palace, get away from the compound and the madness. I'll shower you with beautiful things, whatever you want. Just tell me how I can make it up to you. Please."

Tatiana crossed her arms, turning her back on him. "Are you freaking kidding me?" She laughed. "You've had your chance."

She jumped when the granite bookshelf crashed onto the floor. Yet he was there in a flash, his arms tucked around her waist and lips caressing her neck.

She waited for the promise to kick in and make her all lovey-dovey again. Typically, her pulse would be performing aerial stunts in her veins over this, but nothing happened. Absolutely nothing.

"I care for you, Tatiana. Let me show you," he said against her ear.

She leaned into him anyway, just to toy with him. "Oh, Azor," she crooned. "You're so right. How could I not see your love for me? And how wonderful you are? I'll never second guess you again."

"That's right. You were only hearing things." He brushed his hand down her hair. "So beautiful. So perfect. Have I told you that?"

She laughed inside at his manipulation. Before, every cell would have been alive and screaming, begging for him to hold her, to love her, to promise he'd be her lover forever.

"No," she said with a fake whimper.

"I can't remember a day I didn't want you. All that time when you were in Tahoe; I waited so long to make you mine."

He pulled her into a tight embrace and his heat drove into her body, proving his desire for her. Her stomach churned, unable to handle the knowledge that he'd been telling Xirene the same things.

With a sigh, she snuggled into him. "You promise me you're not cheating."

"Of course not," He took her hand and kissed her fingers. "Let's go in the bedroom."

"Over my dead body," she hissed. She punched her elbow into his ribs and jumped off the couch before he could grab her.

Azor groaned and clutched his ribs. "Why in Hades did you do that?"

"Because you're a slimy sea snake. I caught you, red-handed and…" She eyed a bundle of white fabric under the couch. With a quick snag, she produced the offending garment. Azor's face blanched at the sight of a white skirt, trimmed in blue. "You have the audacity to deny it? This is a servant's skirt."

Azor leapt up, lunging for her hand. "Tatiana, you're jumping to conclusions."

"Am I?" She pivoted and ran to the kitchen, keeping the island between them, vividly aware the knife was within reach.

"Yes," he said, holding out his hand. "Please. Don't let that spoil the moment. I love you. I need you."

"You need a cold shower." She remained poised, ready to bolt the opposite direction or stab him if he came closer.

"Please, let's go home," he held out his hand.

Tatiana laughed. "I'm not going anywhere with you—" Her eyes snapped to the black promising tattoo on his finger, vibrant and visible.

She held up her unchanged ring finger toward him. "If you haven't cheated, then where is my promising tattoo?"

Azor's face blanched. "Uh—I"

Even with the truth, clear and undeniable, he wouldn't admit his wrongdoing. He *had* kissed someone else before Tatiana and the thought sickened her.

She scanned the doorway, plotting her escape, when Xirene walked from around the corner, her eyes narrowed. In her hand was the white pillow.

Tatiana blinked, slow and deliberate. Her gaze focused on Xirene's naked belly, round and firm. Filled with life. Pregnant.

At the revelation, Tatiana almost passed out.

30

Truth

A scream quelled in Tatiana's throat as a rush of wind sped through her mind and slammed into her, stealing her breath. She couldn't tear her eyes away from Xirene's stomach.

A baby? She's having his baby.

And then, her eyes darted to Xirene's bare hand. There, under the golden glow of the sun-tunnels illuminating the kitchen, a promising tattoo shone—bright and shiny as a new dime.

Tatiana's eyes glazed over, the rejection hitting hard. If he was already promised before the ceremony, why kiss her? Why torment her?

"Riri." Azor held his hand to Xirene.

The sound of her name on his lips oddly hurt. When their hands interlaced, Tatiana's limbs began to shake and her vision blurred. He'd captured her by stealing her soul, imprisoning her spirit, with no intention of ever loving her.

"Don't freak out, Tatiana," Azor said simply.

"Freak out? Why would I freak out? I honestly couldn't care less about *her*, you bastard!" She splayed her hands on the island to keep upright, her own untattooed ring finger mocking her. "This is my house, for God's sake. My house!"

Xirene gently slipped under his arm, molding into his side. Her satisfied smile made Tatiana's face burn. The jet-black locks of her hair were adorned in pearls, white against the evil that she was. Tatiana could picture them together, encircled around each other as humans in *that* bubbled room, while Tatiana slept alone. Tatiana almost hurled on the tabletop, thinking of the abuse she'd suffered this entire time.

I'm going to kill him, Tatiana thought as she envisioned a hundred ways to choke him, starting with the strand of pearls from Xirene's head. She curled her fingers into fists, the knife inches from her hand.

"Why?" Tatiana asked, her voice raspy, her eyes filling with tears. "Why have you tortured me like this?"

Azor's evil grin perched on his lips. "To finally show you what it's like to care for someone and have them reject you. And when your father made a fool of the King, I couldn't think of a fitting punishment than to steal his daughter, make her mine. Too bad I couldn't steal your virginity, too." Azor took a deep breath and stroked Xirene's lustrous curls. "But I'd never do that to my Riri. She's the only one who has loved me for me and knows how to make me happy."

Tatiana's breath came out short, relieved they'd never actually mated, though she'd thought they might have. "How long were you planning on keeping this up?"

"Until our merling came. My son," Azor said with a lift of his chin. "And won't it be so tragic that your abduction by the rebels caused you so much trauma you died in childbirth?"

She blinked, speechless, her heart lurching. He still was going to kidnap her. Kill her. A cold sweat broke out over her body. Together, they'd set this all up: the excuses, the drugs, the ambush. It wasn't a royal Azor was talking to that first night in the hall, but Xirene. This whole time Jacob had been right, so terribly right. And since Jacob hadn't come for her, where was he?

Without a further thought, she ran. Straight for the porthole, straight outside, and right into the arms of an awaiting Dradux.

"Oh, no you don't," he said, latching his arms around her, grinding his pelvis into her backside. "Hmmm, this'll be fun," he lisped in her ear. Her skin crawled knowing the cymothoa parasite on his tongue could touch her, lick her.

With a full body shiver, Tatiana opened her mouth to siren when his other hand clamped over her lips. But he didn't cover her mouth entirely, and she bit him—hard. He wailed and Tatiana was free. With a hard pump of her tail, she sped away from him, spitting his flesh.

She darted left, then right, zigzagging between houses, looking for a place to hide. With no other mers around to dilute her smell, the Dradux followed her scent like footprints in the sand. Escape would be impossible. Why did she take off the cape?

With repetitive looks over her shoulder, Tatiana moved between the houses, hoping to confuse her trail. Water filled her gills, rough and erratic, which didn't help matters as she sped from him. She flitted toward the compound, when another group of guards came into sight—dressed in green cloaks with scythes in their hands. *Dradux.*

They're going to kill me.

With a yelp, she maneuvered down and slipped behind a rock wall to catch her breath. But the Dradux's heads turned in her direction in unison and flew at her.

Holy crawfish!

She darted between more houses and headed toward the palace, then turned east.

A gate. If I can only get to a gate!

On her wrist, the gold bobbed against her skin, fighting the current. *Chiton!* She'd forgotten the poison. She cursed Azor's name under her breath. His plan of revenge was so revolting that she couldn't imagine anything worse. She'd never wanted Azor to feel unwanted, but she couldn't force herself to like him. How could he unleash such evil on someone?

The closer she swam to the Bermuda gate, the more she hoped the poison wouldn't kill her immediately. Maybe she'd have time to get to the safe house. With the Dradux hot on her tail, she didn't have much of a choice.

She pressed on, ready to embrace what was to happen. With the cadenced rise and fall of her hips through the current, her heart settled into a fast rhythm. She had to make it, or maybe there wasn't any poison at all. Just a threat. She tried to slide the bracelet off her wrist. A barb poked into her skin. Withholding her scream, she slowed, cradling her wrist.

Something grabbed her tail. Sirening, she recoiled and folded at her waist. A zigzag of twine snagged and pulled at her arm. Tiny knives pulsed into her skin all at once, bursting fire into her limb. She opened her mouth to scream, but nothing would come out.

"Princess," the voice said, "what are you doing out here?"

Her eyes fluttered to find the voice. Concerned eyes stared back at her from under a green cloak. She tried to siren again, unable to find her voice, unable to free herself of the net.

"Oh, Princess," he said, defeated. "Hold still."

Fogginess covered her vision as the Dradux cut the twine away from her arm. Bright green fluid mixed with the wafts of blood rising like steam from her skin. He grabbed her torso, lifting her body against his. He was going to take her back—to him—to the monster. She wanted to tell the guard to let her die now, to leave her alone.

Weakness consumed her muscles. She couldn't fight anymore. Death would be the best and she willed her aching heart to stop beating.

⁂

At Badger's warrior cry, Jacob startled awake. A battle ax twirled above Badger's head, aimed to smash into the intruder wading in his porthole.

"Wait!" the Dradux called out and flipped off his hood. "It's me! Grommet!"

Badger cussed and strained to stop the weapon, slamming the ax into a nearby trunk with an ear splitting crack. "Oye, mate. Whatcha be doing wearing that getup? I almost sliced open yer head like a coconut."

Jacob exhaled; his head fell back onto his pillow.

"It's a long story." Grommet popped up on the porthole ledge with the Princess flopping helplessly in his arms.

At the sight of her, Jacob struggled to sit, pain jolting through his chest. "Tatiana," he croaked.

"Aye…" Badger froze. "Sandy, come quick!"

With a gasp, Sandy rushed to Tatiana's side and ripped off the blue vial that dangled around her neck. She tilted Tatiana's head and poured the contents into her slack mouth. At first Tatiana fought the liquid, then she swallowed hungrily.

"I need towels and soap. Quick!" Sandy shrieked.

Badger brought the supplies. Working frothy foam in her hands, Sandy cleaned the cassava off of Tatiana's arm. Then the two of them helped Grommet move Tatiana to a chair. Sandy smoothed her hair aside, and Tatiana's eyes finally fluttered open.

"You're one lucky mermaid," Sandy said with a smile, wrapping up her arm in a white bandage.

"Sandy?"

"Yes, darling. I was just about to get you, but you're okay now."

"My wrist aches," she groaned.

"Oye, the tea," Sandy said, jumping up and disappearing in the kitchen.

At Tatiana's raspy voice, Jacob gripped the side of the couch, unable to see her through the small crowd. "What's going on?"

"I tried to stop her before she hit the nets, but her arm got tangled. She's a speedy little thing," Grommet said in a rush.

"I thought you were a Dradux," she said softly, her voice weak.

"No," he said in disgust. "I wanted to blend in, so... There's no more guard, as of the ambush. And after I heard what they were planning, I'm glad I found you first."

Tatiana groaned just as Sandy reappeared, clattering a teacup on a saucer.

"Princess, you are no longer safe with them, with any of them, especially Azor," Grommet continued. "He staged the ambush to make it look like the rebels had mer-napped you for a ransom. And since you got away, the Dradux are searching every house right now for you."

Jacob's body tensed. He knew what she'd say. That she'd stay at the palace, that she'd ask for Jacob to guard her. She'd never leave Azor or Natatoria, even if she did believe Grommet. And he didn't have the strength to fight her anymore—make her see reason.

"Princess," Grommet said softly, his voice more urgent while she sipped the tea. "We won't be able to hide you. I can distract the Dradux from your location for now, but…" He paused a beat. "I know it will be difficult, but you must leave Natatoria. We'll take you with us. We'll find Jack."

Dreadful silence lingered on. He couldn't bear to hear her excuse this time.

"Where's Jacob?" she asked in a whisper. "I won't go without him."

What did she say? At the admission, Jacob's heart stopped for a beat. His eyes popped open. Deep happiness filled his wounded spirit. He turned and reached for her, willing Grommet and Badger to move aside. He wanted to touch her, be sure this was real.

"I'm here," he grunted. "Tatiana."

"Jacob?" Tatiana set the teacup down with a clatter and rushed to him. Her gentle fingers met his hand and squeezed. She kneeled beside the couch and pushed aside his hair. "What happened to you?"

Jacob looked up at her, taking her in, studying every inch. He reached up with his free hand and caressed her face. She leaned sweetly into his palm. "When you didn't come, I didn't know what to think. Oh, Jacob."

"You should see the other guy," he said quietly.

Her eyes creased in concern, and she scrutinized the mound of gauze on his chest. But he didn't care about his injuries. He had to know what had changed, why she'd finally decided to run.

"Tatiana." He turned her face toward his, searching for answers.

She fell to his chest, sobbing. "I should have trusted you from the beginning. I'm so sorry. This is all my fault."

"No." He clutched her to his chest and sighed, squeezing her. "Don't think that."

"But it is."

Jacob closed his eyes and held Tatiana tight. Though he tried to tune out the disruptive noises from the others, he couldn't help hearing the shuffle of fabric, the metal clang of weapons. With one eye open, he watched Badger and Grommet head for the porthole.

Grommet leaned in, but his sad smile didn't touch his eyes. He simply mouthed, "We'll be back."

"I'm going to get the rest of the stored herbs," Sandy whispered. She rested her hand on Tatiana's shoulder. "Once we get the bracelet off of you, Princess, we'll leave for the Scotland gate."

Tatiana breathed a sigh of relief, and Jacob couldn't stop his heart from pounding. Things were coming together, finally.

Then all at once, the house emptied. Jacob's heart thumped harder at the silence. He squeezed her shoulder.

"They're gone," he whispered, kissing her hair.

She looked upon him with her radiant blue eyes, rimmed in red from crying, and his heart practically galloped out of his chest for the want of her lips.

31

Proposition

Tatiana studied Jacob's face and rubbed her hand over the stubble on his cheek down to the multiple new scars on his neck and chest. He'd been there for her all along—honest and forthright—in spite of her vicious attacks and promise-induced mood swings.

"What is this hell that we're in?"

"Don't worry about that. You're with me now. You're safe." He touched her cheek, catching a tear on his finger.

"I should have never fought you to begin with." She reached for his arm, grazing her fingers over the faded bite scar. Goose bumps rose along his skin from her touch. "I'm sorry I did this to you."

"I'm not," he said with a coy smile.

She blushed, not sure how to take his comment. He pulled her into his shoulder and she crawled onto the couch next to him, nestling into his side. Their heat pulsed into one another—strong and hot. He gently touched the bandage on her arm.

"What were you thinking?" he whispered into her wet hair. "I asked you to wait for me."

Her heart stuttered at the memory, the rush of emotions, the confusion, the hate, the betrayal.

"Azor found me at my parents' house, because he was there looking for Xirene." She stopped, a lump forming in her throat. She couldn't admit the worst—that he was behind the ambush, that he'd betrayed her this entire time.

Jacob groaned, tightening his arms around her as she hiccupped in sobs. "Oh, Tatiana, I'm so sorry."

"He never wanted me…"—she paused, her body shaking—"and I've been such a fool not to see it, not to leave with you sooner."

"Hey." He wove his hand down around her chin, tugging her face to look at him. She fought him, embarrassed. "I'm serious, look at me."

Reluctantly, she sat up, flicking off her tears with her fingertips. His hand remained, blood pulsing, fast, matching her own.

"You did the best you could, and now that you know, you can break free from him. Locked inside you is a strong and independent woman, the one I heard about from your dad. You can be that again. You just have to want your freedom from the bond."

Fire lit Jacob's blue-grey eyes. Hot. Smoldering. They darted to her lips and back again. A few short hours ago she'd mentally begged for this moment, for his lips on hers. But after seeing Azor with Xirene, knowing the power the kiss brought two souls, she wasn't sure she wanted to jump into another promise so soon. She licked her lips, unsure what she felt anymore. Why would anyone want to bind themselves to someone when they could turn around and hurt you like this?

Jacob's forehead creased, new concern touching his face. "And kissing me might ease that pain, but I don't want to be his replacement. You have to break the bond on your own first, to know for sure."

She startled and pulled away from him. What did he mean

her strength and independence was still locked inside her? Couldn't he see she had broken the bond? Or had her crying shone she was still weak and dependant. Swiveling her legs off the couch, she sat up and wiped away her tears. She didn't need him, or anyone to save her. She was fine on her own.

"Don't worry. I don't need your help. I've already broken it," she stated plainly. "He kissed Xirene first, so I was never really bonded to him to begin with."

He sucked in a breath, then squeezed her thigh. "Tatiana, I didn't mean it like that—"

At the splash in the porthole, Tatiana pulled away from Jacob, embarrassed. And she most definitely didn't want to look like she'd moved onto Jacob when in fact she hadn't. She wanted to be single for a while and they'd remain strictly friends, until they parted ways in Florida. And there she could move onto a new path in life—maybe even become human so she could forget how humiliating all of this had been.

"Finally," she said to the three green hooded heads that had emerged at the porthole. "Nice getup."

All at once, they launched out of the porthole, phasing in mid-air. One landed before Tatiana, trapping her arms at her waist, while the other two apprehended Jacob.

"Glad you approve," the Dradux before her said with a sly smile. "You should see what's underneath waiting for you."

Tatiana screamed. But the siren, trapped inside her human form, only came out as a shriek from her lips.

"Get your hands off her!" Jacob yelled while struggling against his captors.

"I'll do the talking," a fourth Dradux lisped from the porthole.

Like the others, he flew up into the air and phased before touching down on the floor.

Tatiana's captor slid his hand over her mouth. "No biting," he whispered in her ear. She kicked and grunted, but her assailant only held her tighter.

"Chauncey," Jacob growled, "I should have known."

"And I should have killed you earlier, traitor." Chauncey flipped off his hood to reveal his scarred face. "What are you doing alone with the Princess anyway?"

"My job," he seethed.

Chauncey's acerbic laughter echoed off the walls. "As if you could guard Princess Tatiana in your condition. I'll take over from here."

"Don't do this, Chauncey."

"Or what? You'll throw your bloody gauze at me? Sic your rebel friends on me? On the new master of the Dradux?" He waggled his new parasitic tongue. "Guess again."

"Let her go!"

Chauncey snapped his fingers, and the Dradux pulled Jacob to a sitting position. He groaned, favoring his left side. Tatiana tried to lunge for Jacob, moaning in desperation.

"As of this moment, you're relieved of your job, Jacob." Chauncey gestured and the two yanked Jacob to his feet. "And I'm formally arresting you for being improper with the Princess."

"Improper?"

A coy smile met Chauncey's lips. "Like we don't know what you two were doing."

"You'll regret this, Chauncey. I promise you. I will hunt you down and make you pay." Jacob's captors forced him toward the porthole; one grasped his hair and the other prodded his back with his scythe.

"Not after what Azor has in store for you, rebel." Chauncey clicked his tongue. The disgusting noise he'd made against the soft body of the parasite echoed in the room.

Tatiana groaned, struggling in her captor's arms. She couldn't allow them to take Jacob. She had to stall. Badger and Grommet were returning.

Jacob shot her a look of despair and mouthed, "I'll come for you."

"Keep moving," one of the Dradux said and the other pushed Jacob forward into the porthole. Together, they pulled him under the waves.

"No!" Tatiana's cry was muffled through the Dradux's smelly hand.

Chauncey moved to her and traced his finger over her cheek and down her neck between her breasts. A smile crooked on the corner of his lips. He rested his finger on the edge of her skirt waistband. "I've heard you're still pure."

She leaned in with angry eyes and stomped on his foot with her heel. He yelped and moved away, cursing. He took his scythe and aimed it at her legs. She winced, expecting him to slice into her thigh. Instead, he took the sharp blade and lifted the corner of her skirt. She splayed her hands over the fabric to stop him.

The two men laughed at her feeble attempts.

"I'll find out what's under there soon enough."

"Like hell you will." With a swift donkey kick to the Dradux's knee, a sickening crack filled the room. The Dradux doubled over and Tatiana's arms were free. She pulled the battle ax from the trunk and wielded the heavy object around in front of her. "Stand back, you sea sacks!"

Her injured arm ached under the strain of the weapon, but determined, she held the ax outright.

"Or you'll cleave me?" Chauncey pushed up one brow. "So brave."

You bet your vent, I am.

Tatiana jumped into the porthole and submerged, searching for Jacob's scent. She had time to stop the two bastards from taking Jacob to Azor's compound. They could still escape Natatoria together.

She whipped her head around at the musk of rotting oysters and freshness of essence, and froze. A sea of Dradux guards were all that she could see. And just beyond the neighboring house were an entire group of mers, chained with sacks over their heads.

She picked out Badger before they tied a sack over his head. Their eyes met briefly—angered and frustrated. She wouldn't let the mass of enemies stop her. With her siren scream, she swung the ax around with all the courage she could muster, aiming to knock the Dradux down like bowling pins. Someone behind her plucked the weapon from her hands and another restrained her around her waist. The sack plunged her into darkness as something secured uncomfortably across her gills, making breathing difficult. She choked, her siren silenced.

"Take her to the captain," she heard a merman say from behind her.

"No!" she yelled, thrashing.

Then fire burned up her tail, the all too familiar stab from a merman's tail barb. She cried out, heart pounding, but fell limp in the current as the merman dragged her away.

※

With a sudden rush, she was yanked into an air-filled room and dropped. Her knees clattered onto the hard stones. She winced, kneeling prone, gasping and choking, fighting to suck in gasps of oxygen through the wet bag over her head. "Do you mean to suffocate me?"

At the silence, she straightened, trying to gain leverage with her wrists bound behind her. "I know you're here, Azor. I can smell you."

Someone lifted her arms, tugging her to her feet. Then they shoved her forward. Her leg burned at the wound site where the Dradux had nicked her tail, making her foot numb. She slipped on the cold uneven tiles, unlike the palace marble. Where was she?

After walking a few steps, she was turned and roughly shoved into a chair.

"Remove the sack."

Azor.

Tatiana grimaced at the recognition of his voice. With a quick tug of the rope around her throat, light burst around her eyes. She sucked in a breath and focused on a poster of Vincent van Gogh's *The Starry Night* hanging on the wall in her room in her parents' house.

"Azor," Tatiana said in disgust, watching his lips smirk in victory. She couldn't believe how with each interaction, the broken promise peeled back new layers of loathing hate for him. "Really? You're going to tie me up and treat me like a prisoner now?"

"I don't seem to have much choice, considering you run every time I try to talk to you."

Tatiana snorted. "Maybe that's because you cheated on me, then threatened to kill me."

"Careful, Princess." His nostrils flared, and he gestured to the Dradux handler next to her, dismissing him. He waited a beat then walked closer to her. "As far as I see it, in order to get what we both want, we have to work together."

"What I want?" Tatiana laughed. "Since when do you care?"

Azor raised his brow, amusement playing on his face. "Oh, I care..."—he twirled a golden key on a string—"I think you should at least listen to my proposition, especially since you've involved Jacob in all of this."

"Jacob?" she parroted, nonchalant. "He was a horrible guard."

"Oh, don't be so coy. I know you two were caught kissing."

"What—?" She blew out a noisy breath and laughed. "That's ridiculous."

Azor frowned. "So it doesn't concern you I'm charging him with treason, and he's to be escorted to Bone Island tomorrow?"

Her body jolted. "Treason for what?"

"His secret loyalty to the rebellion and his inappropriate advances toward the future queen."

Her chest heaved as she focused to remain calm. "And what about you?"

"Me?" He snorted.

She leaned forward in her chair. "Do I have to state the

obvious?"

He pressed her with hard eyes. "I make the rules, Tatiana, but frankly, I'm not angry at him for kissing you. I'm relieved."

Relieved? Her face crinkled at his statement.

"Yes," he smiled as if to read her mind. "It solves your clinginess problem, though, I'd forgotten how mouthy you can be otherwise."

She gritted her teeth. *You haven't heard anything yet.* "You're one to talk."

"Yes, well…" He walked over to her dresser and uncovered a blob of something—a jellyfish?—missing its tentacles and bloated. "Time to brush up on your acting skills."

She shook her head, already knowing where he was going with his proposition. "Oh, no."

"Oh, yes," he said. "It's just for the week."

"Are you suggesting I wear that? Pretend I'm pregnant? Yes, we mermaids gestate quickly, but we've only been promised for a little over a week, Azor."

"And we were so naughty." He smiled evilly. "Unless you have a better idea."

Did he not know the gossip mill at the palace? She was surprised Xirene's bulging stomach hadn't been detected yet.

"Pearleza knows. She *inspected* me."

"And she knows to keep quiet, or we'll dispose of her."

Tatiana gasped. "You'll what?"

"Like I said, if it's for the betterment of the kingdom, then I make those tough decisions. It's all part of being king."

"You are not king yet."

"I will be soon."

"How about you fall on your trident and dispose of yourself, you slippery oyster," she said with a smirk. "I'm not wearing that... *thing!*"

Azor leaned forward. "Oh, yes you will and this is why. Every minute you don't cooperate is another Jacob will go without water. He can only last for so long before he dries up, and we wouldn't want our hero to turn into a bag of bones, would we?"

She sucked in a breath. "I want to see him first."

"You will, Love."

"Don't call me that," she said, teeth gritted, "*ever.*"

"Fine. You'll pretend you're pregnant, give birth, then... you can see Jacob. After that, I don't see why we can't keep our private lives separate from our public ones... all for the sake of *our* kingdom, of course."

"What are you suggesting? We pretend we're promised to one another, but have secret lovers on the side?" She laughed. "What happened to killing me off in childbirth?"

"This way is less messy." He quirked a smile. "Besides, you still need a bodyguard and I, a handmaid doubling as a nursemaid for our new merling. It solves both our problems."

Tatiana cringed at the lengths he'd go, all for power. Like the dreaded deep-sea angler fish, he dangled Jacob's life like a bioluminescent lure before her, thinking she must have kissed Jacob since she clearly was free of his bond. But Azor had assumed the wrong thing. Though she cared about Jacob and would do anything to save him, Azor had underestimated her. She was free. Free to think clearly. Free to outsmart him.

"What's my guarantee you won't *dispose* of Jacob or me when we're no longer of use to you?" She gauged his reaction.

"Without Jacob, I'd be stuck with your whining love-sick self, trailing me around, begging I spend more time with you. I can't stomach that again, Tatiana. And what's a kingdom without their jewel that is the queen?"

Her lips pulled into a light line, angered at how cruel he was, tricking her with his kiss, then purposefully making her suffer. He had no value of life, of love, or even the promise. He only looked at the mers as objects to do what he wants.

"Why can't Xirene just be the queen instead?"

"Xirene?" He laughed. "Now that's funny. No… you'll cooperate, or I'll resort to using drugs, plain and simple. Your choice."

She cringed. "You wouldn't."

"Oh, I would. But you have my word; I'll return Jacob unharmed after we pull this off, My Queen. Freedom for your mere cooperation."

His word? She wanted to spit in his face. His word was worthless "It doesn't bother you that it won't be my child? Or Xirene?"

"Does that really matter? It's mine, and he'll be of royal blood, so the question of his mother won't need to be discussed. And Xirene will still raise him."

Tatiana tilted her head to the side. How could Xirene be okay with this?

"And what if you have a girl?"

The curl on his lips faded to a frown. "It'll be a boy."

"Confident much?" Her jaw tightened.

He leaned forward and stared her down. "I always get what I want."

She glowered at him until he turned to leave the room, letting out a short whistle. She jumped off the chair when her leg—still throbbing over the merman's sting—convulsed in a spasm of pain, tripping her to the floor.

"Aren't you going to cut me free?"

Instead, two Dradux appeared with an iron gate. They fastened the monstrous thing over the doorway with homemade hinges, locking her in place. She rolled over and peered down the hall.

"Let my hands free at least, Azor! Azor?"

She slumped against her side and wiggled her wrists against the ropes. *Your word, my fin!* She knew better than to trust him, and she refused to be drugged. Her only hope was to pretend the promise paralyzed her, and once free, she'd find Jacob and hightail it out of Natatoria. She just had to wait for the right moment, but first she had to get her wrists free.

32

Bondage

Jacob struggled against the chains binding his hands above his head. Darkness enveloped the air-filled cave, forcing him to remain finned. Only his tail had found solace in a nearby puddle. The water covered just below his lower fins, the amount adequate to keep him alive, just barely—but not enough to quench his thirst.

His eyes fluttered open to the sweet, soft voice.

"Tatiana?" he asked, voice raspy.

"I'm here," she whispered, her arm extended just out of reach. Her body shimmered against the black obsidian wall, flickering in and out of existence.

He pulled on the chains in attempts to get closer to her. "Tatiana."

"I'm here…" In a fleeting wisp, her image disappeared. "Fight for me, Jacob. I *do* want you."

Jacob groaned, slumping into the wall, his mind floating in and out of clarity. What happened? Where was she? How long had he been here?

On his torso, the wet gauze no longer held the blue iridescent liquid. Only his blood, red and bright, dripped from his wound down his chest. If he survived, he'd have to depend on his own healing.

His thoughts fell back to Tatiana, the fullness of her lips, her beautiful smile, Chauncey and his goons taking him from her. Had he missed his only chance to kiss her? Why did he wait?

He'd insulted her instead and assumed otherwise, when she'd already figured out how to break the bond on her own. *I'm so sorry, Tatiana.*

His eyes slipped shut, his heart racing again. He had no idea where she was, what Azor had planned, or if she was even alive. He had to remain hopeful, and somehow outsmart the chains than bound him to the rocks. Where was Grommet? Did anyone see?

A throbbing ache radiated from his brow. They'd bludgeoned his skull before covering his head with the sack. After that, he'd blacked-out from the pain.

"Ah… the lucky bastard lives." Azor emerged from the watery pool, a smile plastered on his face.

Jacob snarled in response. "What is this?"

"Justice."

"For?"

"For kissing my mate."

"What?" Jacob threw his head back and laughed. "Yeah, right."

"You can deny it all you want, but within a week, all will know for sure. That is if you survive that long."

Jacob groaned. "Don't look too closely for a tattoo because when I get my hands free—"

"You'll what?" He leaned in aggressively. "Murder the King?"

"Among other things," Jacob grunted.

"Brave coming from a man whom I could finish off right now."

Jacob snorted, curious why he hadn't brought a weapon with him. "You're too much of a coward to do your own dirty work."

"Ha!" Azor glowered. "You know nothing about me."

Jacob leaned forward as best he could. "I know enough to infiltrate your army, to gain your loyalty, to guard your most precious possession and take your girl from under your nose. Don't underestimate the rebels."

Azor gritted his teeth. "And it's all worked in my favor, Jacob," he said, mockingly. "You've lusted after *my* princess for nothing. I'll be crowned king Friday and Queen Tatiana will proudly swim at my side. Once you're dead, the promise will return to me and she'll become enslaved to my wants again, and do anything and everything I say."

"Like she did before?" Jacob said with an ironical tone. "She's too smart for that and has figured out a way to break the bond, Azor, and you know it."

"There's no such thing." Azor laughed, his voice echoing off the cave walls. "Your kiss has muddied her mind, that's all. It's only temporary."

"She didn't need my kiss to break it. But then again, I don't even think you had a soul to give." Jacob landed him a hard smile.

Azor's face reddened. "Tatiana was mine and you stole her from me."

"Think what you want, but your chance with her is over and she'll never be yours."

Azor's nostrils flared. "Don't lie, Jacob. You stole her kiss and my guards saw you do it. And for that, you'll be executed, next to your brother, Jax, in the square. We'll purge your family's blood from our colony once and for all."

"That doesn't solve anything." Jacob chuckled. "She will still own her soul, even if you kiss her again, and she'll hate you even more if you take my life."

"Believe what you want; I know the truth. She's mine," he said while spinning on his fin. "And I always get what I want."

With a plunge underwater, Azor disappeared.

33

Pact

At the sound of metal scuffing against stone, Tatiana opened her eyes with a jolt.

Xirene stood in her doorway, her belly impairing her ability to straighten quickly. They briefly made eye contact before she moved out of sight.

"Xirene," Tatiana called out to the soft, slow footfalls leading away from her door. "Please, I want to talk to you."

Silence lingered. Only the occasional laugh from a guard broke the quiet.

The smells of the food on the tray distracted her, whetting her appetite: two flaky croissants, fresh berry jam, a cup of strawberries and a poached egg. She walked slowly to investigate, leery of what drugs might be lurking inside.

As of yet, she'd remained strong and hadn't eaten anything. And like clockwork, in spite of Tatiana's stubbornness, Xirene took away the untouched tray and delivered another for each meal since she'd arrived two days ago. The bedpan, embarrassingly enough, she had used, which someone faithfully emptied and cleaned.

She slumped down before the tray with her legs folded under her, and took a small sip of water and waited, testing to see if she felt woozy. Unable to control herself, she added a miniscule bite of the croissant along with it. The bread, flaky and buttery, slid down her throat easily, breaking her dam of self-control. With feral bites, she engulfed every speck of food and licked the plate clean.

With a burp, she leaned back and waited for the drugs to set in. Nothing happened.

Hearing heavier footsteps, Tatiana's heart lurched, and she stood, expecting Azor.

"Princess," Chauncey said with a wolfish grin. "How wonderful to see you again."

Tatiana gave him a frosty glare and moved backward, pretending to busy herself with a book.

"What? Nothing to say to your rescuer? I'd be nicer to your potential bodyguard if I were you."

"Bodyguard?" She spat, remembering Azor's commitment she'd see Jacob if she cooperated. "As if."

"The job is still open, but then again, after what's been told you like to do with your bodyguards, I assume it won't be open for long." His eyes roved over her, making no subtlety at what he'd like to do if the bars weren't in place.

Tatiana crossed her arms. "You aren't qualified."

He finally looked at her eyes, amused. "As head of the Dradux, my duties extend much further than your safety. And today, I'm to supervise your bath before I escort you to the palace. Azor wants you fresh and not stinking like a caged fish."

Tatiana glowered. "You've blurred your job titles, Chauncey. You are a pathetic substitute for a handmaiden. But I'm sorry to say, you've come for nothing." Tatiana smelled her armpit and smiled. "I've already washed and smell fresh as a rose. Do you even know what a rose is?"

Chauncey's smile drooped. "You must change, at least. You've worn that tired thing for three days now."

"Oh, Chauncey. You must think I'm stupid," she said. "Prince Azor would never approve of me undressing in your presence. Now go, and send Nicole, my true handmaiden."

"You haven't heard?" Chauncey lifted his brow, curious. "She's dead, Princess. Killed when the rebels attacked the compound."

"What?"

"Oh, I guess you haven't heard then. Too bad." He laughed, disappearing out of view. "I'll see who I can find."

Tatiana's legs wobbled. *Dead?* She moved to her desk, grasping onto the tabletop for support, her breath coming out too quick.

"Milady?" Xirene said from the doorway. "Are you alright?"

"I'm…"

Xirene put down her rag and a bowl filled with water, fumbling with the silver key tied on a ribbon around her neck. She padded over, waddling with her belly and maimed foot, and placed her hand on Tatiana's shoulder.

Their eyes met; a look of pity crossed between them.

"I just heard about Nicole," Tatiana said in defeat.

"Oh." Xirene's eyes hit the floor. "She pretended to be you, I heard. She was very brave."

Tatiana bit back her tears, amazed this was happening. All around her was grief and strife, war and death. And now birth. Why, of all mers, did Nicole have to be the one who died?

She couldn't hate or blame Xirene for their predicament, both of them stranded in Azor's riptide of power. The only difference was he loved Xirene—something that would keep her alive and useful to him. Tatiana nor Jacob, on the other hand, would have that same security once Azor was crowned king.

After they'd secured a sheet over the doorway, Xirene removed her gloves and started Tatiana's sponge bath. The warm water felt refreshing on her skin, but her conscience ached to make things right between them.

"I'm sorry," Tatiana whispered while Xirene held up her hair and soaped her back. "I didn't mean to be so cruel to you at the compound."

Xirene blew out a nervous sigh. "How were you to know?"

"That's not me." She drew her arms into her body. "The promise messed with my head and—"

"I wasn't any better toward you." Xirene stopped scrubbing once she reached Tatiana's waist, and dropped the sponge into the bowl with a splash.

Tatiana's eyes slipped shut. Though she could understand Xirene's position, never being allowed to show her love for anyone and honored to garner a promise from the Prince, she was still angry at the horrible things Xirene had said, and did behind her back. What she didn't understand was if they were promised, why was she so surprised to see Tatiana in her promising gown the night they'd met. Hadn't she known what Azor had planned? Even with having a honey on the side, he'd pursued Tatiana—right up until the ceremony. Did she steal his kiss?

After Xirene rinsed her off and placed a fluffy towel over her shoulders, Tatiana turned to search her eyes. "Is it true? Did Azor only kiss me out of revenge and plan to murder me?"

Xirene's gaze darted fearfully to her stomach. She held onto her unborn merling, as if for dear life. "I don't know when his plans changed," she stated simply. "All I know is I can't be the queen."

Tatiana pulled away, drying herself off and wrapping up in a robe. "And because you love him, you're okay with that?"

"No." She swallowed, her voice hoarse. "You may think I'm running a brothel at the compound, but I'm not. I wasn't one of *those* servants who swam around topless to please every guard who'd look. Azor pursued me and for the most part, I resisted his charms. Well, I tried to. And once we were together and found I was sterile, I became his lover, secretly of course. Considering my station, I graciously accepted.

"But Azor still wasn't happy. All he talked about was being king and having an heir, something I didn't think my body was capable of providing. So I knew another woman would come eventually... But when I discovered I was expecting, he was overjoyed and..."—she looked down and touched her lips—"kissed me. After that, I believed I would be his, that he'd chosen me. But he followed through with the ceremony anyway... and though he swore nothing would change, I knew my position."

Tatiana recalled the conversation outside her door, his promise to her that nothing had changed, that he had a plan. She sighed. "Azor should have just chosen you to be his princess, regardless of your *position*."

Fire lit Xirene's eyes. She swiveled around, pulling up her dress. "How? Do you see the royal mark on my hip?" she snarled. "He barely touches you and it shows right away, 'cause you're perfect and I'm... I'm a servant."

Tatiana sucked in a gasp, cupping her hand to her mouth, shocked at her abrupt response. Why didn't she have the mark?

"There has to be an explanation."

Xirene laughed scornfully. "Yeah, right. I should have known you'd say that." A tear slipped down Xirene's cheek. "The fact is I don't deserve him and I should have never allowed…"

Tatiana looked into her dark sorrowful eyes, at the pleading hidden within them. "I don't think the mark should matter."

Xirene kept a stiff upper lip. "I don't make the rules and now *you're* to be my merling's mother."

"I don't like this anymore than you do." Tatiana's stomach burned.

Xirene stumbled over to the chair, clutching her belly, and took a seat. "Azor is not entirely to blame. He made a horrible decision in a time of battle and now he wishes to make things right. We all make sacrifices for the betterment of the kingdom. If you pretend, you'll still get the man you want, and the title, and your freedom."

"I am far from free, Xirene," she said with a glower, gesturing to the bars on her door.

"But you're about to be." She circled her hand in the air. "As queen you'll have whatever you want at your fingertips. Power. Love from your people. Respect of the king."

"But Azor loves you."

"And yet he still kissed you." Xirene laughed. "Don't you see? The truth is I embarrass him, and this is the only way he can truly have what he wants. A beautiful queen by his side, a lover in his bed, and a child to spoil."

Tatiana lowered her head, grieved. Xirene believed she was the root of Azor's unhappiness. That if she looked like Tatiana, Azor would finally truly love her. But Tatiana knew that even with the crown, Azor wouldn't be happy. Something else would consume him later.

Xirene grimaced. "But that doesn't matter anymore. I must trust you, now. Trust you'll treat my merling as your own, My Queen." She dipped into a curtsy.

"No." She pulled on Xirene's arm, wishing for a way to knock sense into Azor and have Xirene take her rightful place as Azor's chosen. "You should be queen."

Her eyes dropped. "Right. A queen with a gimpy fin and no royal mark."

"There's no law that says Azor can't choose you. Your worth isn't based on a mark, or a birth defect. Maybe we could fake it. Tattoo you with a fleur-de-lis. Technically, *you* are the princess and about to give birth to a royal heir. It is I who should be bowing to you and giving you a sponge bath." Tatiana fell to one knee.

"No. Stop." Xirene tugged on her arm. "Please. I don't want anyone to know and it's too late. The kingdom will just think me a harlot, now. I just want my son or daughter to be taken care of. Not live an orphan's life."

Tatiana closed her eyes, feeling the weight of everything, of her lot in life, of the people's prejudice. She was right. The people would never accept the relationship now that he'd kissed Tatiana. Azor had allowed his thirst for revenge to get in the way of his happiness, of love, of peace. Tatiana outstretched her hand to Xirene, clasping her hand around her fingers. They were at each other's mercies, now.

"I have no idea how we're going to pull this off, but I'll adopt your child as my own," Tatiana whispered.

Xirene's shoulders sagged. She nodded with tear-filled eyes, kissing the back of her hand. "Thank you, Princess."

They embraced and the strife between them melted away. "Of course."

"I'll try to find out where Azor is holding Jacob, but in the meantime… I made you a belly."

Tatiana sighed, her heart rocking at the mention of Jacob's name. She remained focused on the iridescent blob in Xirene's hands, marveling at how smooth and natural the outside felt.

"Here, let's try it on." Xirene motioned she turn and fastened the stomach to her waist.

She kneaded at the spongy material in awe. "What is this?"

"I'd rather not tell you, but I thought it would be easier to wear than that stinging thing he brought you."

She smiled, but on the inside wanted to scream. How was she to pull this off now? With Jacob, Xirene and the baby, and the rebels. There were no easy answers

34

Submission

Jacob barely had the strength to flip his tail again, torturing himself with yet another spray of miniscule droplets of water on his parched scales. He leaned over and licked the wet wall, dying of thirst.

"Azor!" he bellowed.

At the silence, he slumped against the chains, helpless. Was this how things would end? He recalled the day when he first laid eyes on Tatiana, through the door leading to the coronation room. So beautiful in her white promising gown, decorated head-to-fin in jewels, blonde hair shining. But she swayed like seaweed, half-lidded on King Phaleon's arm. Anger had sped through him once he figured they'd drugged her. Their attempts to make her compliant had been an abomination, such cruelty.

From what he'd heard about her from Jack during the mission, he couldn't help but fall for her. Her spunk, her fire, her zest for life and an attitude to go with it. Jack had feared the entire time he was away that in his absence his daughter would lose her choice. She abhorred Azor. And though Jacob knew Jack wouldn't allow his famous land-walking twins to be promised this way, waiting for his signal had been torture. He'd gripped his trident, his hood over his head, muscles poised, ready.

He thought he'd be the hero that day. Save her. But in the tumult, Jacob watched in horror, as Azor stole what wasn't his to take.

But now, knowing she'd broken free of Azor, he knew what

he'd dreamt of all the days he'd heard Jack's stories. What he desired most: her free will. That she'd choose him. Want him above all. To rise above and fight the chemicals warring within her body. To be stronger than the kiss.

But now? To be rewarded like this? He'd helped the girl of his dreams free herself from her promise, then die? Allowing Azor to still win? How was that fair? How was that right?

Then he thought of his mother, a beta-mer and a Christian, who never prayed to Poseidon like the rest of the mer. Instead of placing hope on Poseidon, God of the Sea, she said her God had a plan, to trust in Him, to choose to do the right thing and let Him do the rest. Jacob only placated her beliefs, thinking her cross and prayers useless. He believed in a god, yes, but he didn't think that her God really cared; too far away to actually see the gritty details of all the people on the planet; too busy to be bothered. And who would want to beg help from Him? Jacob didn't need God anyway. He created his own fate, he could choose to do what was right on his own, he was a good person, he'd always landed upright… until now. He didn't deserve this. He'd sacrificed everything to protect the woman he loved, to bring healing and justice to his people, only to be abandoned and left to die.

"Why, God?" he called out through cracked lips. "What did I do?"

In exhaustion, his eyes rolled back into his head. He cursed God's plan and his mother's stupid hope. But even when Jax was led away to Bone Island for an unknown crime, she still had faith. And Jax had lived. Why would his brother, who'd only indulged his selfish desires his entire life get to live, and Jacob, faithful and loyal, be punished?

Deep down, in his heart he felt a tug. To let go. To let Him work.

"But I can't," he said softly, his soul still fighting. "I want to live."

Jacob sighed. Chained to the wall, he didn't have a choice. Time would take his life. He had to trust. If it was his time, there was nothing he could do about it. And if not, he'd need to wait.

Tatiana was no longer his charge. Someone else needed to protect her.

"I give her to you, then," he whispered. "Protect and keep her. May your justice be done."

And for the first time, peace filled his broken soul and understanding of what his mother was so passionate about suddenly made sense.

35

Pillow

Tatiana sat on the chair for what seemed like forever, dressed in a cream colored, full-length gown, hair pinned to perfection in beads and jewels. If it weren't for the bulbous stomach protruding across her lap and the pungent smell of fish that soured her nose, she might have looked forward to the part she'd play at the palace.

But in all honestly, all she cared about was seeing Jacob. He'd be her guard again. He'd be by her side every step of the way. Then she could prove to him how strong she really was. She just had to control her excitement and not make it to painfully obvious she'd developed feelings for him. Then, she wished for Nicole. Sweet Nicole who'd lived such a short and tortured life.

At another whiff, she guessed Xirene had used fish innards to make the skin of the rounded appendage. Something from the shark? She tried not to guess further.

"Tatiana?" Prince Azor said before he appeared in the doorway.

She bounced up, looking over his shoulder. "Where's Jacob?"

Azor's eyebrows squished together. "What?"

"You promised I could have Jacob as my bodyguard. Where is he?"

Azor forced out a laugh. "Not before the celebration, Love. No, I'm afraid you're mistaken."

She leveled her gaze, incensed. "You promised if I acted pregnant, you'd free Jacob."

He grabbed her arm, his voice lowering. "Do you take me for a fool? I have to ensure you'll cooperate fully and only then will I return Jacob to you. Besides, he's not ready to take up his old position yet."

"What—?" Tatiana sucked in a tortured breath. "Why?"

"Don't you remember? He's still healing from the rebel attack, but I assure you, since you've been good…"—Azor took her hand and patted it—"he's enjoying his stay like you have. Food and adequate sleep is all a merman needs to recover. After the coronation, he'll be good as new."

"Coronation?"

"Oh… I have spoiled the surprise." Azor pressed his lips into a smirk. "Wouldn't it be something if my father gave me the crown for my eighteenth birthday?"

"But, how? You don't have a child yet."

He caressed her fake belly. "I will soon enough, and I think he's finally seeing reason, considering his health. It's sad his days are truly numbered, but no one wants Mother to lead the kingdom when I'm perfectly able."

"But—"

"Coralade." Azor snapped his fingers. "Come."

Coralade bounced into the room, her curly brunette hair fanned over her shoulders, and stopped abruptly. Her eyes widened when she took in Tatiana's form.

"Assure the Princess that Jacob is just fine and that in his stead Chauncey will make a perfectly fine guard."

"I'll say," Coralade purred.

"What?" Tatiana backed up, bumping into the chair behind her, toppling it over.

Azor clasped onto her arm before she went down, preventing her fall.

"Can't have my princess injuring herself." He righted her, then leaned in, whispering. "Coralade knows nothing. See to it that it stays that way or the deal is off."

Tatiana brushed her hands down her dress, now keenly aware Azor had no intention of fulfilling their deal. She knew the King wasn't on his deathbed as Azor had implied, and after the merling was born and he was crowned king, why would he need to keep her around? Xirene met all his needs, physically and otherwise. She was expendable and knew too much.

Tatiana glowered, trapped. "And if Chauncey so much as looks at me inappropriately, I'll out you to the kingdom, got it?"

Azor yanked his head back, stiffening his stance. "Chauncey?"

Chauncey appeared in the doorway, out of breath. "Yes, Captain."

"You haven't been inappropriate to my mate, have you?"

A surly smile lifted his lips. "Of course not, Captain. Never. Or should I say, my Lord." He gave a curt bow to the Princess.

Tatiana sneered at the both of them.

Azor merely studied his reflection in a nearby mirror. "*My Lord*... that has a nice ring to it, doesn't it."

"Yes, My Lord," Chauncey said while winking at Coralade, who kept giggling.

"Speaking of rings. I have something for you, Love." Azor left the mirror and took something from his pocket.

Tatiana's skin crawled at the term of endearment and she almost jerked away when he clasped her hand.

"A gift for our firstborn," he said and slid the ring onto her finger.

Tatiana studied the gem-encrusted ring covering her naked finger and cringed. Azor hadn't forgotten anything in this sordid ordeal, and now with Xirene and her merling trapped in the sea anemone that was his heart, Tatiana wasn't sure what she'd do. Run? Tell the truth?

Azor ignored her hesitation and propped out his arm. "Come, my Queen. We have a kingdom to lead."

Reluctantly, she accepted, and as they walked down the hallway of her parents' home with Coralade and Chauncey in tow, Tatiana looked for Xirene. She worried for her, so close to her delivery date. But she wasn't anywhere to be seen.

Through the current, Tatiana swam, lugged down by the dress and her wayward stomach. Without both hands holding the contraption firmly at her waist, it would have swiveled around and become a hump on her back.

She searched the horizon, looking for any signs of mer-life, of Jacob. Only guards dressed in green hooded cloaks dotted the sand dunes.

Jacob, she called out telepathically. *Please fight and don't lose hope.* She bit her lip, embarrassed over their last interaction. At the time, she'd been confused, and now, the more her soul distanced itself from Azor's bond, the more her feelings for Jacob surfaced. She did care for him, deeper than her lust over his sexy chest, rippling abs and piercing blue-grey eyes. And her fear that Azor really was depriving him of water, somehow made her chest tighten. Her glare found Azor's smug smile as he stared at the palace. He was finally getting everything he'd ever wanted. But if he hurt Jacob in anyway, she didn't care what she needed to do.

There'd be some serious hell to pay.

Upon approaching the palace, Tatiana stiffened. Could she do this? Pull off the biggest deception ever?

"Are you ready?" Azor asked, gauging her response.

"Of course." She forced a smile. If only she had her butter knife now.

They all swam through the northern porthole. The weight of the dress, along with her task, bore down on her shoulders, stealing her very breath. On the other side of the seaweed privacy curtain, she heard Queen Desiree's voice.

She closed her eyes, her limbs shaking. She wanted Jacob. She needed him by her side. His words came to mind.

You can do this, Tatiana. For Jacob. For the kingdom.

Tatiana wrung out the bottom of her skirt and squished her stomach, before standing. With a smile, she exited the curtain.

"Princess," Queen Desiree said sweetly, arms opened. "When Azor told me, I didn't believe him. And to look at you now… You're so beautiful." She crossed the space and enveloped Tatiana lithely, careful not to get wet, and whispered in her ear. "And you'd kept it a secret. You sneaky girl. I knew you had it in you."

Tatiana shrugged, speechless she'd met the Queen's approval.

Azor's hand met the small of her back, causing her to tremble in revulsion. "I asked her to keep it a surprise, Mother."

He caressed her waistline, rubbing right over the spot where the knot held the stomach in place. Tatiana tried to smile, her lips still frozen in fear they'd discover the truth.

"That it is," the Queen agreed.

"Tatiana?" Girraween's voice bounced off the walls before her energetic body appeared at the archway. "Oh. My. Poseidon. I came as soon as I heard. They told me you're pregnant." She blinked, disbelieving for a beat. "You *are* pregnant!"

"Yes," the Queen said, snagging her daughter's hand and pulling her under her arm like a mommy bird. "She's kept it a secret."

"How did she—?"

"Girraween, please." The Queen squeezed her daughter's arm. "I'm sure Princess Tatiana is exhausted, this being her final days. We should get her to her room."

"Oh, yes. We must." Girraween walked forward to take Tatiana's hand, but rushed her for a hug instead, squishing into her wet clothing and stomach. Unannounced, she kneaded her hand against the mass and hummed. "I can't wait to see your stomach," she whispered. "Does it hurt?"

Azor pulled his sister away and pressed against Tatiana's back at the same time, propelling her forward. "Enough with the questions, Girra. We need to get Tatiana off her feet."

He directed Tatiana into the hall, and he ignored his sister's protruding tongue. The entourage of mers filed on as well. Though Tatiana didn't mind Girraween's curiosity for the most part, things couldn't be left to chance this time.

Together, the bevy of mers filled the hall. Only Girraween's questions about gestation periods and if she could watch the birth were heard from the group. Her mother cut her off, curt in her responses. Water trailed down her legs and pooled onto the floor with each step. She tried to gain Azor's attention, but he ignored her, pressing her on.

When they rounded the corner of the hall, the King's

bedroom door called to her like a beacon and a lump formed in Tatiana's throat. His blue eyes, hot and fiery, singed her memory, making her quiver. She gulped down her discomfort, hoping they'd all just pass by. Surely they weren't going to visit, not today.

And against her greatest wish, the group collectively stopped before his door. Tatiana's pulse pounded, anticipating what the King would do this time, what he'd say. However, instead of knocking to go inside, they merely bowed. Tatiana lowered her head with them.

"Long live the King," Queen Desiree said, low.

Everyone repeated the chant, then straightened.

Inside, she could hear a muffled voice, but they ignored it and marched past. Finally, they rounded the last hall and stopped at her door. Upon first glance inside the room, everything appeared the same, except a small cradle sat in the corner. But once she entered, Tatiana had to bite back her tears. Folded neatly on the bed, along with other items of clothing, was the wisp of fabric she'd worn the first day to the palace, the day Nicole had rescued her with her skirt. She grabbed her mouth and turned away to hide her grief.

"The Princess is moved by your generosity, Mother," Azor said. "Thank you."

"But of course," she said sweetly.

Tatiana straightened and wiped her tears, applying a smile to her lips. Azor moved past her and started barking orders.

"Coralade, your quarters. Chauncey, mind the door. The Princess will not leave her room, unless she's chaperoned by me. She's to eat in here and rest until her time of birthing, understood?"

A cacophony of *yes, sire's* resounded from the mixed group of royals and servants. Tatiana's eye caught Pearleza's. Her blood froze. What was she doing here?

"I've assigned Pearleza to the birth, Azor," the Queen said, motioning for her servant to move forward. In her hands was a black bag. "She's here for Tatiana's exam."

Tatiana gulped, looking to Azor for help.

"Fine," Azor said with a sigh. "Everyone outside."

The group quietly shuffled out and Azor gave Pearleza a stern nod before shutting the door.

"Quick." Pearleza rushed to open her bag. But instead of doctor's tools, she pulled out a rounded pillow and white undergarment. "Put this on."

"What?"

"I said put this on," she whispered between her teeth, harsher.

Tatiana grabbed the items and moved to the changing screen.

"No." She grabbed Tatiana's hand. "We don't have time. Come here."

She lifted Tatiana's soaking gown up and over her head, dropping the wet garment onto the carpet with a thud. Tatiana let out a relieved breath, happy to be free of the weighted dress, then clutched her fake belly, embarrassed. Pearleza ignored her, and pulled the bow, freeing the stomach from her waist.

"Starfish, that was so heavy."

"I'm sure it was." She handed Tatiana the undergarment, and secured a new pillow around her stomach. "Crawl into bed quickly, and whatever you do, never take that off, you hear?"

Tatiana frowned, watching her stuff the old stomach into her bag and zip it up. Then she took the dress and hung it on a rack. After a moment, the drips splashed onto the floor.

"We need to get a bucket or something—"

"Will you get into bed already?" She pushed into Tatiana's side, shoving her toward the bed. "I'll take care of the dress."

Tatiana ran to the bed and ripped back the sheets.

"And act pregnant, for Poseidon's sake," she said with gritted teeth.

"I don't understand. Why are you doing this?" Tatiana asked.

Pearleza marched over and slammed her hands on the bed, putting her face inches from Tatiana's nose. "Because, if Xirene doesn't give birth by Friday, Azor is to use my son as a decoy. And if I don't cooperate, he's as good as dead." Tears filled her angered eyes. "That's why."

Tatiana's body shivered, her eyes watering. A son? She had a son? But how? Her gaze fell to her clenched fists. "Okay."

Pearleza lifted her hands and smoothed the blankets over Tatiana's stomach, then inhaled deeply and smiled. "You can come in," she called sweetly.

The door opened and the group reconvened.

"Mom and merling are doing nicely. I'm pleased," Pearleza announced, clutching her black bag filled with evidence.

"Good," the Queen said, nodding to her.

The whirlwind after, of people and the new royal merling's layette, rushed past her in snippets. All she could think about was Jacob, and how, if she happened to survive, would she escape this nightmare with him undetected? From servant to royal, lies were all the kingdom was built upon, and if she didn't watch it, her body would be smashed between the bricks and mortar as Azor built the next level.

She kept breathing, in and out, holding a perpetual smile. Such deception, such control. Azor had blackmailed everyone to take the throne. She couldn't let him. And, though, Xirene loved him, she had to stop him. She had to do the right thing.

※

Restless, Tatiana rolled over with a moan and arched her sore back. A tummy sleeper, she couldn't wear the stomach any longer and be comfortable. Giggles coming from Coralade's servant quarters woke her up further.

She sat up quickly and her stomach fell off the bed with a thud. A series of shushes followed.

Tatiana held her breath, listening. Silence lingered.

"Princess?" Coralade asked through the door.

Tatiana scrambled to grab the stomach and slide it under her gown before Coralade's head peeked out from the doorway.

"I'm fine," Tatiana said to her. "Just need to use the water closet."

"Oh." Coralade yawned, but watched her with wide-eyes.

Tatiana maneuvered herself off the bed, holding her belly and feigning great effort. She waddled to the bathroom and closed the door. A small chuckle escaped her lips. Her body apparently enjoyed the act and had taken on the roll of being pregnant all on it's own, from her sore bones to her need to pee.

Upon returning, Tatiana stared at Coralade's door and stopped to listen. *Was she alone in her room? Could she and Chauncey be—?* She gasped; firmly aware her perfect opportunity to escape had presented itself. Her heart sprinted as she tiptoed to her door. Upon turning the knob, the handle seized.

"The door's locked," a voice boomed from Coralade's room. *Chauncey.*

Angered at being caught, Tatiana immediately went to Coralade's room and threw open the door. "What is this?"

Coralade squeaked, hiding under the sheets.

"What do you think?" Chauncey said, his voice smooth.

"You need to get out!" Tatiana demanded, stabbing the air with her finger. "You're place is *outside* my door!"

"Or you'll what?" He leaned back onto his elbows. "Tell me. What laws are we breaking?"

Tatiana stuttered. "I—I'm the princess and this is my maid's quarters and if Azor—"

"Azor lets us do this all the time." His lips curled into a grin and he coaxed Coralade out from under the sheets. "Who says we can't have a little fun?"

Revolted and wracked with fury, Tatiana balled her fists. How dare they? Next to her room of all places. Powerless, she peered into both of their smug faces. They weren't going to budge. Tatiana would have to listen to them all night.

Then an idea hit. In an instant, she doubled over and held her fake stomach, groaning. "Ohhhh, I think it's time. Get Azor."

Coralade gasped as Tatiana continued to wail. They waited a beat, unmoving, listening to her groan louder when Chauncey broke out into applause. Coralade quickly joined with a cheer.

"Great acting," he said with a laugh.

Tatiana still held her stomach, horrified. Sure, Chauncey knew, but not Coralade—or at least that's what Azor had said.

"I'm not acting. I need Azor," she said, breathless.

Coralade snickered. "I think you need a lesson about where merlings come from, Tatiana. You have to do far more than just wear a strand of tulle and wiggle your tail."

Tatiana's legs weakened. "How do you know about that?"

"I know everything," she cooed. "And you clearly aren't aware of the peephole in the kitchen."

Tatiana's stomach seized as if Coralade had punched her. Her hands fell to her sides.

Coralade bounced up from the bed, holding a sheet against her body. Her hand darted out, squeezing Tatiana's belly.

"Don't do that." Tatiana moved away.

"What?" Coralade snorted. "I know it's fake."

Behind her, Chauncey's hairy body laid strewn out on the bed. Only a mere pillow covered his groin.

Tatiana looked upward and an embarrassed flush covered her cheeks. "I want you to return to your station outside the door, Chauncey."

"Why?" He laughed, standing up and parading past. "The door's locked. Besides, I think I'd rather sleep out here on this comfy bed." He moved to her bed and sat down, squeaking the springs. "What about you, Cor?"

"I think I would, too. So much bigger than my tiny cot."

"No!" Tatiana said adamantly. "I'm serious. I want you out Chauncey. Both of you!"

Chauncey ignored her and slid on the princess's robe. He inhaled the fabric at the collar. "Smells like roses."

Coralade giggled nervously, almost fearful, and crawled under the covers next to him.

"I mean it!" Tatiana stamped her foot.

Chauncey threw the pillow he'd used to hide his groin and tossed a blanket a Tatiana's feet.

"No, *Princess!* You'll do as I say now. You're to sleep in the servant quarters where you belong, or we'll let it slip that Cor knows the truth about your faked pregnancy. And you'll never see your precious Jacob again."

Tatiana gritted her teeth for a moment, eyeing them evilly. She had no choice, hijacked from her room and her bed. With fiery disdain, she bent down and clutched the blanket, abandoning the pillow, and turned on her heels. Once inside the servant quarters, she slammed the door behind her.

Outside, the giggling resumed along with what sounded like Coralade bouncing on the bed. Tatiana stuffed the lone pillow over her ears and tried to block out the noise, but Chauncey's oyster stench had infused everything, making her gag.

36

Tradition

At the rattle of the lock, Tatiana pried her eyes open.

"Tatiana, this isn't funny. Open the door," Coralade said through the wooden panel. "I'm sorry, okay? We'll let you sleep in your bed tonight. Please."

Tatiana shook her head, her pulse pounding at her temples, and stood, bleary-eyed.

She unlocked the door and Coralade bounded in, a sheet tied around her torso, and pushed past her. She grabbed Chauncey's manskirt off the floor and threw it outside, then pawed inside the dresser drawers. She threw on a top and skirt, and pulled her hair back with a tie.

"Come on," she said, straightening Tatiana's belly, and placing the robe Chauncey had worn over her shoulders. "Get into bed. Azor's coming."

Disgusted by his fishy musk tainting her robe, Tatiana dropped the thing on the floor and took a new robe from the rack just outside the servant quarters. Sheets and pillows lay about the room. She crawled in bed anyway, trying not to think of what they'd done on her sheets. Quick as a flash, Coralade made the bed with Tatiana in it.

She looked apologetic. "I'm sorry. I lost my head last night."

Tatiana blinked at her, a frown on her face. "You're horrible, both of you."

"I know," she said. "I didn't mean to get that carried away—" she huffed. "You won't tell, will you?"

"Tell? You're worried I'm going to tell?" Tatiana laughed. "Do you realize I'm about to be the queen? That I could make your life a living hell?"

Coralade kept silent, her eyes low and her hands trembling at her sides.

Revolted at her behavior, Tatiana was tempted to make her suffer more, but at this point she needed a bargaining chip. "Where's Jacob?"

Coralade pressed her eyes shut and swallowed. "I don't know. I never saw him. But I know he's not at Bone Island. No one is. There is to be a public execution tomorrow at the ceremony. The rebel leader confessed."

Tatiana gasped. "Who?"

"I don't know. That's all the guards are saying."

Tatiana cupped her hand over her mouth and turned away, choking back a sob. Who confessed? Surely not Jacob. Was her father here?

Just then the door to her room opened, the visitor unannounced. "Well, look who's up," Azor said with amusement playing on his face.

Tatiana couldn't withhold her grief. She threw back the covers and stood. "Who are you executing tomorrow?" she demanded.

"What?" Azor's eyes zeroed in on Coralade, who was slowly retreating backward. "What did you tell her?" he said through gritted teeth.

Tatiana interrupted, rushing him and grabbing the front of his breastplate. "There's to be an execution! Tomorrow! At the ceremony!"

"No, no, no," Azor said, pulling her off of him and sliding his hands down her arms. "That's a rumor. I plan to pardon the rebels and end all of this tomorrow. It's time to show our unity with our…" Azor's eyes darted to Coralade, "merling."

"What?" Tatiana wiped away her tears, confused. Did Xirene give birth already? "But someone confessed?"

Azor screwed up his face. "No one confessed."

Tatiana gasped. "You don't have my father?"

"Of course not. Calm down." He landed Coralade a glare. "No one confessed and I've decided I'm done with this war. When I take the throne, I want peace, the song again and better food."

Tatiana's hands fluttered to her neck. Azor could lie to her and say anything. But tomorrow, he could say Jacob had confessed he let the rebels free from jail, that he'd set up the ambush. Azor could kill him right in front of her to torment her. All because she didn't want him, didn't love him.

"Stop." He rested his hands on her shoulders, leaning in. "We made a deal."

She peered into his dark eyes, untrusting. But instead of his typical discontent, happiness and joy radiated from within. Had the merling been born? Had he really intended to go through with the deal and let Jacob go free?

"I've actually come to fetch you for your fitting. You need a dress for the ceremony to match this…" He walked her over to the mirrored closet doors and snapped his fingers. A servant appeared with a box. Azor pulled out the golden gemmed crown and set it on her head.

Eyes still blurry from the tears, she tried to focus on the sparkling object on her head. Confused at his new behavior, she remained straight-faced, unable to pretend she liked it.

"It's heavy."

"Heavy?" Azor trilled his lips. "Underwater it'll feel fine. You know, it's been passed down from generations. You should feel honored."

He quickly removed it and handed it to the servant, who scurried out of the room.

"Come on," he said, taking Tatiana's hand. "You'll feel better after you've had your fitting with my mother."

He entwining his fingers with hers, and led her through the door. They passed Chauncey on the way out and Tatiana bristled, leveling him a glower. His lip curled in a smirk, then he had the audacity to give her a wink.

I'll deal with you later, she thought.

Alone, Tatiana let out the breath she'd been holding. "Did the merling come?"

"No, not yet."

"Is she okay?"

"Uncomfortable, but fine."

"Do you think today is the day?"

"Most definitely."

His arm tightened around hers, but not in a possessive way. More like an excited way. Tatiana momentarily peered at his beaming face. He looked ahead, eyes shinning, just like that of a proud father.

"Tatiana," the Queen said, rising from a padded chair sitting in front of a vanity. "So good to see you."

"Yes, my Queen," she fell into an awkward curtsy.

"Still pregnant, I see." Desiree's hand gently caressed the top of her stomach. "No having that merling on stage tomorrow."

Tatiana chuckled, rubbing her belly protectively. "Oh, let's hope not."

"Come. Let's get you off your feet."

The Queen gestured to an open chair next to hers. Together, they sat as the maids preened and primped their hair. In the mirror, Tatiana spied a pastel rainbow of colorful gowns they were about to try on. Any other time she'd be thrilled to wear such lovely attire, but Tatiana dreaded the coronation ceremony.

Though Azor seemed like a completely different person, happy even, and he'd suggested he wanted to let the rebel war go, and acted as if he'd still planned to fulfill the deal, she knew better. Like a switch, if it suited him, he could easily change his mind. And unless she found a way to make herself indispensible until she could rescue Jacob, they both could lose their lives shortly thereafter.

Pearleza assisted Tatiana behind the dressing curtain, and finally, after ten dress changes, the Queen decided on a beaded blue dress for Tatiana for the coronation. Then the Queen shooed away the maids and pulled Tatiana aside.

"I have something to show you," she said, once they were alone.

With a gulp, Tatiana met the Queen's gaze. Seriousness plied into her from Desiree's soft blue irises.

"As the new queen, I must share with you a tradition we've passed down from generation to generation." From within the vanity, she pulled a small box with a golden fleur-de-lis on the cover. Inside, two metal fleur-de-lis stamps lay, one an inch in length and the other three inches, next to a vial of brown liquid.

Tatiana's hand flew to her neckline. "What is this?"

"I think you know."

She blinked, unbelieving, staring at the two intricate stamps. "The fleur-de-lis mark doesn't actually appear, does it?"

A giggle sprung from the Queen's lips as she removed the larger stamp. "It's a tradition shared only among queens from a tale that dates back to as long as our people have swum these waters, starting with late Queen Esmernda. She had an unsightly birthmark on her hip and tried everything in an attempt to cover it. Her sister, though, had visited land and seduced a man who inked skin with art. He took Esmernda's blemish and crafted a wonderful fleur-de-lis using this—" She lifted the tool. "And then, magically, her daughter and every royal daughter and queen thereafter has had one since."

She brushed the end lightly, reminiscent almost. "To think if this could talk, the stories it would tell." She blinked, pausing for a moment. "So… what you do is heat this end, then pour the liquid on first, then brand the skin to infuse the ink."

Tatiana gasped, remembering the night she'd dreamt of stinging bees prior to her mark showing up.

"Oh, it doesn't really hurt. I mean, you don't remember, right?" The Queen touched Tatiana's hand. "And since we heal so quickly, the skin locks the color inside. The larger one is for adults and the smaller, for merlings."

"But why? I mean… everyone thinks the mark appears after the promise or you're born of royal blood." Tatiana's chest heaved, thinking of Xirene. She hadn't been flawed after all.

"Exactly," Queen Desiree said with a wink. "Marks appear only on those who are royal and the others cannot claim otherwise."

Tatiana let out the breath she'd been holding, her mind still on Xirene. "Wow, so you…"

"I tattooed you and all my daughters. And if you have a girl, we'll tattoo her together." She leaned forward. "That's why I've insisted, not only myself, but Pearleza to be your midwife."

Tatiana held her hand over her mouth, not only horrified they'd purposefully burn a merling, but that Pearleza knew, too. And how were they going to fake the delivery if the Queen insisted she be present.

The Queen pressed her hand on Tatiana's leg, sudden and urgent. "You'll be forced, in your lifetime, to make tough decisions, Tatiana. Things you might regret, but just know… you must do everything in your power to keep the ways of our people going and keep its secrets. The mers depend on it, like life. Otherwise, we'll be bound to chaos, and if we're found out by humans, our punishment will be extinction."

Tatiana's eyes grew. She shook her head and mouthed a simple "yes," finding her voice a bit too late. "Yes, my Queen," *I know all too well the secrets I must keep.*

Queen Desiree sucked in a deep breath, a peaceful smile replaced her concern. "Good. My son loves you and his people. He's been groomed for this day his entire life. And it's a shame what's happened to Phaleon. But, by passing the crown early, he'll live to see his grand-merlings. Most kings—" she dragged her teeth over her bottom lip, "—*expire* before the crown is passed. But since Phaleon cannot lead in his condition, he's wisely chosen a permanent sabbatical instead. And Azor's taken up his duties already, so it seems fitting to give him the crown, too."

Tatiana wanted to ask if her son was so honorable, why he was spreading rumors the King was dying? Or if she's even been out of the palace walls lately? Audience should have clued her in that Azor hadn't lead well at all. His desire for revenge had far outstretched his so-called love for his people. He only loved himself, hence his desire to force her to look pregnant and keep his real mate in the shadows.

Tatiana steeled herself. "What do you mean by expire?"

Desiree's eyes turned hard again. "Princes have been known to *help* their fathers onto the afterlife for the crown, Tatiana."

Tatiana's cupped her hand to her lips, withholding a gasp. The King had predicted he'd die, and she thought him crazy to believe that. But hearing the story, she realized he hadn't meant his health would take his life, but his own son. Did Azor even know his dad was going to give him the crown early? Azor had merely bragged he'd make the tough decisions, that his father's days were numbered. Her heart pounded, hoping the Queen hadn't waited to tell Azor their plans, wanting to surprise him instead on his birthday.

Tatiana grasped her hand, determined to help her see reason, when Queen Desiree clutched her chest and stood. The kit tumbled off her lap and to the floor. With a crack, the vial split, oozing brown ink onto the carpet.

"No!" she screamed, kicking off her beaded flats and running for the door with her new gown on.

"My Queen?" Tatiana reached for her, but Pearleza and her

other maids had flung open the door and were at her side.

"No! NO!" Desiree's voice careened through the halls. She pitched the girls off and ran from them.

Tatiana followed, running behind them when Pearleza took her hand and forced her to slow down. "Act pregnant, Princess," she warned.

"Phaleon!" Desiree bellowed. "Phaleon!"

Just beyond her, Azor walked out of King Phaleon's door. Blanchard leaned against the wall, watching on with a curious white bundle in his arms. Azor ran to his mother. Blood covered his hands.

"Mother, I tried to stop him," he said, anguished, arms outstretched.

She collapsed into him, sobbing. "Please, no! Tell me you didn't."

"Mother, I'd wanted to see if he'd attend tomorrow, but I was too late. He said he couldn't bear to look upon himself anymore." He wrapped his arms around his mother's sobbing frame, his eyes, though, were on Pearleza. He nodded to her and Tatiana stopped walking, a sickening dread washing over her.

Pearleza squeezed her hand and whispered. "It's time."

Tatiana couldn't listen, or comprehend what she meant. She stared at Azor, then to the Queen's convulsing form, then to the tiny hand reaching up from the bundle in Blanchard's arm.

"Go into labor, now, Princess," Pearleza prodded firmer.

Tatiana watched Blanchard turn and walk away with the bundle—a baby. The horrible sounds of the Queen's grieving made her cringe. Did Azor actually say he'd tried to stop the King? Implied he'd committed suicide? Nausea hit when a firm punch landed into Tatiana's side and she bellowed, crumbling over. Pearleza crouched around her, pouring something in her hand. Water splashed at their feet.

"It's time," Pearleza called out. "The Princess is in labor."

Maids surrounded them, escorting her past Azor and the Queen as Desiree fought to gain access to King Phaleon's room. Through the doorway, he lay strewn, maimed body exposed, a dagger in his chest. Desiree pressed past and fell to Phaleon's bedside.

"Why, Phaleon?" she sobbed. "Why?"

Tatiana turned away, tears pouring down her cheeks.

"Do your contractions hurt?" Pearleza asked, digging her nail into her palm.

Tatiana grunted and tried to pull her hand away. Pearleza held on tighter. "I've got you. Breathe through the pain. Don't worry."

Tatiana mumbled something, her voice stolen from her lips. If Azor killed his own father, just to ensure he'd get the crown, he was capable of doing anything for his own gain. Her chest constricted, her heart about to burst. She couldn't do this, couldn't continue the charade.

In Tatiana's room, Pearleza took over, immediately clearing everyone out. Blanchard appeared from hiding in Coralade's quarters and handed Pearleza the merling.

"Thank you, I've got it handled," she said before shooing him out the door.

Once alone, Pearleza gave Tatiana the baby. The small bundle looked up, dark eyes and lashes, his lips smiling. And an adorable shock of black hair puffed at his crown. A little Azor.

"Wail," Pearleza instructed, her voice hard. "You're supposed to be in labor."

Tatiana groaned, but kept getting distracted by the adorable bundle in her arms, cooing at her. She already saw herself bonding to the child, teaching him to swim, to walk, to run.

"And if anyone asks why you birthed in human form, tell them you didn't have time to get to water."

"Wha—?" Tatiana momentarily tore her eyes away from the boy as Pearleza stripped the bed, then nicked her finger with a knife and spread it on the sheets.

"It hurts more the human way." She wet her hands in the finger bowl and touched Tatiana's hair and brow. "Again."

Tatiana blinked, then remembered her task and groaned.

"Louder," Pearleza said through her teeth.

She pressed her voice harder, startling the baby. "Sorry, little one," she said quickly, offering her finger, which the merling suckled.

Pearleza took the baby from Tatiana's arms, and he started to cry.

Tatiana pouted, holding out her arms. "I want to hold him."

"Sh-h-h," she patted the boy's bottom and moved to a nearby chair. Lifting her top, she placed the child to her breast.

Tatiana gasped as the child stopped whimpering and nursed, hungrily. "I'll give him back in a minute. He's hungry and I have no clue where Xirene is. Besides, you need to get into your nightgown and into bed."

Tatiana watched on with awe before she obeyed.

Pearleza closed her eyes and leaned her head back with a sigh.

"What I do for this kingdom."

"Do *I* have milk?" Tatiana asked, curious.

"No," she said simply. "I have milk because I'm still nursing my son, but there are herbs in my bag. If you take them, you'll produce milk if you want."

She jumped out of bed, and found the herbs. Grimacing, she ate one of the bitter weeds and put extra in her pocket for later.

"How old is your son?"

Pearleza's face lightened. "Ike is only a few weeks old."

"How—?" Tatiana blanched, catching herself for asking such a stupid question.

Pearleza laughed and shook her head. She removed her glove, careful not to disturb the baby, and showed Tatiana her tattoo. "I'm not one to break the law, but we couldn't help it. Love is a very powerful thing, and since Ike's father is a widower, it's not like anyone would find out."

Tatiana blinked, stunned for a moment, before crawling back into bed.

Pearleza looked at the babe and broke into a smile. "When Queen Desiree found out after my pregnancy, she turned her head to it, because I've been a good servant and kept many of her secrets. And since I'm to serve you now," she gestured to the child, "you must know the truth. And it's difficult to remain celibate, Milady. Especially when there's nothing wrong with your feelings or your parts."

"I can imagine," Tatiana mumbled, suddenly thinking about Jacob.

"So…" Pearleza's head turned to the door, listening to the small murmurs outside. "You might want to do one final labor cry."

They both looked at the sleeping babe in Pearleza's arms and sighed, deciding against it. Reluctantly, she finally handed the boy to Tatiana.

"He is sweet," Pearleza said, sniffing his head and kissing his brow, "for now."

Tatiana cringed, remembering the horror they'd just experienced with Azor. If he turned out anything like his father, Poseidon help them all.

Pearleza took one last hard look at Tatiana. "Are you ready for this?"

Tatiana sucked in a breath and held the bundle tighter, reminding herself that this wasn't her son; that she was merely there to play a part. She'd care for the boy today, but she couldn't get attached. Her plans were to escape with Jacob, not get caught up in a mess too big for her to fix. Why had she eaten the blasted weed?

Pearleza replaced her glove and touched Tatiana's arm. "It's an honor to serve you, my Queen," she said with a bow.

At the title, something pinched inside Tatiana's conscience, and her spine stiffened. Although she didn't hold Azor's promise anymore, she held the coveted fleur-de-lis along with the responsibility. And with Azor acting irrationally, she couldn't run away to leave the kingdom to his wrath. So many innocent mers needed her help—the rebels, the servants, the maimed and the orphaned, the babe and his mother. They were all counting on her. They needed freedom, not only to love whom they wanted, but freedom from tyranny, and at the ceremony, they were going to get it, one way or another.

"Yes," she said with a heavy breath. "I'm ready."

37

Homecoming

The briny water pulled in and out of Ashlyn's gills, her heart pounding. She gripped Fin's hand tighter as the light at the end of the tunnel from Tahoe grew larger. She'd finally see Fin's underwater world. Her kingdom. Natatoria.

She'd heard so much about the city, all good things in the past. Right before leaving her home in Tahoe, Fin explained the possibility of a lot of crap that could go wrong, of problems because the Prince stole Tatiana's kiss, of a war. She'd already experienced some of it when his uncle Alaster forced himself on her and kissed her, but she'd never let Fin go to Natatoria without her. Their mission was clear: rescue her best friend from the clutches of the Prince. Problem was, from what Fin had said happened before, under the power of the promise kiss, Tatchi wouldn't be compliant.

With her foreign appendage propelling her along to the unknown, she felt lost. And her scales, something new and tingly all over her body, wouldn't stop quivering in excitement and fear.

"Is that it?" she asked, in English.

"Yes," Fin said softly, patting her hand.

"Uh," Jax said from ahead of them. "Sorry, guys. I—I kinda forgot to mention, things are a little different."

"What do you mean *different*?" Galadriel asked, her voice terse.

Jax filled everyone in on what had happened since they'd been in Natatoria last. From the rebel attack, to the shark eating the King's fin, to Prince Azor running everything with the help of his Dradux goon squad.

Galadriel halted, creating a bottleneck in the tunnel for Ash and Fin, Fin's cousin Colin, and his uncle Alaster, who was bound at the wrists by Ferdinand, the mute. "And you didn't think to tell us to bring weapons?"

Jax turned to her, his voice cracking. "I thought we'd get them in Natatoria."

Galadriel snorted nervously. "And where exactly will we find them? Azor's compound?"

Alaster's hoarse laughter filtered through the water behind them all. "Fools. You have no idea what you're up against."

"Silence," Galadriel demanded, and Ferdinand yanked Alaster's tied wrists. She moved her tail, coming inches from Jax's face. "I should have been informed of this a lot sooner than now."

Jax's mouth floundered, opening and closing. "I—I wanted to. I—I was just so happy to see you again. It kinda slipped my mind."

She closed her eyes a beat, then turned to Fin with a frown. "Is there anything at the house we can use?"

Fin laughed, incredulous. "A few spears, but they're smoldering in the ashes in the basement."

Galadriel huffed and pushed her hair away from her face. "I can already see running this kingdom is going to be difficult. Don't keep stuff like this from me, Jax, please—"

"I'm sorry, Princess." Jax reached for her and took her hand.

She closed her eyes again, softening to him. "Well it's not like

I'm deft at using a sword or anything. But I do have one heck of a siren. Besides, Darrellon and his two goons are scared of me anyway; so is my brother."

Jax pulled Galadriel close, hugging her.

"Darrellon is dead," Colin said quickly while his pectoral fins flared. "Chauncey is in charge now… and there are more than just two Dradux guards."

She pushed Jax away, her eyes lit. "How many are there?"

Colin sighed. "Pretty much all of the true-blooded mermen who chose the King's side over Jack's were inducted."

Fin's face fell. "Azor drafted all the mermen?"

"Yeah." Colin grimaced. "He blackmailed them after they saw what he did to the rebel families. Kind of like, be loyal to me or else. The rebels are awaiting punishment in the square."

Alaster's laughter returned until a loud "oof" filled the air, silencing him. Everyone turned to see Ferdinand looking off to the side while Alaster leaned awkwardly over.

"Call him off, will ya?" he begged, his voice pinched.

Galadriel chucked, shaking her head. "Thanks, Ferd."

A slight smile played on Ferdinand's lips.

Fin's hands wove their way around Ash's middle, pulling her close. "Don't worry about all of this," he said in her ear. "I'll never let anything happen to you."

Her heart thumped anyway. The Dradux guards sounded fierce, and without weapons, she had the impression they were sitting ducks.

"Come on. Let's face the music," Galadriel said, leading the charge.

Ash fluttered her tail, propelling herself out of the cave into—

beautiful didn't do the vast land and palace in the distance justice, with its vibrant spires and tiny lights in the windows. Palatial. Heavenly. And inside, her spirit felt whole. Home.

Next to her, though, Fin cussed. "This isn't the place I wanted you to see, Ash. This is—"

"Where's the song?" Exasperated, Galadriel's hands flew upward into the current, then fell down, clutching her head.

Once Alaster and Ferdinand cleared the cave, Fin whipped his tail and grabbed his Uncle by the throat. "What did the King do? Why is it like this?"

Alaster's face turned red, his beady eyes bugging out. "Your father is to blame."

"My father did nothing. He hasn't even been here."

"Stop it," Colin interrupted, pulling Fin off his father's neck. "He may be a son of a bass, but he didn't do this. Azor did and we have to stop him."

"Azor," Fin hissed through gritted teeth. He pressed his hands against his knuckles, cracking them. "I can't wait to see him."

"What's that stink?" Ash asked. "It's like rotten oyst—"

A bag slipped over Ash's head and she thrashed about as someone's hulking grip surrounded her middle, trapping her arms. A pinch sent fire racing up her scales. She cried out unsuccessfully, unable to make any sound with the bag wrapped around her gills.

"Get the other girl," a gruff voice said.

Grunts and groans punctuated the air when an earsplitting scream flooded the water. Instantly her hands were freed. She untied the sack at her throat, and removed the bag, shrieking a blasting noise herself. Fin, Jax, Alaster, Colin, and four mermen dressed in green cloaks were all doubled over, holding their ears and moaning. Though the sound was hardly tolerable to her, the mermen all seemed pained over the noise coming from Ferdinand's mouth.

Galadriel freed herself as well and removed the cloak from the first guard.

"Quick," she said. "Get their clothing and their weapons."

Ash flexed her weighted appendage, wincing in pain, and somehow managed to maneuver herself over. She removed the cloaks from the two nearest thugs without any struggle from them.

Ferd's eardrum-shattering screech continued, loud and long. Galadriel put on one cloak and propelled herself forward with the spears under her arm, dragging Jax behind her. She motioned Ash to do the same. "Come on!"

She took Fin's and Colin's hands, towing them slowly behind Galadriel with her gimpy fin.

"I can't," she whimpered, feeling herself losing strength.

But as they distanced themselves from Ferd, Fin and Colin were able to swim alongside her. Colin pulled his hand away.

"I can't leave my dad."

"But Colin," Ash said, nervous. "You can't go back there, and what about what your dad did to you…?"

"I'll be fine. Go ahead. I—I'll distract them."

Fin shrugged and took over, taking the weapons and pulling Ash with him. "Let him go," he said.

Together they disappeared over the ridge.

38

Instincts

At a wail, Tatiana's eyes popped opened and a weird tingle passed over her breasts. Without a thought, she jumped out of bed and ran to the cradle, scooping up the child.

"There, there, baby," she said, rocking him. "I'm here. Don't cry."

She looked around for Pearleza, whom she had more affectionately nicknamed Pearl. Where was she?

"What's that racket?" Coralade peeked her head out of the servant's quarters.

"The baby—I need Pearl."

"He's hungry, feed him," Coralade grumbled.

"I know, but I just need help!" At her yelling, the baby wailed louder.

Coralade groaned and threw on her robe. She banged on the locked door and once Chauncey answered, she marched forward without a word.

Desperate, Tatiana offered her finger, which the boy accepted, sucking hard, but that only lasted a second. He let out another frustrated cry. Her breasts ached with each howl and she was confused why, until two wet circles soaked the front of her nightgown. Did she have milk already?

With shaking arms, she sat on the nearby chair and hitched up her gown. Holding the baby's mouth to her bare breast, she was unsure what to do. Rooting around with his nose, the babe nuzzled against her, and clamped onto her.

She yelped, feeling a pinch and an ache, then held her breath, watching the merling suck in deep gulps. Pearl had made this all look so easy, relaxing even. She winced, imagining he'd take her nipple right off. *How long does this last?* The merling, though, breathed between swallows, completely content. She remained tensed, her arms aching, as she waited for him to release when the door opened.

Tatiana snapped her head up. "Pearl?"

"No," Azor said, "it's me. I came as soon—"

He stopped and gaped, blinking at her, at the merling.

Tatiana pushed the gown over her bare legs, hiding herself from his curious gaze.

"How are you—?" he started, then stopped.

She didn't want to tell him she'd taken Pearl's secret herbs. She wanted him to need her, to think her valuable in this twisted situation until she figured out a solution. He had to trust her.

"My body must have thought I really was pregnant," she said softly.

He moved closer, caressing her lovingly with his eyes. A few days ago she would have killed for him to look at her that way, but now... a shiver crossed her skin. Why was he watching her like that? He held out a small bladder to her, dazed.

"Pearleza gave me this earlier... but it appears you have things handled."

"Guess so." She gazed down at the baby, who pulled away from her and drifted off to sleep. A mustache of milk covered his sweet lips. Quickly, she pulled down her gown to hide herself from Azor's roving eyes.

"I'll say," he mumbled. A look covered his face,—joy? She

couldn't be sure.

"Where's Xirene? I thought she'd be here by now."

"Oh, she's…" Azor's eyes glazed over for a beat. "Recovering. She'll take over after the coronation, tomorrow."

At the words, Tatiana's heart sunk. Reality. The brief bubble of bliss the merling gave popped. Things were about to get complicated and very ugly. Uglier than they'd already been. She had to remember the merling wasn't hers. "And Jacob? Will he be joining me as well?"

Azor stiffened, his face stern. Tatiana would have guessed he was jealous if she didn't know better. "Afterward, yes."

She bit her lip, gauging whether or not he told the truth. She'd cooperated, and then some, going so far as to nurse the child. But then everything rushed in. Queen Desiree's grief, the King lying impaled on the bed. She didn't believe Azor when he'd said the King committed suicide, not after what Desiree said about past princes. He'd murdered his father for the crown, and he could do the same to her and take the baby.

Instinctively, she pulled the babe close to her body. "I think you should go."

He furrowed his brow, hurt almost. "Yes. Tomorrow is a big day, my Queen. Rest." He waffled in which direction to move, either to her side or the door. He stooped over her, petting the boy's hair. But he wasn't looking at the merling. He stared at Tatiana's lips. "I want you to look your best for the coronation, Lovel—" He stopped himself, then stepped away. "Good night, Tatiana."

Only after she heard the door lock did she exhale a relieved breath.

The morning came with a bustle of activity: hair, makeup, and nails for the big event. Tatiana tried to remain composed, twisting her hands and pressing against her flat stomach as each second ticked on. Azor, a ticking time bomb, would get his final wish—the throne. She'd hoped he wouldn't do anything rash in front of his people, but then with his past behavior, she wasn't sure. What more would he want from her afterward? She ached at the thought of leaving the merling forever. She'd bonded with him. She'd miss him.

"You've recovered so quickly, Princess," one of the mer matrons said, breaking her spiraling thoughts. "And to have a human birth, I'm impressed."

Tatiana smiled appreciatively.

"We are lucky having mer blood," another said. "I've heard human women carry their young for practically a year, then afterward, they're riddled with stretch marks and fat. Can you believe it?"

"If I had to carry my thirteen around for thirteen years, I'd tell Gunderon to keep his clasper far away from me. Oye vey!" Mama Ondia, the eldest of the mer matrons in the colony, said with a chuckle.

Tatiana laughed, too. She'd never known a human who'd given birth, but the length of gestation sounded dreadful. Weeks of pregnancy she could handle, but the lack of sleep? Just being awakened once during the night was difficult enough, not to mention her nipples felt rubbed raw with sandpaper and her boobs so full, like they were about to explode. But everything seemed worth it for the sweet nameless boy.

Pearl sat close, cooing at the merling wrapped in her arms.

"What's his name?" Mama Ondia asked, admiring on.

Pearl startled, jostling the babe awake. In response to his cry, Tatiana's breasts began to leak, soiling her robe.

"Oh, um." Tatiana bit her lip, taking him from Pearl's hands. "Azor—we haven't chosen yet, but I do like Landon."

"Hmmm," Mama said, "that's different. Sounds human."

"Oh, really? I'm not sure," she chucked nervously. "I'd like a moment to feed the baby, though," Tatiana said to the women. They all cleared, but Pearl. "Its okay, Pearl. I've got this."

Pearl's hands kneaded together, worry taut on her face.

"I promise." Tatiana laughed. "I did it last night perfectly fine."

"Okay," she said with a quick bow. "I'll be back."

Alone, Tatiana blew out a trapped breath and bit her lip, sucking air through her teeth once Landon latched on. Things felt a little easier this time. Then reality hit. She had no control over his name, his life, or anything. What was she doing still pretending? Landon belonged to Xirene. She needed to find Jacob and the others, and escape from Natatoria. She bit her lip. Could she do it now? Was Chauncey even guarding her door?

She glanced at the babe again and her heart softened. She cared for him too much to just leave.

"Landon, I promise to figure out a way around this."

The baby smiled up at her, blinking his long dark lashes.

"Tatiana?" The door opened a crack.

"I'd like to be alone—"

"It's me," Lily, Badger's niece, whispered. She rushed inside and closed the door. "I need to talk to you."

Tatiana blinked at her *almost* sister-in-mer's form. A small bump protruded at her bellybutton. "Are you pregnant?"

Lily yanked her head backward, eyes zeroing in on Landon. "You're one to judge." Lily flashed her tattooed finger. "Yes, I am. After Fin *left me* at the alter, Kiernan asked for my hand. And we were promised before we *did it,* if you're wondering."

Tatiana sucked in her gasp, as small snippets of the promising ceremony came to mind. Hardly lucid, she barely recalled what they'd talked about when she'd gotten ready with Lily, or hardly anything.

Lily's glare turned frosty. "What I don't get is if you hated Prince Azor so much, why would you bed him before your ceremony?"

Tatiana did a double take. "What?"

Lily laughed cynically. "You had us all fooled."

Tatiana peered down at the child, wanting to protect him. No one had made any snide remarks about his sudden appearance as of yet. Was the gossip mill talking? Would they think him illegitimate his whole life?

"—and now Jacob? What do you think you're doing?"

Jacob. What was she insinuating and how did she know anything about him?

"Now wait a minute." Tatiana's shoulders straightened. "Look who's judging whom—"

"I don't know what twisted line you've got these mermen dangling on, but people are in danger. You need to pick the side loyal to your father—to Jack."

"I am loyal to my father," she defended.

Lily closed her eyes, her face marred with anger. "Well, you could have fooled me. Uncle Badger and the others have been stuck in pillories all week awaiting today's sentencing while you're here…"—she waved her hand around the room, finishing at Tatiana's perfectly coiffed hair—"playing dress-up. You cannot let Azor do what I think he's going to do."

Tatiana's mouth gaped. "Pillories? He said he was going to pardon them."

A caustic laugh escaped from her lips. "And you believe him? I thought you were smarter than that. But after seeing this—" She gestured to the child. "Does Jacob even know? Did you tell him?"

Tatiana bit her tongue. What had the others been saying about her and Jacob for Lily to come at her like this? Did they think she kissed him? Tatiana pressed her eyelids shut. Even though Lily had gotten her facts wrong, too many lives were at stake at this point, including Landon's, for her to confess the truth. "I'm not stringing anyone along, and I have it under control."

Lily raised a brow, then just laughed, shaking her head. "Control? Right."

"Is Jacob with Badger?" Tatiana asked.

Lily looked away, disgusted. "No. I don't know where he is. Rumor has it they've locked up the rebel mer matrons in the dungeon and confiscated all the ink, so they can't come in a sirening mob and rescue the men. People are terrified and hungry, and there's no end to the Dradux torture." She looked away, as if ashamed of Tatiana's ignorance.

Tatiana lifted her chin, her chest constricting. "Thank you for telling me. I'll do my best."

Her eyes fell into slits. "Your best?" She huffed and slammed her hands to her sides. "Then why are you still sitting here? You clearly don't care you're promised to the enemy." With a quivering lip, she said, "I can't believe you're cowering under Azor's tyranny. I had faith in you."

With tears falling down her cheeks, she ran from the room.

"No, Lily. You don't understand."

She brushed past Pearl as she opened the door.

"What was that about?" Pearl asked, confused. "Wait, miss. You dropped something."

Pearl disappeared after Lily. Tatiana clutched the baby, trying to withhold her tears when something wet sopped her hand. The liquid came from Landon's bum.

She tsked, never having changed his diaper before. Taking Landon to the table, she unswaddled him and looked for a new diaper. But once she uncovered him, she discovered Landon wasn't a boy at all. He was a girl.

"Mother of pearl," she said, breathlessly.

39

Ruby Slippers

Ash wriggled her toes and stared at an oil painting of a ship, the *Sea Queen*, hanging on the wall over a fake fireplace. Underneath on a mantle stood a golden trophy and a spyglass, all human things. Pipe smoke lingered in the air along with garlic. *Garlic?* Being fish, the whole concept of air-filled homes stumped her. Why did they act so human? Her eyes darted once again to the bloodied sheets on the couch. She tried not to think about who'd lain there not so long ago.

"What's going on, Jax?" Fin yelled. "It's like a ghost town. There's no song! Hardly any sunlight! And who were those freaks that just jumped us?"

Jax had his back turned to Fin as he rummaged in the closet, pulling out black robes and broken oars. "There's got to be some face paint in here somewhere."

"Are you kidding me?" he barked, slamming the flat end of the scythe against the brick floor. "How are you and I going to fight those *things*?"

Galadriel pulled Ash aside. "Where'd Colin go?"

Ash frowned. "He stayed behind."

"Really?" She blew out a breath. "And Ferd?"

Ash shrugged. "Don't know."

"Gah," she grumbled. "This is crazy. Stop, Jax. Even if we do find something, it's useless. What are the four of us going to do?" She threw down the wet Dradux cloaks.

"I won't leave without Tatch. Colin said the rebels were all in the square. We just need to sneak up, pretend to be the guards and set them free," Fin said. "Badger should be there. He'll know what to do."

The scene in the Wizard of Oz where the Lion, the Tin Man, and the Scarecrow snuck into the castle dressed as guards to free Dorothy came to Ash's mind. She'd crossed into the Emerald City, with strange new creatures, both scary and exotic. But what was next in this crazy world? Flying monkeys? Should she click her heels and wish for home?

"Where do you think Tatiana is?" Ash asked.

"Probably the palace." Galadriel put hands on her hips, her eyes zipping around the room as if looking for answers.

The deep vibration of a horn penetrated the sea; everyone's spines stiffened.

"What was that?" Ash looked to Galadriel.

Galadriel's face fell. "It's the signal for everyone to gather at the square. There's to be an announcement." She brought her fist to her lips and stared at the Dradux cloaks. "I think you're right Fin. We can blend in. Then once we know what we're up against, we'll form a plan."

Jax and Fin hummed in agreement and each took a weapon and a cloak, but Ash's stomach turned aerial stunts. How was she to blend in when she didn't even know the first thing about being a mermaid? Let along holding the weapon of choice for the Grimm Reaper?

40

Baby Blue

At the signal horn, Tatiana stood from her vanity, dressed and ready to go. Her eyes met Pearl's who handed Tatiana the sleeping merling girl, dressed in a long gown. "I'll be with you the entire time, my Queen," she said before she bowed. "Anything you need, just ask."

Tatiana nodded, unable to catch her breath, her heart pounding. In a daze, she walked forward and moved into the hall. At once, the guards surrounded her and escorted her to the front of the palace. The entire walk, the soft shush of her beaded gown hitting her bare legs echoed against the stark walls. Her coronation day and she still had no idea where Azor held Jacob.

The group stopped before a porthole leading to the staged area outside in the square. Through the windows Tatiana could see the dais decorated with pillars and sprays of anemones and coral. Oberon, officiator of the ceremony, stood next to three vacant thrones. To his right, the boys' choir sang the anthem while the women and children below huddled together, frightened. Rebels were bound in pillories like Lily had said, flanked in long rows on either side of the square.

The women watched on in horror and hid their children's eyes while Dradux guards draped sacks over the rebels' faces. As far as Tatiana could see, the Dradux hovered menacingly in the current with their scythes crossed over their bodies, uninviting green hoods over their heads.

The last to be covered was Badger. Tatiana gasped, covering

her lips with her fingers, her limbs shaking. Was Lily right? This didn't look like a pardon. More like a massacre. What did Azor have planned?

"Ready?" Azor said behind her, startling her.

"Azor." She forced a pleasant expression, dropping her hand. "Yes."

He smiled, eyes still shining. "What? No happy birthday?"

"Oh, right. Happy Birthday." She curtsied.

He laughed and proffered his arm. "You know you'll have to kiss me to make this believable," he whispered while escorting her to the porthole.

"I know," she said, revolted at the thought of his lips touching hers.

With a quick plunge underwater, the baby awoke. Under her gown, a tiny baby-blue tail flipped out of the blanket and wiggled. Tatiana quickly wrapped her fin up and out of view, looking to see if anyone saw.

"Ladies and mermen, welcome to this glorious occasion. I give you Queen Desiree, Prince Azor, Princess Tatiana, and the newest Prince, Treviathan Jacques," Oberon bellowed.

Tatiana's head whipped to Azor. Jacques was her father's formal name.

Azor leaned in. "Appropriate, don't you think?"

She shuddered, keeping a firm hold on the rambunctious merling. Of course, not having to change the babe, she'd assumed the merling to be a boy. But how could that have slipped by Azor? He would have found out the instant he took her underwater when her blue tail thrashed around anxious to swim. But most important, if she didn't keep a firm hold on the child, she'd flit away and all would see.

※

Staring at the dais, Ash pulled a ragged breath of water through her tensed gills at the announcement of names. The Prince's name struck her odd. Did the Queen just have a baby? Another son?

She squinted hard, staring out from under the stinking green hood, while the people cheered flatly around her. A beautiful woman with white-blond hair floated in first and took her seat, stealing Ash's breath. In her soul, she felt the instant connection and knew instinctively who she was—her mother.

Azor appeared next, smug with his jet-black hair and dark, sinister eyes. Then Tatchi swam in with a gorgeous pink, purple and blue tail, and Ash's hand flew to her mouth, one in recognition of her best friend and another for the small bundle in her arms.

The guards around them broke into cheers, smashing their weapons together.

Ash jumped. "Holy crawfish!"

Fin moved in closer, taking her hand, but his face portrayed horror mixed with confusion. He looked to Galadriel and mouthed, "What in Hades—?"

Galadriel shook her head, just as stunned. "Maybe she did like him," she whispered.

"No," Fin said adamantly. "She hated him up until the moment he kissed her. And, it's not possible. We left only two weeks ago. Unless…" His nostrils flared. "If he even so much as touched my sister improperly—"

Touched her? Didn't like him? Were they implying the baby belonged to… not Tatchi?

"Hold up," Jax interrupted quietly, grabbing Fin's wrist. "Rumor was they weren't even, you know, *together*, so I'd say no… I know my brother wouldn't have fallen for her otherwise."

"What?" Fin turned to Jax, his eyebrows pressed together. "How do you know this?"

"I was in the dungeon with the rebels, man. We talk." His eyes canvassed the line of shackled hooded men. "Jacob's not with the Princess, though, which is odd."

"Jacob?" Fin asked.

"My brother is Tatiana's bodyguard," Jax corrected.

Ash's eyes snapped to the front when Azor began to speak.

"Welcome all," Azor started. "I'm glad you've joined us. Though today is to be a happy time with the announcement, my birthday, and my son, Treviathan…"

Murmurs and gasps came from everyone in the group. *"Son? How could he have a son? They've only been promised for two weeks. How improper."*

"—It is also a sad one to have to inform you that my father has indeed passed."

"W-what?" Galadriel clutched her neckline, gasping. "Nooooo… He didn't!"

At the Queen's wail, Ash gripped Galadriel's arm, trying to withhold her own sorrow. She responded and embraced her. She knew the King to be a cruel man, chopping off Galadriel's fingers to hide her promise, but she couldn't handle seeing her mother so upset, robbed she'd never meet or confront her father.

The Queen continued to sob, interrupting Azor's concentration, and the crowd broke into confused whispers. Azor's side fins flared and he motioned to his guards. With a quick bow, he lowered down in front of his mother while two guards manipulated the Queen's arms like a puppet to place the crown on Azor's head.

He rose and waved to the audience. "So, without further stress added to the Queen, I accept the title as your king," Azor said, hurriedly.

"Long live the King," the crowd mumbled half-heartedly.

"That son of a bass," Galadriel grunted. "When I get my hands on him."

Ash was still confused, unsure what this all meant and his reference to *his son*? Did mermen have more than one wife? But at hearing her mother's desperate cries, her heart ached to comfort her. She flitted her tail and rose slowly upward, her head tipped backward so she could see the Queen better.

"And with that said," Azor continued, "for my first order of business, I'd like to address the mermen before me."

Ash shook her head, releasing the hood for a better view, and stared blankly, out in the open, hoping to gain eye contact with her mother.

Out of nowhere, someone placed the crown on Tatlana's head. She startled momentarily, then held her breath and prayed the next words Azor spoke would be to pardon the rebels. If not, she'd let his daughter swim, thus giving the power back to

Desiree to lead.

If only she'd stop crying and take the lead.

Desiree's sobs, though, visibly interrupted his concentration; his face reddening and jaw clenching.

Nevermind. Let him have it. He deserves this, she thought with a vengeful smile.

The Queen suddenly stopped mid-wail and her eyes glazed over. Staring into the crowd, a flicker of hope hit her face. Tatiana scanned the audience for why, for the source, hoping for a miracle, and blinked in disbelief, and blinked again to clear the mirage. But the redheaded girl that was her very best friend didn't fade away.

"Ash?"

Azor continued on unaware, his body relaxing in the sudden void of grief. "As agents of harm, you've been found guilty for your acts of treason, for attacking the compound and attempting to kill your Queen, and you'll be punished under the full letter of the law. Beheaded—"

"Lies!" the Queen shrieked, rising from her throne. "All lies!"

The crowd gasped.

"Mother?" Azor said, reaching for her.

She sirened and all the mermen doubled over, holding their ears. The merling sent out a small siren of her own. Unthinking, Tatiana placed her hand over the babe's mouth.

"You will not touch me!" The Queen screamed to the approaching guards. She continued to glare at Azor, pointing. "You are not of royal blood. You are not my son! I replaced you. I replaced you with her, my daughter." Her finger shifted to the new target; to the redheaded girl fluttering in the current, wearing a Dradux cloak. To Ash.

Ash reached out for her mother, the two of them propelling themselves to meet in the middle.

Fin? What is going on? Tatiana screamed in her head. *Get Ash out of here!*

We're here to save you! Fin yelled back telepathically.

She scanned the people surrounding Ash's tail and didn't see an army, let alone Fin. What were they doing? *I don't need saving, idiot! Ash does. Get her out of here! Now!*

Dradux guards darted toward Ash the same time Azor swam to his mother, yanking her back by the tail from the crowd.

"Do not say another word, Mother," he threatened. He released her to two Dradux guards who grabbed her arms and pulled her off the dais.

"Silence," Azor bellowed, lifting his hands. "That's only my sister, Galadriel. She'd returned to serve me. And of course I'm of royal blood. Queen Tatiana has the royal mark." He gestured his hand to Tatiana. "Go on, show them."

Galadriel? Tatiana panned the crowd again to find Ash. She was gone.

Fin? Fin! She mentally called.

She knew she hadn't imagined seeing her. They had to be somewhere. She'd spoken with Fin even. What did Azor mean she was his lost sister, Galadriel?

At the siren scream beyond the dais, Tatiana's head whipped around to find her mother-in-mer struggling against the guards. She couldn't keep up the charade anymore. She had to find Ash. She had to rescue Jacob.

The squirming merling, as if understanding it was her turn to shine, bopped her tail just right and wiggled out of Tatiana's shaking hands. The blanket fell away, revealing the colorful tail signifying a girl. The crowd gasped.

Tatiana fell back into her seat, watching her twitch her body in the current, happy as a clam.

"It's not a boy!" someone in the crowd yelled. "Imposter!"

"He *is* an imposter!" Ash yelled, surfacing from the crowd once again. Her hair like fire framed her head. "I'm the royal heir to the throne! I'm your queen!"

Queen? Tatiana gasped. She'd never seen Ash so vocal before, so brave.

"Arrest Galadriel!" Azor shouted.

And in a flash, Tatiana saw two girls. Two redheads. Two Ashes.

A skirmish broke out around and between the Dradux guards. Siren screams parted a sea of mers, scurrying to find safety as the green hooded figures mobbed in. She spotted Fin and another merman in a Dradux cloak, releasing rebels from the pillories. They'd come to save the day, with backup and look-a-likes apparently. She unbuttoned her beaded gown to release her weighted garment and straightened her black get-a-way dress that had been hiding underneath, when a hand tightened around her neck from behind.

"You did this," Azor seethed, yanking her from her throne and lifting her off the stage. "Deal's off."

From the corner of her eye, she watched Pearl pluck the merling from the current and scurry away, but as for anyone else, she couldn't see them through the stars flickering in her eyesight.

Fin! she screamed telepathically *Fin! Help me!*

41

Toll

At the splash, Jacob peeled his eyes open to see the intruder. He'd heard the announcement horn and knew it was only a matter of time before Azor would come to gloat, then finish him off.

The dark silhouette only stared at him. After another hard look, Jacob recognized the blond merman, the odd one from the practice field.

"Hey," Jacob said, straightening. "Ferdinand?"

The man only tilted his head, birdlike. Hope pulsed through Jacob anyway. Badger had said he'd let all the rebels out of the dungeon. Had he come to save him, too?

"Ferdinand, it's me. Jacob. I'm Badger's friend. I—I need help." He rattled the chains over his head. "I think if you hit that rusted spot with a spear, they'll break free."

Ferdinand looked off to the side, sniffing the air. Then without a word, he slipped under the water.

"Ferdinand? Ferdinand!" Jacob yelled, slumping against the slick wall. "Red Tide!"

42

Lost and Found

Azor slammed Tatiana's wet body against the wall inside the palace.

"I did no such thing!" Tatiana yelled once her gills faded from her neck and she could breathe from her nose.

"You let the merling go!"

"The baby wiggled from my hands. And she's a girl, Azor! There's no denying that."

"Don't you think I know that? Pearl was supposed to keep that hidden from you!"

Tatiana laughed, still struggling to free herself from his hands. "It's over, Azor. The mers know you're a fraud."

He moved inches from her face. "I'm not a fraud and the crown is now mine. You'll give me the son I need eventually and I'll take my birthright."

He pressed his lips to hers, hard and forceful. His soul, deceptively sweet and beautiful, slipped inside her and wove its fingers around her fighting spirit, plucking the delicate strings of her soul. But knowing who he was and what to expect, Tatiana fought back. The darkness, cloaked in a promise of love everlasting, pushed into her harder, demanding her free-will.

"No!" she screamed, seeing the promise's beguiling hold for what it was—lies. And before succumbing to him, she rammed her knee firmly into his groin and tore her mouth away from his. His soul ripped from her, empty handed.

Azor doubled over, groaning. Tatiana clambered up from the

floor and ran around the corner directly into Chauncey. He grabbed her around the waist, securing her arms.

Tatiana shrieked. "Let me go!"

Azor marched up to her with a limp. "If you weren't pregnant, I'd beat you!"

Tatiana sucked in a breath. "What?"

A coy smile spread over his evil mouth. "You know that you are. Couldn't resist me, could you?"

Tatiana spit in his face. "You're disgusting and I'd never mate with you, ever!"

He winced and wiped away the spittle. "Oh, but you did. How do you explain how you can nurse?" He reached out to fondle her breast.

"Don't touch me!" She reared back, flailing her legs, kicking Azor in the stomach. He backed up and grimaced. She then stomped on Chauncey's foot, but he didn't let her go.

"So feisty," Chauncey said in her ear. "I'll hold her down if you want her. That'll take out some of her fight."

Azor glared, his chest rising and falling. "I just need to get rid of *him*, then she'll be mine again, beg for me, like it was supposed to be."

"What about Xirene?" Tatiana asked through gritted teeth.

Azor lifted his chin. "She's dead, Tatiana. You got your wish."

Tatiana sucked in a gasp. "Dead? I never wished that. How? Did you kill her, too?"

Azor clenched his jaw. "What do you take me for? She birthed the baby alone, and… " He looked away, his nostrils flaring.

Tatiana's chest heaved. His ardor the night he'd found her nursing the merling made sense now. With Xirene's death, he'd been freed of his promise to Xirene and could feel his connection to Tatiana. He'd hoped by kissing her, the promise would rekindle for her as well. But she didn't let him. She'd broken the original bond. She'd chosen freedom over the promise spell.

"I'll never love you, Azor. Ever," she seethed. "You're evil and you're…" She remembered what the Queen had said, that he wasn't her son. That she'd switched him for the girl, for Ash. "Not even a royal!"

"What?"

"Xirene doesn't have the mark. Your own daughter doesn't have the mark." She laughed. "You were adopted and you didn't even know it!"

Azor's head pulled backward, his eyes falling into slits. "I don't know what was wrong with Xirene, but you have it. You have the mark!"

A grin pushed up on her lips. "Because your father kissed me…"—she lifted her chin in defiance—"that's why."

Azor's face fell. "What?"

She felt despicable for lying, but she couldn't tell him the truth—that the girls had been branded, royal blood or not. She had to trust Desiree's confession was true, otherwise he'd never let his quest for power go.

Chauncey's grip slackened and Tatiana's arms were suddenly freed. Chauncey believed Tatiana, too. And that he could choose whether or not he still wanted to be loyal to Azor.

"You're an orphan," she said plainly. "I bet the Queen couldn't birth Phaleon a boy, so she stole you from a human family and converted you. Ironic, isn't it? You're a beta-mer."

Azor's hands slipped down to his side. "It's a lie," he

whispered, searching the floor.

"Desiree used you to secure Phaleon's throne, just like what you tried to do with your *daughter*... but the people know the truth now."

"When? When did the King kiss you?"

"While you were trying to avenge my father. I visited him in his room and he told me everything. That you'd left him there to die. He called you a fool and even predicted you'd murder him, that you'd steal the crown. I didn't want to believe him. Sea stars, was I wrong!"

Evil crossed Azor's face. He straightened, his eyes canvassing her body. "After your mark showed up, you still wanted me." He grabbed her hand and pulled off her ring, flinging it across the floor. "If he kissed you, then where's your tattoo?"

She pulled her hand back. "You don't get the tattoo when you're kissed by someone who is already promised, idiot!"

He grabbed her arm and swiveled her around, lifting the hem of her dress. "*I* gave you the mark. Me!"

Tatiana pulled away and slapped him across the face. "Don't touch me!"

"But Jacob kissed you, too."

"He didn't!" she screamed and ran down the hall. "Get away from me!"

"Kill him. Kill Jacob," she heard Azor demand to Chauncey behind her and her heart lurched. She looked over her shoulder and watched Chauncey march in the opposite direction.

"NO!" she screamed, doubling back.

Azor grabbed her by the hair, pushing her to the floor. "You're wrong, Tatiana. You will *love* me! I will *make you* love me!"

Tatiana pawed at him, kicking and screaming.

"Azor!" Fin yelled, charging their way with a scythe in his hand. "Unhand my sister, you bastard!"

A group of mers followed behind Fin, all rebels. Azor stood up and bolted in the opposite direction.

"Tatch," Fin said breathless, helping his sister to her feet. "Are you hurt?"

"I'm fine." She dusted her hands on her skirt.

Behind them, Badger barked orders to the rebels to split up and search for Azor. "Aye, girl. Good job. We'll get that mangy pain in the arse in no time."

"No!" Tatiana did a quick double-take at the twin Ashes standing with Badger—one confident, the other shook up. "Ash?"

The less confident girl smiled and ran to her, embracing her neck. "Tatchi!"

Tatiana relaxed into her, finally feeling safe, when fear about Jacob's safety coursed through her once again. "Wait. We have to find Jacob before Chauncey does. He's going to murder him!"

"Aye!" Badger whistled with his fingers. "Grommet, round up yer men and search da eastern side. The rest of you, come with me. Is there a jail here, Princess?"

"What?" Tatiana asked.

"No," the other redhead interrupted. "If we ever had prisoners, we only kept them at the compound."

"We're foostering. Let's go!" He ran forward, down the same hall Chauncey escaped, toward the northern porthole. The rest of the group followed and Tatiana explained briefly what happened along the way.

Fin cursed after she finished. "That son of a bass. When I get my hands on Azor—"

"You'll be havin' time later to bleed dat gobsite, but fer now, don't be wastin' yer energy," Badger said. "Jacob needs findin'."

Outside of the palace, while Badger barked orders to search Natatoria in pairs, Tatiana tried to smell the water for Chauncey's stench, smelling everyone else instead.

"Return here in an hour!" Badger called out to the rebels.

"We're too late," Tatiana exclaimed, flopping her tail, defeated. "I've lost Chauncey's trail."

"Don't ya be worrin'. He can't be far. Split up and search the caves. If he's not at the compound, I'll come help ya look," Badger said over his shoulder.

"Azor, that jackfish!" yelled a dark-haired merman, one who had a striking resemblance to Jacob. "If my brother's anywhere, it'll most likely be the caves. You three search the northern wall and we'll go to the southern wall. Chauncey couldn't have gotten far. Come on." He charged ahead while holding the hand of the confident redheaded girl.

"Let's go." Fin motioned, holding Ash's hand.

"Tatchi!" she exclaimed, reaching for her.

You okay, sis? Fin asked telepathically.

I think so, yes.

Tatiana pressed the water she'd been holding through her gills and clasped onto Ash's hand, the three of them speeding north. "You two practically gave me a heart attack. What are you doing here?"

"We're here to save you from that... asshole!" Ash exclaimed.

Tatiana sucked in a startled breath, stunned by her best friend's attitude, not to mention her tail make-over. Actually, she'd resembled the other princess down to her green fin and—?

"Whoa... how'd you get that?" Tatiana pointed to the fleur-de-lis.

"Cool, huh?" Ash said with a smile, motioning to Tatiana's matching mark. "Means we're princesses."

"I know that... but you're not supposed to have one. Why haven't I ever seen that?'

Ash blushed. "'Cause I always wore a one-piece to cover it, I mean, who had a birthmark that looks like a fleur-de-lis? But I just found out why. Queen Desiree switched me for Azor when we were babies, 'cause she needed a son. Your uncle thought I was Galadriel and stole me, then kissed me..."—she grimaced. "So disgusting. And it's why I swim fast and—"

"Wait? Wha—?" Tatiana's mouth gaped open.

Ash tsked. "There's too much to tell. We need to find your friend, first. Come on."

Tatiana ran her free hand through her hair, her brain spinning. This had to be some crazy-ass dream. There's no way this was happening.

"And you thought high school has drama... *girlfriend*," Ash said.

Tatiana choked on a gulp of seawater and pinched her eyes shut to refocus. *Jacob. We need to find Jacob.*

43

Slice of Life

"Ah, Jacob. Still alive and flipping, I see."

Jacob's eyes startled wide at Chauncey's calm voice. "And Azor's still making you do his dirty work."

Chauncey laughed, slithering in from the pool. "If you mean King Azor, then, yes. Yes I am."

Jacob snorted. "Yeah, right."

"Didn't you hear the horn toll?" Chauncey sneered. "Oh, forgot you can't hear it, locked up in this lovely place." He gestured around the cave.

Jacob gave a dismissive nod. Of course he heard the bell and had been curious. But king? Chauncey had to be lying.

"Here's a recap," he continued. "Phaleon's dead and King Azor and Queen Tatiana are now in charge."

Jacob laughed. "How is that possible without an heir?"

"Didn't you know?" Chauncey threw his chin up and shoulders back. "Tatiana was pregnant this entire time. Gave King Azor a son just in time."

Jacob's eyes narrowed, disbelieving. How long had he been locked up? Couldn't have been six weeks, could it? He would have died without food. "You and I both know he paid more attention to Xirene than Princess Tatiana, with her bubbled room and secret exit."

"Did he now?" Chauncey raised his brow, touching his finger to his lip. "I wouldn't know, considering she's dead, too. That leaves just one loose parasite to dispose of in order for Prince

Treviathan and his parents to live happily ever after."

Jacob pulled his head backward and seethed, "Azor will never be happy."

Chauncey leaned in, his eyes flashing. "That's King Azor to you." He lifted his scythe, swiping it across Jacob's fin.

Jacob yelled as the blood spurted out. "You can kill me, but you won't get away with it! The rebels will revolt! Jack's coming back!"

Chauncey laughed hard, and sliced Jacob's fin again.

Jacob roared, writhing in pain, fire burning down his fin.

"The rebels have all been beheaded in the square. King Azor has won. And even when I was leaving the palace on strict orders to dispose of you, Tatiana couldn't control her joy over the crown. I watched her and Azor *celebrate* naked right in the middle of the hallway."

Anger ripped through Jacob's tail at the thought of Azor touching Tatiana. He reared back and knocked Chauncey over. Then with a hard jerk of the chains, he broke free one of the chains above his head.

"Chauncey, you coward!" He yelled, yanking the other, which held firm. "Make this a fair fight and let my hands free!"

Chauncey grunted, pulling his body upright. He sliced Jacob again, this time across his chest. He then removed the parasite off his tongue and placed it on one of Jacob's wounds. Jacob flicked his tail, but the thing latched on, anxiously drinking his blood.

"Naw," he said with an evil smile. "I'd rather watch you suffer first."

44

Silence

As Tatiana, Fin and Ash swam off toward the caves, Tatiana began to lose hope. She kept smelling the water, unable to pick up anything. Without Chauncey's scent, finding Jacob would be like looking for a diamond on a sandy beach. As they approached the northern walls of Natatoria, Tatiana's eyes canvassed the obsidian rock, looking for caves or holes, not finding anything large enough to hide inside.

She cupped her hands to her mouth. "Jacob!" she called feebly. "Jacob!"

Out of answers, she felt her optimism crumble. Pressing her eyes shut, she prayed as a last resort. *I don't know where Jacob is. Please help me find him before it's too late.* She inhaled the water deeply through her nose, hoping to catch Chauncey's stink again.

"Are you sucking the water through your nose?" Ash asked, confused.

Tatiana stopped and opened her eyes, embarrassed. "I'm smelling the water, actually. Chauncey reeks kinda like—"

"Oysters?" Ash finished.

"You know the scent?"

"What scent?" Fin asked.

Ash wrinkled her nose, then looked to Fin. "Like rotten oysters. It's disgusting."

Tatiana frowned and shook her head. "Fin's sniff-blind."

"Oh." Ash's eyebrows furrowed as she paused a beat when hope filtered into her eyes. "Then let's split up. I'll go and smell the water this way with Fin, and you scour the cliffs that way. Call out if you find anything."

Tatiana perked up and nodded, propelling her tail to the left, while Fin and Ash disappeared to the right. She knew eventually, she'd hit the shark tank to the eastern side. Thinking back to her interaction with the sharks before, her stomach quivered. She'd just swim around and continue on. Quitting wasn't an option.

The desolate caves, inky and cold, led to nowhere and she had no clue if Jacob was even alive. The thought of losing him brought tears to her eyes. She couldn't see herself without him in her life. All the times he'd been there, saving her, making her see reason, showing he'd cared, his selflessness and honor—to be blind to all of it because of the kiss? Her skin crawled in disgust. Had she even thanked Jacob? She groaned, recalling their last awkward conversation. He lay rotting somewhere, accused of kissing the Princess when he hadn't, and she'd never forgive herself if he died for her selfishness and stupidity. She had to find him and finally tell him her feelings.

Find anything? she telepathically asked Fin. At his silence, she knew he was too far away for communication.

She continued on, stopping at the dreaded shark fence. In the distance, she could see the compound, but to her surprise, there wasn't a mer or shark in sight. Where did everyone go?

She ventured to the shark tank door, swinging wide on its rusty hinges, creaking a sound of doom, and froze. Had the sharks escaped into Natatoria again? Then the scent hit her. *Oysters. Chauncey.*

With a kick of her tail and a pounding heart, she propelled herself inside. On the sea floor, the trident she'd used earlier poked precariously up from the sand with rotten shark flesh still attached. Snagging and clutching the metal for dear life, she flung off the bits and headed straight for the Pacific Gate. Her heart whooshed in her ears. With the bracelet on, she could only go so far inside. Had Chauncey taken Jacob to the Pacific Ocean? To Bone Island, wherever that was?

She skimmed the surroundings for help, fearful to call out and attract the wrong attention. The eerie quiet made her scales shiver.

Fin?

With quick breaths across her gills, she entered the tunnel anyway, accosted by Chauncey's boggy scent. Then she heard him. Shrill laughter. With a hard pump of her tail, she swam further inside, prepared for the horrible stinging poison that could pierce her skin at any moment. Then the scent veered off to the right toward a hidden cave.

She surfaced, unprepared for what she was about to see.

Staring down the scythe pointed at his heart, Jacob knew without a miracle he was done for.

"What the—?" Chauncey started, turning to the pool.

Jacob blinked, unbelieving of his eyes. Now he had to be dreaming.

"You!" Tatiana bellowed. With a side-swipe of her trident, she smacked Chauncey's left side. Losing balance, he toppled onto the rocks and smashed his head.

"You'll pay for that, Princess," he bellowed, reaching for his brow. Blood trickled down over his fingers.

"I'm your queen, you son of a bitch, and I won't allow you to treat my bodyguard like this!" She pointed the trident directly at his gonads. "Give me the key, or you'll lose your precious claspers."

Chauncey's eyes widened. He palmed the inside of his waist pouch and chucked the key to the other side of the cave.

When Tatiana's eyes followed the arch of the throw, Chauncey's tail reared up and stung her. She yelped slightly, but snapped her head to him.

Oblivious, Chauncey laughed, attempting to sit up.

With a twist of her wrist, Tatiana pierced his skirt, nicking his manhood with the trident.

"What the—" Chauncey wailed, grabbing himself. "Why'd you do that?"

"Honestly? After everything?" she sneered through her teeth. "I think you'd be smarter than that. Actually, I should give you one slash for every sick comment and every grope you've done. Or maybe I should cut it off right now and save the world of your seed."

"No, nooo," he begged, crying. "I promise. I won't—"

At the blood seeping from between his fingers, a sick satisfied smile played on Jacob's lips.

"It's too late for promises." With a quick slash of the trident, Tatiana side-swiped the blunt end into Chauncey's skull. A dull hollow thunk landed him on his back; his eyes rolled back into his head as he passed out, unconscious.

"Tatiana," Jacob gasped. "What are you doing?"

"Saving you." She moved, as if to phase, but lurched forward on her hands, slithering over to locate the key.

He blinked at her, amazed. Jack had said she was bold and courageous, but this? He couldn't contain how turned on he was.

With the key in her hands, she moved to him, balancing precariously on the uneven ground, reaching high to unlock the cuffs. With his head tipped back, he inhaled her skin—sweet like fruit. He couldn't stop the fantasies of what he'd do to her if he wasn't chained. Instead, he leaned forward, allowing his lips to brush her stomach.

"Hey." She giggled, wiggling away.

Once his other hand was free, he groaned. But her energy gave him a second wind he hadn't predicted. With a crack of his back, he stretched out his arms toward her. "That feels so much better."

She met his rough cheeks with her soft warm hands, sending a tingle over his skin. "You're alive."

"Barely," he said hoarsely, smiling back at her, working to contain the indescribable joy rocking his nervous system. "I'm going to miss my own private Bone Island."

"I'm sorry I didn't come sooner." She bit her lip and allowed her eyes to rake over him, sad. Her fingers trailed slowly over his bandage and down his chest, to the healing gash on his stomach. "Did he do this to you?"

"Yeah, well—"

Tatiana's shriek interrupted him. She knocked away Chauncey's pet parasite. "Disgusting. What was that—? Don't tell me. I don't want to know. Come on. We need to get you out of here."

She tugged on his hand, but he didn't move. He only grasped

her fingers tighter, bringing them to his lips. Indescribable awe filled him. Who was this girl in front of him? Taking charge? Rescuing him? Fighting with weapons and attempting to cut off enemy claspers?

"Are you even listening to me?" she asked, studying him.

Desire singed through his body, hot and demanding. He wanted to kiss her. Now.

A curious smile tipped on her lips. "Why are you looking at me like that... and... doing that?"

"What?" he said, kissing each finger again.

She pinched her lips together in a cute puckering sort of way, clearly flustered.

"It's like you've never seen a girl kick ass before."

"I haven't." His lips continued to turn up at the corners.

"Well, it needed to happen, so..." She shook her head. "We should really go."

"Go?" He massaged her hand, unable to put into words how much he wanted her, to wrap his arms around her, touch her, crash his lips to hers. Her newfound confidence was making his head crazy and his heart pound.

When he didn't move, she rolled her eyes and chuckled. "You know, the girl can be the *hero* sometimes."

"I know but... *wow.*"

She blushed, but still prodded him to leave. "You can thank me later. We should go."

"Wait." He grabbed her hips and slid her onto his lap. "I have to tell you something." He waited a beat, struggling to choose the right words. "I'm sorry about what I said before—about being your replacement. That was insensitive—"

"No." She stopped him, placing her fingertip on his lips. "Jacob, I understand," she paused, her beautiful blue eyes sweeping over his rugged face. "I know who I want."

At her confession, he took her face between his hands and held her there. "Then promise yourself to me," Jacob whispered. "And never leave my side again."

"Yes," she whispered, breathless. "I promise."

Without waiting, he covered her mouth with his and his soul exploded into light, feeling her, breathing her. Her mouth, so soft and warm, sweet and tangy, trembling and deepening. He was hers and she was his. They were one soul. Alive.

45

Choices

This time, when the sweet pull came for Tatiana's soul, she allowed herself to be free and afterward, the connection was so much deeper than anything she could have imagined. Her soul exploded into a song filled with all the goodness that was him. And everything about him felt right. To hold him close, to be with him, to treasure him for all eternity, she could think of nothing else, completely engulfed in his love.

He buried his nose in her damp hair and inhaled as if he couldn't get enough. She mentally pinched herself. Could this really be happening? Or had they died and gone to heaven?

She giggled, her face still trapped between his hands. "Why didn't we do that sooner?"

Jacob laughed. "I don't know." His unending grin stretched his face with indescribable joy.

He playfully pulled her closer, smothering her lips with his once again, his hands moving down her torso, tugging at her skirt. Her eyes rolled back in her head as his lips made their way down her neck, tasting and moaning, breathless and whole. Filled with longing, she wanted nothing more than to be devoured by him, but at Chauncey's moan, Tatiana startled.

She stayed his hands. "We need to get you out of here."

Jacob's shoulders slunk.

"I know, but we have to," she said as his hands freed themselves and grabbed her again, pulling her to him, leaning his lips out to hers. She indulged one more kiss before forcing him in the pool,

He fell underwater, reemerging with slicked back hair. Tatiana gnawed at her lower lip, moved at how quickly his skin was reviving, and how incredibly sexy he looked. The faint reminder she needed to restrain Chauncey tickled the back of her brain. With a quick pivot on the ledge, she leaned back, grabbing the chains.

"What are you doing?" he asked.

She winked, putting the cuffed end around Chauncey's wrist. With a smirk, she tossed the key over Jacob's head. The splash echoed in the cavern.

"Chauncey needs to dry out a little."

He chuckled and as soon as she met him in the pool, they both slipped under the water, unable to keep their hands off each other once again. Tatiana felt Jacob's scales soften with each breath of briny water over his gills. Then he pulled her in tight, sending a rush through her heart once again. Yes, she'd kissed Azor and allowed the promise to trick her into having feelings of attraction for him, but this… this was a whole new dimension. She molded her tail around his, pressing her heat into him, feeling her pheromones ignite. The urge to escape out to the Pacific verses returning to Natatoria, sped through her. If only she didn't wear the blasted bracelet…

"Here?" He tilted her chin, a coy smile on his lips.

Wanting nothing more than to indulge their greatest fantasies, the reminder they were still in the shark's domain hit her gut. "Not yet… not here."

"Where are we anyway?" he asked, looking around.

"Inside the Pacific Gate."

"We are? What about the sharks?"

"I have no idea where they are," she said nervously, panning the wider part of the tunnel.

He pulled her close again and nibbled at her earlobe. "Then let's go somewhere else…"

"You don't have to ask me twice." Tatiana laughed nervously; still vividly aware they couldn't get distracted. "If only I didn't have this bracelet on."

He brushed his hand down over her backside and squeezed. "If only…"

She moaned to tease him, melting momentarily under his hot touch, wanting more, so much more.

Once they cleared the cave and entered the dreaded shark enclosure, a screech sent her scales on end. They turned to see Jacob's brother being pulled through the current by some blond merman, grabbing tightly ahold of his fin.

"Ferd," he yelled. "Let-t-t me-e-e go-o-o!"

Galadriel swam after them. "Let Jax go, you big lug!"

Tatiana and Jacob let go of each other momentarily and held their ears on his approach, expecting him to drag Jax past them through the Pacific Gate. Ferdinand only stopped abruptly, letting Jacob's brother go free.

"Whoa," Jax righted himself and did a double take. Tatiana's stomach flipped, hit with awkwardness, and she released her tail from Jacob's.

"I—uh—you're okay, huh?" Jax eyed them up and down.

Jacob took Tatiana's hand, zinging an electric current up her arm. "Yeah, all because of *my girl*."

Tatiana's heart burst in joy at the endearing title. Everything was falling into place, finally.

Tatiana! She heard Fin say in her mind.

Over here! She called back.

Ash and Fin swam up, gills flapping extra hard. After quick introductions, a brisk conversation erupted catching everyone up on what had happened. Tatiana remained quiet, secretly marveling at the circle of siblings brought together by love: Jax and Jacob, Ash and Galadriel, her and Fin. All promised. All family.

"Aye," Badger called from the ravine. His hands were filled with weapons. "Are ya all daft? Whatcha be doin' in the shark tank? Yer all as useless as a lighthouse on a bog. We need to be gettin' back to the skirmish!"

Tatiana's spine stiffened. Reveling in her *real* promise, she'd forgotten her responsibilities, the merling, everything.

They swam to meet up with him and Sandy hovering in the current. Badger bowed at their approach. "My Queen, what would you have us do?"

"Oh, well I thought we'd—"

Badger gave Galadriel a hard look. "With all due respect, I don't be meanin' you, Princess. But our queen, here." He motioned to Tatiana

The blood in Tatiana's veins froze, as all eyes trained on her.

"She can't be queen," Galadriel interrupted. "Azor's not of royal blood and I can prove it."

"Aye." Badger's bushy eyebrows pressed together. "That don't matter, now, doll. You've been right gone this entire time and Queen Tatiana be acceptin' da crown in front of God and everyone and as far as da mer know, she *is* their queen."

"No!" Galadriel barked.

"Baby," Jax started, reaching for her hand.

"Don't *baby* me!" She pushed Jax away. "This is my heritage. My birthright! My responsibility! I came back to fix this!"

Tatiana's heart pounded. She'd love nothing more than to give the headache over to Galadriel, but she couldn't—not yet. Galadriel had no idea what had transpired since her absence and Desiree had empowered her with the brand and the crown. Too many things needed to be changed, starting with laws regarding the promise, then with the servants' rights, and especially with the class warfare. Too much responsibility to entrust to someone else.

"Badger's right. I am queen," Tatiana said confidently, feeling Jacob's hand reassuringly squeeze hers. "I need to return order. Azor and the Dradux need to be punished for their crimes. And the rebels pardoned. I need to set everything straight."

"How, when you don't have the mark?" Galadriel asked through her teeth.

Tatiana lifted her chin and kept her cool. Knowing lives were on the line, she merely turned and showed her hip.

Galadriel gasped. "I don't understand. How—?"

"She's also birthed Azor an heir, which trumps ya," Badger said plainly. "So we must get goin'. There isn't much time."

At the mention of the merling, Jacob dropped her hand.

"It's true?" he asked simply, disbelief on his face. "How?"

"I…" Her eyes flickered to him for a moment. His devastation crushed her. How did he know about the merling? She closed her eyes a beat, hiding her frustration. In any other circumstances, she'd explain, but with Galadriel there, peace in the colony needed to be restored first.

She merely turned and said, "Sandy, can you reopen the essence pool, then find the wounded and treat them? Jax, Fin, Badger and Jacob: I need you to lock up the Dradux guards in the pillories, including Azor. Ash, stay with me. We'll see to it everyone is okay. Once I get control of things, I'll speak to the people and makes things right again."

"Got it," Badger said with a bow. When no one else moved or said anything, Badger's face turned into an ugly scowl. "Where's your loyalty? This be yer queen! She earned this from her blood, sweat and tears! You will honor her! Bow!"

The group startled and everyone but Galadriel bowed. Instead, she glared with her arms crossed over her chest. "I will not serve an imposter."

"So be it," Badger said while handing out the weapons.

In a huff, Galadriel spun on her tail and swam off with Jax following behind her.

It's okay, sis, Fin encouraged telepathically. *She'll simmer down. You're doing the right thing.*

Though Fin's words helped, Tatiana wanted Jacob's reassuring hand in hers more. She looked for him, hoping he'd swim by her side. But he chose to swim on the outskirts of the group instead. Wishing she could mind talk with Jacob like she could her twin brother and explain everything, she kept looking toward Jacob's permanent scowl, hoping to catch his eye. Then her heart punched against her ribs in anticipation of what they'd find.

The skirmish at the square took her by surprise. Sirens and wails punctuated the crowd as mermen fought, dark green hoods against black. Among the crowd, bodies floated unconscious. In horror, she watched Dradux guards kiss unpromised mermaids, then witnessed the maids changing sides and taking up swords against their friends.

"Oh my starfish," Tatiana mumbled, seeing the carnage and blood.

Without a thought, she charged, sirening, and held out her trident to the nearest maid. "By order of the Queen, I command you to stop!"

The woman swiveled around and pointed her spear at Tatiana. "Imposter," she squealed and rushed her.

Jacob appeared from nowhere and parried the woman's blow. "What are you doing?" he yelled at Tatiana. "Get inside the palace at once!"

"No! My place is here!"

Someone pulled her hair, spinning her around in the current. Tatiana shrieked, staring in the face of a Dradux. "Lookie who I caught."

His tail whipped around and stung her in the side. She winced, but felt nothing more than a pinch. With her talons, she ripped into his startled expression, shredding his skin to ribbons. "Unhand me!"

Then Jacob was there, piercing the Dradux in the heart with the trident that had been in her hands.

"Come on." He grabbed Tatiana's arm and swam her from the square.

"No! I want to fight."

He put his face inches from hers. "You're the queen. You don't get to fight. Now get inside."

He shoved her up through the porthole and swam off. But instead of air, she surfaced into water. Water everywhere.

"No!" She clutched her neckline, spinning around. The palace was flooded.

46

Lost Ones

"Enough!" a male's voice—rich baritone—boomed from outside. Immediately, the noise of the fighting diminished.

Tatiana returned to the square, awed at the response. Some of the mers bowed, while others remained speechless and gawking. Murmurs of a name tumbled through the crowd. *Merric. It's King Merric.*

"What is this? Explain yourselves!" the man yelled, his white hair floating around his head in the current like lightening. Though weathered in his appearance, he lifted his trident with ease and waved it over the crowd, pointing to people at random. No one dared speak, petrified in his presence. "Where's Phaleon, my son?"

My son? She'd remembered seeing a bust of King Merric in the library and hearing stories of his greatness, but he couldn't be the same merman. The King had died ages ago when Phaleon took the throne, and he looked so... old.

A staccato of gasps came from the mers, then a lone courageous voice cried out, "He's dead."

"Dead?" He scratched at his beard, his face suddenly pained. "I see."

Behind him, a whole host of merpeople hovered, wrinkled and aged just like him, and yet they carried weapons, eyes alert, ready for battle. Then she spotted her parents in the crowd with Fin and Ash, anxious but steadfast. Why wasn't her father rounding up the rebels to attack and capture Azor's men?

Nervously, Tatiana watched, refraining from swimming across the square to them. She caught her mother's eye, at the concern filling her face.

"Then who's in charge?" King Merric bellowed.

"King Azor," a merman in the crowd said.

"Hmmm." He thought for a moment. "I'd like to speak with him. Have my grandson explain this mess."

Grandson? When no one spoke, he moved forward, whipping his golden fin behind him. "Well, where is he?"

"He left," a mermaid replied timidly.

Tatiana's heartbeat boomed in her ears. After her speech earlier and with Azor's absence, she had to account for what had happened, to make things right, to be the one she'd professed herself to be. Queen.

"I'm in charge," Tatiana said with her head held high, voice quivering.

A rush of whispers filtered through the water. Her family gasped and moved forward, objecting. The King waved them off with a flick of his trident.

"Mighty brave for one so young," he said as he crossed above the crowd toward her.

"I can explain." Tatiana momentarily pinched her eyes shut. *I hope.*

She rehearsed her defense, intending to reveal all of Azor's secrets and lies. But upon opening her eyes, she locked onto Pearl who hid in the nave of the palace entrance. In her hands squirmed Xirene's merling, the blue-tailed girl. Responsibility hit Tatiana. If she told the truth, she'd criminalize the child's father, ushering the babe into a life she'd promised Xirene she'd protect her from.

With a gulp, she turned to Merric, lost for an explanation. "We have no excuse," Tatiana said grimly. "Azor and I have been at odds since our promise and, in light of King Phaleon's death, he hoped by becoming king, he could create peace again."

An angry murmur pulsed from the crowd.

"They've only been promised two weeks! How could they have a child so soon?" an array of voices yelled. "Harlot! Tramp! Whore!"

Jacob waited impatiently in the audience for Jack and the Lost Ones to attack. That was why they'd come, hadn't they? But he couldn't help himself from staring hard at Tatiana, hurt and confused. And how could she have kissed him and not told him about the child? She never even really showed. Was her pregnancy the whole reason why she'd hesitated to kiss him to begin with? Why she wouldn't leave? Anger surged when imagining Azor forcing himself on her. Crossing his arms over his chest, he watched her grimace at the accusations as she fluttered her tail in the current.

"I think after everything," she continued, smoothing her trembling hands down her skirt, "we should start by freeing the rebels and disbanding the Dradux."

A collective gasp flowed around Jacob, silencing the attacks against her virtue. But Jacob only saw Azor for the animal that he was. He sucked water over his gills, trying hard to slow the blood crashing through his veins. Azor would suffer for hurting her, mating with her, then forcing her promise—die miserably.

"—and actually, I've since discovered I wasn't promised to Azor to begin with..." She raised her hand as proof, but light caught her ring finger. She clasped her hands, to hide the evidence. Jacob's heart stopped for a beat as he studied the black shards of light erupting from his hand, evidence of their bond.

Hissing and vitriol worked its way through the crowd again, condemning her.

"Liar! She is *promised*," someone yelled behind Jacob.

Chants broke out all around him. "To Bone Island with her! Arrest her! Off with her fins!"

"No!" Jacob kicked his tail, bulleting himself above the crowd. "I'm the one. The one who should be punished! Not Tatiana!"

"Jacob, no!" Tatiana gestured him away with her hand, then someone yanked on his tail, pulling him down.

"Hover somewhere else, sympathizer!" a woman screamed in his face.

Jacob scowled, putting space between them. He bumped into another mer, who shot him a look, wary of his trident. "I'm here. Find your own spot!"

"Jacob," Grommet said from behind, pulling him backward. "What are you doing?"

"Silence!" The people hushed and looked up, frozen in a trance under Merric's hard gaze. "It seems we have a discrepancy of who's responsible."

"Ya think?" Grommet mumbled.

"I'll kill him," Jacob seethed quietly. "If he's even so far as touched her—"

"You and me both," Grommet agreed.

Azor interrupted from the other side of the square. "And who are you?"

Jacob panned to his voice, his body shaking with adrenaline.

Merric raised one brow. "I'm your grandfather."

"I highly doubt it, old man." Azor snorted.

Whispers from the mers flew around. Was this actually Merric? Or was it someone else?

Merric postured, bristling his fins. "I've come to help you."

"What?" Azor smirked. "Help me? I think I've got things under control!"

Jacob grunted, flexing his fingers around the shaft of the trident, arching his fins. Why was Jack waiting? Why were they entertaining this idiot?

"Imposter!" someone yelled from the crowd. Jacob and Grommet followed in suit, "Imposter!"

"Ahhh, now." Azor sneered and moved into the light. With a stretch of his neck, he displayed the crown, and floated down towards the stage opposite Merric. Six Dradux guards flanked him, scythes pointed outward. "You all saw Queen Desiree crown me today, and as you know, an heir doesn't necessarily have to be a male to make one king."

All Jacob could focus on was Azor's pulsing jugular and how he'd love to slice into it and watch him bleed in the current.

Merric's gills flared. "In special circumstances, yes, but you have passed her off as a boy—"

"I accepted the crown on Tatiana's lies." Azor pointed his spear toward her. "Struck with grief over my father's sudden death, I wasn't there for the birth. How was I to know? I took her word."

"You murdered King Phaleon after he wouldn't die on his own," Tatiana interrupted. "And you're not of royal blood! Your mother confessed she switched you at birth!"

Azor threw back his head and laughed. "We've been through this already. My mother is grieving and—" He scanned the crowd and pointed. "How was I switched with my sister Galadriel? Explain that."

"Because I am not Galadriel!" A girl yelled behind them as she rose in the current. "I'm Ashlyn Frances Lanski, born mer and switched at birth because I wasn't a boy! So my father could be king!"

"Ashlyn?" Azor yanked his chin back, then shook his head before readdressing his people. "Are you going to believe this nonsense? The mad words of a woman? Or your King?"

The crowd murmured, unsure. Without hard proof, they couldn't decide what to believe, who to follow. Jacob stared at Tatiana, at the woman he loved, withholding his desire to yell out and demand Azor's death. But if she didn't say something soon, the crowd could turn on her and even with Jack's army, she could lose her life in the upheaval. Her eyes briefly met his, flashing fear.

"Tell them," Jacob mouthed.

Her chest heaved as her chin rose. Courage replaced her fear. "Then explain why your daughter doesn't have the mark of royalty, Azor?" she yelled.

Jacob watched fear cross Azor's face. "The what?"

"The mark of a royal. This—" she turned and lifted her dress, revealing her fleur-de-lis.

"Of course my daughter has the mark—"

Heartache thudded in Jacob's chest, watching the merling girl in Pearleza's hands as she swam to Tatiana's side, the daughter she shared with Azor. But when she lifted the babe, the merling didn't have the mark of a royal.

How can that be?

Hope pulsed into Jacob. Hope that the whole thing had been a ruse to look like Azor's kin. Hope that his girl was still untouched. Hope that they could get out of this alive.

"Arrest them!" Azor called abruptly.

Madness broke out as mers swarmed in all directions. In a brief glimpse, Jacob saw the Dradux guards surround Tatiana, holding her arms and mouth. He kicked his tail, unable to gain ground as the massive crowd squeezed and pushed him, trapping him under their bodies and tails.

"No!" Jacob called, elbowing against those around him, ready to sting anyone who'd get in his way. Trapped in the sea of moving mers, he couldn't free himself from the angered horde's path, when suddenly the mers broke apart. He found himself face to face with Azor.

Azor's shock was briefly entertaining, until his Dradux guards pushed Jacob away.

"We meet again," Jacob said with a wry smile. *And it's not going to end pretty.*

Tatiana thrashed against her handlers when King Merric held out his trident.

"Silence!" He waved his weapon over the swarming crowd.

"We will handle this civilly!"

"I am King!" Azor yelled. "Arrest them all!"

In the tumult, Tatiana scanned the crowd, unable to see Jacob. She panicked, calling out to him. But the older mers couldn't compete with the Dradux strength and weapons. She pinched her eyes shut to think, then reopened them, spotting Jacob next to Azor, held off by the Dradux guarding him. She lifted her chin, infused with courage, and yelled, "Azor cannot be king because the merling is not mine!"

Jacob's eyes widened as a hush overtook the square.

"What? No—" Azor began.

"It's true!" Pearleza called from the nave. "This child is Xirene's, Azor's handmaiden. They were promised first," she said, pointing at Azor. "I kept the lie because Azor threatened to kill my child. I swear to you, Tatiana did not birth this child."

The crowd murmured in anger and confusion.

Then Queen Desiree's voice floated from behind Tatiana. "It's because I switched Ashlyn with Azor as a baby. He cannot produce a child of royal blood." She lowered her head. "I'm sorry, Azor. But it's true."

"Lies! All of you!" Azor seethed. "The King wouldn't have accepted me as his son if I wasn't. I've fulfilled the law and produced a child. I'm the king!"

"But you broke our law!" Tatiana interrupted. "You kissed me while promised to another! You must pay for that crime!"

"I—" Azor looked around nervously. "Well then, where is she? This other woman, Tatiana? You have the promised tattoo and so do I." He raised his hand.

"No!" Jacob yelled, gritting his teeth. "She's promised to me!

Tatiana's tattoo matches mine!" He held up his hand as well.

Another gasp fell over the crowd. "Bone Island!" they yelled. "The shark tank! Off with their fins!"

Tatiana's heart rocketed blood through her body. Her promise to Jacob was going to be their doom. She looked to her father for help. He kept a conflicted expression, holding off a band of Dradux determined to get to Merric.

"And what's your defense, Tatiana?" Merric asked.

Tatiana's head whipped around. She blinked, unbelieving the blame was being pinned on her.

"Defense? It's my word against his," she said plainly.

A sneer filled Azor's lips. "And I did nothing wrong."

She leveled her gaze to Azor. "You stole my choice, Azor."

"I did no such—"

"I'm not finished!" she interrupted. "You claim you didn't kiss another, but this war is evidence you did. If you were bonded to me, you would have understood why my father interrupted our ceremony and forgiven him. But no! Even against King Phaleon's advice, you went after my father. And when you didn't find him, you punished the people instead by starving them and taking away their loved ones. And even today, you deceived them with this child and tried to behead the rebels in the square!

"But before our ceremony, you *had* unconditional love. If you would've been honest and told them you'd fallen for a servant, they would have accepted her as their queen. Your bigotry and impatience killed that love. And in these last two weeks, we've watched you pit mer against mer and suffocate the song, killing the Natatoria we all loved and fought to preserve."

Azor laughed. "I was not in charge. Queen Desiree drove us

to this ruin. And how can you, a land-walker, think you've got this all figured out? By bringing Merric and his bag-of-bones army to usher us into a utopia again? You've only graced Natatoria with your presence for a month and proven your worth by committing promise polygamy. Everyone knows you, the rebels, and your father have created this war. If you think by letting the mers decide between you and me who is at fault, then let them. They've experienced hell under Desiree's leadership, and now they need a man. And I will start with the removal of the rebellion!" He gestured to Jack.

Tatiana pulled her shoulders tight, fear pulsing through her veins as the crowd, newly energized, began to chant, hate behind their eyes. They were going to kill her dad.

47

Revenge

Mers surged around Jacob, pushing and pulling, chanting for Azor's, the rebels' and Tatiana's deaths. Jacob's fear spiked. He had to get to her before anyone else did, save her from this mess.

A siren emanated from the rush of bodies as a clang reverberated from the center of the square. Bodies tumbled outward from the spray of blue essence, previously trapped behind a gel dome. Like magic, the Lost Ones around the spring became youthful once again. Jacob sucked in a cleansing breath of the water, feeling his muscles rejuvenate.

The tide of the crowd turned like a snake looking for something to devour. In the distance, Jacob spotted Azor and the four Dradux fleeing behind him.

"Let's get him," Grommet growled, charging ahead. Fin, Jax, and Badger filed in next.

Jacob panned backward to Tatiana, watching her flee with Jack and Merric. He faced forward; joining in the cry with his fellow warriors, weapons raised.

"Get back!" Azor yelled, whipping his tail in attempts to stab anyone who dared get close to him.

The four pressed onward, corralling Azor and his men like fish caught in a net. Acting as if they were fleeing for their lives, Azor and his men swam with all their might. But instead of hiding in Azor's compound like Jacob had suspected, he and the Dradux entered the shark tank, slamming the door behind them.

Azor turned with a smile, hate brewing in his eyes. "You think you've won," he said with a laugh, eyeing the four of them. "But you haven't! I'll live to see another day. You're idiots to listen to Tatiana's lies!" His glare pressed into Jacob. "She's incapable of love! All she cares about is the crown!"

Jacob glowered at him from between granite spires of the shark tank. "I pity you, that you still can't admit you were wrong. You'll pay for what you've done to her."

"Done to her?" Azor swam off laughing, holding his sword out as they crossed through the swarm of sharks. "I'll see you in Hades, Jacob!"

"Come on," Fin said, grabbing the door of the shark tank. "Let's follow them!"

Badger flashed his cuff. "You go right ahead, but I can't."

"Red Tide!" Jax cussed, gripping the bars. "But I'll be damned if I'm following him in there."

Jacob shook his head, angered. "That sorry son of a bass won."

"Aye," Badger said, gripping onto his shoulder. "He might have escaped, but he didn't win. He'll be back, mark me words."

At a screech, everyone doubled over and held their ears. When it stopped, they lifted their heads and stared across the pen. Ferdinand appeared and stood guard at the mouth of the Pacific Gate.

"Ferdinand!" Jax yelled. "What the hell is he doing?"

At each attempt of Azor's men to gain ground, he shrieked, paralyzing them. The sharks, antsy and angry at the noise, began to dart about, passing closer and closer to Azor and the Dradux. Everyone watched on; fear tightened in Jacob's gut.

"Stop him!" Azor yelled, pointing at Ferdinand.

The Dradux attempted to swim faster. But a shark turned, barreling toward Azor as he hovered behind the pack.

Jacob turned at the last second when a sickening crunch filled the water. A bloodcurdling keening followed in short choppy bursts and Jacob winced, watching the shark whip Azor's lifeless body in the current. Blood coated his gills as the rest of the Dradux were attacked, and after several minutes of chilling screams the water was silenced, finally.

"Aye," Badger said, palming his beard. "What a way to go."

Jax swam to the spires, yelling for Ferdinand. But through the murky waters, no one could see anything.

"Tatiana!" Jacob yelled, swimming up to her, his gills flapping out of breath.

"Jacob!" she called back, leaving the shelter of Merric and her father's circle.

They crashed into one another, their bodies pressing so close that nothing was between them, their lips hungry to know their lover was alive, safe.

"What were you thinking?" he asked, pushing her hair from her face, studying every inch of her skin.

"I don't know. I just had to do the right thing."

"And the merling—?"

She frowned. "I know, I'm sorry. She's Xirene's, but there wasn't time to explain—"

He smothered her with another kiss, his soul alive and awake, whole in her presence. "If something had happened to you—"

"I'm so sorry." A small sob escaped her lips. "Is it—?"

"Yes. It's over," Jacob exhaled, pushing the grim memory from his mind. "Neither he nor his Dradux will be bothering you, or anyone in Natatoria again."

She exhaled, whooshing out a breath of relief.

"And I promise to never, ever be apart from you again."

"Me neither," she whispered.

"What happened?" he asked, touching her again as if he didn't believe she was okay. "The crowd wanted to crucify you."

"I don't know. One minute they were charging me, threatening to drag me to Bone Island, but then my dad and Merric were there, holding them off. And the crowd pulled backward, then turned and headed after Azor… like his retreat was his admission of guilt. And then the screams. Everyone stopped in their tracks. But you should have seen it. It was like something heavy had lifted off everyone. And then the servants came out from the palace and took off their gloves, looking for their loved ones. There were so many… and they've been promised all along. Look."

Jacob turned and sure enough, in the square, mers were embracing and kissing: servants, guards and pure-bloods, betas and rebels. It was as if there wasn't ever a caste system to begin with.

And directly in front of them, Pearleza kissed Council member Fendole, a merman he'd believed to be widowed. And in her arms she held onto Azor's daughter and a boy. Jacob's mouth gaped.

Tatiana grabbed him, piercing him with fire behind her blue eyes. Unable to control himself, he covered her mouth with his, and she molded into him under his touch. His heart rocketed in anticipation of the moment when they'd finally be alone so he could show her exactly how much he loved her.

"I love you," he breathed against her lips.

"I love you, too."

Epilogue

"Do you, Jacob Vanamar James take Tatiana Renee Helton to be your lawfully promised mermaid?" Oberon asked.

Tatiana's fin trembled as she gazed into his blue-grey eyes, making her stomach quiver. He was very soon to be hers and she was his, lawfully, intentionally, forever in bonded bliss.

"I do," Jacob said with a smile, his voice husky.

"Heck, yeah," Jax, the best merman added.

Giggles sprung from the audience and promising party as Galadriel, one of Tatiana's bridesmaids, glared at him. "Hush."

"I'm just sayin'." He winked at her. "It's about time."

Oberon continued, "And do you Tatiana Helton, take Sir James to be your lawfully mated merman?"

She stared up into his face, adoringly.

"I do," she said with a coy smile. *Sea stars, do I ever.*

"Then by the power bestowed upon me by Chancellor Merric and the United Mers of Natatoria, I now pronounce you mermaid and mate. You may kiss your maid."

Cheers from the audience flowed from the square as Jacob brought Tatiana's lips to his, kissing her deeply, lovingly. He finished by pressing his forehead against hers, looking down at her through his dark eyelashes. "Now you're really stuck with me."

She wove her hands around his neck, restraining herself from weaving her tail against his, too. "I go where you go."

They turned, hand in hand, and Ash, her mermaid of honor, handed her official sister-in-mer a seashell bouquet as the boys choir broke into a soft ballad. Tatiana glanced down the line of mermaids dressed in soft purple, until she found Galadriel and Pearl. She beamed and mouthed a heartfelt, "Thanks."

Badger's catcall rose above the crowd, "Let's get this hooley started!"

A mix of young and old rose on their fins and clapped for the newly promised couple. She marveled at the support of so many mers, in awe of the response after what had happened just a week ago. Merlings swam down the aisle, scattering starfish on the sandy runway. In the back, Fendole, Pearleza's mate, held the little blue-tailed merling squirming in his hands toward Tatiana. The baby reached out and pulled on a tendril of Tatiana's hair.

"I wasn't sure how I'd feel about this, but she's just too cute not to love," Jacob said as the girl wrapped her tiny hand around his finger and brought it to her mouth.

"So," Jax said, after Grommet and Fin joined them, oblivious to his interruption of the sweet moment. "When do we get a move-on to the promisetide?"

Galadriel nudged him in the stomach. "Is that all you can think about?"

"Heck, yeah." Jax snorted. "We're all going still, aren't we? I'm dying for a break after all of this work."

"Well, of course we are," Galadriel said. "After we stop by Tahoe for a quick visit, so Ash can check on her parents, then we'll be on our way to Hawaii—in a plane, mind you." She wrinkled her nose at Fin.

Fin smirked back at her, then turned to Jax, flapping his lips. "And you thought this was work? Just wait 'til my dad gets us going on the rebuild in Tahoe. He's not going to build your house for you."

"I can't wait," Ash said, sighing, snuggling into Fin's side.

Fin raised a brow. "Me neither, my ginger girl."

"And then our *official* wedding, too, under the evergreens." Ash batted her eyelashes.

"Most definitely," Fin said. "Though, I should ask your dad's permission first."

Ash shook her head. "You'll have to sing his permission, you mean. He does own a gun."

The group laughed.

"Only if I'm your mermaid of honor, of course," Tatiana shot Ash a grin, "and we don't forget our scholarships to Florida Atlantic University."

"College? In Florida?" Galadriel blew out a breath of water. "No thank you."

Ash chuckled and moved next to Tatiana. "I don't see why we can't go to FAU, but you'll have to share me with Georgia."

"Georgia?" Tatiana wrinkled her nose.

Ash sighed then winked. "She was my *you* when you were gone. My human friend."

"Oh, I see."

The girls laughed and hugged each other.

Ash whispered, "We'll be married and living next to each other like we'd dreamed so many years ago."

Tatiana responded by breaking apart from her and offering a pinkie swear. "Super spy #2."

"That felt like ages ago," Ash said while looping her pinkie around Tatiana's. "So much has happened."

"Yes," Tatiana agreed, gesturing to merling Nicole. "But I

think things will be better now, with Fin and Jacob by our sides, and honestly, I wouldn't have dreamed of a better way for you to find out about the mer, minus kissing my gross uncle. Where has he been, anyway?"

Ash wrinkled her nose. "Who knows? Without Azor, he's kind of like a fish out of water."

With a laugh, Tatiana shrugged and shared a seashell off her bouquet for Nicole to play with. "I guess you're right."

As the audience of mers started a single file line to congratulate the happy couple, the promising party moved aside so Tatiana and Jacob could greet the guests. Smiles filled the faces of her parents, Desiree, Badger and Sandy, Sissy and Hans, the Lost Ones who'd returned to help rebuild their colony. She returned the waves of the retired servants hanging out of the windows of the palace, from rooms renovated into apartments. Though Azor had knocked out the northern entrance windows in his attempts to escape Grommet and the rebel army, flooding the second story, most everything above was able to be saved. Thinking of him, her eyes panned the landscape, noting the pile of rubble in the distance that used to be Azor's compound. With the song in full bloom and the sharks locked away, Natatoria had morphed into an even more glorious place than it had once been.

"Such a beautiful promised one, you make," Merric told Tatiana and kissed her forehead.

"Thank you," she said with a blush.

She admired the returned youth of the once king. After the skirmish, Tatiana discovered King Merric, one of the surviving Lost Ones, didn't die on Bone Island when Phaleon had escorted him there eighteen years ago. With the help of Sissy and Hans, he and so many others were saved from the banishment, living free and undetected on land, just waiting for the right time to return.

Merric had been elected Chancellor, overseeing the Council of the new governing body of Natatoria. After a brief stint as queen, Tatiana couldn't be happier to see the position abolished, deciding she'd rather teach than lead. Her most attended class? Land-walking 101.

"Dad," Tatiana said, encircling her arms around his middle. "I still can't believe this all worked out."

"You know, I'm still shocked myself. But I've never been more proud of you, or your choice in a mate," he said, eyes shining. "To overcome the bond is an extraordinary feat."

"Thanks, Dad," she said, her tears dissolving into the current.

He touched the merling's nose "And I'm proud of you, too."

The child cooed, blinking her long dark eyelashes at him.

"Let me hold her," Tatiana's mom said, arms outstretched. "And you have nothing to worry about. Blue is going to have a wonderful time while you all are on your promisetide."

"Blue?" Tatiana pursed her lips.

Her mom, Maggie, laughed. "Well, what else are we going to call this nameless child?"

"I actually decided to call her Nicole."

Jacob, overhearing, pulled away from some of his rebel buddies and squeezed her shoulder. "I can't think of a more fitting or more beautiful name."

Tatiana smiled, molding into his side. "I can't either."

After the audience gave the happy couple their blessings and began to feast on a meal Sandy and her friends had put together, Jacob pulled Tatiana away from the group and into his arms. She peered up into his blue-grey eyes, her heart aflutter. And like always, a familiar fire crackled between them—one of loyalty, of understanding, of unity of purpose, with a dash of pheromones.

Acknowledgements

I first want to thank God, for grooming me for this. This has become a career I ever love. To my husband Mike, for your endless love of me, our family, and our home. Your promise to me is my greatest treasure. To my boys, for being persistent when competing with the characters screaming in my head and showing me what unconditional love means. To my family, for your never-ending support and encouragement, and forcing the occasional distraction from my imaginary world.

I'm never prepared for the journey a book will take me on. The characters always push me off a moving rollercoaster, but I'm astounded at the friends that come into my life as a result of these imaginary people.

I have the most amazing editing team ever. To Janille Dutton, for being there in a pinch, for your vernacular, attention to detail and wit. To Kristie Cook, for being my BAFF and saying it like it is. To Chrissi Jackson, for being my pseudo "B" to my lone publishing world here in Cali. To Lisa Sanchez, for pointing out the obvious and swooning over the hero. To Valia Lind, for cheering me on the entire way. To Darci and Savanna Soldano, for keeping me PG-13 and loving Aaron so I can indulge time in my imagination. To Karen Hedger at Crain Editing, for finding my mistakes and laughing with me over *mermatrons*.

Thanks to Amanda, the winner of the title contest, to Kelly Ford Powell, winner of shout-out, and Nicole Hanson, winner of the name contest. May you enjoy your embodiment of a mer of great courage and strength. And to you, my dear readers and book bloggers, I write for you!

Follow Brenda

brendapandos.com

Twitter: @BrendaPandos

Facebook: Facebook.com/brendapandos

More from Brenda

The Emerald Talisman
The Sapphire Talisman
The Onyx Talisman

About the Author

Brenda Pandos lives in California with her husband and two boys. She attempts to balance her busy life filled with writing, being a mother and wife, helping at her church and spending time with friends and family.

Working formerly as an I.T. Administrator, she never believed her imagination would be put to good use. After her son was diagnosed with an autism spectrum her life completely changed. Writing fantasy became something she could do at home while tending to the new needs of her children, household, and herself.

You can find out more about what she's working on next on her blog at brendapandos.com.